DREAMS BELONG TO THE NIGHT

Novels published by Midnight Fire Media

Your Own Fate
Night on Earth

The Janus Clan series:

The Defenseless
The Slaves
Birds Flying in the Dark

Poems:

Amos Keppler: Complete Poems 1989 - 2003

(A few of the) novels to be published:

The Afterglow trilogy
Season of the Witch
Alarums of Reality
ShadowWalk
Thunder Road: Ice and Fire
Falling
Black Dragon

For a «complete» list of current and current future Amos Keppler and Midnight Fire Media projects see the back of the book and the Midnight Fire/Midnight Fire Media web pages.

Dreams Belong to the Night

by

Amos Keppler

MIDNIGHT FIRE MEDIA
2011

Midnight Fire Media

http://midnight-fire.net/mfm
For more about Dreams Belong to the Night:
http://midnight-fire.net/dbn

E-Mail:
ak@midnight-fire.net
manofhood@yahoo.com

Cover, text, design, art, premedia and photos Amos Keppler

ISBN 978-82-91693-11-8

Part one:
DREAMS IN DARKNESS

«Revolution begins with the misfits».
Herbert George Wells

CHAPTER ONE

A light flashed in the dark.

A woman stood by the edge of the forest. Her features suggested that she was not quite fully developed. But she was indeed well grown. Strength and agility were very evident in the tall, slim body. Her thoughts returned briefly to a time when this hadn't really been that evident. She turned her attention to the forest, the one she had watched from the mountaintop above. It had an oval shape, surrounded by large fields of green grass. She saw the night between all the trees as impenetrable and threatening. Only by straining her eyes she was occasionally able to glimpse the campfire she knew was burning therein.

The wind howling in the night, seemingly coming from everywhere and nowhere roughed up her short hair. The forelock just about reached her eyebrows. The sound of drums, beating slow and thunderous, reached her, close from behind and more distant in front, on the other side of the forest. She listened, concentrating, attempting not to merely listen with her ears, but seeking beyond the thunderous beat, in the hope of hearing the other drums, those that Jonas had spoken about, that weren't sound at all.

– Listen, listen and you can hear them, he said in her mind, even as she strived to keep herself from being distracted, – the heartbeats of the gods.

She set off into the forest with a sinking feeling in her stomach, but with a fire burning in the eyes. Her point of incursion took place where the gathering of trees was the thickest and the crossing had to be from one point to the other, where there was the farthest to go, like walking the longest route possible on a circled road. It was tough, but that was how they were taught here. The girl smiled.

The wind blew along her body. Her feet hardly seemed to touch the ground. She was dressed in simple fabric, a set of warm and functional clothing making it easy to breathe. She hardly noticed its weight. The forest was breathing mystically and invitingly, but also traitorously. She knew that. Even though the journey between trees was swift she planned every step in her mind before actually taking it. Body and mind were tense. Earlier in her life, before coming here, there was no way she could have imagined that such a focus was even possible, but now it seemed almost a mundane task, like breathing. She imagined a spider spinning its web somewhere ahead. Except that she was no longer thinking in such a manner. Slowly unnecessary thoughts faded from her consciousness. The words appearing in her mind were «spider» and «ahead». She recalled that animals were supposed to think like that, in images and directions.

She took long and fluid strides across the forest bed, sliding between the trees, allowing herself to momentarily recall the first time she had crossed this shore, and to reflect over how noisy she had been. Now, she was confident that the man awaiting her ahead couldn't hear her, even though he knew she was coming.

«When you move through the shadows», he had told her, told them, «be as quiet as the shadow, be the shadow. Always expect the unexpected». He repeated it often. «You may avoid the whirlwind by crawling into a hole in the ground, but you will never be safe. It will always catch up with you».

The darkness momentarily touched her. She shivered lightly and got goose bumps all over. Understanding didn't escape her. In spite of her youth she wasn't unfamiliar with the darker shades of life.

Her foot froze on the spot where it had touched the ground. Against bare skin she felt it, the trap. She jumped, far spryer than a deer. She felt it like that, felt it had to be like that. The trap sprung the moment the foot vanished. She registered how the rope touched her toes. Tree and branches rose violently from its confines and leaves rained everywhere. There was a thunderous crack as many guns fired simultaneously and a rain of bullets, rubber bullets ignited the air above her, while she was rolling away. They were harmless, really, hollow and filled with red paint as they were, but they hurt, like Bergli had initially assured them they would. Hurt more than being hit by a real bullet.

«To die quickly doesn't hurt», he insisted. «The healing does».

Distractions made by these and other stray thoughts faded. Focus returned. She hadn't taken many steps further when the ground suddenly felt unusually soft under her foot. A pitfall. A major one. She grabbed a stick, a cleaned branch and passed the grave crouched and almost on all fours. She moved it like a blind man's stick in the air and the ground before her. It had to be done fast. She was in a hurry. Time was about to catch up with her. Metal screamed against metal and the stick was stuck. Bergli didn't play games. His students had quickly become familiar with the particularly constructed fox trap. It was made to not snap too hard, but afterwards remain firmly around any given foot or whatever it caught. The girl recalled its lessons well.

Time moved within her. Like a cat she jumped up in the nearest tree. She remained on the branch for a second or two. Nothing transpired and she jumped back down. The traps obviously increased in numbers on the ground, but were certainly even more numerous in the trees, particularly where she could easily walk from branch to branch to the target area. He who had set the traps had strived hard and knew the forest intimately. She moved further into the forest's deep night, alert with her entire animal power.

«Lights.» She raised her head and sniffed in the air. «Right hand.»

«Fire?»

«Fire.»

Nothing more of significance transpired. She reached the open area in the forest's midst. Four small fires burned, one in each corner. Between two of them, almost at the opposite side of the clearing an old man sat on a flat rock. The long white hair reached to his shoulders. His head was bent forward and the shoulders lowered. Before the fire closest to him a sword was pushed into the ground. The girl moved with careful steps towards it. She pulled it up and lifted it above her head. In the steel's silvery surface she saw her own silver hair. She locked her eyes on the old man. His eyes seemed… haunted. He sat still, so very still, as if he had never moved at all. The skin had a thin layer of sweat. She moved towards him with the sword raised. Their eyes were like locked on to each other. Yellow leaves danced around him. Spring's juices flowed through her. The blade's silvery surface flashed, mirroring the hot fire. She turned away from him and walked towards the square's center. The fires were all exactly the same distance away from her. She placed herself there, on a small rise. A soundless whisper reached her. She heard the barely audible sound of friction against his clothes and turned abruptly. The time had come. This was the moment. She suddenly sensed the silence. The thundering drumbeat had halted. She couldn't tell the precise moment it had happened, but it had happened well after she had entered the square. She had arrived in time.

A crack, and heavy timber hanging from a rope raced through the air. She threw herself aside, just in time. The moment the log passed her she swung her sword and cut the rope that would have made the thick log swing back and forth like a pendulum. It fell harmlessly to the ground, rolling away from her, over one of the fires. The burst of embers rose in the air. She faced the old man with her feet apart. He held a little bow in his hands. Before she could even think about it, register it he had effortlessly cocked it and sent off an arrow. The arrow raced towards her. She knew it had a blunt point, but in her mind she imagined a sharp metal point that stung and tore flesh and turned red with her blood. She took one step to the side. The blade flashed as she brought it down at the passing arrow, cutting it in two. Its two harmless pieces fell silently to the ground.

He sat still once more. It seemed to her just then like he had never moved at all. In the black clothes his body seemed almost indistinct, while his face was well lit, and finally she was able to glimpse a shadow of a smile there.

In one single, swift move she threw the sword. It hit the tree right above his head with a loud crack and remained there, vibrating, deeply within the tree, within the ground. The broad smile transformed her face. Light on her feet she walked past the man in black and disappeared into the forest. In there, where she saw nothing but darkness, she imagined she could almost hear the heartbeat of the gods.

+++++++++++++++++++++

There was a fire burning on the other side of the woods. Seven youths gathered around it, accompanying the old man. Of the seven there were four girls and three boys, something of a coincidence, according to he who had gathered them. It could just as well have been the other way around, or an even number. They kept their eyes fixed on the old one. He seemed different and in a way less imposing now than in the forest. In another way he seemed and had always seemed overwhelming. During the entire time he had trained them, pushed them at and beyond their ultimate potential they had felt an enormous amount of respect for him.

He was also a tormented man. They could see that clearly now, with their newfound awareness.

– My condolences, he, Jonas Bergli said, with his dry, hoarse voice. – Some time ago, encouraged by me, you set goals for yourself, goals you have now reached, together and as individuals.

Happy and laughing they congratulated each other. They had had a great time here and also felt sadness because it was over.

– I've been pushing you, and tormenting and hounding you, everything to remove layers upon layers of illusions put on you by your surroundings. I'm not sure I've done you any favors.

One of the boys leaned forward and spoke:

– I think I can speak for all of us in expressing my gratitude, sir, for everything you've done for us. We lived only… half-lives before meeting you.

– Hear, hear, one of the other boys said.

The sentiment was echoed by them all.

– But I remain curious. I believe we all are. We wonder about your motivation, about your possible ultimate intentions.

– Formal Olav, one of the girls chuckled.

The conversation was in English, the language tying them together.

– I'm not sure I have any truly satisfactory explanation to give you. Jonas Bergli breathed deeply. – I guess I saw much of myself in you. Let me say it with flowers: The simple truth is that you are rebels, strangers, odd birds, exiles in a society weaving invisible strands around a person from the cradle, strands turning to ever thicker chains as a person grows older. You stand outside what our culture sees as holy and what a culture can't assimilate it destroys. I have enhanced this strangeness in you, instead of muting it. I've taught you to fight and you've learned to know yourself, and thereby learned compassion. Therefore you'll have an even harder life than you would otherwise have. You'll probably be forced to destroy that little soft spot inside simply to survive.

They sat outside their host's small cabin, all of them recalling the bloody hardship they had endured inside and around the old, but well kept building. It already seemed like a distant memory. In the shimmering light from the fire they saw it in a completely different light, as a source, a spring of hidden knowledge, a path to untold wonders. Their eyes were open, had been forced wide-open the last few weeks, and thus they pondered and grew at this remote, unknown place, one that could be anywhere on Earth.

– You *live* here, Anya said slowly. – But you must be rich. Otherwise you would never have been able to travel and… gather us the way you did.

– Money can be useful, even though it truly has no value at all. He shrugged. – In my search I traveled far longer and wider than you've been led to believe. I didn't decide upon any advance number. Eventually I ended up with seven. It was a better chance that way, for you to learn what you had to learn.

– But where did you get the money? Judith asked humorously.

– As I've explained there is a difference between robbing a bank and a defenseless old lady.

Laughter, a silence too deep for words.

– I don't want to say much more, he drawled. – It's important that you start drawing your own conclusions. Don't look at this as an ending, but rather yet another beginning in an unending number of beginnings. You must never stop learning, and you must do it with reason in mind. It's important not to be stuck within a given framework. Life is hard, ruthless, but instead of bending to it you should challenge it. Remember that only desperate situations demand desperate actions. The present day condition of the world is pretty grim, of course, but I meant on a personal level. I can't tell you where to draw the line. You must do that yourself. But I will emphasize one thing: I'm convinced that you, sooner or later will be driven into a corner, pushed against the wall. I can't say when or how, but I know, when push comes to shove that you won't back away. One must concern oneself with oneself before concerning one self with others. There's a fine line here, you see.

He heard them mumble in agreement. He saw the frost in their eyes, of thoughts not yet fully realized. He felt a heart-wrenching compassion just then, in a way he hadn't felt for many years.

– You all did well, but Judith truly surpassed you all. She's your leader, if you should ever, ever need one. He waved with his hands. – That's it, the last class is over and done. From this point on, you're on your own. I'm through with you assholes.

– We live as we dream - alone, Anya intoned.

She was the nature child and the poet among them. They laughed some more, loud and hot chuckles mixed with worry. Increased understanding didn't necessarily lead to good things.

Not in the world as it was.

They ate and drank, practically gorged without gorging on food and wine, enjoying themselves. The meat they digested, an elk they grilled on the open fire, its scent, its very essence… invaded them. Each bite brought another flavor. All seven had participated in the hunt and kill the previous day, in the enormous forest to the east. Before they nourished themselves on the proud animal Bergli led a ceremony they felt was ancient. The elk had given its life so they could live, and they felt boundless gratitude. They fed, honoring the animal, and the meat tasted so much better, better than they could ever have dreamed. This entire final day and night carried with it something magical. The memory overwhelmed them in such a way that they would never be able to forget, even though they might want to. The heat from the ground, from the Earth turned alive within them, and along with the cold from the life-hostile world outside, it made them shiver and burn. They felt close to ancient times, when humanity lived close to the fertile Earth.

The fire burned in their hearts and the blood boiled in their veins. They had learned more this short month than during their entire life previous to it. Judith was seventeen, the others not much older.

– There's so much… work to be done, Anya said. – Too much talk and not enough *action.* The world needs that, needs it desperately.

– The world is screaming for our services, Judith grinned, the intensity beneath the banter only thinly veiled.

Shouts of agreement echoed and multiplied among the small group.

– Swear that you will make a difference in the world, Judith said abruptly and with huge and eerie eyes. – Swear that you will contribute with more than phrases.

Everybody did, one by one and together.

Far more, Olav thought, added in his minds what everybody knew everybody was thinking, while toasting with Judith, looking into those huge innocent eyes of hers.

– I would have loved to help you further, beyond this modest beginning, Bergli said with regret, – both financially and otherwise, but because of various *distinct* reasons it isn't a very good idea. I'm a marked man, and if you're seen with me you will be, too. If not, and you're lucky, you could avoid it for maybe ten years or so, when you'll know better how to deal with it.

– You've evidently done a lot in your time, Anya said cheerfully. – What did you do when you were our age?

– I was a deckhand on a ship, he replied a bit preoccupied. – In those days it was one of the few ways a boy of a poor family could leave the country. Girls had, of course even fewer opportunities. But a few years later I met a group, both men and women sharing my view on life. A wonderful time followed then. I guess we didn't achieve that much, not in the grand scheme of things, but sufficient for us to become famous… or shall I say infamous. At that time rebels had even fewer ways to express their anger and everything compared to today. You should know that nothing comes easy… All of you seven will surely experience periods and moments of doubt. Then it will be more important than ever to remember why you do what you do, and that you rise to the challenge, show what you stand for. Action must follow thought, or freedom will be no more than an illusion.

They knew about doubt, even if it felt like only yesterday since their eyes had started to open. They sensed what enormous odds they had against them, in a world dominated by bleak forces.

The fire rose towards the night sky and less wood remained.

– Is something the matter, Jonas? Judith asked carefully a while later.

– I'm tired, the old man admitted.

She realized he didn't mean physically tired. She moved herself closer to him and lowered her voice.

– We don't know much about you, Jonas. She spoke in Norwegian, now. That made Olav the only one who could understand anything of the conversation and he wasn't around at the moment. – What are you? Who are you?

– A kind of teacher, I suppose, Bergli replied. – Nothing resembling any ordinary one, mind you. I believe it's important, even crucial to teach youth what they aren't taught in ordinary schools.

He grinned. When he realized she wasn't satisfied with the fullness of his reply he continued.

– I left Norway after The Great War, the First World War. Yes, I am that old. I was sick and tired of «the job age» and the wave of stock speculation directly glorifying the hierarchy. I wanted to travel the world, to observe all the changes happening there. I did return to Norway occasionally, like a salmon always returning to its birthplace, but I never felt at home there. Out there, between the borders, I gained a certain perspective, clearly unsatisfactory… in more ways than one… but better still. You see, I don't believe there is any true answer, any unified solution to the problems. No matter, they can't be solved in only a generation. I've learned that much. Teacher and student learn together, because both are in truth… both. That's the best way to learn. Remember that.

– My thanks, teacher. She put a hand on his shoulder.

The old face looked more wrinkled than ever. He was in excellent shape, but the years were like cut into his features.

Suddenly, before she could react or even notice, his eyes changed and a hand grabbed her arm, grabbed it hard.

– You are what I was hoping for, what I feared and hoped, he whispered. – One final message: Have you noticed the bolted room beyond the wine cellar? Do you have it enshrined in your mind?

– Yes, actually I have… She strived to keep a light tone. – I've wondered what…

– A dark secret is waiting in there, he hissed. – Awaiting *you*. Something for the utter desperation and despair. When the day comes, and it will, when no other path is left for you, you'll return there and everything will be ready.

– I will remember, she said, half in a stupor. – Remember…

– Good. He loosened his grip on her. – Good…

His eyes were dead. She shuddered in a paralyzing cold. Dead!

In deep thought she left him. She realized that Jonas Bergli had died bit-by-bit, year-by-year, until there was little or nothing left. He had lived in hopelessness and despair his entire life. And now his life had ended. If it hadn't in truth ended long ago.

But that didn't have anything to do with her. Uncertain steps turned more assured. Her life was just beginning and she would enjoy it. The entire world waited for her out there.

– Our fearless leader, Olav joked when she sat down with the others.

She blushed, fully aware of the fact that she was the youngest. But it didn't really faze her, because she knew it didn't matter.

They studied the old man as he entered the cabin and closed the door behind him.

– He has said everything he wants to say, she stated firmly.

Wilhelm filled her glass and gave it to her. She sipped the wine while attempting to eye-flirt with him. It was a rather failed venture. They called him Willy. He was nice enough, but there was something about him she just didn't get.

She carefully swallowed the red wine and sensed it slip down her throat. It was different from anything she had previously tasted. Jonas had an entire, expensive collection in the cellar. It wasn't the kind of stuff you got drunk on, but she sensed a pleasant warmth spread through her body. Somebody had turned on the cassette player and she started rocking, swaying, following the music's beat.

The Storm waited for them out there…

– The world is at our feet, Olav said. She danced with him and snuggled close.

– Judith and Olav are true, she heard Anya tease them.

The night embraced them darkly. Of the fire only embers remained. The stars in his eyes were the only lights Judith could see. He ruffled her silver hair. Kissed her hard and demanding. She wetly returned his kiss. They were alone now. The others had gone to bed or spread out across the forest.

– I know about a place, he whispered into her ear. – There is soft and dry moss there. There are four special trees. They will enclose us. They will surround and isolate us.

She sensed something explosive be released within and she clung to him. Tonight she would enjoy herself, in wild and uncompromising ways. He liberated himself from her, took two steps back and reached out a hand to her. She reached out hers, and allowed him to take it, and they walked to the forest, walked so fast that her forelock was pushed back from her brow and they almost ran.

TEN YEARS LATER - COPENHAGEN

CHAPTER TWO

Judith Breen walked on the right, heading north on the busy and incredibly broad and long Vesterbrogade. Long, silver hair fluttered in the wind. The wind was always blowing in this town. The thought, the experience made her smile and frown simultaneously. She had just finished working for the day. The stench, the sounds, the voices of people fond of giving orders, the constant hassle and oppressive working conditions stayed with her, as she hurried away from the stinking burger joint.

She took one look at her watch and started running. Autumn's first yellow leaves flowed around her legs. She refused to wait for the light to shift to green and stormed across the street towards Tivoli. Traffic raged in both directions on the broad road, but the cars didn't even come close to her. Still, there were people on the other side casting angry looks in her direction. She turned the corner at the end of Tivoli and discovered that the bus had arrived. A heavy hand hit her shoulder and stopped her in her tracks, turning her around. It belonged to a female police officer. Judith struck the hand, pushing it away.

– Wow, that's some temper we have here, the woman noted caustically.

– You got no excuse to touch me, Judith breathed. And then calmer: – Listen, the bus has arrived, can't we…

– You crossed the street outside the zebra stripes, on a red light, she was told quite pointed. – Such an act may be accepted by a juvenile, sniveling kid, but you're definitely too old for that kind of behavior.

– I must catch that bus, Judith protested. – No cars were even close to me, sergeant.

She looked towards the stop. The last passenger had entered the bus.

– Haven't I seen you before… The policewoman twitched her mouth in an obviously false thoughtful expression. – Yes… NOW, I remember. You were at the illegal demonstration outside ICI. Well, you didn't manage to say much…

– We applied for permission well in advance, but we never received a reply. This is what's it all about isn't it? You don't give a damn about the rest.

The bus left the stop and drove towards the stoplight, towards them.

– To be brief, Breen: You and your likeminded are garbage. You're nothing more than irresponsible children upsetting the natural order of things. You can't do much actual damage, but you're irritating, like a buzzing fly, and not worth more.

– There will always be flies, no matter how many you swat. Judith replied with a naughty grin.

– You got no *productivity,* the policewoman snarled. – You're not contributing anything to society's progress. How does it feel to belong to the lowest of lowest scum? You will never make anything of yourself. You are a disgrace to those who raised you. You will always be the bottom of the barrel, a loser among losers.

The bus stopped for the red light. Judith hammered on the door to make the driver open it. He ignored her. The bus drove on.

– I would like to go, now, sergeant, Judith said calmly. – If you wish to make me listen to more of your disgusting crap, I suggest that you bring four or five of your colleagues next time. Or you might discover that I'm not one of your typical lambs fit for slaughter.

A large crowd of curious people had gathered around them. When the uniformed woman discovered this she stopped playing with the club hanging from her hips.

Judith crossed the street, doing so very deliberate on the zebra crossing, and on green light. There was laughter. She enjoyed that and started whistling. She walked inside the chilly and spacey Hovedbanegården, the Copenhagen Central Station, carrying the rage as a constant inside, wearing the calm as a mask outside. It was an okay place, this, to calm yourself.

Somebody approached her from behind. She turned abruptly, facing a smiling man. She relaxed a bit.

– You're Judith Breen… Uncertainty turned to certainty in his seeking eyes. – You are Judith Breen. I knew it!

– Judith «Silverhair», she confirmed cheerfully, cheerfully like him. – What can I help you with?

– I saw and heard you speak at the ICI protest, he said eagerly. – You were fantastic. It was a fantastic protest. Or… it could have been, I guess…

– You were at the protest, and you speak to me, now?

– Yes, he confirmed a bit vain. – My name is Ole Sivert Olsen. Delighted to…

– Congratulations, Sivert, she said dryly and took his outstretched hand. – You've just earned yourself a place in the Secret Service's hallowed computer archives.

– Sivert? He said, raising a brow.

– I like Sivert, she said merrily.

– I'm honored, he said. – About the computer stuff… I'm older than you and have wanted to make a name for myself for quite some time.

He smiled. She caught herself returning the smile.

– Uh, may I get you something… a drink perhaps?

– I'm an alcoholic, she told him straightforward. – It does surprise me that those computer guys, in their eagerness to drown me haven't made sure it has been «leaked» to the papers yet.

– I guess it's just a matter of time, he said with a gleam in his eyes. She hadn't sensed any disappointment in him. – A coke then?

– Perhaps another time, she teased. – Seriously, though, I have to go, or I will miss this bus, too. Friends are expecting me. Nice to meet you… Sivert.

– Where can I see you again? He cried after her, as she reached the exit.

– Come to «The Green Rose» in Fristaden Friday next week, she returned the cry.

– But that's a ten days' wait, she heard him complain aloud through the glass door.

She couldn't stop giggling and laughing for a long time after that. It had been a long time since she had enjoyed herself this much. He was funny. So funny that he had almost made her forget what had happened just before. Almost.

She (finally) caught route 40 from Central Station. While the bus was driving north she thoughtfully looked out of the window, at the streets, the gray, heavy clouds. Thoughts drifted. Everything she saw was burned into her brain. She had always been blessed or cursed with something approaching photographic memory. The last few years she had felt even stronger the need to train herself in any ability or talent, physically as well as mentally. She had traveled this route countless times. There were always new things to discover, new things to *feel*. The mere registering was no trouble, no feat anymore. It was only when she could, like now pull detailed memories from her mind she could feel she was burning with knowledge.

The man at the bus stop had been wearing a gray coat yesterday, not the gray and black he wore, now. The woman crossing the street had carried a nondescript bag.

Countless other mementos, both from the bus route and not raced slowly through her mind, making her feel good, making her feel bad.

She lived with four others in a loft «apartment» in Classens Gade. None of the five earned much on their jobs. They shared expenses and income, both sporadic and erratic. The sharing was simply a necessity, in order for them to manage from one month to another.

The image of the tears of frustration and despair in Yvonne's face halted the movie being played behind her half open eyes.

The bus passed the botanical garden. Its scents tore into her olfactory sense strong and good. Judith sniffed in the air, wanting more. No one else on the bus bothered to do that. She felt sorry for them.

But she didn't look down on them. From there the road was too short to outright arrogance. A thought making her innards turn violently and her head hang low in despair. She had so absolutely, definitively learned humility, and learned it well.

She left the bus on the second stop in Classens Gade, almost at the end of the street. Silence reigned here, as it almost always did. She breathed the silent mood. Her light steps and the careful way she closed the entrance door echoed in the hall. The stairs reached far, to the distant ceiling, and she ran, all the way to the top. She had promised herself she would always run these stairs.

Well at the top of the stairs she was only sweating marginally. The pulse rate hadn't really been rising much. In fact she could hardly detect any rise at all. Good. A useful test, this, whether or not she kept in shape. She carefully, silently turned the key in the door. Moving silently was usually a matter of honor to her.

The inner hall was dark, dank. They couldn't afford using any electricity beyond bare necessity. The contrast to the living room, as she opened the door and light flooded her eyes, was almost overwhelming.

They had arrived all four of them, way before she did. Willy, Kathy, Yvonne and Jemma. The five of them were, in more ways than one, even though Jemma and Willy had Danish citizenship quite the international bunch.

– You're late, Yvonne greeted her with a lewd smile.

– I can explain. Judith raised her hands in a protective gesture. – First Manning «talked me into» working overtime. Then he made a pass at me. I escaped, even though it took its sweet time. Afterwards on the street, Chief Sergeant Elsa Andersen *delayed* me.

– Jeez, that's enough, Kathy moaned. – Another one listing you in his or her book. How many more enemies will there be before you stop?

– I suppose there will be a lot more, Judith replied lightly.

– Hugo M is giving chase with his big, fleshy hands again, Yvonne said. – You may recall that I warned you about him?

– I have encountered Elsa occasionally, too, Willy grinned. – She doesn't like me. I wonder why.

– We have all encountered countless versions of Hugo and Elsa, Jemma stated.

– Is there any hot water left in the shower? Judith asked, humbly pleading her case.
– We saved something for you, fortunately, Kathy replied kindly. – You clearly need it the most, the way you smell of hamburgers and body odors.
– I've been behind the counter and in the kitchen in «Hamburger Hell,» in a steaming heat for two days, and Manning has kept his fleshy slabs close most of the time. What do you expect, for fuck's sake?
She writhed out of the down-jacket. The rest of the clothes followed suit on the way to the shower. She just dropped them on the floor, so tired that she was unable to do anything else, diving, stumbling under the lovely, shower. The water started out hot, but quickly turned cold. She didn't allow that to bother her, didn't mind that much, as long as there was enough of it. She rinsed herself thoroughly. The drops whipped so lovely against sore skin, cooling her body, her sore mind. Yet, when turning off the water she felt tired enough to sleep a whole week. She wished, in that moment she could have remained under the waterfall forever.
Willy and the three girls helped drying her. They saw how exhausted she was. Willy rubbed her thoroughly but softly with the lovely Turkish towel. As usual she looked for a reaction in him to her nudity. As usual there wasn't any. Willy was gay. Even though he was the only one who had an entire bedroom to himself, none of the girls cared if he saw them naked. They treated him almost like another sister. If he just hadn't been so damn manly. Judith sighed. She had long since realized (in her infinite wisdom) that he didn't have it easy either. There had been the occasional lover, but they had thrown out in disgust his previous failed attempt at a meaningful relationship a month ago.
– You need rest. Willy rubbed a hand across her cheek. – That's obvious without really looking. You should stay here and relax. There's no need for you to *accompany* us to the bank. We'll take care of it.
– No, she mumbled. – You need my wit. I should go. I'm not that tired.
You look like shit, Kathy said brutally. – We'll take care of it.
Kathy was the model in their ranks, the fashion model. She had been a flight attendant when she had been stupid enough to participate in an «illegal» protest. They had fired her. That fact had made her ongoing mood somewhat caustic.
They virtually carried Judith to bed, ignoring her halfhearted useless objections, and covered the sore body by the down. Yvonne kissed her softly on the forehead.
– Sweet dreams, she said cheerfully.
Silverhair didn't hear them leaving the apartment. She slept and sleep came to her filled with confusing and chaotic dreams. They made her moan

in distress and bewilderment, holding on to her for quite a while, before finally, temporarily letting her go.

She woke up, somewhat fresh and rested. It was dark outside. Yvonne sat by the bed. One blink, two and Judith was fully awake.

– What time is it? Where is everybody?

– Seven. Jemma and Kathy are having an evening out. Willy hasn't left for work yet. He's taking a shower.

– So he hasn't dragged his body out of here yet? Yvonne confirmed it by shaking her head. – That's great. I've told him repeatedly that I want to go with him and tonight I feel really up to it.

– Why, Yvonne wondered roguishly, – do you want to go with him?

– I wish to understand him, Silverhair replied. – And why not? It might be fun. You've been there yourself, right? Cheap drinks and nice and interesting clientele, you said.

– You wish to understand the whole world, the French woman laughed. – Throwing yourself at anything. I thought I was pretty curious myself, but that was before I met Silverhair.

– I guess there is a need in me in to keep climbing mountains, Judith said, a bit preoccupied, a bit vulnerable. – Everything that has happened hasn't changed me, but has instead encouraged that. Grandmother used to say I had a great appetite for playing and living. I didn't realize then why she was often sad while saying that.

They were momentarily lost in thoughts, falling into silence.

– How did it go at the meeting? Judith asked suddenly.

She sat up in bed and held Yvonne's eyes with her own.

– Not b-bad. We got the payment postponed. But it doesn't solve anything. In a month we will be stuck in the same mire. That is, if our general situation hasn't taken yet another turn for the worse by then.

Judith didn't make any comments. She just kept looking at her friend.

– We spoke with the chief executive like you said. It was a surprise that he agreed to see us… but that surprise didn't last long. He started making suggestions, implying that we could earn major relief on the rent if we were willing to offer certain services in return…

Judith smiled. Yvonne had seen her that way before. It was a dangerous smile.

++++

Willy worked at the Pan Discothèque as a combined bartender and bouncer. The entrance was found in an old courtyard close to Strøget, Copenhagen's main entertainment district. It looked like any other disco. Judith sat on a stool by the bar on the ground floor. Willy served her her third free coke. She looked at herself in the mirror behind the bar. She was dressed in a dungaree jacket and pants, and she wore running shoes. Several other guests were similarly dressed. People here didn't really look different from guests in any other informal disco or entertainment establishment. What surely looked strange to those who didn't know better was the fact that the couples by the tables and on the dance floor usually were of the same sex. Judith felt neither more nor less estranged here, compared to other places.

She felt attached to Willy, like he probably was attached to her. They had been in love until he found out that he was gay. This fact had naturally put a halt to intimate contact and closer attachments. But they were bound together. As far as she knew they were also the only two of Bergli's seven presently living close to each other.

– Isadora is dead, she said quietly. – There are only five of us left, now.

Willy knew she didn't count Olav among the seven anymore. He also knew why.

– I heard that Anya left you and Olav, he said carefully. – What happened?

– She returned to Ireland, Judith replied tightly. – She wouldn't say why. I haven't heard from her since.

She turned towards him and put her hands on his big ones, obviously eager to change the subject.

– What about you? What did you think and do when it dawned on you that… you know… when it dawned on you?

– It took a while until I managed to fully step out of the closet, he replied relaxed. – But after a while I truly felt that I had found myself. It felt good in many respects, in any that counted.

– You realized yourself, she stated. – I can understand that. Please don't misunderstand, but I think it's great. You accepted your inner being and didn't want to hide it, but stood up for yourself. Like putting up a poster, isn't it and saying it out aloud: «Take me as I am or fuck off».

You're a marvel. He shook his head.

– That's good, she said hotly and devilishly. – Then I won't ruin your reputation now.

She gave him a tongue-kiss on his lips. It happened so fast that he couldn't have avoided it even if he wanted to, and he didn't.

– It's already ruined and has been for some time, he laughed. – In both camps. And by the way: I didn't misunderstand.

He was busy for a time with many orders. It didn't matter to her. She had decided to mingle anyway. Before leaving the bar she allowed herself to admire his mixing technique. He was truly a master and could have had a job in any bar, including places with far higher salaries.

Music was as deafening here as other places and went in thud-thud-thud mode. Sabrina, Sabina, Samantha… It didn't make it easy to engage in a conversation and the surroundings could not be said to be encouraging close contact between people, even though discos were supposed to do just that. In a pig's eye, perhaps.

With passionate moves she threw herself out on the dance floor. Silverhair enjoyed, loved dancing, moving the body, in rhythm and display. When she turned around she sensed the drums in her body, the elastic body. She wanted to howl in joy, really, in this display so rare. There wasn't complete abandon, but close. She realized no time and place could be better. There was quite a high risk of making a fool of herself in her own eyes. No major reward without major risk. And tonight she was ready for it, for it all. She felt awake and better than in a long time. For a long time, now, she had wanted to initiate a new phase in her life. Tonight was the night where she took the first step.

The silver hair glimmered in the light from the spotlights. She attracted attention. Even in the dim light it was impossible not to be fully conscious of that fact. She wondered if she went too far. What if she received… an invitation? She had no idea how to deal with that.

Happily out of breath she left her jacket in Willy's care. He looked sharply at her, knowing fully well how unpredictable she behaved. They rarely knew where they had her.

– Why did you throw the jacket?

– It's hot as hell in here, she laughed.

I surprise people all the time, she thought. It's so great.

Very conscious of playing with fire she returned to the room with the lights and the dance, to the mass of bodies slipping across the floor. She stopped in the portal leading to it. There was virtually nobody dancing just then. They all stood in a circle, watching. Six men and women were moving on the floor, but one alone drew attention to herself.

The wild dancer was dressed in a skintight, black snake-dress. She had oriental features, but a flow of fair blonde hair, all of her a sight to behold. Judith slowly ascended the stairs to the above floor. As she had pictured in her mind one could look directly down on the dance floor from the top. It was exactly like she had fantasized about. She locked her eyes on the smooth hair whirling to the sides by the body's rotation, the body with its smooth and firm limbs, quite visible from where Judith found herself. From this place somebody, perhaps *she,* had studied her in similar ways. The dancer turned her head abruptly and met Judith's eyes. Judith blushed and rushed into the bar. She got a bit confused when she didn't find Willy there, until she realized she was one floor above his station.

A table was available in a corner. She sat down by it and leaned her back against the wall. It calmed her in a way. Huge, wary eyes looked back and forth across the room. She was able to sense the air sliding in and out through her nose, the scent of night from the open windows, mixed with the stench of sweat, smoke and alcohol. A bit in the background she sensed the scent of perfume and bile. She had always had a sharp sense of smell, even though she had grown up in a city.

The image created by smell, sound and vision changed. Before she looked up she knew it was her. How could she be so sure?

She could dream about her.

The woman approached in her tight dress, sliding in night moves, straight to Judith.

– I saw how you enjoyed the dance. Perhaps you would care to dance with me?

She spoke the Skåne-dialect from southern Sweden as if she was born to it, and she obviously was. Judith blinked. She was unable to hide her surprise. It ended up with her nodding silently and rising to greet the other, the other woman taking her hand and leading her away.

– My name is Kimberly Russel. There was a sweet melody in her voice, singing in Judith's ears. – I must tell you, I'm truly excited to meet you.

– Judith Breen. She put a slight, but clear warning in her voice.

– I rather thought I knew you, Miss Russel said cheerfully. – I've just recently arrived in town, so I wasn't completely sure. But I've certainly heard about you from time to time. You're different from the herd, in several ways. And by the way, I meant what I said when I said I was exited to meet you. I'm pretty sure I'm already listed in less public archives.

– You said you knew me, Judith pointed out, insecurity evident in her voice. – Not that you recognized me.

– Don't we know each other? The other's confidence made Judith dizzy.

They began the dance, and it felt right from the first step. Their dance would last an eternity and they would be legends in life and beyond.

Judith couldn't stop observing, and she studied Kimberly discretely, without being close to revealing it. The blonde was almost as tall as Judith herself, substantiating that she was a rather successful mix of Eurasian ancestry, in both her face and body. And the less obvious about her, what was behind the façade revealed similar characteristics.

Music was wild and crazy just then, and they took advantage of this in full, generous in the display of moves and strength. With eyes half closed Judith looked at herself in the mirrors, at the white blouse with shoulder straps clearly a size too small, the pants tightening around thighs and hips. She turned giddy by it all.

– Let’s take a break, she said.

Kimberly could only look at her, naturally, not hearing shit. She pointed at the stairs.

They returned to the upper floor. The corner table, strangely enough was still available. Even though there were other tables they could have chosen Judith did feel strange. They looked cheerfully at each other.

– What about a drink? Kimberly suggested.

– I’ll take care of it, Judith said quickly.

She went down in the bar, to Willy.

– Do you have the red wine? She whispered. He looked surprised at her.

Kimberly didn’t reveal any surprise, merely cheerfulness, when Judith put a big glass in front of her and just a small one in front of herself.

– I don’t drink very much, Judith said shyly.

A confident, calming look from the other woman. A light touch of the cheek.

Silverhair had no intention of drinking more than the one glass, and didn’t. She didn’t get the slightest intoxicated either. Not by the wine.

– My parents were Americans. A while later she was about to reveal things she had never told a soul. – They settled in Norway and Bergen before I was born. I believe they were running from something. They never talked about it. It didn’t end well.

– You were lucky, Kimberly pointed out. – My father was English and mother from East Asia somewhere. I never got to know where or when. I was born in Sweden. Daddy had the house full of «maids». One of them was probably my mother.

Color and lights, Lights in spots and every color. *Fog*. A mist in the surroundings and the soul, in every shade of gray. Judith opened her mind and her heart. Such were her thoughts, and it didn’t have a sentimental feel to it. Not now. She had never done it to this degree before. Now she spilled everything, or that was how it felt, and to a total stranger to boot.

But… in more ways than one she sensed that Kimberly wasn’t a stranger. It twinkled in the well behind the distinctive eyes. She felt a pleasant warmth spread between them and beyond. The surroundings turned indistinct in the fog.

– I guess it’s unnecessary to mention that I was called «silverhair» with more than a derogatory implication at school…

– But you’ve grown beyond and won over that patronizing nickname, the other pointed out energetically, – and turned the name into something honorable. You’ve grown beyond your limitations while the pests bothering you have stayed nothing more than bricks in the fucking wall.

– Well, one of them is a council member in Bergen. Judith shook her head. – I've heard his name be mentioned now and then.

– A slightly bigger brick then, Kimberly shrugged.

– I was called «the old wise woman», too, Judith said, a bit more subdued. – I guess it fits in a way. Since I was little I've had an uncanny ability to see the big picture.

– You have an old soul, Kimberly said excitedly. – I saw that instantly. They are very often good at seeing through illusions: or if they wish it so, to create them. But you, you're just as good at living life as to thinking about it. May I call you Silverhair, please?

– That would please me, Judith replied a bit pulled back. Praise had always embarrassed her.

A moment later she started speaking lightly, deliberating stifling her familiar and draining anger.

- The many supporting the government and the system of things it maintains don't find people like us very responsible and wise, of course and not the previous mentioned kids either, now. Their definition of responsibility is to be a smaller wheel in the bigger, contributing in the most effective way possible to keep an oppressive, destructive system ruining all life, including humans, one ultimately *doomed* going. If that is responsibility, I won't have anything to do with it.

She allowed herself a bitter, sarcastic smile, mixed with the inherent joy inside herself and also in the girl by her side, the girl taking her hand.

– So, I wonder, when looking at the world, she continued, in a more somber moment, aware that she was making a speech, inevitably, – how much I can stand to adapt to the standards of a society so cruel, so inhuman and destructive. I find myself so lost sometimes. We have knowledge, lots of pure information. The question is what we should do about it all, how to break out of the impasse we suffer from. Knowledge isn't necessarily synonymous with understanding, with clarity.

So sharp, so clear the thoughts were. What had turned and turned in her thoughts so long achieved form, substance and rough edges. The smile blossomed. She sensed a connection between them, far beyond the grins and light touches and nods of agreement, and strangely enough it didn't surprise her. It was just there. It needed neither questions nor answers.

And they kept up a certain irony between themselves, to keep it from becoming too sweet.

When they once more took to the dance-floor, they danced tight and they embraced each other. Several other couples did so, too during the soft parade. But even if they had stood right in the middle of Vesterbrogade Judith wouldn't have given a shit. She breathed in and out the close to soft skin and turned dizzy and crazy. Two pairs of pouting lips met and none could later say who had taken the initiative - if any.

– Humans are creatures of passion, Kimberly breathed softly, shaking her head. – We're born to love.

They pulled towards the exit, hardly conscious of the fact. Judith had no idea where Kimberly had found her purse, but it hung from her shoulder. Willy, with his sharp eyes approached and handed Judith her jacket.

– Are you okay? He asked.

– I feel great, she assured him.

He couldn't avoid noticing the abandon and stars in her eyes and didn't know what to believe. She waved to him from the entrance.

Just a wave and she was gone.

They walked a while on the cobblestone. Kimberly was wearing high heels and had to watch out not to fall.

– Aren't you cold? Judith asked and touched the naked arms, legs under the dress, and mumbled. – No, you're warm. Glowing hot…

They moved away from Strøget and towards Nyhavn.

– What shall we do the rest of the evening?

– I'm blond all over the body, Kimberly whispered into her ear.

Judith felt her own heat move beyond any reasonable potency.

She looked at Kimberly, looked again. A cab turned a corner somewhere behind them.

Available…

She took the other woman's hand and waved. The cab stopped and a door opened, as if by itself, and not by their hand. She registered preoccupied that it started raining the moment they sat down.

– My place or yours? She giggled.

Jeez, she behaved like a precocious adolescent girl on her first date.

– I live alone, Kimberly said, bending forward towards the driver. – Drive us to Vesterbro Torv.

It was suddenly pouring outside. The wind whipped the raindrops at the windows. The weather did not influence Silverhair's mood the slightest. She crouched in the seat and gave the female by her side a long, sultry kiss. The driver obviously watched them in the mirror, but she ignored him. She didn't care about the surroundings.

After Kimberly had given the driver further directions the cab stopped straight outside the entrance. The two girls ran the short stretch inside. It didn't take more than a few seconds. They still turned soaking wet.

The apartment was on the lower floor. A small, partly derelict, but nice place, Judith thought. It reminded her of her present home, not containing much more than basic necessities. There was no phone, TV, stereo or other luxuries.

One entered the combined living room and kitchen directly, without going through any other room or even a passage. There was no other room, except for the «bathroom». Judith grinned, before turning solemn, turning her eyes towards the other end of the room, to the bed.

Kimberly shivered visible in her wet dress.

– They cut off electricity a week ago. I don't know what I will do the coming winter. I just don't know…

Judith walked to her, brushing off some hair and kissed her shoulder. Skin was still red hot.

– The night mirrors our dreams.

– Yes, and by day we have to live them.

Judith bit into the shoulder muscle. Kimberly shuddered weakly and with half closed eyes she bent her head backwards. Judith stopped apprehensive for a moment. Kimberly smiled. She grabbed the dungaree-jacket and pushed it off the other's shoulders. It slipped down the arms and fell to the floor. It seemed like a hard knot, a fist loosened somewhere inside Judith. *Free, I'm free*. She lifted Kimberly with surprising ease, carried her to the bed, lowering her down on it. She pulled off her dress. Kimberly helped with impatient moves. Judith tore and pulled off her own clothes. Exposing herself to the other woman hardly felt awkward at all. She held her urges back for a moment, deliberately, posing, before joining the other in bed. Kimberly welcomed her with kisses and touches, moaning and eager in joy. There was a minor hesitation, no more, before Judith responded, before she stroked hands and tongue down the firm body, until reaching the blond mound of hair. Kimberly, her eyes half closed stretched the arms behind her head writhing her body and hips in the bed.

The Eurasian opened her eyes wide, pools of shadow. Judith choked startled, feeling it as if she was swallowed whole.

Rub yourself against me, Kimberly instructed. – Back and forth, back and forth…

Eager hands pushed at the butt. Breen lowered herself. Their groins met, and she shuddered in sudden pleasure. She felt playful hands on her breasts. Bodies pushed at each other, rubbing and caressing. They spent eternity like that, in a sharp and clear intoxication, until touches turned fast and uncontrollable, until hands clasped, and everything turned unbearable. Her body tensed and the heat inside exploded.

Kimberly pulled even closer to her after they had rested side by side for a while, pushed herself at the bigger body, and kissed and patted it with a wet tongue and invasive hands.

– You're such a beautiful pet, little Kim, Breen mumbled preoccupied and stroke the fair hair.

– NO! Don't say that, please. The head was pulled back.

Breen touched carefully the other's skin, damp, now, tight as leather.

– You do have a problem with those words, don't you? I'm sorry.

– You got no reason to be sorry, of course. A sickly, convulsive smile. – It isn't your fault.

– Come, Silverhair called. – Let me make it better, make it up to you.

Kimberly hesitated. Judith pulled her impatiently closer, grabbed the other's hair, pulling the head backwards. And they kissed. Skin glowed and warmed anew. They sighed content.

– It is I who should be sorry, scaring you like that.

– *Hush!* Nothing more was said.

Sweaty bodies glistened in the light from the street outside. Kimberly, laughing and out of breath, kept the other at bay for a moment by holding up a hand. She turned on the bed, so the girls had their heads by each other's hips.

– Perhaps I can still teach you something, she mumbled.

They pulled tight together. Judith allowed her to snuggle a while. But it didn't take long until Breen took the lead. Kim shook her head and surrendered. Eventually it didn't matter. They could no longer decide who was the one touching, and who was being touched. All their moves intensified, and they began to moan wildly, uninhibited. Active hands and tongues explored with impunity wet thighs and holes.

So good, so good, so indescribably wonderful. Oblivion and joy haunted them. They whirled round and round, towards the black hole, deep into night's dreams…

CHAPTER THREE

Dark clouds, a strange grayness, a storm approached straight from the north. Wind blew right through the walls. Humidity outside easily found its way inside and made the room grow even colder by the minute. The cold and more made Judith cover herself well with the down.

Her… bed companion the night before stood by the window, fully dressed. Cars drove by outside, roaring and noisy. Walls were thin and sounds were easily heard, but the sounds still felt muted, dulled. Kimberly turned towards the bed. Judith kept looking into the wall, avoiding the other's beautiful but opaque and eerie eyes.

– Tell me, are you just as clever in everything you do?

– I feel so *embarrassed!*

– Don't worry about it, Kimberly replied cheerfully, spiteful, just a tiny bit aggressive. – It's completely normal. I don't take offense. You're a friend. Friends are honest towards each other.

Friends… The woman on the bed tasted the words, felt how right it sounded.

– It pleases me to hear you say that, she said. – I've thought a bit about it since I woke up. You see, I'm an alcoholic. Just on very rare occasions I drink red wine, like I did yesterday. It was a special occasion.

– I saw the signs in you, Kimberly said, smiling pointedly and enigmatically, – not about your alcoholism, but the other… thing. You've discovered something new about yourself. But I can tell you that you have no reason for being worried. My hunch is that you prefer men, even though you now and then may taste the other… fruit.

– I said I felt embarrassed, Judith said. – I don't feel ashamed.

– I know. The face surrounding the skewed eyes softened. She walked to the girl on the bed and kissed her on the brow. – I've made breakfast. Pull your lazy butt out of bed and get dressed.

Judith had always been eager to harden herself, also against cold. While removing the down the chilly air didn't give her any discomfort. But it did sink in after a while, as she knew it would. They both had jackets on during breakfast.

– Weren't you supposed to be at work? Kimberly asked.

– I'll be fired soon, anyway. Judith put an entire sandwich in her mouth. She was hungry. And thirsty. She drank the entire glass of orange juice in one try. – I can just as well take a day off. I stopped being a nice and compliant girl a long time ago.

– Me, too. Isn't it great? I'm so happy.

Two pair of hands clutched each other. In each other's eyes they found not merely understanding, but also mutual understanding and interdependence, a connection beyond appearances.

– What I feel for you is almost as strong as what I feel for Willy. It was spoken slowly, probing.

– The bartender at Pan? Kimberly wondered.

– Yes, it's comparable in more than one way. That, too, can never be anything *more*.

– You've known me for less than twelve hours, and you already speak this candidly to me. Your sincerity is strengthening our ties. Do you know what? I'm happy with that. I knew almost from the start that we're soul mates.

– Perhaps we've been lovers in a previous life? Silverhair joked.

– Perhaps, the blonde giggled.

They would never forget these first, precious hours, the mood and the strong emotions during the night, and the morning after, when they confirmed their ties just by talking.

It turned dark before they were ready to leave the apartment. Kimberly brought only one single bag, containing clothes change, a cassette player, a few commodities and nothing more. Most of the stuff in the apartment didn't belong to her. Judith sent her an encouraging smile. Out in the streets they breathed deeply. The wind and air felt fresh on her face. Yesterday they had been breathing and moving, but now they felt truly alive.

They started on the walk towards Central Station. It was almost the entire broad street of Vesterbrogade. The tiny bit Judith used to walk from the opposite length was only a minor distance of the long, straight stretch. Kimberly danced on the sidewalk. She had her arms stretched to the side, the bag in one hand and the cassette player in another. Judith caught herself in moving to the beat. Kimberly's bright mood was infectious.

The blonde stopped her friend and moved her hands like conductor's sticks. They cried in unison:

– LIFE CAN BE GREAT! Eager nods. Laughter.

They stopped a moment by Vesterport, embracing the sense of the night and their own moods. Judith always felt a slight worry when she let herself go like this. She had burned herself on it before. And worse.

She looked weary around her.

– What is it? Tell Kim. She's a good listener.

– I'm just pondering a bit over the fact that I always find myself in *cities*. It's a kind of paradox to me, no doubt about it. I… dislike these… heaps of concrete and hostility, even those I like. They are anathema to the human spirit, making it fade away slowly and horribly.

– Perhaps it's your fate, or rather your chosen destiny? Kim, the good listener mused. – You're a *warrior*. Perhaps it's in the cities, the stone deserts the future awaits you, for good or bad.

– The «stone deserts», huh? That's so sad and so poetic.

Hands grabbed hands again and held on.

They had walked for a while when Judith raised a hand in warning, and they stopped.

– Turn off the music.

Kimberly promptly did as she was told.

– Something feels wrong, or not right, I don't know…

Judith couldn't point at one piece of the picture before her, and say for sure it didn't fit, but the worry persisted, as they moved on

On the bridge by the Central Station a woman dressed in fur stood in their way. She held out something resembling caramels. Judith narrowed her eyes slightly. Something was indeed not right about this picture. Someone had gone to a certain length to present this woman as a drug dealer. They hadn't done a very good job.

– I got something for you girls. The voice was slick and smooth as oil. They who had instructed her had seen too many gangster movies. – It's good stuff. You're even allowed an initial sample.

– You are in our way, Judith said coldly. The woman wasn't really. The broad sidewalk made it an easy task avoiding her, but Judith did no longer felt like tiptoeing.

– If you try it, I'm certain you'll enjoy it. There's no need to be upset. Uh, you should of course be eager, but...

Judith and Kimberly glanced at each other and grinned.

– You should consider giving up this line of work, Judith told the woman, almost softly. – You're virtually useless.

– You aren't abusing the stuff yourself, Kimberly said. Why are you doing this?

– You snotty insolent half-breed.

A powerful hand was raised in anger and in a flash it rushed at Kimberly Russel's cheek.

Kimberly met the fleshy hand with one of her own hands. With the other she grabbed the woman's arm, almost by the shoulder. The big body flew through the air. The powerfully built woman in fur showed how well physically trained she was when she landed in almost perfect balance. But she didn't regain it completely before Kimberly rushed in and gave her an elbow in the abdomen. A painful gasp and she was left as newly butchered meat in the street. Judith was thoroughly impressed by the speed in which it had happened. Kimberly had looked as fast and as invisible as the wind.

– Let's get the hell out of here.

Kimberly had lost the bag. Judith grabbed it and one of her friend's arms, pulling her away. People who had seen the incident applauded. Kimberly curtseyed while tiptoeing away.

Judith held hard around the arm, so hard that it would probably result in bruises. Kimberly moaned in pain.

– What is it? She asked weakly. – I didn't do anything wrong, did I?

– On the contrary, you were fabulous. An apologizing smile and the grip loosened. – I just have an ugly, prevailing suspicion about that «drug dealer», that's all. There was a number of things not right about her. I studied her as we approached the scene. She made no attempt to sell to or enlist anybody else, and there were *lots* of possible candidates. I'm willing to bet she had been there on the bridge for some time, probably since we left the apartment.

– You mean she was waiting for us? What reason should there be…

– You're so damned naïve. A shaking of the head. – You should outgrow it. It's probably one of two: Either my *ex* is behind it or it's *official*. They've wanted to get me for something, anything for at least six months now. So far it has been half-hearted and unorganized. But I'm confident they'll be moving me up on their list of priorities fairly soon. On theirs, or on that of those with both money and influence. Their lists are pretty much blurring together anyway.

They passed by the SAS Royal Hotel in a hurry. Unprepared for the sudden pace Kimberley needed to run a bit to keep up with the whirling silverhair. She turned her head, looking back just before they turned the corner. Furwoman still fought to regain her footing on the other side of the street. She made no attempt at following the two.

– Where are we going?

And then adding jokingly:

– Quo Vadis? Where does the road take us?

– Let's go see… a movie. Judith made a dramatic gesture, speaking fluent Swedish: – *Gå på bio, flicka.* Let's let our hair down some.

Kimberly covered her mouth with a hand in an attempt to contain a giggle. She seemed completely starving for joy and laughter, so very vulnerable. Just now her face looked like that of a little girl. And her voice could be like a bird singing. Judith was overwhelmed by amusement and emotion just then. She managed to contain it. The blonde was probably a couple of years older and her body certainly didn't belong to that of a girl.

They crossed the plaza leading to the Palace Theater cinema complex, one that could easily and favorably be compared to the larger ones in major cities throughout the world. An impression enhanced as they walked inside. There were twenty cinemas at the most under one roof and for once the advertising fit the reality: There was always one good movie.

A poster on the wall caught their attention and interest.

– That one, Judith said categorically, reading the Danish movie title of the American film. – «A cellar black as coal».

– «Prince of Darkness», really, Kimberly sniffed.

– Yes. Judith nodded. – The Danish, «translated» titles are just as stupid as the Norwegian.

– And the Swedish, Kimberly agreed. Her face lit up. – So you're a John Carpenter fan, too? I've seen all his movies. They're wonderful, aren't they? He he. I mean… terrifying and wonderfully different, up there with all the best.

– At least the film is featured here, Judith's face lit up, too. – It will probably never be shown in Norway.

– Or in Sweden, Kimberly laughed out aloud.

When they left the cinema two hours later they felt cold, shuttered and yet with an enormous clarity of vision. Ten thousand thoughts ran through their mind and yet they were able to think. The frost awoke them.

Lights and neon blinked through the darkness. Judith Breen both felt and saw the gray buildings behind and around her. She nodded to herself.

– I've moved a round a lot, she told the woman, the smiling shiny-eyed kid in her presence. – Copenhagen is neither the best nor the worst city I've lived in. I've wandered my entire life. I am a wanderer. Since Jonas Bergli let us loose in the world I have, both by choice and not, moved from place to place, alone and with others, and learned a lot. I would've liked to learn more, before… before everything, but it's time to make a stand. Not against the winds of change. I… embrace them. No, make a stand against the powerful and righteous building walls against them, walls of violence and blood, inequality and injustice. Places like these, the stone deserts, where freedom is a four letter word, are indeed my fate.

And she grabbed the beautiful form accompanying her and kissed its lovely lips.

They got as far as Central Station. When they passed through the portal and were about to cross the street towards Tivoli to catch the bus two police officers appeared by their side. It happened quickly, effective, mechanically, as if the uniformed men were machines, not people.

Both grabbed Kimberly hard and turned her around. She made no effort to resist, just looked attentively at them.

– Your passport, one of them, the woman grumbled. – We wish to see it.
– Hey, Judith exclaimed. – What's this about? You have no right to do something like this or speak like that. HEY, I'm speaking to you.
– It's okay, Kimberly said evenly. She put her hand on her friend's arm in a calming gesture, before once more turning to the unformed thugs. – I don't have a passport, have never had one, but I have an ID.
– That will probably not come close to be sufficient, the man said brusquely. – No matter, you have to come with us to the station to clear it up.
– Clear up WHAT? Judith shouted. – She's a Swedish citizen, damn it, born and raised there. You may not be aware of this, but you don't need passports within the Scandinavian countries. No Scandinavian citizens can be forced to carry a passport within the five Scandinavian countries.
– Stay out of this, the woman said pointedly.
– I'm a Norwegian citizen, Judith said acidly, her eyes mocking them. She was really rocking now. – My parents are from the United States of America, but that's probably not *foreign* enough for ya?
– That does it, the woman snarled. – You're under arrest.
– You're such assholes. Suddenly Kimberly's behavior was just as aggressive as her friend.
– You, too. Up against the wall!
Judith sensed the cold metal from the handcuffs close around the skin. The arms were caught behind her back. The two women were led away under lock and key. Curious bystanders watched and listened. And some of them listened and watched well. She recognized the light in their eyes. They recognized her. That pleased her somewhat.
The two of them were pulled away in quite offensive ways. She turned and cried:
– Will someone be so kind to call Yvonne Bastian at the crisis center for violence victims and immigrants? Tell her I'm in desperate need of assistance.
There were shouts and laughter. Enough shouts of support to make her hopeful.
Entire groups followed them, mostly from a safe distance. But very few turned back, no matter how much the police officers shouted at them, scolded and threatened. It led to extensive delays. When the two of them were finally led into the police station's processing room it didn't come to any surprise to Judith that Yvonne was already there. Behind her was her friend, the lawyer. Journalists - from newspapers, radio and TV stood poised all over the room. More pushed on to get inside.

The French woman embraced Judith. For quite natural reasons Judith couldn't return the embrace.

– What happened?

– I have no idea, Judith replied dryly. – We had been to the cinema, and not long afterwards they grabbed us.

– Must have been some film.

– «Prince of Darkness», Judith said, both sober and dreamy. – It gave the audience the overwhelming sense that there just isn't any place to hide. That's so very, very correct.

– Well, the other one sighed. – I hope you didn't give them anything but name and number.

– Not even that. There was no need. They knew it already, and have for some time, I gather.

There were flashes, as photos were taken, sounds of whirring from tape recorders and video cameras, a true chaos, but not so much out of control that it gave the police an excuse to clear the premises.

– Hey, Judith, a journalist called to her. – This is the second time you're arrested in a week. How does it feel?

– I would have been higher on the list if I had run faster, Judith replied, showing what she felt about such stupid questions.

– What was the *reason* this time?

– I can hardly begin to guess, she replied laconically. – You'll have to ask them. Just because I was there, I guess.

Roaring laughter. They liked Silverhair.

– Yvonne and Morten, she presented casually. – This is Kimberly. She's with me.

– What is GOING ON here? The on duty desk officer shouted.

Based on his facial color he had evidently spent a considerable time and effort nursing his annoyance before releasing the pent up aggression.

– We have arrested these two, the male police officer claimed weakly.

He obviously didn't feel very confident being the victim of his superior's eagle eye and the focal point of everybody else in the room.

Morten walked to the desk, presenting his card, his only one.

– I'm representing these two, he stated, in an even voice. – I believe it will be easier on all of us if we can agree that this was all based on a *misunderstanding*.

– Certainly not any misunderstanding, the female cop snarled at the lawyer. – They resisted arrest… Yes, they did. Resisted arrest. We arrested them.

– On what grounds?

– On what grounds, what? What do you mean?

The woman blinked.

– On what grounds did you arrest them? Morten wondered.

He had a smile on his lips. So tiny that it almost didn't show. Almost.

– Just because they were there, they heard a fair voice from the crowd.

Cackling. Loud cackling.

The officer behind the suddenly not so comfortable desk glared at his colleagues. What the hell was wrong with them? You would have to look long and hard to find such clumsiness. He intended to grant their request, but if something went wrong later he would certainly make sure they took the fall. He reached for an arrest form…

A man forced himself through the crowd to reach the desk, followed by quite a few other men and women. The desk officer had seen the expression on their faces many times. Too many times. His hand fell on the desk, conveniently far away from the arrest form.

– Listen, I saw what happened, the man said, his jaw very, very set. – And you can bet I'll be in court and that I'll *testify*.

– Me, too… me, too… me, too, people repeated in the ever growing queue.

The female cop opened and shut her mouth endlessly, unable to utter a single word. Her face was contorted in rage, but she had enough sense to remain silent.

– Release them. The man behind the desk waved his hand.

Judith and Kimberly were pushed hard against the desk. Keys were turned and the cuffs harshly removed. The male cop placed himself behind Kimberly.

– You won't get away with it, he hissed into her ear. – Don't think coloring your hair helps you any.

– What was that, officer? Morten straightened. – Do you care to repeat what you just said?

– Go straight to hell, the man grinned.

– I got it all on tape. A man stepped forward. Judith recognized him. It was Ole Sivert Olsen. He smiled eagerly at her.

– I did, too, was heard from several dry throats.

Sivert played the tape. And they all heard it clearly, every word.

– *«You won't get away with it. Don't think coloring your hair helps you any»*.

– Do you care to explain what you meant by that remark, officer? Sivert asked innocently.

He was instantly followed by his colleagues, rushing towards the foaming cop, armed with notebooks and microphones.

Chaos erupted all over the place.

Judith smiled from ear to ear. Her bad mood vaporized in an instant. She felt a vitality she had hardly felt in ten years. Perhaps she had been withering lately, fading without realizing it? Outside she even took great pleasure breathing the polluted air. Yvonne, Morten Falck and Kimberly gathered around her. She embraced them all. The journalists had finally discontinued their assault. Only one remained on the battlefield. Ole Sivert Olsen. He stood there waiting, some distance away. Judith brought her three friends with her to him.

– Guilty as charged. He lifted his hands in a mockingly protective gesture. – I'm a journalist. Will you exterminate me now or sooner? I know how you feel about journalists.

– I've never been one to generalize, she said lightly.

– I hope you'll never doubt that I'm on your side, he said more somber and quiet.

– Don't be silly. I know you won't do anything to hurt me.

She looked so much like a queen then. He had to swallow hard. He knew she wouldn't like to be called that or be seen as one. And that was what really made her fit to lead.

Two pair of eyes met and remained in contact. She desired him. That comforted her, in a way.

They made a trip to Tivoli, the huge amusement park in central Copenhagen, needed to relax after all the ruckus. Relax with more ruckus, Judith thought. Fight fire with fire.

Carousels turned. Lights blinked from every angle. Only minor areas of the gray roads and the green grass in the park were poorly lit. They encountered lots and lots of people virtually anywhere they went. The mood wasn't bad, Judith mused, and they had fun. Yvonne and Morten snuggled tight and constantly. Judith felt no desire to do it, either with Kimberly or Sivert. They respected that. The amusement park was certainly special in this town. One might get the sense of being isolated from the world outside. If one imagined and listened with head, hands and heart this could be a place independent of time and space, something that could be a good thing. Even though the clocks were ticking and humming, the numbers and markers moved, time had frozen and the world outside didn't exist.

The entire world, all its many and varied parts awaited them.

Judith rose and howled on the rollercoaster, one brief moment of boiling blood. She was breathing hard and her cheeks turned red well before she dismounted the coach. One step seemed timeless. She sensed the wheel of Life turn in her depths.

One of the restaurants offered today's special at a very low cost, even less expensive since the season was about to end. The five of them grabbed the opportunity wholeheartedly. It didn't happen too often that they had the chance to eat as much as they could handle.

– I'm *starved,* Yvonne stated. – I could eat everything on the table.

Judith easily noticed that she didn't eat with much enjoyment. She had behaved overly cheerful and eager the entire evening. Judith didn't push her. Pain mixed with vitality always broke the surface.

They tasted everything fully this night. The mood in the room in general and among the five of them in particular would have to be described as… spirited. Perhaps they were merely imagining that everybody else present had a good time, too, but they couldn't help it. They sensed something unknown and fantastic awaken somewhere inside. The longer time they spent together the more it seemed that they, in truth belonged together. Kimberly and Sivert seemed to fit in, as if they had always been there. All five of them felt it the same way. As if they had always been together.

– The bank's chief executive called me at the office today, Yvonne said. – You should have heard the sleazy voice. *Horrible!* He told me that there might be problems. There would certainly be major problems. But he would be able and willing to handle them… in exchange for certain services.

– By damn, Kimberly exclaimed and whistled.

– I managed to keep myself from giving such a reply, Yvonne said, shaking her head, smiling slightly. – I played so virtuous and innocent that I almost threw up on the spot. Wasn't everything settled? What did he mean exactly? I complained and wailed, telling him in intimate detail how difficult life was. I even let him experience my cute-little-girl persona.

– Did it work? Morten queried, very interested.

Contrary to some, he didn't believe women were weak, frail creatures that had to be protected at any cost. But there was a clear narrowing of his eyes, showing his anger.

– I realized that he wasn't a pedophile, Yvonne replied dryly. – He didn't fall for any of it. «You and the other tramps shouldn't take too long to reach a decision, Miss Bastian».

Judith turned to her with a conspiratorial look engraved in her features.

– He meant everybody in the apartment, then? Tell me… did he include Willy, too? Did it seem like that to you?

– Yes, Yvonne replied, pondering. – The way he said the word «tramps» I would definitely say so. Yes.

– Good, Kimberly said pleased.

She had more than an inkling of what Judith had in mind. She had already been given ample demonstration of the remarkable ways Judith's mind worked.

– If he calls again you tell him we accept his terms. Judith enjoyed herself thoroughly by observing the shocked expression in the faces of Morten, Yvonne and Sivert. – On one condition. Demand that he gets himself a certificate of health first, and that we get to pick the doctor in question. Or the deal is off. And keep the conversations you have with him. He may not know that you have the opportunity to record what's being said. It's possible that we won't get more trouble from him, but it never hurts being prepared, right?

The others looked speechless at her. She smiled innocently.

– What if he doesn't buy it? Sivert asked.

– He will. The temptation is too much for any such smalltime tyrant. He won't take the chance that we're bluffing. It's a game to him, too. If we... move out he loses any chance he might have.

Enlightenment changed first Yvonne's face, then the others'. The four of them gave Silverhair their best smile, admiring her from ear to ear.

– We've talked for so very long about changing our lives, Judith told them. – It's about time the dream becomes the reality. And this is also a good opportunity to give a true asshole a sledgehammer poke on the nose.

– Nobody fucks with us, right? Yvonne's smile both hardened and softened. – You're right. They've done it for too long. We have let them do it for far too long.

– They strike at us ever harder, Sivert said serious minded. – I've seen it coming. It's just a matter of time until something... worse happens. We won't always be as lucky as we were today. One day they'll throw away their masks, and they won't give a shit about procedure and the illusion of democracy. I've seen it happen before, in Italy and West Germany.

They weren't surprised by his «us», but he was himself. Judith put a hand at the top of his. Three other hands joined in, and there would be more to come. With hand, head and heart they bonded, and they rejoiced, did so in spite of the bugs crawling under their skin, a stifling impression they couldn't rid themselves of... that destiny had caught up with them.

CHAPTER FOUR

September had passed, virtually undetected, vanished into mists of Time and Shadow. Winds blew harder and colder. This evening in seething darkness it wasn't raining. In the area surrounding the tavern The Green Rose in Liberty City - Christiania the wind was also quite absent. One might spot clouds of mist in the air, between and above the buildings. Circling the house with the rundown façade was both fresh and yellow leaves. The place seemed like the eye of the Storm.

Beyond the front of the building air and flesh pulsed with life and heat. People had been looking forward to this meeting for a long time. It had been announced, but not initiated, started, but not concluded. It had been disrupted, delayed, disrupted and delayed time and time again. Such meetings often were. Now was the time. Darkness descended on the streets outside. No electrical lights, either outside or inside disturbed the peace, the roaring mood flowing from almost every single human being present. Lights from torches, kerosene lamps and other non-electrical sources danced across the gathering. Everybody allowed inside had dressed in dark robes and hoods. The scent of Marijuana and alcohol from previous evenings lingered in the air, but there was no fresh, sweet scent of Marijuana present tonight.

– Why can't I bring my stash? A man complained.

– Because the public servants shall not have any excuse for a raid or to stop anything going on inside, one of the sentries said. – One hopes they will decide they need one this time around. No matter, no one has come here to eat, drink or smoke, or dance. No, tonight, my friend we seek another dance, another tune.

There were six sentries by the entrance. Their torches lit shadowy faces. Most people were allowed to enter, but not everybody. The sentries didn't really have a hard task. There was no queue, even though there was some curious and less eager potential attendees on the opposite side of the street. Some of them even dressed in cloak and hood. Some for fun. Others just didn't dare take that crucial step forward. Crossing a ravine was a big step. There was a shimmering of movement in the unruly line. A figure divided from the mass, and set out across the street. The man was visibly hesitating, but he didn't turn back. He had realized that one couldn't cross a chasm in two small jumps.

They stopped him in front of the open door. One of the six standing there shoved a torch forward to reveal his features. Then it was pulled back, and he saw nothing but darkness ahead.

– I'm Charon - the Ferryman, an ice cold voice stated. – I don't know you, and I know everybody here.

– Kurt, he coughed. – Kurt Mørch. I…

– Hold your horses, we don't need your life's story, he was cut off, – just tell us… why you're here.

He thought about it, if nothing more than a short moment.

– I've been patient for too long. I'm tired of just talking, of hiding my head in the sand.

– You may pass - by your own recognizance. «Enter ye here, and let all hope fade».

He realized that the words and subsequent laughter weren't malicious, and he also realized the further implications, the deeper meaning. He had done more than enough thinking in his thirty-year life.

The darkness inside embraced him, but not the silence. He had visited this place briefly once before. Everything seemed so very different now. The similarities were just superficial. The roses on the wall meant something. The patterns on the wall, the scent in the air, everything he experienced meant something, had some deeper significance. He stood before two entrances. One ended in nothing. There were naked trees and human skeletons. The heading above said: «No hope here». Above the other opening the heading said: «There's still hope, hanging from a thin rope».

– *So* poetic, a girl marveled.

He knew there were people who had turned and left at this point. He knew people. There were those who couldn't stand to hear the truth. Not that he was always completely secure in his beliefs and in himself. Only very narrow-minded people believed that about themselves. But he crossed his Rubicon, threw himself into the raging river, and walked through the portal more certain of anything than ever before in his life.

The ceiling was pretty high up here. Originally it had probably been lower. Most of what would have been the upper floor had been removed. Stairs led upstairs along the walls. The entire room resembled a mix of a saloon in the American West and a tavern from the Dark Ages. Life seethed everywhere. In contrast to that the level of noise wasn't too bad and conversation was low-keyed, muted. Kurt easily realized why. What was being said didn't need to be emphasized. Not here.

Inside any given green rose the guests were free to contribute to the entertainment, and to entertain themselves. They sat by the tables or placed themselves on the small stage. Just now, one sat on a stool in a corner and played solo-saxophone. Grieving tones, longing tones filled the room. The music reached all present, and reminded them all of a time before the present day world, emotions from a state that had hardly existed other places than in humans' dreams.

Kurt saw that the man playing wore a half-mask, and that the hood covered most of his forehead. Several of those present had covered their faces. Only by the entrance they had shown themselves. Kurt worked, had worked as a production designer in movies and theater.

– I enjoy the costumes and stage I see here, he grinned to no one in particular. – To me art is something true and real, something to be savored everywhere, something wild and vital needed in any world, any society, to keep it from stagnating and fading.

He smiled to himself when he saw one wearing a genuine monk robe.

Others spoke close enough and loud enough for him to hear without straining his ears.

– Very few of those present tonight enjoy hiding, a girl argued, somewhat heated to a cluster of fellow visitors, – but it's necessary. The secret services could have found a way to photograph the visitors. It's both a means and an end to make it hard for such people, isn't it?

– She's absolutely correct, a boy stated hotly. – You know she is. Scandinavia is the land of milk and honey, and no serpents are allowed.

– I'm a serpent, the girl cried. – I'm the Lizard Queen. I can do ANYTHING!

More laughter, hearty and loud rocked the house and its people, hearty and loud enough to wake the dead. Kurt slipped ever deeper into the present stream of consciousness and excitement and furious expression, a catching gathering in his throat.

Judith and Sivert sat by a small table by the bar. They had placed themselves on that exact spot, to easily view the entire room. It was unnerving in some ways, almost like they sat outside it all, able to see behind them… sitting inside it all. The entrance was just a few steps away, and they were able to study everybody entering up close and personal. They saw Kurt enter and seat himself. They smelled him, heard the sound of his breath.

– Another one setting out on the Thunder Road, Judith said, shaking her head. – Poor guy.

Morten, presently among the sentries spoke to them as he passed by.

– Nobody here knows him. He spoke softly, just loud enough for the two of them to hear the words. – But I believe he's okay. I recognized something in him, I think, a longing, the burning impatience.

– Just the possibility for him belonging here should be sufficient, Judith said decisively. – It's better to deny one too few than one too many. One may never see in advance which seed that may grow.

– Most people with potential to think and act for themselves, may need two, three or more encouragements, and even hard pushes first, Sivert said.

– I know. Judith nodded. – I've had many.

– We're all brainwashed and rinsed from birth, the journalist said solemnly. – It doesn't have to be a conscious, focused force behind it. It's just the way present day society works. We're taught to think, or not in certain ways, and to deny all other ways. And the noose is tightening ever more. The Soviets and the Americans have conducted «research» in behavior control and modification since the fifties, at least that long, and it's very naïve to believe it doesn't happen here, too…

He stopped when it dawned on him that he had made a speech.

She took his hand. It didn't cost her that much.

– Those thoughts have been burning you up inside, haven't they?

– Yes. The softness and understanding he read in her hard eyes made him even hotter. – Yes…

– As they have in many others.

She looked around her, a bit preoccupied, thinking about what had happened earlier in the week.

Yvonne sat by her desk, in the worn down office. The others stood around her. Judith, Kimberly, Morten, Sivert, Kathy, Willy, Jemma, Steve, Kees, Renni and Karine.

The man in the other end of the line spoke very loud. They all heard him easily.

– *You agreed to it*, he said furiously. – *I've kept my part of the bargain. You better stand by yours, for your own sake.*

– As I said, Yvonne said with an unusual, triumphant smile. – We've changed our minds. We no longer want to give in to sickening, little men like you.

– I'm not alone. Something you will discover if you don't come to your senses. My partners have also put this on their schedule.

– Ask *them* to suck you off, little Caesar. Yvonne put all the scorn and sarcasm she could muster into her voice. She held nothing back. It worked.

– *You five will appear at my home tonight. You will all dress casually, very casually, and you will obey our every command. Or we will do much worse to you than throw you out in the streets.*

There was a «click». Not from the phone. From the tape recorder. Yvonne played it back. It turned very quiet at the other end of the line.

– *You five will appear at my home tonight. You will all dress casually, very casually, and you will obey our every command. Or we will do much worse to you than throw you out in the streets.*

– If it's agreeable to you, this concludes our relationship, Yvonne said. – Goodbye, Casper.

She waited. Nothing more was said. She hung up.

– Why don't you move in with us? Renni had offered.

They had gratefully accepted the offer. The apartment in Classens Gade had lost its final charm after a few days in their new home. And they no longer desired to play the landlord's game, whether he was in cahoots with Casper the friendly bank manager or not.

When he came to throw them out the next day, they stood in the hallway with their luggage. They presented the key to him before he managed to open his mouth. Six nomads left the place as quietly as they had moved in. They felt tons lighter, infinitely better.

The room, the mist and the glimpses in it in the Green Rose turned real for Judith once more.

Kimberly waded around and served, and smiled. She held the huge glasses of beer in an easy grip, as if they were much smaller. The visible parts of her face seemed to glow. Judith would have been willing to swear she saw her smile even when she had her back to her.

They had found themselves a new life here, the six who had lived in the apartment in Classens Gade. They had joined those who had already lived here for months, for several of the Moon's phases. Nobody seemed to own the building and nobody cared whether anybody owned it or not. Five of those still living here had been participating in the great moving in party six months ago. They had «refurbished» the house and made it their home. For the time being, counting the newly arrived, fifteen souls lived within these walls. Not many dared live here, not even people visiting often. There was a lot of room. Willy and the girls had been made more than welcome. Morten and Sivert would rather have lived here, too. It would just be a confirmation of the actuality. But it was decided that there could be an advantage that some were living outside. If the worst should happen it could be a major benefit to have a group of «independents», someone seemingly outside what was perceived as the hardcore ready to act if trouble arose.

– How weird.

It was hardly audible. Sivert only noticed her skewed smile.

– May I inquire what's amusing the maiden?

– A few days in this paradise, she grinned, – and we turn paranoid. In a way it is sad and scary, but exciting, too. We all sense it, the danger, the quiver in our innards.

She squeezed his hand harder. He sensed the jolt, not as electricity, but something far more fundamental.

– And I've realized a long time ago that paranoia is just another word for vigilance.

And then there wasn't even a jolt anymore, but like blood, flowing from her into him, spreading slowly through his veins.

Willy sat by the adjacent table, seemingly in deep conversation with two guys who were absolutely not comfortable in tonight's particular chosen clothing. He spoke loud and noisy. He had a well-developed sense of humor in Judith's eyes. It pleased and stimulated her.

– I recognize one of the two, Sivert whispered, faking a surprised tone. – He was intelligence officer at the embassy in Bonn years ago. What business can he *possibly* be conducting here?

– We're affectionately calling them snitches, Judith commented dryly. – We allowed them access tonight, to give their masters the illusion of control over us. They won't hear anything of consequence. And as you know the belief in control is one of the greatest illusions there is.

– I can confirm that, she added serious minded.

He laughed. Then he laughed even more, at his own, ironic taint. Where was this reckless mood coming from? He had to look far back into his own past to find anything resembling it.

– Perhaps it would've been better if we could have sailed away on a green wave, she said more solemnly. – But I doubt it. And the world is as it is. We can dream, but we can't hide. There are no more big holes in the sand to hide our heads.

He nodded, thought about it, and nodded again.

Smoke, lights in the air. It's easy to lose ourselves in the mist and the glimpses in it. You can study the pattern forever. You may learn much, but you may also disappear into the infinite and eternal. Lights blink, and smoke is rising from the ashes. Lights blink again. No beginning, no end. There is one simple rule: Energy can't be created or destroyed, just changed into another form.

Energy in many shapes moved around them tonight.

A powerful built man, covered by cloak and hood jumped up at the bar. Judith blinked. She had been surprised. It pleased her. She hoped she would retain her sense of wonder, even after a thousand years.

– The time has come, the guy at the bar cried. – We must either dig ourselves a hole, a big, deep hole, or make a stand. To us there's no longer any middle ground.

One rose from a chair, a woman. She tore off her hood. It was Yvonne. The black hair flashed around the sparking eyes. She cried out in a loud voice:

– Who's guilty when a poor man is breaking and entering a rich man's home? Many would stumble and give the wrong answer to that one. The tyrants and their eager servants are paralyzing us with lies and deception. They're so good at it that they're fooling almost everybody.

Rejoicing and shouts of agreement, salutes and the thunder of feet against the floor bathed her in pleasant heat. The gathering celebrated both themselves and the fact that they had come here at all. It was worth celebrating, in their opinion.

Silverhair made herself seen. The sound of the saxophone faded and the room turned virtually silent. She didn't remove her hood. If she did there was more than a good chance that everybody would. Yvonne had removed hers as a challenge, but so many here were innocents. They did yet not want to believe the worst. But the mood here… it was something special. Judith felt she faced something… fundamental. The moon shone for her tonight. She could almost *see* it, through the ceiling and the clouds. She said:

– Fear does something to us… Fear leads to passivity, spiritually as well as physically. They don't like that we *dream*. People without dreams are easy to lead. They're easy to keep in place.

– Everything in nature is connected. What we need more than anything else to get across is a holistic worldview, cause and effect, effect and cause. Everything in society is connected, South Africa, multinational corporations, industry, public and private governments, parliaments, injustice, lack of freedom, destruction of nature, of *Life*, the world-encompassing world community where we've grown to adulthood. Both medically speaking and otherwise the classical approach is to attempt treating the symptoms of the disease, instead of the disease itself… The gun is directed at those dependent on drugs. There are only asked minor questions as to why this dependency exists in the first place. Those who steal a little are jailed, while those who steal a lot are made into kings and dignitaries. The law is made by the rich and powerful, to benefit the rich and powerful, against those who have little or nothing, and those who are resisting the system. Environmental work is merely cosmetic, more of a joke really. It's like using a plastic axe to chop down a huge tree. The masters wish it so. Why should they change anything? They don't suffer. At least that's what they keep telling themselves. It's a charade, a masquerade. With the difference that the audience is forced to stand up straight and applaud them most of the time. Bush is smuggling drugs while he, as one of the most popular actors expresses his animosity concerning its popularity. The Norwegian government preaches conservation and defends environmental issues while heavily supporting car traffic and subsidizing power hungry industries. Danish authorities support a super corporation like AP Møller, one repeatedly fucking and stamping on the ants. The Swedes sell weapons like hell. Maggie takes the attack on the freedom of speech one step further. The Germans are photographing and registering protesters. In Eastern Europe, at least people are shot with full disclosure these days. Video and movies are blamed for the increasing violence in society. As you know it's very common to blame art when everything becomes too much to handle for the poor tyrants and those before mentioned eager servants. Now, as ever, art is merely a mirror image of the society it's portraying. There are those who will ban anything not supporting their narrow view on life. Censorship is something sneaky, often concealed until emerging fully, shockingly. There's certainly something very wrong with all nations needing censorship and secret police. There are people claiming that those things are necessary for the «defense of the realm» and many more «good» reasons. *And that's true.* Kingdoms and nations do need stuff like that to survive, a horror as they are to the living Earth. Surveillance is indeed directed inwards, against a country's own citizens. «Damaging» movies, books and people are very handy to blame, when not everything goes according to plan. All these illusions and conceits need to be exposed. Einstein said that nationalism is a children's disease. We must leave this narrow belief behind, and approach a broader view. We must no longer allow ourselves to be misled, must stop calling people from other cultures «Enemy». The enemy is usually far closer. We must stop fooling ourselves, no longer allowing ourselves to be fooled, to live in imbalance, inequality and poverty. From now on there will be no more turning away. No more compromises.

– Let me hear your cry. She raised a fisted hand. – No - more - compromises.

– NO MORE COMPROMISES!

The present individuals listening to her originated from virtually every corner of the globe. Except for the two provocateurs everybody listened intensely. And they had a taste and a touch of the strange, seething mood. Something extraordinary happened here, this night. Only the two spies and a few others failed to realize that. Important words were spoken. It was so strange, how people from all over the world had gathered in this place, in this backyard, where history was in the making.

Among them was Jemma, from Jamaica, by way of Fascist Britain, Kees, a white from South Africa, running from forced military service, finding that he had to leave his limited country of birth behind to fight effectively against oppression. Here had also come former, basically peripheral members of the Baader-Meinhof Gang, Red Brigades, Action Direct and other rebel groups. They felt at least something resembling renewed hope this night. It burned in the wind and through them, exploding inside. They had thrown off the shackles of nationalism, and taken a giant leap further on their way.

Judith lifted and lowered open hands, up and down, up and down, lifting the very mood. It turned wild after that. They imagined they glimpsed the silver hair, and the crooked smile beneath the hood.

– *Where do we go from here?*

– *A beginning in a long chain of beginnings,* Jonas Bergli had said.

Judith and Willy looked at one another. They felt the sweet itch of expectation.

There's always another mountain to climb.

++++++++++++++++++++++++++++++++

The heat and humidity broke her down, slowly and inevitably. They had warned Judith against Hugo Manning, but she hadn't listened. She could defend herself, she had told them cockily, so sure of herself.

She toiled and suffered in one Hamburger Hell, the kitchen in Manning's fast food chain. It was her second turn of three this night, and it was HOT, so terribly hot. Like all the other girls she spent a lot of time drying her forehead. She had lost count of how many times she had done this in the course of the evening. The thick sweatband had been penetrated by sweat hours ago. Her vision turned foggy and her eyes burned because of the sweat. Quite often she turned the burgers without seeing anything beyond the fog in her eyes. Occasionally they ended up on the floor. She threw them disrespectfully back on the plate.

The ventilation had been out of order a long time and Hugo was in no hurry to have it fixed. It was whispered that he actually wanted it this way. He was notorious for things like this, and far worse than this. Instead of correcting bad working condition, he perfected them. Judith believed it. People did quit, occasionally. The way she heard it they moved far away to escape even the memories of this place. Some even vanished without a trace. They who stayed he treated ever worse. It proved to be a vicious circle. Eventually everybody was so broken that they didn't dare quit, and put up with ever more to keep their job. But Judith didn't let herself be harassed.

Perhaps I haven't been here long enough, she thought, deeply disheartened.

She knew he was targeting her. Precisely because she wouldn't let herself be harassed. Still, she began to grow tired of it. His persistent competitive viciousness would always outdo hers. She wanted to quit. And she would have. If not for the fact that she needed the job almost just as bad as everyone else here.

He obviously enjoyed his game, but most of all he enjoyed playing her, perhaps because she enjoyed a certain status as a rebel and because of her distaste for him. One she didn't bother hiding.

She did her best to distract herself, and to raise the rage within. She feared this monster in her innermost being, but most of all she feared it would fade away, die of exhaustion. All this made her so… so *furious*. She occasionally played with the idea of… No, he wasn't worth it and his death would hardly be a gain to anyone. He was only one among so very many. She couldn't kill all of them. There had to be a better way. One had to strive to see the big picture. Manning just represented his peers, one symptom among many. It was like that with everything concerning the coldness and alienation. The human beings lived far from their original surroundings. Hunters and nomads had become farmers and city dwellers, two sides of the same, jagged coin. The attitude was what needed to change. The vicious circle had to be broken. The children, with a few exceptions grew up to become what the parents and society made them. She was one of those exceptions, she hoped, downtrodden and desperate. But more were needed, many times more than everybody with an attitude like hers around the world today. Humanity no longer personally harvested what they sowed. Or better: They sowed and thereby there was no perceived need for spilling game's blood to survive. The close-knit relation to everything living was gone or forgotten. Sometimes Judith Breen felt she could reach out her hand and touch it, but it always slipped away. They had to become many, she and her like, like an army of lemmings, unstoppable.

Finally it was her turn to stay behind the counter. Out here the air felt cool and fresh. Almost too much so, when the door opened and the wind and the icy gust from the east filled the room.

A group of youths, just arrived and about to order recognized her. She saw it clearly, and she saw the characteristic surprise. They whispered to each other. She smiled in despair.

– Are *you* working *here?* One of them asked as he approached the desk.

– Why shouldn't I work here, at a burger joint? She wondered.

– Errr. He drawled a bit and stopped.

– You evidently see the work behind a counter in a hamburger café as inferior, she stated softly. – This in spite of your usually very open-minded outlook on life. If I were you I would have realized that nothing is inferior in itself. Our artificial society puts artificial values on everything and everyone, everywhere.

– Fuck, we're sorry, one offered, – but it isn't that important, is it, to justify a lecture?

– A similar process of thought is justifying racism, she pointed out, more solemn now.

– We know that, a girl said. – And I've heard you speak before. But it's so hard out there, so hard to fight, so difficult to keep everything from slipping away. It's such a sad, bottomless pit out there. What do you think we should *do?*

– Fight on, Judith said instantly. – It's that simple and that hard. Work with yourself so you don't submit to the sadness, because then everything becomes even sadder. Protest against what you feel is wrong, not necessarily in the same way, using the same methods as others. All of us must find our own way. The most important is to feel good inside, within oneself. Then use the positive impact that creates to reach out into the world.

Reach as far as possible, she thought. Sometimes one may reach too far. *Some* may reach too far.

With the sadness often overwhelming her, disheartened as she usually felt, she wasn't sure she was in any position to give advice.

– I think I *understand*. He who had spoken first spoke up.

– A hamburger café doesn't have to be that bad, she grinned with doubt in her voice. – Who the owner is does matter. This one is certainly bad beyond belief…

Their hearty laughter made her feel good. She couldn't actually tell if she had softened the despair in their souls, but their shiny faces made her feel better. Jonas Bergli had done the same for her so long ago. By merely looking at her he had instilled in the searching young girl a sense of pride, a hope that Life was worth living. It pleased her that she was able to do the same.

That's why he had picked them, their ability to encourage joy.

Stimulate excitement.

Their lethal devil may care attitude.

She watched the youths sit down and wolf down the food. They joked and laughed while casting the occasional shy look in her direction. She made herself hard. It was true that they had to find their own way. They were not yet ready. But some of them would be.

She watched them vanish out of the door. From darkness to darkness, in all et… No, she wouldn't think thoughts like that. They were so… bleak.

One of the girls turned there on the sidewalk and waved. Judith waved back.

– Hi, do you have change? Dorte asked, out of breath. Judith felt as if she was pulled back into reality. – I'm out.

Dorte was far advanced in her pregnancy, the baby almost ready to pop out. She had been plump as long as Judith had known her. Now she was close to fat. She shouldn't have been here at all. The uniform sat tight on her body. She shouldn't have worked, and this work was hard and tiring. The pains often riddled her. She had been forced to stop working occasionally, on her doctor's orders. Then she was harassed by her superiors, and forced herself to start up again. Judith gave her change, disheartened and sick to her stomach.

– This can't be good for you. Are you okay?

– I'm good. Dorte replied with wavering eyes and hurried back to her spot.

A while later they both found themselves back in Hamburger Hell. Dorte strived on, mechanically and effectively. Judith was suddenly overwhelmed with dizziness and feared she would faint on the spot, as everything turned black. Kirsten, their immediate superior, Manning's «man» in the kitchen scolded and generally mistreated the employees. But it wasn't actually her position that made her feared. She wasn't the typical pea-brained person, enjoying the sound of her own voice. The reason was that she quite simply so enjoyed her work. Her eyes… Like all the others Judith got goose bumps all over when she had those eyes staring at her.

Kirsten ordered Dorte to fetch more raw meat. Dorte obeyed, her head bowed, her spirit cowed. She returned shortly, with her hands full and short of breath.

– That wasn't much, Kirsten stated sourly. – We'll quickly run out again. Take another turn.

– I'll go, Judith said decisively.

– The Good Samaritan? Kirsten spat. – So predictable. Just don't expect anyone to thank you for it, Breen. Okay, let it be a large pile.

Judith put down the kitchen tools and headed towards the storage room. She was very conscious of not hurrying, and she made sure Kirsten and the others knew it. None of the others moved from their designated places, not Dorte either. They knew that this time the fearsome eyes hadn't been directed at them. They bowed their heads and breathed a sigh of relief.

The storage room was huge and dark. Only a single bulb in the ceiling high above kept it from being completely black. Fortunately it had the habit of actually working. Manning, the greedy asshole probably feared they would set the door to the kitchen too much ajar and waste too much in heating expenses. Judith opened it wide. Perhaps the draft would make Hell more livable.

Her steps echoed through the room as she walked across the wooden floor. There was a small staircase going up to the food shelves. To her amazement and fear she noticed that her legs turned weak almost instantly. Yesterday had been her first hard bout of exercise in a week. She had struck a sparring partner down fairly quickly, but it had still happened slower than it should.

She realized it was hot in here and had to smile. Somebody had turned on the heat. Hugo M would have a heart attack.

It amazed her that he had installed heat in here at all.

The bread was always placed in the worst possible location, as deep as possible on a shelf, far from any reaching hands. The burgers were, in contrast placed on the floor. She placed the boxes on her left arm. The potatoes and other stuff she put in a plastic bag she carried by left hand's little finger. She had developed her own, unique method. She was worried that she had learned it too well. Perhaps it was truly time to quit?

She went for the bread and put down her load. As always she had to bend forward and stretch her upper body flat on the shelf. Her butt would inevitably be pushed up. If she didn't know better she would have suspected Hugo of hiding in a well-hidden spot in here, in order to watch the show. The thought brought a cheerful twisted grin to one corner of her mouth.

Somebody had put them impossibly far out of reach this time. She couldn't see anything, but stretched as far as possible without having to lift her feet from the floor. Her fingers touched the naked wall. There was nothing there.

She felt hands on her thighs. Big, fleshy hands… The realization squeezed her a moment, squeezed her hard, until she started moving. He moved his large frame and countered her resistance remarkably fast. A fleshy fist struck her in the back between the shoulders. The blow pushed air from her lungs and paralyzed her completely. He grabbed the waving, powerless arms and forced them behind her back. He held them like that, with only one hand, in an iron grip. Feet were pushed at the wall by his thick brick-like legs, and she couldn't do anything effectively with them. She was trapped.

– What the hell are you doing? She gasped for air. – Let me go!

– Let you go, such a fine piece of meat? The sick laughter made her sick. – Then I would have to be quite stupid, and I'm not.

She screamed for help with everything she had. She didn't like it, but sometimes pride had no place in this world. He had her, there was no way around it. And the fear of what he was about to do to her made the panic something tangible inside.

He grabbed her hair, causing flashes of pain in the scalp and knocked her head into the wall. She saw stars and the dizziness overwhelmed her. She could no longer see the door to the kitchen, but heard the sound of running feet… that suddenly stopped. Why did they stop… so far away?

– Close that fucking door, Manning shouted coarse and raw.

The door closed *fast*. She heard it amazingly clear, even though she didn't immediately realize it. Nobody would help her. No one would come to her rescue. She had to make it on her own. She was held so hard. He was so much stronger than her. She twisted her body desperately and kicked out as hard as possible from her awkward position. He turned her briefly over on the side and a fist hit her deep in her unprotected abdomen. She almost lost consciousness. He had her pliable once more, never really losing any of the control he had over her.

– Now, cunt, now you'll get what you've been begging for.

He pulled down her pants. She lay there paralyzed, like prey before the predator. She imagined she sensed thousands of needles on the naked skin. How quiet everything had become. The only sound filling her ears was the ever-higher disgusting breathing. She was unable to hear herself breathe. She attempted to mobilize soul, thought and body to one desperate act, in vain. Panic made her absolutely frantic. She made one, final attempt. It failed completely, was no more effective than a finger moving with the hands tied. The whimper of despair rose from her innermost being. Was she truly this weak, this helpless? As if confirming that stray thought he pushed a hand between her thighs and she moaned. She failed to keep it inside. He laughed in satisfaction and anticipation. She heard how he fumbled with his belt.

– So, you're being turned on, huh? He spat it out, in contempt. – I knew you longed for this. Don't worry. Soon you'll be warm and willing all the time. Your time as a bitch giving lip is over, trust me.

… *do something*. She had to, couldn't allow this to happen.

But there was nothing she could do

And he wasn't going to let her go afterwards either. He would never let go of her. She gasped in thick, paralyzing fear. He was laughing, scorning her. She gasped again.

His pants slipped down. She noticed clearly the slight, beyond sinister sound.

The door to the kitchen opened with a loud crack. Lights flooded the room.

– THIS IS THE POLICE! A female voice. – LET GO OF HER AND TAKE THREE STEPS BACK.

He didn't see the figure clearly. Just like a silhouette against the harsh light. He glared at it and took a step back. Judith remained in her position, gasping and frozen. Slowly, painfully it dawned on her that he wasn't holding her anymore.

– What kind of bull is this? He cried it out in anger, and didn't seem particularly worried. – What are you doing here?

Judith had recognized the voice. It belonged to Dorte, as unlikely as that was.

It was time to act. Now… or never. She twisted sideways and around, and kicked out with her foot. It hit him in the chest. He backed a few more steps, but otherwise he looked pretty unfazed. She threw herself off and away from the shelf.

– A trick, huh? Pretty clever. He smiled in his usual abominable way. – Well, it won't help you, and she will pay. Oh, how she will pay.

– Get away from here, she shouted to Dorte. – Go far away and never look back.

She heard the pregnant girl leave. She focused all her attention on Manning. Pulled her pants up the same time he did.

– What were you going to do… afterwards? She asked it hissing at him.

– I have many choices at my disposal, he snarled. – You're worth far more alive than as a corpse.

He attacked. She didn't underestimate him anymore, and as she had expected he was quick as lightning. She avoided him, and kicked the gross stomach with all the force she could muster. He merely grinned at her. She shook desperately the sleeping foot. It had been like hitting a brick wall behind the flesh. He struck again. She just barely managed to avoid the crushing blow. The fleshy fist grazed her temple and made her vision even foggier. She swayed.

Her back and stomach still hurt. She didn't believe he had damaged her with his brutal blows, but she felt stiff and far from her best. As she pulled back panic, rage and hatred fought for dominance in her. It had ever been thus. But now there was balance. Until this moment it had weakened her. Now it strengthened her.

When he raged forward once more she feinted. He grabbed the right hand, the one she used to distract him. She struck her hard, half fisted left at his larynx. She succeeded well enough to make him halt abruptly. He released a gargling sound and had to struggle to keep breathing. Like a machine or a wild human beast she stepped close to him, within the reach of his crushing grip, and struck in a raging triumph. Her right elbow hit his neck directly and with full force. He fell like a tree. The floor thundered, as the thick lumber hit it. The head hit just a moment later, with a dull sound.

He was breathing, that was easy enough to see. She couldn't tell if she was relieved or disappointed. She could kill him now. He was at her mercy.

She spat on him and smiled in a cold rage. He looked at her with unfocused eyes while attempting to make the muscles and limbs work. She turned her back to him and left.

Like a fury contained in dark flames she marched through the kitchen and the dining room. The help stared at her in shock and even the customers gathered something had happened.

– I quit, she told the manager. – I'll be sending the clothes by registered mail. Goodbye, damn assholes.

The wind outside was cold compared to the safe heat inside, but it was worth it. She kept breathing in and out. Dorte waited for her.

– May I go with you? She asked.

– Sure. Judith grabbed her hands and squeezed them.

Dorte hesitatingly returned the big girl's smile.

– You did it, Dorte said. – You're so strong.

– I almost gave in, Judith whispered.

Dorte nodded. She understood.

– What must I do? She worded her query carefully. – At your community?

– Do? Judith lifted a brow in surprise before she, too understood, shaking her head with a wide smile. – Be yourself, that's all.

– That's GREAT! Two palms met, as she clapped her hands like a little girl. – Everybody else has always wanted something from me. Is there… nothing you desire?

– Nothing but your true friendship, Judith replied, slightly ironic.

They realized they were still standing outside Manning's place, his domain. He himself was nowhere to be seen. They assumed he felt he had lost face and didn't want to appear to his «employees» in his dishonor. His terrifying reputation would suffer a heavy blow when this got out.

Not a bad outcome, Judith thought.

She knew she would never be able to get him convicted for attempted rape. Dreams are the first casualty in a human being. Reason and realism dominated in the world.

They had taken no more than a few steps when a strange, covered figure approached them. Judith wasn't alarmed. She recognized the woman in spite of her alien clothing and sent Dorte a comforting glance.

Anya.

The two old familiars faced each other across a gulf of years.

– I went to the apartment at the address you gave me and rang the doorbell. You had moved and had left no forwarding address. So I came here.

Anya said.

– You were lucky, Judith said tightly. – If you had arrived here a minute later you wouldn't have found us.

They stood there motionless and didn't really know what to say to each other.

– We're headed for the crisis center close by, Judith finally said, clearly hesitating. – One of us is working there. I have… a need to speak to her. I can give you a guided tour afterwards, if you want?

She wanted to, that much was certain. It was there in her features, even if her stoic face always had been from difficult to impossible to read.

It usually took fifteen minutes with fast walking where they were heading. This time it went faster. If Dorte hadn't stumbled by their side they would have reached the place even sooner.

Judith felt the restlessness crawl under her skin. It had been a constant bother since leaving Manning and his toys that certainly weren't, shouldn't be toys. That sense of impending doom grew stronger way before they turned the last corner and saw Yvonne stand with her back to them, with hands curled into tight fists in front of the darkened building. This image festered in them, grew to a cancer inside. Yvonne spotted them as reflections in the window, where they, too, saw her face of wrath and despair. She turned towards them. Now the face seemed sadder, more somber.

– I'm so PISSED I can hardly EXPRESS it, she screamed at her friend and the two familiar strangers.

– They closed it down, Judith stated flatly.

– By damn they did. Not that it wasn't in the marked cards, but still, it's so… bleak.

She cried a bit. The three supported her as they left the place. Tears swiftly dried in the merciless wind.

– And who are these fine ladies? She queried a while later.

She had started speaking English for Anya's benefit as soon as she had realized her language.

– Two new banner scribes, Judith replied in wicked irony.

They crossed Rådhuspladsen, the city hall plaza, at the start of Vesterbrogade and rushed into the warmth in and by Palladium Theatre. It was possible to do late night shopping there, of a wide variety of goods and foods.

– Allow me to pay, Anya offered. – I have some money.

After shopping their arms full of bags they watched «Cry Freedom». Judith wasn't sure if they needed to be further excited, at this time. The movie made one sad, encouraged and seething, boiling angry. She gathered that besides experiencing a wonderful story in images and sound, she had a need to see that people other than she and her close ones suffered, too. It was bleak, but it was a bleak world. Every time she saw the children being gunned down in Soweto she was boiling inside. She wanted to be reminded of the injustice ruling the world, reminded so hard that she never forgot.

– A man spoke to me outside the city hall, Yvonne told them afterwards, not raising her voice. – A man in a dark coat. We protested outside the hall and were being chased off. Only I was given the sordid honor of remaining. Funny, huh? Yes, you should be laughing, Dorte. It is comical, a tragic comedy. He told me in an unexpected clear language that the center would achieve renewed license if I broke with the Green Rose and adapted a more positive attitude to society in general. I told him in even clearer terms what he could do to himself. I have never seen him before, but no one was allowed to take his photo. If anybody carried a camera unconcealed it was confiscated and destroyed instantly. The pigs stormed and cleared our premises *half an hour* later. They confiscated everything. We were permitted to leave with not much more than clothes and skin intact. One of the pigs snarled in my ear that I would never more find decent work in this town. I wasn't too crushed about that. After all, you've been in the same rut, Judith.

– I found a job at last, but you won't convince me to recommend it.

Laughter.

They faced the usual problems when they wanted a taxi. The first driver barked at them through the window the obvious fact that he didn't drive just anybody. He was one of the most encouraging. Many didn't stop at all. The usual reason they were given was that many wouldn't drive them to Christiania, to Liberty City, especially those that recognized them and knew that they were living there.

– The funny thing, Yvonne grinned curtly, – is that it isn't that many days since Judith and I moved in. Well, I guess they've marked us years ago.

– And I, Anya said. – Definitely I.

– And I, Dorte exclaimed excited and ironic simultaneously. – If not yet, then soon. I can hardly wait.

Laughter.

Distractions. Judith considered the post movie text, the long list over everybody who had been jailed without due process in South Africa, and had died there. She had noticed one particular case. One was supposed to have fallen off a chair and broken his neck. Hilarious. She had laughed out aloud. Sure. Just like those who had been given their public due process in West Germany about the same time Biko had been murdered in South Africa. Andreas Baader, Ulrike Meinhof, Jan Carl Raspe and Gudrun Enslin had officially speaking committed suicide in the Stammheim prison. No difference. And no one cared. Most people didn't give a shit anywhere.

Finally they found themselves in a comfortable, warm taxi. The driver, a nice old fellow, often graced them with skeptical eyes. By each street with bad or non-existing lighting his nervousness increased visibly.

Anya had removed some of her headgear, now, when they were closer to home. It made her look no less alien. She had a flower-patterned scarf on her head and large, swinging earrings hanging from her large earlobes. Around her neck she wore a thin scarf, exposing some weird signs. But what really underlined and created the exotic impression was quite simply the face itself, and the long coal-black hair.

– You look like a Gypsy, Dorte giggled. – Do you work as a fortuneteller?

– Aye, Anya replied. – It's a living, right?

– Ain't that the truth? Judith extended the circle of her eyes as far she managed. She made eyes a la Marty Feldman. The four cracked up.

– I'm not a Gypsy, Anya explained. – But we Celts have at the very least a history just as interesting. And especially some of us. Some of the madmen in our family claim we're descendants of ancient elves…

The taxi driver halted abruptly in front of the Green Rose.

– That will be 65 kroner, please. He turned towards them, more than visibly nervous.

– I have only forty or hundred, Anya said. – Do you have change?

– *Forget it,* just get out. I'll take forty. I'm not greedy.

Not right now. The girls chuckled and took their time leaving the car. All doors closed and locked the second they were out. The car disappeared in a roar of dust and exhaust.

– Perhaps we should spare these suckers some stress and worries in the future, Yvonne stated very worried.

– Not as long as it is so much fun not sparing them…

Judith danced off, and they followed her.

They headed inside, from night to deeper night. Judith noticed that Anya closely inspected her new home. From step one it was as if her eyes penetrated the very walls. But a smile played on her lips.

– The place is unfortunately closed for paying guests a few days, Judith told her. – A few nights ago uninvited guests visited us. Definitely uninvited. Until they were *stopped* they completed quite a thorough redecoration…

– A life of action, Anya exclaimed. – Great!
– Don't be so sure, Yvonne replied solemnly.
Willy and Kimberly led the restoration work. Both looked very cute in workers' threads.
Judith whistled with four fingers in the mouth, with an intense look at Yvonne. Everybody turned towards the four. Judith pushed Anya forward.
– Take a look, she cried cheerfully. – We've gotten ourselves a genuine fortuneteller.
+++++++++
She ran beside the black elf in a silvery gray, bluish landscape. The yellow disk cast its cold light and warmed them. The Moon was both friend and foe. Or perhaps more correct: Neither foe nor friend. It had been, was and would always be many things, be vengeance, lovemaking, desire, retribution, attraction, hunt, love, motherhood, hatred or all of the above, and more. Not indifference. It was either warm or cold. It was change. Through every cycle it changed its look until it returned to its previous incarnation... *But not quite*.
It wasn't oppression. Breen, in heat and despair threw herself back and forth on the bed, and was about to fall down into the wide and deep black hole. She saw Him everywhere in her dreams. He ravaged the shadowland hunting her. She was scared. That was an undeniable admission coming easily to her. But fear made her crouch close to the black hole. She felt so small, pathetic and frail, so horribly vulnerable, haunted by insecurity. He shook her convictions. To her, in more ways than one, he personified the black hole. The sunlight could shine straight at him without him feeling it. He had fallen into it himself and wanted to pull her there with him.
She woke up screaming, sitting straight in the bed. Greedy hands reached out of the shadows for her, but she saw to her relief that those gathering around her, around the bed were her friends.
The scream faded. She wanted to dry the sweaty face and push the wet hair from her forehead and cheeks. They tenderly, but decisively captured the waving hands and did the pushing and drying for her. Breath, pulse and thoughts slowed down. She sensed clearly those who looked worriedly at her. She shook her head. The entire building had evidently been awakened by her howling. She relaxed, allowing herself to be coddled. The worst ruckus died and most of those present were led out of the room. Three remained. Kimberly, Willy and Anya sat down in the bed beside her.
– Where's Yvonne? She asked with a hoarse voice. – She's experienced in dealing with stuff like this. It's her I should be talking to.

– I attempted waking her when I heard your beautiful song, Willy sighed. – I guess she filled herself up yesterday. To the point of being intoxicated beyond caring, I'm afraid…

– What were you dreaming? Anya asked carefully, anxiously patting her shoulders. – Tell us.

– That Manning forced me to give in to him. He made me kneel before him and made me his slave. He branded me and caged me, and put me on display, and then… he sold me. It felt so real. The bars, the smells, the auction, the eyes thick with desire and implied ownership… So close to how it could have been. Or perhaps it did happen that way, in another world, a parallel existence, dimension…

– But he failed completely, Kimberly interjected. – And if that wasn't enough, you made him the laughing stock of the town. He didn't do you. You did him, did him thoroughly, reducing him to a wet spot on the floor.

– You don't understand, Judith exclaimed exasperated. – It's not Manning. I'm through with him. Olav, my husband… grew ever more eager in his desire to practice his own, private form of behavior control - and then I did give in.

– But you liberated yourself completely from him, too, Anya said urgently. – You're free of him, now.

Judith's head fell down between her knees. They saw that the usual glow in Silverhair's eyes had turned pale and lost its brilliance. She closed her eyes and the memories rushed back. He had taken her dreams and reduced them to something brittle. Just by touching them she feared they would burst. He had exposed her pain. She had loved him, exposed herself for his sake. And he had seduced her. Not by making her love him, but by making her continue to do so. She had asked herself if he had been like that, sly and manipulative all the time. And if so, what did that say about her?

They who were with her, now, didn't put any price on their emotions. They didn't expect to get anything in return for their friendship, other than it being returned.

– You know as well as I do that abuse victims often develop guilt and self-recrimination, Willy said angrily. – You don't need Yvonne to tell you that.

They remained, talking with her, comforting her, as time slipped away. She discovered how good it felt. She had never really done anything like this before, not even with Olav, certainly not with him. He had never shown any interest in deeper emotions.

– I feel much better, now, she said. – Thank you. I love you all.

She rose and kissed them in gratitude.

– You may go, she said cheerfully. – The bed is a flood and disaster area. I'll attempt to sleep on the carpet. If we're lucky we'll yet get a few hours sleep before breakfast.

The three of them glanced at each other. Then they nodded. She looked at them, as they walked through the doorless opening in the wall, leaving the bedroom.

– Why did you leave? She whispered it unheard at Anya's back.

The hammering started well before the cocks crowed in the distance.

– Remember, people, Kees cried, – today is the day our modest tavern is gonna be reopened to paying customers… with emphasize on paying.

– It has turned out to be important, hasn't it? Renni said. – I can't say I like that very much, and yes, I know most of us have lost our jobs and that we need the money badly.

– The worst part to me is that what seems like an organized campaign isn't really organized. Karine shook her head. – The noose is tightening, that's «all». An already hard world is turning harder.

They all knew that imagination and independent forms of expression were ever less tolerated and appreciated. They felt it on body and mind every day.

– Most people have enough with themselves, with their own financial troubles and stuff, Anya said. – Many of the rest would rather spit on us than help. We, like a few others lead the way and show them the path to personal growth and true freedom, but the vast majority rejects it with a snarl. Those in charge show them every single second how terrible it is not to grow… and almost everybody prefers that.

Anya, with her clarity of vision and passion and taint of bitterness was welcomed and comforted by her peers.

And what about us? Kimberly thought. How many here will be caught in the web the mighty, with their dead souls is weaving and throwing into the river?

She hit her final nail, as the sun was about to set. Others also lacked nails to complete the job. They had to get more. Sometime. Tomorrow. What they had done would stay that way for a while without further work, hopefully until tomorrow. She shrugged and danced down the steps of the old wood ladder.

– Let's take a small comfort, like good capitalists in the fact that the notoriety the place has gained will assure the sound of coins and crackling money, of cash flowing behind the counter, Judith said dryly, grinning wider by the amused look in the others' eyes. – And keep in mind that we don't take credit cards, no matter how the somewhat wealthy tea drinkers accidentally dropping in may object to that…

– Plastic is just useful for *major* withdrawals, Kimberly cried and raised, as the first of many her fist, greeting Silverhair's presence.

One hour later major noise rose from the filled to capacity building. If there had been as many guests every night they could have bought a Pacific Island after a year.

That did comfort them, in an ambiguous way, one reflected in their eyes and musings.

Kimberly had to run a gauntlet between the tables and had difficulties balancing the trays of pints. Steve, standing behind the counter with Jemma and Willy grinned at her.

– Why do you think you get far more orders than everybody else? He asked her, exposing his teeth.

– I can't imagine why, she replied just as pleasant.

She exposed her teeth, too, and they shared the moment.

– I can't help it, Kurt shared his thoughts with Willy later, – I envy Scandinavian men and women hundred years in the future, people able to enjoy the spoils generations of racial and cultural mixing will provide.

– It is indeed disgusting that some people are opposed to such a mix of colors and cultures, to such a glorious development, Willy agreed.

He overdid it slightly, deliberately, to test the man. It pleased him when Kurt nodded in solemn agreement, in gestures and passion impossible to fake, at least to a bartender with lots of experience in reading people.

– Today, there is so much fear of strangers, of the unknown, and so little humanity, you know, Kurt said, sipping more beer.

Willy nodded with a catching in his throat. He knew this well.

Kimberly saw Judith and Ole Sivert talk. They seemed awkward in each other's company. She sent them encouraging and ironic smiles, but it didn't seem to help much.

Beatles, The Doors and Bob Dylan were played, not too loud, through the speakers, and by those who entertained acoustically in-between. She swayed her hips to the timeless beat. The time of rebellion in the sixties stood for the majority here as something great and nearly legendary, a unique experiment, even though one that failed. She sensed the mood, the music and the hot stares the males in the room sent her. It didn't bother her. Almost all of them were sweet and kind. She would certainly have looked favorably at their advances, too, if she had been interested, but she wasn't.

It didn't keep her from enjoying their company. Besides, it pleased her to observe how hard and fast they attempted to swallow the beer before she brought them some more…

It was prosperous, too.

The last was a fleeting stray thought from a somewhere practical part of her brain. It wasn't truly important, she comforted herself. That thought made her smile inside.

She passed Yvonne and Morten. Yvonne drank a broth of herbs. She constantly held hands to her head, swearing repeatedly that she would never taste another drop of alcohol ever again. Kimberly whistled very, very telling.

Kurt searched for some time, until finding a group staying a bit away from most others.

– So, who is Head Honcho around here? He asked.

– Kees, Renni and Karine over there by the door used to run the place, at least that was the impression, before the mass migration started. A boy shrugged. – If they feel any animosity towards the new blood they're certainly concealing it well. It seems to me that they're quite pleased because they've finally received some help.

Kurt glanced at them. The three did indeed seem to enjoy themselves, even more so than everybody else present.

– Some will claim it is Judith, now, a girl said. Her teeth flashed in white.

– Or perhaps it is Jemma, another snickered, – or Kimberly… or Morten?

He stopped a bit, frowning.

– I really don't know.

Kimberly rushed at them, giving them all, including Kurt more glasses of beer.

– The question is really quite simple to answer, she pointed out, stunning them. – There is no head honcho.

He stared at her, couldn't do anything but wonder how she could have heard them.

– It might sound corny to some, she kept pointing out, – but we've all found companionship here, one only strengthened by every new attack directed at us by the power hungry. The divide and conquer approach they employ usually works. It has worked on countless occasions throughout history. But not here, not yet. We know our history and are strengthened by it. It will take some doing on their part to break us and break us up.

He danced with Anya. Shadows twinkled in her earrings and her eyes.

– I'm also new here, she said quietly. – A lot seems… new here, right? And already the companionship is well under way on becoming unbreakable. There's no possessiveness here and I've also noticed something else.

She thought about it a bit, before continuing.

– Many here have stopped… bending.

– That's right, he said. – That's so very right.

– They won't give in when the collective hatred is directed at them, or when an individual or a group's fear of change and the unknown strikes them either randomly or in a well-planned manner.

He nodded and they nodded together.

– Or perhaps we're fooling ourselves, he said reluctantly, – delaying the inevitable, one way or another.

– I experienced something similar some years ago, with a similar crowd, Anya said rigidly and sadly – We were indeed fooling ourselves.

– I haven't tried before, he whispered. – Never. At least not anything like this, and I've wanted to do so, for so very long.

Her eyes twinkled at him.

The dance and the room seemed to move like one, in a slow, slow whirl of motion.

The two human beings seemed to… join, to melt into each other. There was something painful, desperate in them both. They kissed and the room faded around them. In one blink of an eye was an eternity. Later, when later came an eternity had passed in moments. They rested on a couch, snuggling tight, enjoying the heat and contact of the other, while people were slowly leaving the place. Among those staying there was a noticeable, palatable informal outlook. Nobody seemed to care that the two of them, and many others spread around the place lay there half naked.

Bright lights had been put out. Flames, living fire rising from candles and flickering in the wind (there was no wind) cast its shadows in the room. A room that had seemed so big, even when filled with people, and now seemed both small and infinite.

Silence… finally. Jemma and Kimberly stretched tired limbs. Around them, where there just a few minutes ago, ages earlier had been chaos, there was nothing now but echoes from moist walls. Kimberly enjoyed life and ruckus in her immediate vicinity, encouraged it any opportunity she got, but enjoyed equally the silence, this kind of silence, in the aftermath of such potent celebration. She didn't really feel tired, but rather lucid and awake. As she had always believed there was no need, in a stimulating environment, to drag oneself up by the hair every time one wanted to have fun. Fun, visible in features and movement burned within her.

– I'm going to bed. Jemma managed a stiff smile. – I just hope I'll actually reach the bed before I fall asleep.

Willy was cleaning glasses. He and Kimberly waved to Jemma. She quickly faded into the shadows. They saved as much electricity as possible. The entire room was Shadow. He quite enjoyed that.

He didn't see any difference concerning Kimberly's hair in the badly lit room. It looked as bright and shiny as ever. He looked around. There wasn't a single soul close by. Everybody was busy elsewhere.

Kimberly watched his hands while he was cleaning the glasses. He showed himself to be quite skilled. But she felt he took longer than he usually did, doing it. She waited patiently.

– Eh, Kimberly? He began hesitatingly.

– Is there anything I can do for you, Willy?

She turned towards him and smiled, more than a bit ambiguous. She didn't want to make it easy for him.

– I have no right to ask anything like this, but… Damn… I've thought about it for some time, but nothing has come out of…

– Of what, Willy?

He behaved quite strangely. Usually he didn't beat around the bush like this. Damn!

– I would like to have a kid, he charged.

– Damned logical, she mumbled and closed and opened her eyes. I thought it would rather be something like that, she thought. Eyes opened once more and the smile turned roguish. The face turned rigid, though, like a mask. – Such a coincidence. I have, for some time, in fact entertained such a thought myself.

– I don't blame you for being sarcastic.

– Your place or mine? She offered in a practical manner.

The slight irritation turned to compassion when she saw how he was searching for words. It ended by her smiling encouragingly.

– I don't know how to go through with it, he said calmly. – Women have never turned me on.

– And it won't be any fun artificially, will it now? She took his hand. Both shook their heads. – We must find another way, then…

She drawled a bit.

– Tell me, do you like Sivert, is he your type?

– Yes, but he isn't… An exalted expression lit his face. – Yes, that could work. I'm actually quite confident that it will. But… is he willing?

– I'm convinced he will, she grinned. – Especially when we whisper in his ear that Judith will join in, too.

– But should we bother her with this? He said, clearly worried.

– *Bother,* are you nuts? She needs the encouragement. Perhaps she needs this far more than we do. Besides, I need her there. I've never been any good doing it with men.

– I'm sorry, he reddened, – I didn't want to insult you.

– I wasn't insulted. She kissed his hand seductively. – You're too nice for that, brother.

He nodded, something once again catching in his throat.

– Shall we? She pulled him with her.

She was so natural. To him she looked like a sunbeam just then. But he realized that she, too, needed this, that they both needed it, as a way of softening the creeping unrest they felt, and also because they wanted it, as a natural way of living their life.

They joined their other, suffering siblings in the shadows, while the sense of impending tension increased, while smoke whirled and whirled ever faster in the vortex that had become their lives.

CHAPTER FIVE

Women look at men. Men listen to women. Or the other way around, in countless ways and none. Humans sensing each other, listening in ways that have nothing to do with the common, limited use of the five senses.

An evening in late November the cold wind blew across Rådhuspladsen, the city hall plaza, hotter than ever. Torches in the close confines of the assembled masses flickered, but didn't blow out. Dream and life pulsed between everybody present, some older people, mostly young, everybody still retaining their humanity. Those who still carried life's fire inside and weren't dead, like those who were, even though they were still breathing and walking. Virtually everybody from the tavern was there, and life and fire burned hot in them all. It was something visible. One was able to actually see it, if one looked, if one stared, by a casual glance.

It was all a boiling and explosive cauldron of a witches' brew.

– *I can't…* Judith pulled away from Sivert's touch, his swollen, raised limb.

The four of them stood naked on their knees, on the bed, facing each other. Kimberly patted Judith's dank skin and comforted her with tiny kisses.

– *You haven't done it with any man since…?* Something caught so hard in Willy's throat that he was unable to complete the sentence.

Judith shook her head, unable to speak. Deeply ashamed she didn't dare meet their eyes. She covered herself as much as possible with her muscled, but yet thin arms.

– *One, two, but it didn't work. And then H-hugo came. His deed reminded me of everything. Everything! He exposed the wound, laid it bare anew. And then... then... He, he made me enjoy it.*

She stared insane at them.

Willy, too, started touching her in affectionate ways, trying, carefully. It didn't cause vomit to get stuck in her throat, but she didn't feel anything either. Neither did Willy. She knew that. He did it for her sake, as an obligation.

– *No wonder you made those passes on me,* he finally said, – *I'm no threat to you.*

– *It's no good,* she said, bowing her head, – *I'm sorry.*

– *Don't feel sad on our behalf,* Kimberly said pointedly, ambiguously. – *You're the one suffering, not us. Perhaps you should drink a glass or two, to calm your raging* ***nerves***.

– *No!* Terrified Silverhair straightened herself. – *No…*

She pulled Sivert's head to her and enraged she kissed him on the lips, so hard that she smelled blood. He forced himself to remain passive, as hard as that was. The reward was the warmth from ember eyes under the silver hair. He noticed playful fingers below and that the power was building down there. Until he realized that she was using both her hands to hold on to his hair. He looked down, at the much bigger male hands. He reddened and any excitement went out like a candle. Chin and most other things fell like a tree.

– *Sorry,* Willy said with regret.

All four of them laughed so hard that they screamed, and collapsed in a heap on the bed.

A time not possible to measure hummed while they rested there, enjoying the skin-to-skin contact and closeness.

Kimberly started stroking Judith between the thighs, slowly, methodically. Judith stiffened at first, but then slowly she began stretching her body and pushing against the invasive hand… and then she moaned. Kimberly used her tongue, ever closer to the awaiting wetness. Judith laughed, low-keyed at first, then stronger. Kimberly crawled on top of her. She waved. Willy and Sivert lay down beside her, on each side. Sivert's cock grew big anew, eventually on display on Judith's belly. Willy didn't take his eyes off it, and his, too, started twitching. Kimberly rubbed her cunt hole against Judith's. She kissed Judith on the lips. Both released tiny moans of excitement. Kimberly shook herself and began fumbling until she found Sivert's hand. She met his eyes and pulled the hand over to Willy. He knew where she wanted to go with this. His hand decisively closed around Willy's cock and started patting and pulling it. Willy moaned abruptly and violently. *Jeez, the guy got to be starving.*

– *Now,* Kimberly cried out alarmed. – *Take me now!*

– *What…* Willy looked as if he had half awakened from a dream.

– *Now,* she repeated with clenched teeth.

He hardly managed to think. He had been so focused on Judith that he hardly noticed it until he found himself in Kimberly's hot nest. He stood behind her and slapped his hips against her butt. It happened so unexpectedly and brutally that he feared it would paralyze him. But the hunger overtook him completely and while he almost blackened out he sensed that he was ejaculating a part of himself into her. Kimberly cried out and fell hard on Judith. Willy moaned just as loud and fell at the top of the heap.

Judith let them stay on her sweaty body a few seconds, before pushing them off her. They remained on their backs with arms around each other. Judith pushed Sivert back when he attempted to rise. She placed herself on her knees above him and descended on his waiting body. He saw clenched teeth part as she made him push himself into her. She sensed something, very little disgust, a glimpse of growing joy and pain. Perhaps merely a pale echo of how she remembered it, but she did feel something. He hardly moved, did no more than moving his hips up and down, up and down. She controlled it all, bit into his lips, as her hips started moving by themselves. And then she controlled nothing anymore. Both lost all sense of time and when they pushed against each other with all their might, all sensitivity returned, a busted dam, a high, high tide. He was over her, pushing her down. He had emptied himself into her for the second time and had not pulled out afterwards. She didn't mind. It was so good, so good, good.

– *You sleaze,* she heard Willy tell Kimberly.

– *I may have to be even more of a sleaze the next time,* Kimberly giggled.

– *Or perhaps not,* Silverhair, *Silverhair* overheard Willy say far away.

The memory brought a huge smile to her no longer so rigid features in the cold heat at Rådhuspladsen, among the protesters and the cops.

– *Not that it is any of my business,* Kimberly had asked Wilhelm when Sivert and Judith had fallen asleep by their side. – *But why didn't you first ask Judith if she wanted…*

– *It is indeed your business,* he had replied. – *At least now. I think we both have thought about it. But it would have been too painful to us both, if you know what I mean…*

– *I think I do,* she nodded.

– *I thought you might. You're good at empathy, without obliterating yourself.*

– *I learned early the value of the Self. She spoke low-keyed, without pretense. – It is needed more than ever, in this cold, hard world, one not black or white, but gray, one who doesn't realize it's doomed. But... that just makes it more important to spread life and joy.*

But it is hard. Why is it so hard?

A sigh, a desperate cry in the night.

Police officers in black, protective uniforms and helmets covered the entire line around the gigantic square. Everything was set to collide and burn between the neon lights, the concrete and the endless sky. Judith blinked. She looked out through the holes in her mask, looked at the representatives of the Law and Order might, with its clubs and shields raised, and she felt a strange, hardly noticeable and non-strange many-colored notion of predestination, and abruptly a tremendous clarity, not merely for this night, but far beyond.

The good mood of rage and happy savagery was rising in her, swelling inside, filling her to the brim.

– We did the right thing, deciding to wear masks, Kathy whispered. – Take a look in the binoculars. Damn me, if there aren't Shadows taking photos in every building around here. I can always tell. Old habits, you know. And now I can feel the prickling in my entire body. The pigs would have loved having us for themselves, naked and passive, don't you think?

Judith put the binoculars before her eyes and tiled it along all the dark windows. It wasn't easy discovering people inside, not even with the bright lenses, if one didn't look. Judith moved her attention from camera to camera. She watched them while they clicked and hummed without interruption. She heard them.

Unaware people watched her curiously. They shook their head when she started playing air guitar, pointing at the windows. She heard that, too.

– There are so many people here, Dorte exclaimed, sighing happily. She moved easily through the crowd, a lot skinnier now than just two weeks ago. – They can't possibly be able to register everybody?

– It's a full time job, Kurt Mørch said ironically. – But we're talking registration here. They don't need to do it all tonight. Everything is loaded into a computer, and they can sift through it all in their own time. Let the computer gather, go through, compare and select.

– Such a bother, Dorte cried out.

The other two exchanged cheerful glances.

– Who's taking care of your kids? Judith asked.

– I brought them to my mother, Dorte replied. – I heeded your advice of expecting the worst tonight.

Somewhere ahead a young man climbed the temporary stage, raised for the evening and occasion. Everybody looked in that direction. An expectant roar rose from the gathering. Judith, suddenly, shockingly realized she experienced it even more pronounced than all the others present. She could see his eyes, see them very clear, very near, as if she had seen them before somewhere, in real life, not just on television.

Roland Vallens placed himself behind the microphone, exposing his usual, cheerful grin. This man was so much that his overwhelming reputation quite simply didn't, couldn't do him justice. Just a teenager he was already a living legend, putting all others to shame. A rock musician, composer and expressed mystic. Rumors claimed he both participated in and led black masses. Countless other «worse» incidents were whispered about. None of it confirmed. Mystery truly surrounded him like a veil of unreality. He was seen as something of an enigma. But he didn't isolate himself like others, who had a tendency towards the «eccentric». If he in any way wanted to hide, he did it by not hiding.

Several teenage girls, who had come here to experience their idol screamed and fainted. They were swiftly removed on stretches.
People cackled and grinned. Vallens, too. He had never been afraid to show - and stand by - his convictions.
The long, dark hair flickered in the wind. He raised his hands above the head, and the very air turned quiet and eerie.
He held up a mask. Slowly, deliberately he pulled it down on his head and pulled forward the hood of his jacket. The Hooded Man from countless legends stared into the eyes of them all.
– Call this a protest, if you will, he shouted. – Against those who are watching us from their hidden positions, from behind their heavy curtains, in their dank rooms.
He halted for a moment and everybody in this sea of people felt like he touched every single one of them.
– The ember of greatness is in every one of us. The voice would have carried far, even without the aid of the microphones and electronic equipment. – Most of all in those of us breaking out and thinking independently. It's the end, now, of the turning away, of accepting that people with a different skin color or inclination are blamed for every bad thing under the sun and moon. That the Earth is sullied, and we are alienated from it. The multinational company AP Møller has «earned» close to a billion Danish kroner on soliciting garbage and alienation this year. This is just a number, of course, without any true value, but it says a lot, is very illustrative, of how far people of power are willing to go to destroy us…
The cheering broke like a dam the moment he ended the speech. If anybody had thought he was just another bigmouthed rock musician, the remains of that notion vanished with this moment. The cheering he had literally pulled forth from obscurity transferred to several of the other speakers. The mood went ever higher.
– What is more important? Another asked rhetorically, one who didn't wear a mask. – To be a law-abiding citizen or save humanity from oppression and extinction?
– Jeez, Jemma cried into Judith's ear. – I've seen that guy speak more than once. It's Giovanni Rossi.
– I'm SICK and TIRED of how the very language is used against us, the man on the stage roared. – That a self-correcting mechanism is attacking everything different, everyone falling through the cracks, everything valuable. A Human Being is free the moment it realizes it, realizes that all barriers, all boundaries are false. BUT… action must follow thought. Otherwise the freedom turns hollow and meaningless. I'm challenging you:

The circle of cops rattled and threatened with their clubs and shields, but they couldn't overwhelm Rossi's voice or the cry of rage drowning their noise.

– Stop any attempts at changing society from within. Stop any attempts at changing the system. Don't be that STUPID. Stop believing in such an unfruitful venture. A system can never be reformed, only destroyed, and democracy, so priced today is the slickest tyranny ever, because it gives a given population the illusion of participation and independence. The rotten root must be pulled from the soil. Let Phoenix rise from its ashes, free and wild.

He's crazy, crazy like a wolf. Silverhair howled joyfully.

She imagined him nodding to her across the vast distance.

People changed places up there, slipped in and out of the gathering's attention. There was fluid movement, a mystical quality to it all making Judith even more excited.

– I will speak about prejudice, Laurie Isherwood began. She also counted among the more well-known speakers this memorable night. – We aren't born with it, but from the cradle and the older we become we learn ever more of it. Our waking dreams are condemned to darkness and so is our humanity. Yes, we live a sleep of reason producing monsters. We stumble through the day half asleep, easy to lead for those who want us thus. They are turning us against each other. Immigrants are blamed when old and young starve. Those who have chosen to jump off the bandwagon are also used as punching bags, as a way of distracting an unruly population. These are characteristics of an advanced technological society, of «our» society.

– We can talk about leaving an Earth to live on to our descendants, but this line of thought is really wrong, stillborn from the beginning. At the very least it is unnecessary and unsatisfactory. The disaster isn't coming. It's here *already,* and has been for along time. Our health is deteriorating. Radioactivity, chemicals, medicines and treatments are destroying it. It happens slowly, it happens fast, but it is happening. The number of sterility cases is increasing exponentially. As usual the proposed solution is an endless desert walk around the bush. Artificial insemination is increasingly developed as a response, but what if there are no longer any more people who can inseminate or be inseminated? Genetic and biological research do nothing more than further undermine our much needed respect of nature, of the natural processes that has made us what we are. This is one more step on the tailspin suicide run. We must stop fooling ourselves. All releases of artificial compounds must *stop.* Everything interfering in nature's balance must end. Plutonium and Dioxin and the countless other lethal compounds must be stopped from multiplying, to nevermore rise again. As with everything else in society, science is governed by the need for turning a profit. Everything can be excused if there's money in it. The rich and powerful are playing the stick and carrot game with us. They're merrily developing, expanding upon their system of greed and corruption, because that's their milk and blood. In their ignorance and foolishness most of the little cogs needed to run the machine do so willingly. They don't realize you don't need to be corrupt to be a part of a corrupt system.

– From when we're very young and throughout school we're taught to discard the big picture, to be good servants. We're told that to toil the ladder of the hierarchy is the only acceptable way. There are those who are embracing this conduct as a way of life. Like the uniformed men with shields, clubs and helmets surrounding us.

The police officers instantly started hitting their shields in more than a threatening way. In spite of the lack of guns, Judith found no discernible difference between them and those she had seen portrayed in «Cry Freedom».

– The big picture is an environment in balance, not in the balance, Laurie Isherwood continued. Incredibly enough virtually everybody present heard her voice through the ruckus. – Nature must only be used in such a way that the ecology is sustained. Attitudes must change. Everything in nature must be guarded. Life on Earth isn't a toy, existing for our amusement. We must use what we need to survive, but nothing more. Besides, to guard life is to guard human life. Of course it is. And I'm honestly sickened by witnessing the abundance the oppressors are drowning in, without any consideration for the consequences. They talk so sweet about responsibility. Work hard, don't be a parasite. While they, in truth are the irresponsible parasites. They don't give a damn about anything not elevating their stature. It is about time for the oppressed of Gaia to *rebel*.

The fat circle of policemen made their move. Just like that. There was no advance warning. It started as if by an invisible, silent signal. They charged forward with horses and dogs, raised shields and sticks. Shouts and roars rose from the crowd. Some scared, some angry and some enraged.

– FIGHT them, Roland Vallens shouted incredibly loud. He no longer spoke through the powerful speaker system or any enhancement. – They have no RIGHT to obstruct our exchange of ideas and thoughts. Even less right than their own law gives them. C'mon, let's strike back just a little.

The law protecting those who have much, Judith thought, against those who have little or nothing. A law made by the rich and powerful, to benefit the rich and powerful.

The uniformed thugs, on their feet and on horses mercilessly charged into the crowd. Some in the crowd had prepared for confrontation, others hadn't. A man attempted to run away. A club hit him on the head, and he fell like a ragged doll, remaining there, still and dead. During one blink, perhaps two, total chaos ruled the Copenhagen streets. People ran in all directions. Those in uniform struck everyone within their reach. Judith saw blood flow from heads. She saw people on the ground scream in pain. And she wondered when the same would happen to her. She was hardly more than a good step away when a club hit an arm. She heard the bone break. There was hardly a conscious thought in her head when she ran and ducked, and howled in thunderous, savage rage. The bullies on foot, with their dogs followed eagerly the first line of riders, but had to retreat when a large group met them with torches, torches burning with tall, intense flames. The dogs growled and whined, and they turned on their masters when those very masters attempted to push them further forward. The brainwashing occasionally failed. People ran to the center of the plaza, and they ran off it. Most didn't know where they were running. A horse got a torch close to its eyes and reared in panic. The rider was thrown off. A bunch of cops attacked the torchbearers, striking wildly and furious. The plaza was amazingly fast transformed into a battleground. Humans writhed on the ground, beaten bloody. The battle spread out from a kind of central point, in an uneven, circular shape. Judith stopped at the beginning of Strøget. She hardly recognized her surroundings. They had turned alien, practically unrecognizable. Another uniform masquerading as a human being attacked her with his tongue sticking out of its mouth.

– I'm not a lamb, she shouted at him, enraged, – and I WON'T allow myself to be treated as one.

She ducked the whistling club, and kicked viciously the arm holding it. There was a loud CRACK. She grabbed the club, tearing it out of the powerless hand, and pushed it deep into the soldier's abdomen. Something broke there, too. The man's howl of pain sounded like music in her ears. She pulled off his face cover while he crouched there on the tarmac.

– Your armor didn't help you much, this time, she cried contemptuously. – Did it, *pig?*

She left him there, even more helpless then those he had struck down. There were a huge number of civilians on the ground, but a substantial minority was also wearing uniform. Unexpectedly many, and when they realized that, they gathered in groups. Five repeatedly struck a teenage girl crouching and crying on the ground. She begged and howled desperately for mercy. The big guys merely grinned and laughed while they cuffed her. Without the slightest mercy she was thrown into an open police van with other unfortunates.

A woman, Laurie Isherwood, crouched on the ground, too, with one foot twisted at an impossible angle.

– My foot, she shrieked. – MY FOOT. Pigs! PIGS! I CURSE you!

Two servicemen, one male and one female started pounding her. They jumped and danced on the foot while releasing insane shrieks of laughter. Laurie's shrieks turned into whining, weak, sickly. Several people covered their ears. Her screams sounded almost as disturbing as what the long arm of the law did to her.

– I curse you, she whispered weeping, as they dragged her off.

What she witnessed, everything she witnessed made nausea stick like a hard ball in Judith's throat. People around her had a similar, frozen visage, as if what happened wasn't real. She had believed, fooled herself into believing she was pretty hardened. But she now realized that what she had experienced to this point in her life had been like nothing. What had been shown on TV, from the areas Israel occupied in Palestine, from South Korea, Chile, Prague, Beijing… it couldn't truly be *appreciated,* until reality came crashing down on you, in your living room, your tiny, protected slice of the world. She felt it, now, the Stormtroopers terror on body and mind. Realizing it was something she should get used to, that it should please her. And it did. They had revealed themselves, now, their true face. There were no guns or teargas, but only because they had deemed it unnecessary. Judith felt a gathering ecstasy because they had been wrong.

– *Gestapo, Gestapo*. A group halted a moment in their flight, chanting to the uniformed thugs. Instantly others cued in, and the cries spread like wildfire in the night. – GESTAPO, GESTAPO, GESTAPO

The police had won the battle, but it had cost them. The effective, battle ready force had dwindled considerably, and the chaos didn't wane, even though they had achieved an illusion of control. Among the protesters there had also been quite a few «average» citizens, and not just the usual «riff raff», used to getting their skulls kicked in on a regular basis. It was a loss of prestige on more than one level.

And it was about to take a turn for the worse.

The patrol vans were quickly filled with guests, and many were forced to sit handcuffed on the sidewalk. Then there were no more handcuffs currently available. The vans didn't dare drive off without escort. One made the attempt. Fifty meters down the street two cars deliberately crashed into it and *stopped* it cold. The uniforms disguised as human beings were pulled out and dragged off. They were undressed and left naked. Some were carried all the way to the harbor and dumped into the ocean. The cops left to guard the prisoners had their work cut out for them.

Many of the arrested, both with and without handcuffs attempted to escape. Many made it.

Judith saw several of her friends be captured and dragged off. She realized there was nothing she could do about it, and with known and unknown she sought hiding. Now was the time to bend.

She spotted Giovanni Rossi, and ran to him. She stopped, uncertain. He sat on the sidewalk, holding his head, looking so absolutely miserable that she didn't know what to say at first. And then it came to her, drawn from the cold, hard place inside.

– On your feet. It erupted in short and scornful snarls, from an oasis in moonlight, from a well, a cauldron she had just vaguely previously been aware of. – Or remain on your knees for the rest of a miserable life.

He rose. She could sense it, see it without eyes. He hadn't looked at her, until then.

– You're correct, of course. One can't give up, right?

One moment the situation seemed totally out of control. Then, in the next it suddenly seemed to be restored. It turned… quiet. The area looked deserted. Only flysheets floating in the wind and a totaled platform remained. The only visible signs of what had happened.

Kurt sat with other prisoners on the edge of the sidewalk. A circle of guards surrounded them. He held his head with both hands. It hurt. It bled a bit and hurt like hell. He was shocked and scared, but from within other emotions appeared, a burning, lasting rage, and a fundamental type of resolve. It showed in his face, in his eyes, unmistakable.

Scared, with a lump in the throat, and several illusions poorer, or richer on fewer illusions people hid in narrow alleys and stairs. Some remained there, before finally setting course home. Many, on the other hand remained, and slowly, virtually unnoticeable at first, they started boiling inside. The human cauldron had done that in minor ways for years, but now the fire grew to encompass the kettle. The ball in the throat transformed into resolve. A weak fire grew strong. Anger and a call to arms rose in them all. Grave injustice had been visited upon them. The more they thought about it the graver they felt the injustice. Injustice had been a dominant part of their lives for as long as they could recall and they had had enough. Addresses were exchanged and oaths sworn.

– I thought I could put the Storm behind me, Giovanni Rossi told Judith. – What a silly notion. It will always be there.

– That's why you withdrew from the Red Brigades?

– No, that came later, when I thought there were no more choices. He looked potently at her. – We developed considerable differences of opinion.

The police vans drove off slowly, followed by walking officers with their captives. The ambulances had first picked up the wounded cops. It had taken a long time before they had returned for the wounded protesters. The main requirement for being taken to the hospital to be treated was near unconsciousness.

The uniforms moved with the greatest caution to one of their fortresses, where safety awaited them like a warm blanket. They imagined they saw threatening shadows in the deep shades of the city. They had seldom felt more unsafe, and never when being part of such a big pack. Threatening figures grew out of the shadows. Elsa Andersen clutched her club. She had lost her shield. The club shook in her hand.

Smoke from many torches was oozing in the dank air. They saw the fire now, and the human beings carrying it. The human being and its fire surrounded the police station. The uniforms managed to get inside just before the circle closed. The ring quickly fattened and more torchbearers arrived. Elsa Andersen recoiled from a horrible vision of a fire that would never stop burning.

By the main entrance a few officers screamed angrily. They were ignored. Every eye of fire looked away, at Roland Vallens. Andersen saw him clearly. He stood in the intersection between the main entrance and the garage. Judith Breen wasn't visible. Not her face, anyway. Andersen burned in the certainty that she hid behind one of many masks. Andersen truly hated the two and the riff raff following them around. They should all have been chained and forced to repay the damage they did to the well-ordered society.

But the worst, the very worst was that she saw no fear in the sea of eyes in front of her, only anger. How dared they? If she had been the top dog she would have made sure they would have been forced to work until they dropped, until they begged forgiveness.

A new line of guards and arrested appeared. The uniforms halted petrified. No one in the wall of masked people took direct action against them, but they didn't move either.

– PLEASE DISPERSE. An officer stood with a bullhorn in his hand. – YOU ARE KEEPING PUBLIC SERVANTS FROM DOING THEIR DUTY. YOU HAVE ORDERS TO DISPERSE AND GO HOME. IF THAT DOESN'T HAPPEN WE WILL BE FORCED TO TAKE FURTHER STEPS.

– You're standing quite still, I see, a scornful voice cried from the crowd.

– Release your prisoners, Roland Vallens shouted, – the people you attacked without the slightest provocation. You've done us all a great wrong. The least you can do is to give us an apology. A release and an apology should suffice for now.

– You… you impudent…

– Elsa Andersen, isn't it? I recognize the voice. An undivided pleasure.

A salvo from many guns was heard through the ruckus and noise. The officers had fired in the air. More came marching from inside with lifted guns. Their smiles were very challenging and triumphant.

– You can never win. Roland Vallens shook his head. He was smiling, too, a very unnerving smile to the already unnerved officers. – For every one of us you strike down ten new will join in.

Judith, standing close by, felt heat flow through her at his words and the way he spoke them. He was impressive, undeniable. She felt enormously encouraged.

– LET THE SERVICE MEN THROUGH WITH THE ARRESTED. WE GIVE ONE MINUTE WARNING. WE WILL START SHOOTING IN THE LEGS, BUT CAN'T BE RESPONSIBLE FOR FURTHER INJURIES.

– That's for sure, a woman cried scornfully.

Something happened then, before the standoff had really had a change to solidify itself. Everybody present kind of sensed it, shockingly, even before they identified the stench of heavy smoke in the air.

– FIRE! A screaming officer rushed forward from the other side of the building. – The fuckers have ignited the wall. They've put the building on FIRE.

Sensible fuckers, Judith grinned, igniting the building on the opposite side of the cellblock.

– We're evacuating the station, a superior officer shouted. And then, as an afterthought: – Those in the cells, too.

In just a tiny moment the chaos had been transformed into a raging inferno.

– Nothing is in vain, remember that. A voice sounded quietly in Judith's ear. She turned and met the man's eyes. Roland Vallens.

– Satan's subversives, Elsa Andersen shrieked. – You're under ARREST.

He didn't dignify her with a reply, neither by voice nor body language. A blink of an eye, and he was gone.

The building was already submerged in fire, and totally unsalvageable. If firemen had been ready instantly with their hoses and water, it might not have been too late, but they weren't. Judith slipped away into the crowd. Everybody who had been arrested ran off. The police had other things on their mind.

Most of them.

– Forget the fuckers in the cells, Elsa Andersen cried hysterically. – Let them PAY. You're gonna pay for this, ALL OF YOU!

– We won't forget you either, a woman cried. Judith recognized the voice. Jemma.

At this point people left the place in droves. Police officers pulled the trigger like hell, now, and not everybody shot into the air anymore. Judith didn't see anybody being hit, though, but she did hear more screams of pain and rage. She ran from the place the fastest she was able. The only concession to that was that she pushed and helped people with their hands cuffed behind their back, coincidently appearing in front of her. She often turned and looked behind her. The huge fire reached ever higher. One brief moment the anxiety grabbed her to the point that she feared it wouldn't let go. This would be trouble. Giant trouble. Then the sinister grin returned, and her rage resurfaced, growing in strength for every step she took, visible in her features and her very body language.

She ran and ran, and didn't get tired. The streets spoke to her while she was running through them. The rock spoke, no longer silent.

– What's happening? A guy she met asked her.

– The police station is burning, she told him.

– Did you say… *burning?* He gasped when he realized she was serious. – Jeez…

And then he ran towards the fire, ruled by his curiosity. He wasn't the only one.

– Don't go too close, she shouted to them. – You may run into trouble.

They ignored her.

It will certainly be an advantage if the cops fuck with them, she thought cynically. More recruits.

Her resolve kept strengthening as she approached the home. The undefined driving her for as long as she could remember roamed her being. It had been better defined tonight. Far better!

She saw exalted faces of fury wherever she looked. She saw it even clearer when she finally reached the Green Rose. Both outside and inside she was bombarded with the sound of enraged voices and the sight of enraged people. There was no one here ready to bow to superior forces.

So many had sought and found this place tonight. It hadn't been filled to the brim, like it should have been, but everybody present fought energetic against the wind battering them. She easily recognized the most obvious emotions, but couldn't ever recall having experienced such a mood of rebellion, and… yes, revolution. It felt indescribable.

She looked anxiously for her friends. It took time, but finally she spotted everyone. Jemma was the last to arrive. Everybody had escaped. Karine and Renni were still cuffed. The cuffs were removed with a certain serious minded cheerfulness. The two of them were carefully embraced. Both had blood and swellings on major parts of their body.

– We started getting worried, Kimberly said with a seriously slanted smile. She almost always made them smile.

– It hurts merely by me opening my mouth, Renni said, clearly in pain. – But all in all…

– … YOU'RE OKAY! The others choired.

It turned quiet for a few seconds after that. Contradicting emotions of despair and fury warred briefly, until the angry buzz of voices rose again.

– Though I don't know if I will ever feel okay after this, he said, after pausing a bit. – Fuck. Inside, I mean, where it counts. I guess most of us had trouble imagining they would go this far.

Judith spoke quietly, pointedly:

– Neither we nor any others on the meeting had done anything even remotely justifying what we suffered tonight. We did nothing wrong, but merely expressed our opinion in words. But we were still attacked, beaten and chained. If the power of Order had its say many of us would have been rotting behind bars now. The attack was designed to demoralize and pacify the protesters, at the very least those who weren't already a part of the rebellious element… *But it failed.*

Her closed fist, her triumphant smile made all the present wild hearts beat faster.

– Still, I can't help but feel the usual fit of… of depression. The policemen won't be persecuted for anything. They will, on the contrary be praised and rewarded. There will be a bit of a ruckus for a time, with strong vocalizations, and such from the liberals…

Her somber expression changed to a snarl of contempt.

– But then it will, as usual fade. And the masters' bullies will be free to do the same again. And *again.* And *again.* Every time the noose is tightening, slowly strangling any open show of protest. In the long run they won't be satisfied with keeping the status quo, and fooling people silly. They want total control. No less. We know this, and I'm sick and tired of knowing it and do *nothing* about it.

Her voice rose slowly to a roar.

– Denmark is the most liberated country in Scandinavia, Karine stated, adding her own intense passionate voice to Judith's. She had lived a nomadic lifestyle since she had left Norway, her native country eleven years ago. She had gained quite a level of infamy and respect among her present peers during that time. – I guess the people running it here, too, are starting to grow tired of that. They can handle a certain number of rebels *easily,* but we're growing beyond their control. We must stop fooling ourselves. It's about time we stop believing the bullshit that they will be kind to us, if we are kind to them.

– I agree, Morten said in measured anger. – Whatever we do, here or elsewhere, as long as the world is as it is, we will always be vulnerable. The time for compromises, the time for talk and the slow, cautious path is a thing of the past.

Spontaneous cries of agreement reached him from both close and afar.

– We must create something lasting, truly lasting, Kimberly insisted. – Something they can't destroy if they kill us a thousand times.

Leftover posters were placed on the walls. The totally inciting sense of aggressive mood they all showed made them wonder. They were scared, but it didn't seem to matter anymore. Their fear no longer kept them at bay, kept them from doing anything. Sivert walked around, recording everything, «for posterity».

– This is clearly a significant historical moment, he said grinning. – Gatherings of people, throughout history refusing to bend usually make history.

The inspired conversations and discussions continued throughout the evening and night. Thoughts were freely exchanged. No one and nothing was held back. And Sivert felt at home. He was home. He realized fully that this was something he had always yearned for.

– I feel like I've been waiting for this as long as the mountains have been unchanged for humans' eyes, he said shyly. – I can't help wondering how long the excitement will last.

– *Forever,* Karine shouted, raising a fist, directing the circle, and they responded: – FOREVER!

– At least as long as the mountains, Kurt said. – We need only to want it.

Sivert sat there, shaking his head in wonder, shaking in emotional turmoil, wondering what would have happened if circumstances had been slightly different. If he hadn't met Judith at the railway station, would he have been here then? What he did know was that the very thought of missing this made cold sweat break all over his body.

Judith would have been logical and said that many small coincidences formed our lives, but he wasn't so sure.

He had been sitting on the sideline, observing, for way too long. That had ended tonight. He was certain of that.

– Most people I have met are so… insensitive, Kimberly said, sitting in one of many circles, groups spread randomly around the house. – I don't know… it's like they are living in a completely different world. We have lived in theirs. We must show them ours.

– I think you're right, Sivert concurred. – We must be heard, come what may. To merely keep discussing among ourselves, and do the occasional public protest, are no good. We will just keep getting clobbered, figuratively and literally. The establishment has long experience in violence, how to legitimize oppression, and discredit true and truly dangerous opposition.
– The secret services are excellent tools for that, Morten said dryly. – I have always said they're directed more towards the people of the nation they're supposed to protect than against other nationals. «Defense of the realm». HA!
– We must rouse the «masses», Karine said. – We must.
– Perhaps also rousing a lot of undesired stuff in the process, Renni pointed out.
– That does exist out there, and has for a long time, Karine replied. – If it is brought into the light it will just more clearly draw the line. I can live with that.
– Wake the dead and to hell with the consequences, Kurt declaimed.
They had heard the loud cries a while when they heard the sound of many people running by outside. The entrance door was opened, and the sound grew far more distinct. A man ran to them sweaty and out of breath.
– The cops are coming, he shouted. – They're doing it like an army, sweeping every «suspicious» place.
He didn't need to say more.
– Thanks for the warning. Kurt rose and walked to him. – How far behind do you think they are?
– A couple of minutes tops. They're methodical in their approach, doing the city from left to right. The rumors say they're mostly looking for Rolland Vallens, but are reining in all they can get their hands on as they go. They have cracked, so pissed that they don't care about anything.
– They show their true colors, Jemma said.
– They have weapons, and I heard shots being fired…
– You made sure others were warned, Kurt praised him. – We won't forget that. Get going, now. If you have friends living nearby, go to them. You will be safe there.
Fairly safe.
The man or the boy, he wasn't much more than twenty stood there indecisive, until he was given one final, calm nod. He turned and ran off.
Silence reigned for a moment, and everybody looked into each other's eyes.

– They will come here, Yvonne said harshly. – In the mood they're in, now, they'd rather charge one house too many than one too few, and we're high on the list.

– Go! Judith cried. – Almost everybody must go. A few of us must remain, in the vain hope that they'll leave the house standing.

– And I reckon you'll remain? Sivert said angrily.

– I must. It's possible they'll be content with just me.

– I'll remain, too, he said enraged.

– You must go, she insisted. – You're one of the few who can write about this, and reach many people.

She placed herself in front of the bar, facing the entrance. That was the way he and many others present would always remember her.

– Consider the logic in it all, Kimberly said to him. – She has. Let's vamoose.

He thought about it and he understood. Understanding struck him like lightning. It didn't make him feel much better. He followed Kimberly and the others into the shadows.

They emptied the place quickly and efficiently. No crowding or hesitation. Twenty remained behind Judith. They saw how the silver hair blew in the wind from the open door.

– Let it stay open, Judith said. – So they won't kick it in.

She closed her eyes briefly and breathed deeply, calmed herself with careful mediation and closed her eyes one last time, before she heard the heavy steps in the hallway. She saw them come rushing in, guns in hands. She imagined they were met by a murderous crossfire, from in front, behind, from the sides, from all the houses in the street outside. That they fell like the tin-soldiers they were, blown away by the wind.

Not now, not tonight. They kept going, all of them, unstoppable toward the target. They were many. She didn't bother counting them. Everybody stopped in front of her. Pushed the breaks like the machines they were. They spotted her first, then the rest. She knew they did their best to convince her she was a tiny spot on their path. It would probably have worked before, but not anymore.

– Is there anything I can do for you, guys? She asked with doubt in her voice.

– We're looking for Roland Vallens. We *know* he's here.

He had probably told that to a number of people tonight.

– There are just us here. Nobody else tonight. Do you want a beer or something?

The authoritative leader gave his troops the signal, and they started *searching* everywhere. Rage and hatred increased in Judith's already seething insides while watching it. They didn't bother hiding anymore. They had thrown the gauntlet.

In bygone days they would probably have cleaned the localities for people before starting the wanton destruction.

– You're Judith Breen? Norwegian citizen, American parents…

– I am, she broke him off, grinning wide, displaying her rows of teeth. – What's this about?

– You're under arrest!

– What are the CHARGES? Someone asked behind her.

– WHAT ARE THE CHARGES? Everybody repeated.

Judith sighed. She wished they had kept their mouth shut…

– Sedition, subversive activities, sale of alcohol without permit, violence against public servants… That should do it for now. Put the irons on her, guys.

They grabbed her hard, and prepared to chain her.

– So big and strong, and unafraid you are, she sneered.

A female officer slapped her cheek and kept it going so intensively that she was unable to let out the curses lined up inside. She was chained from the ankles to the neck. Not cuffed. Chained.

– What are Master or Mistress' fervent desires? She spoke tonelessly. – Everything exists for their taking. They must just make their victims defenseless first.

The roar of laughter from behind warmed her, she willingly admitted that. The male officer, a very methodical man took over the slapping, one cheek, second cheek. More.

– Take them, too. Take all of them. We'll see how they're acting up after a few months in a holding cell.

Everybody was heavily chained. Eventually they could stand, but not walk. Not on their own. They were pulled and pushed outside, and into the awaiting vans like a bunch of long-term convicts. Sharps lights blinded them wherever they directed their eyes. Chained together in smaller groups they were in different cars, isolated from each other. Heavy doors closed with a crack. There were bars between them and the driver's seat, and bars on all the doors and windows, bars everywhere.

Judith stared out the window, as she fell down on the bench, stared at the chains binding her. They fit so well around her neck, wrists and ankles. It was easy to give in, she knew that. Chains fit everybody, everybody allowing it. Her lips tightened. She and the rest were treated like tamed animals. But they were not. Never! Nevermore! They would put her in a naked cage. Pull her out of it at uneven intervals. Speak nicely to her, speak harshly to her, to make her confess. She wished them good luck.

They didn't know whom they were dealing with. She had been to prison before. She could handle it. They wouldn't be able to hold her. If they didn't let her go it was only a matter of time before she escaped. And when she escaped, one way or another she would… one way or another… the next time they wanted to chain her, to imprison her, to put her on display there would be a good reason for it. It wouldn't be for minor offences.

She had just wet her feet on the beach of the vast ocean. They hadn't seen anything yet. They did their game, terror and play, stick and carrot, and probably felt reasonably safe, content in their belief of control. Like the lion tamer…

Grabbing a tiger by its tail.

++++++++++++++++++++

Sivert wasn't discovered, but he hid in the shadows and was able to register what happened. He chased the cars to the police station, the headquarters for this particular operation. He observed as a bunch of nicely dressed, pretty youths applauded as the prisoners were brutally pushed and pulled from the cars to their iron cage.

He had seen enough, and went straight to the newsroom, and started tapping on the keyboard. Words erupted from his mind at a furious speed. He tapped the keys hard, as if he was writing on an ordinary typewriter. He didn't give a damn if he fucked up the entire network.

Two hours later he stood facing the editor, in his office. The fat man in the chair pretended to read the article with the greatest care and interest.

– I can't print this, he finally confirmed.

Sivert had expected that. He had awaited the confirmation.

– I was there, he said through half closed eyes. – I saw what happened.

– You were there, the other agreed.

– The pigs wanted a confrontation, so they could show off their muscles, Sivert continued unabated. – The point is that the people at the Environment and Freedom Gathering fought back, and got their licks in. They're finally fed up with being beaten and kicked all the time.

– Don't be silly. No one in their right mind can make such a statement?

– It was a legal protest. The pigs and support attacked without provocation. Three of the protesters were killed. Two before the attack at the station, which by the way is one of the finest fires I have ever been fortunate enough to witness. I assume the *police* got more trouble than they bargained for. That's the reason for the hysterical reaction in its wake. Are there four who are killed so far during the *operation?* Confirmed killed? Oh, I forgot. One policeman is supposed to be *injured…*

– That's enough! The editor sighed heavily, signaling a fake resignation. – It is clear that this silver-haired girlfriend of yours has relieved you of any reason or objectivity you once might have possessed.

– I've never believed in journalistic objectivity, not even when I was an obedient, tiny sheep. You sick fuck! You and your like are the right ones to speak about reason. Human society and the environment are on the brink of collapse, and you cling, with all you have to the old, wrong ways. Like the two-legged hyenas you are, you exploit those unable or unwilling to protect and defend themselves.

– Save your sanctimonious bull for yourself.

– Or, to be more direct, perhaps there's a link to the money you have invested in certain politicians…

– You're fired. It came quickly, but in a deadly calm manner.

– I had meant to quit anyway, Sivert said even calmer. – Do you know what? I'm gonna take you down. You're at the top of my list. Do you know why? It's personal, I admit that willingly. Far too many hopeful and idealistic youths have come to you because of your reputation as a radical, and you have destroyed them, you damned…

The man behind the desk literally jumped from his chair, red faced with rage. Sivert experienced it as an insignificant breath of wind compared to the Storm raging within him. He had never imagined he was capable of feeling this strongly.

He hit the other in the belly. The hard fist went deep into the soft flesh. And he attacked him. And attacked him. AND ATTACKED HIM

CHAPTER SIX

The day shrugged, as it once again wore a gray coat. Clouds hung heavily over the city. But there was no rain. The sun burned behind the colorless scheme, a seething place of fire and life.

Heat is burning below the surface, Judith Breen thought. It isn't always visible in the light of day, but it's always there.

But most people had great difficulties seeing it.

Once again, for the seven hundred and thirty-fourth time she asked herself why that was. She was, and had been thinking for some time that a lot of the present day shit happened because emotion, passion was systematically suppressed, pushed below the surface and kept there, in desperation.

She found herself at the «processing» office of another police station. It had turned into a habit. *A bad habit,* she told herself. She stood by the desk and looked half distracted at the TV. They interviewed Elsa Andersen.

– But wasn't the Environment and Freedom Gathering actually a legal demonstration? You did give permission, didn't you?

– We considered the situation as extremely dangerous. I assure you that if we hadn't intervened when we had it would have developed into something far worse than what did happen.

– Yes, was it truly necessary for you to use such extreme measures? Wasn't the fire a direct consequence of your attack on the legal demonstration? And what about everything that happened later? All the arrests... Most of them had definitely no apparent connection to the protest and the fire?

– It's necessary, in my opinion to see this within a larger framework. We used the opportunity to do an absolutely necessary cleanup of a lot of dodgy communities inside and outside Christiania. As you know, Gitte, these occupied houses may fall apart any moment, and should be demolished, really. I feel we should help those who can't or won't help themselves. It's about time we start teaching them how decent, law-abiding citizens behave. Perhaps those now living so hopelessly outside everything, everything even resembling decent ways would have behaved differently, if someone had taught them this earlier.

– So you are pleased with the way the police handled the situation?

– Yes, I was pleased...

Judith closed off the voice. She had heard everything countless times before.

The policeman returning her property behaved in a strangely respectful manner. She didn't get it. It was certainly not her he respected... or feared?

He certainly feared her and what she represented, on a deeper level, but this wasn't about that.

– You will be back, he sneered. – Next time they'll lock you up for good.

– Don't count on it, she replied. *To stop me they must kill me*.

He signed the release papers with an unreadable signature. That, too, told her something. Without haste she accepted the plastic bag with her stuff, and walked out.

She almost collided with Morten and Sivert outside. They came through another door. Both brightened visibly.

– What a coincidence, Sivert exclaimed cheerfully, – Arrested virtually simultaneously, and released simultaneously.

– I heard about your arrest, she grinned. – You should be ashamed of yourself.

– I realized I didn't have your experience with prison cells, he returned the grin. – I felt I needed to experience it at least once.

– So, is there one of you or both I can thank for my release?

– I would love to take the honor, but I'm an honest guy.

Sivert's gallows' humor was infectious. She giggled.

– I can't either, Morten said. – As you know I've made several attempts, in vain. There was no problem getting the others out, and even getting the charges against most of them dropped, but every time I mentioned your name I encountered a hostility that made me believe they would take me in, too.

She didn't understand it either. She thought about Roland Vallens, but dropped it. He had gotten away that night, vanished without a trace, but here and within five hundred miles he couldn't show himself. Why did she feel so strongly that she *knew* him? It hadn't occurred to her before, but he had spoken Norwegian to her during the protests. She had never met him before, she knew that. As far as she knew he had never set his feet in Norway. He spoke Norwegian like a native. She sensed that she would probably never know. How could she then sense that he was so important to her?

– And you? She asked Sivert.

– I'm charged with battery and assault. He shrugged. – It doesn't matter anymore, does it?

– That's right, she said firmly. They communicated without words.

Willy and Anya approached. Their rapid steps surprised her. Both the conduct and the look in their eyes revealed their inner turmoil.

– Judith, *he* is here, Willy said, and implied a direction with his eyes.

They had stopped her just before the corner. She knew whom they meant.

She pushed them gently aside and turned the corner. He stood there, by his limousine with dark glasses. She placed herself straight in front of him, face to face.

– Aren't you happy to see me? Olav gave her his widest grin and a mock embrace.

– I can't find one reason, even if I try.

– But there is one, he said, cocking his head. – I got you out of that not so nice, tiny cell.

– I think you rather made sure I sat there as long as I did. She smiled sarcastically.

– Anya, Wilhelm, nice to meet, isn't it?

They voiced no reply. He didn't even try to give the impression of heartfelt emotion. The other two, he ignored completely.

He held her eyes with his. She was never able to stop that from happening. He was so charming, and she drowned in his black eyes.

– Come home with me, he insisted. – The child misses you.

– Of course she does, Judith said subdued and enraged. – She hates you. That's natural, since she's intimately familiar with everything you've done. But you would rather kill her than allow her to come to me, wouldn't you? Or kill me. Of course. I'm stupid. Or you would perhaps not damage your property?

– People must love you, he said caustic. – You always get alibis and people to stand up for you.

– Frustrating, isn't it?

– It might have repercussions to have so little respect for law and order…

– I give as much damn about the law as you do. She showed him her fangs. He had seen them before, but not so distinctive.

– You should know I don't have indefinite patience, he said, as if he told her something she didn't know. – If you aren't with me, you're against me.

– I'm against you. She drew breath hard. – I think you should consider obtaining hearing aid. Haven't I made my position abundantly clear many times?

– He's very thickheaded, Anya said scornfully. – Hard on the outside, soft on the inside, the same old manipulative, arrogant Olav.

– He's certainly even less impressive than he seems, Sivert commented.

They laughed at him. He saw red instantly, and swung at Judith. She parried, fast as lightning, and then the others were by her side.

– Return to the hell you came from, Willy snarled, unusually excited.

– The world is a hell, Olav said with a shrug. – He or she who fails to see this is doomed.

He waved off the quickly advancing bodyguards. They halted their advance. He stepped inside the car's backseat, and closed the heavy door. They got a glimpse of his hand, raised in a greeting, before the car drove off, vanished into the thick, gray fog.

– He's right, damn him, Judith mumbled with a fist pushed at her lips.

– In a way, Anya breathed. – His observations are correct, but his conclusions are way off.

Judith hurt and hurt inside. She was unable to control it. For a moment she almost wished she was capable of speaking with absolute certainty, like Olav. Fortunately, she wasn't.

The dust whirled in the cold and the wind. The five of them stood there isolated and alone, or alone together.

But we aren't, Judith thought, aren't alone. They want us to believe that, but it just isn't so. We're many more, and we shall be many. The task is to gather us all, those remembering we're… Earth's children. We shall never more fight alone.

++++++++++++

Dust whirled in the cold wind and night.

Out of the green and red fog, Judith thought cheerfully. But no joy showed in her face.

She was dressed completely in black. A scarf tied tight around her head hid the hair. Dark and light from the street wove threads around her and reduced her to no more than a shadow sliding over the cobblestones.

She was followed, by one single man. She discovered him the moment she entered Strøget, in a window. A man clearly not skilled in what he was doing, since she had discovered him and she wasn't exactly well versed in these kinds of games. She told herself she should become better.

The first she learned was to constantly move her eyes, to do it, but not to show it. It demanded practice and a resolve still sending shivers down her spine. She had stood before the mirror for days… or had that been weeks by now? Her attention flickered on and off, as everything in her vision flooded her brain. She looked around her, studying her surroundings, as she always did, with both wrath and curiosity. But it was Wrath fueling her this night, Wrath that would continue to fuel her the long, coming night. She welcomed it, smelled and touched it, intent on savoring its taste.

There was very little physical evidence of what had happened here, not long ago. The entire, central Copenhagen area had been cleaned and brushed to the point of irrationality. It had always been thus; evidence of rebellion faded quickly, as the establishment reinforced its hold on the world. Men and women, girls and boys walked in the streets with her. Somebody walked towards her, passing her at a hair's breadth. But everybody moved so clumsily that she easily heard the sound of their feet against the ground. They played by the rules. She, too, had done so. For twenty-seven years. That was long enough. She studied faces, as she had taught herself. Some were happy, most were sad, or at the very least sad inside, in their depths, where it counted, where no one was pleased with themselves and the life they lived. It was so visible and evident that she almost felt surprised.

She speeded up, not heading straight to her goal. Instead she circled inconsistently, making it impossible, or very hard, to gauge any direction. She seemed like a young, swaggering lady, without any particular goal in mind.

Like most of them, she thought.

Virtually any kid grew up with the goals set for them by parents and society at large. She had hardly done anything else herself, until she, after society's standards «grew up». She had never bought the mindset behind that phrase, really, the same way she denied most preset definitions. But it was during that time her inner strength had been strong enough, hardened enough to rebel, and now it had, through suffering and wrath grown strong enough for her to break out and break free, for ever and ever.

– The need for rebellion is fading, as people grow older, Sivert had told her, lightly. – In most people, that is.

– In me, it just grows stronger, she had replied.

Streets turned narrow, the darkness deeper. She turned a corner. A few seconds she was running full throttle, twenty steps ahead and into a pitch-black alley. She breathed faster and her pulse quickened even more the few seconds she hurdled there in the dark. He appeared before she expected him. Probably because he believed he had lost her. She exposed her teeth. He would regret that he hadn't given up.

She had no chance of seeing him. There was just a wall, no windows on the opposite side of the street. But she heard that he was hurrying. She relaxed, knew she was as good as invisible in her hiding place.

He passed her, breathing hard. The tie whirled in the air and his suit was pushed backwards. She tightened her muscles and gave chase. He didn't react at all, before she overwhelmed him with everything she got. She kicked him while still in the air. The foot didn't hit him exactly right in the head. He fell down on all fours. He didn't lose consciousness, but shook his head in order to clear the fog descending on his mind. She struck his neck with both hands. He collapsed and remained still. She gave him a few extra kicks in the body. Nothing that would injure him, but he would remember the hurt for a while. Crouching above him she searched his pockets. He moaned. She grabbed his wallet and hurried away from there.

She didn't find much of interest in it. An ID and references to BREVIK INTERNATIONAL. A few thousand Danish Kroner. She kept the money and the ID, and left the wallet in a trash bin. To keep anything, anything at all was risky, but she reckoned that if the police or anybody else hadn't showed up by now, they wouldn't. Olav had merely wanted to irritate her by sending this man. And remind her of her luck because he chose not to send a more… competent emissary. It wasn't surveillance, just a whim on his part. She knew him rather well by now. And the secret services still didn't see her as important enough to waste time and manpower on. They knew perfectly well she hadn't executed or planned any illegal action, even though the police claimed otherwise.

After another half hour with careful moves and added insurance, circling the area she reached her destination. Music reached her, more than one tune mixing and echoing through the streets. «Huset» or «The House» was a place with a well of different styles and directions. And rarely the *right* ones, as the oppressive society saw it. Judith descended the stairs to the cellar restaurant and bar. It was an intimate, comfortable and moody place. One of the guests sat by one of the tables and entertained the others with his guitar and song. He played and sang Bob Dylan's music and words, The Times they are a Changing, Masters of War and other early acoustic works. She felt it resonate inside, the sound and the lyrics. She hummed to it, joined the humming filling the room.

Dylan had realized what the current world was like, at least in the lyrics he had written in his youth. They were so radical that they usually took her breath away. And he hadn't been corrupted by the system either, at least not as much as most of his peers and everybody else.

Most people did indeed tend to grow more conservative as they grew older. The ideals and fire, and rage of youth faded and were forgotten, replaced by indifference, and even with the adoption of a way of life those once upon a time radicals had once held in contempt. Judith knew well the temptation of adaptation. Her eyes narrowed. Suddenly she was glad she had come here, to this place she hoped would be so crucial to her and her friends.

All tables and chairs were taken. The exception was the one available chair by a small table in the corner. The man she had come here to meet, Tom Rawlins sat with his back to the wall. She sat down in the empty chair without any initial pleasantries.

– Great tune, Rawlins commented with his characteristic, hoarse voice, a memory from South America a few years back.

But as she knew well herself, without being reminded of it: the worst wounds didn't have to be visible or be visible scars.

He wasn't that many years older than her, but he already looked old. Life had done that to him.

She nodded, while looking attentive at him.

– You requested a meeting?

She nodded again.

– I must tell you, I'm a bit surprised. It isn't exactly what I would have expected from you… Or perhaps it isn't very surprising, considering the latest developments…

– I can't pay in advance, she said tightly. – All payment must be from future income.

– Such deals are very often very bad business, he pointed out, quite unnecessary, – but since it's you I won't reject it right away…

– One, complete «cargo», she said, she ignored his bartering. – One delivery. Complete training by you, personally. You may wear a mask. One delivery from us, one week after training is complete.

– That isn't good enough. He shook his head behind the cigar smoke. – I need insurance, assurances. If anything goes wrong, I'll be stuck in the mire, and I seriously dislike being forced to resort to my reserve funds.

She lowered her eyes for a moment before raising them again.

– If the demands are not met, within the time limitation… I'll come and work for you… for as long as you want me to. No preconditions, no limitations.

She hated the catching in her throat, everything exposed in her naked face.

He leaned back in the chair. He was smiling.

– I would love to see that happen, he said pleased. – You're a true asset. I have always said that. Perhaps I should hope you would fail?

– Do we have a deal? She leaned forward, focusing on displaying and conveying the hard look in her eyes.

– What if you should be killed? God forbid, but it can happen to us all… a random bullet…

– Why not take a chance? She said icily. – You're a Gambler. It's about time you take more than calculated risks.

– We have a deal, he said quickly. – As I said: You're a rare asset. So skilled and willing to learn that I won't really risk much. Let's celebrate our partnership with a drink. On me. Are you sure you don't want anything… stronger?

– You're some piece of work, Rawlins, she said with admiration in her snarl.

He made a short trip to the bar desk, and returned with a beer and a cola. She sipped the cola carefully. There was no suspicious taint. He smiled icily.

– So you have finally decided to learn a craft, he grinned.

– To this point we have only talked about me, she said very subdued and timid. – How is business, Raw? Any dissatisfied or *greedy* customers lately?

– All the time. He shrugged. – A bit of excitement is what makes life worth living, isn't it?

– Lots of it, she corrected him, heat and cold flowing through her.

– By the way, who does know about me, except you, about tonight's meeting?

– Only Anya and Willy, what about it?

– Nothing. A tired shrug. – Nothing important.

– Why don't you join us, Raw? Impulsively she put her hands on his big and hard ones.

He grinned curtly.

– What makes you and yours different from everyone else I've given my services? There was no sarcasm or levels of nuances in his voice, no scorn. – Are you willing to bet which one of us who will live the longest? I'm putting it to you here and now: I'll be here long enough to offer my services to your daughter. You see, I've adapted, aligned myself with the world: I'm filling a void, just like the priest, the physician and the policeman. They aren't merely craftsmen, you see, but an arbitrary function within the system. They're all liars, deceivers, though, while I'm not. I just sell to anybody able to pay, without comments, without blame.

– It's just business, right? She saw a small flicker of worry in his eyes. – But I am deserving of your wisdom? I'm touched, Rawlins.

She fought with herself concerning her effort to smile softly, innocently to him. It was difficult. His rock hard cynicism was like a future mirror of what she felt grow within herself.

– I don't understand it. He shook his head. – You're logical, intelligent, bright…

– I'll never give up, she said. – I'll always hope, I hope. That's totally logical. Hope can move mountains. Without hope the world will die, even if we're all walking and breathing…

It irritated her that he had made her open herself. She wasn't in the mood. Not concerning him. He resembled too much the people she despised.

She could enjoy herself in his company. She could. He was funny, and had a sense of self-irony, something Olav, among others, totally lacked. She tolerated Rawlins. She could do that, because she had decided to do so.

The rock hard resolve didn't leave her. It was very much present the rest of the evening as she joked and laughed in Tom Rawlins' company. It hadn't left her many days later when she pulled the trigger, and felt the jolt from the gun. She pulled the trigger in an even and intense flow, while firing countless shots into the many-colored fog, against the whirl of indistinct faces.

– We must find a well-suited training area nearby, she had said to him. – Our travel expense funds are rather limited these days.

– I know the perfect place, he had replied. – Everything to please the customer.

He had brought them to a farm a considerable distance from the city, far from the nearest neighbor. The thick fog made it unlikely that anybody would accidentally hear the sound of the guns. There was nothing surrounding the lone cluster of buildings, except a gray, infinite plain of green, a sight both sad and magnificent.

Judith took a break. The arm hurt. Frozen eyes were moved from a shredded target disk, its numbers hardly readable anymore.

– That's what I've always said, you're a natural. Tom waggled to her. He wore no mask. – And the foundation is already in place. You learned the ropes several years ago and merely need a finishing touch.

– What about the others? She pulled the empty clip from its container. She reloaded it, instead of replacing it with another.

– They're all remarkable students. Not so strange perhaps. It's my experience that you will learn all this that much faster once you've realized you're willing to kill.

She looked at the line up, studying each and every one in it. Jemma fired every shot with lips pulled into a snarl.

– Especially the nigger bitch is highly motivated…

– The bitterness in her is very pronounced, Judith shook her head, shook it hard. – She has learned, even better than the rest of us that there are truly no places to hide. There is no sanctuary, where freedom and justice reign

– Or democracy?

– The dictatorship of the majority, she snarled at him. – At best.

Giovanni pulled the trigger in an even and near relaxed manner.

– Rossi hasn't much use for this, really, Rawlins commented dryly. – It doesn't hurt with a repetition course, though. He is a bit rusty, after all.

– You're good, she nodded. – I didn't imagine there would be someone able to irritate me this much anymore.

She spotted a worried look in his eyes, and loved it. He did fear she would simply shoot him, and keep the money. Nothing kept her from doing so.

– Okay, she nodded, acknowledging his questions as valid, suddenly very relaxed, even more dangerous. – A society with a justified respect for itself and its works wouldn't just accept variety, but encourage it. It would certainly not use any opportunity to stifle it, to strangle life in all forms.

He nodded, wet behind his shoulders, visibly relieved, happy as a bird for not being wrong about her.

They all took a break a while later. Tom stood in front of them, a machinegun in his hands, handling it with practiced ease.

– Behold the UZI, he explained. – Some say it is shit. Others, like myself say it's one of the best and most handy weapons ever designed. It was designed by and for the Israeli army. There's no jolt to speak of. It's extremely reliable and won't fail you, even during the most extreme circumstances. My prediction is that it will still be used far into the next century…

– The deal is done, Kurt joked. – You don't have to sell it twice.

Warm breeze, warm laughter, a final gentle wind of summer, before the inevitable fall.

– Remember… short bursts. Don't fire for more than a few seconds at the time. This is true for any kind of machinegun. As you can see the barrel is short. That makes it very handy in crowds, but not very effective for long-range shooting. At short range, though, where you will use it the most, doing your urban guerilla thing, in streets and inside buildings it's excellent for killing a maximum number of enemies…

They listened, they learned, with serious, attentive eyes. The light mood couldn't hide the underlying sense of dread. They knew why they had come here. It had taken them all a long time.

Judith Breen took the deadly weapon he offered her. It could tear a creature to pieces, extinguish its life like wind did with a candle. She fired a short burst while holding it in one hand. It was easy, even if the accuracy left a lot to be desired. She gritted her teeth. Using both hands she fired again, and the disk fell apart before her eyes.

– We've started on our path, now, Kimberly said in a hushed voice.

Her words invaded everybody present, made them nod to themselves and to every pair of eyes they met.

They gathered as a group around Judith. She sat on her heels by a circle of dead grass. None of the blades would grow in spring. In this eternal twilight she pulled them up one by one.

– Freedom is only a word, she spat. – A four letter buzzword diligently and frequently used by the sneaky tyranny to lead potential rebels astray. It has finally become something more. To us. *Finally!*

They all sensed it, as they stood there, weapons in hand. They couldn't avoid asking themselves how it had come to this, how they had come to this. But they knew. It was just as natural... and inevitable as when night followed day, and day followed night. Even from an early age they had reacted with smoldering anger to oppression. It was unnatural for them to accept it. They had come a hard, long way, before realizing the obvious.

And there was no need to say anything more about it.

Words were... insufficient. At best. And unnecessary. And possibly an impediment. Never again!

+++++++++++++++++++

The silver hair had been tied with needles and clips. She pulled the mask over her head. Her face faded away. Only the eyes and mouth showed in the window. She continued walking down the street and the imprint of her dark clad figure was fleeting, like a ghost in the display windows. The wind was blowing in the dark. Four other, shadowy creatures followed in her tracks. Five hearts, five pairs of feet increased their pace.

The bank had just opened. There were still only the smallest signs of the approaching daylight. The five moved forward dressed in wide coats, hiding the weapons and the big plastic bags. They moved rather quickly, but not so fast that it should cause this short breath, this beating heart and paper dry throat. They felt the excitement and worry, inevitably, in spite of the meditation and relaxation exercises they had completed. It didn't matter. Rather it was an advantage, more than the opposite. Senses sharpened, adrenaline flowed, making them as ready as they could be.

They had never done this before.

Ready or not, here we come.

Judith grinned nervously under the mask. In spite of the most meticulous planning things could always go awry. One could never guard fully against the unexpected. No one could. Judith had learned that nerves sharpened the mind, as long as it didn't go overboard.

They drew the guns and raced through one of two identical doors. Eyes of customers and employees turned round and wide.

– NOBODY MOVES, Sivert shouted in Danish. He had been appointed spokesman. – Don't move a finger. I mean it.

Nobody moved. Strangely enough nobody turned hysterical either or got a case of severe panic, making them do anything stupid.

Kimberly jumped over the counter. One almost had his finger on the alarm. Kimberly shook her head in warning. The hand fell.

– Everybody down on the floor. The command was instantly obeyed.

Willy had fun shooting the surveillance cameras to pieces. The others started filling their bags. Sivert took care of everything in the drawers.

Kimberly, Anya and Judith ran into the vault and cleaned up there. Huge stacks of bills literally fell into the bags. They had known of this place before Judith had met Rawlins in «The House», and since then they had been informed that there was, on certain dates even larger amounts of cash here. The final decision to go for it hadn't really been that difficult.

– One minute, Sivert called. He shook the watch to assure himself it had the correct time. He feared far more time had passed.

He saw Willy make a ring with his thumb and index finger. It was just a minute. Sivert wondered hysterically and cheerfully if there was a scornful grin playing on the damn homo's lips.

This was a quiet street. Not too many cars passed outside, even though there were some. They had spotted a few people before entering the premises. Some could be in the process of calling the police right now. A scenario played itself out in Sivert's mind that he saw as hysterically funny. A pack of pigs in uniform lurking outside, ready to welcome them. He pushed a hand inside the jacket and felt the handle of the machinegun. They had decided to not reveal the heavier guns without it being absolutely necessary.

– Ninety seconds, he called. Everybody heard him clearly.

The three women had put away their weapons and loaded money the fastest they could. All five of them imagined they could actually hear the ticking of the seconds. Time raged. And they didn't see this as a contradiction to previous thoughts. Perhaps more than anything they experienced a sense of timelessness.

– Two minutes, Sivert warned.

It took a moment, or an eternity. Then the women charged out of the vault. A van, their van stopped abruptly on the sidewalk outside. Willy walked out first. He opened the big sliding door, and returned to hold the entrance to the bank open for the others. Sivert was the last leaving the premises. He backed off with the gun in one hand and a bag filled with money in the other.

– This has been fun, he said. – We're more than happy to return at a later date.

He threw himself inside the van. The door closed with a loud crack. Wheels screamed and they drove off.

– Sorry, I was a bit too eager, Karine apologized. She kept the speed normal, after the rather… fast acceleration.

The alarm went off in the bank, much too late. Those safely tucked in, in the runaway car laughed joyfully and with shaking hands.

– It went well? Karine asked, full of enthusiasm, her eyes growing huge when she looked at all the money.

– Jeez, yes, Kimberly stared impressed. – There must be millions here.

– And only used bills, Sivert commented sarcastic and pleased. – I wonder what scam they had going…

– The others were ready to withdraw? Judith grabbed Karine's arm.

– Everything went so smooth that they had already taken the first step, Karine assured her. – Not so far that they couldn't have turned back if there had been sudden problems, of course.

They had driven a while before Sivert finally allowed himself the luxury of celebrating.

– We did it, he cried out.

– And without injuries of any kind, Anya said joyfully.

They met their friends at the prearranged place. Both groups left the cars they had arrived in, and drove off in another that wasn't stolen.

Their hiding place was in the cellar in a house by an old, abandoned gas station a while outside the city. They reached it just as the sunrise had started brightening the sky in the east.

Dreams crumbled and died, lived and thrived.

Salty waves rolled on the beach by the tourist city of Las Palmas, The Canary Islands. They had all traveled here. After a few days of waiting and preparations, they had gone to Sweden and caught a commercial airline from there. They had bought their tickets from different vendors and to different departures, but after two days everybody had left.

Waves rolled over Judith and Kimberly's legs. They had watched the deep water come for some time, but hadn't moved until now. Their eyes met briefly. Then they threw themselves out in the waves, in the salty sea.

After competing a long stretch back and forth, through tall waves they finally ended up back on the soft, sandy beach, completely spent.

– At this point I just want to remain here forever, Kimberly gasped, happy as the sun.

– We listen to the wind, Judith said. – And I have allowed myself to be blinded by diamonds at least once. It will never happen again. Perhaps we are stupid, but we will hear the winds wherever we go.

The beach and the surrounding area were filled with people. The two didn't usually mind crowds, but here there was something stressful and false about it. It started getting really crowded by now, anyway. And it was time for dinner. The thought alone made Kimberly imagine the taste and smell of food. She had acquired quite an appetite lately.

They ran side by side back to the apartments, meeting Kees and Jemma by the gate. Their only other friends in the world they met inside. There were three large bungalows in a circle there. They had rented all three for fifteen days. They could afford it.

They didn't bother to go anywhere that night. This was their current brief-home, where they cooked and fed. They enjoyed themselves. Time flew. Before they knew it the night had come. The dark arrived faster than they were used to this far south, but it was more than that. They had their campfire in the garden. Judith, Anya and Willy were reminded of another campfire, ages ago. Embers ascended the vibrant air. Judith looked at the sea. White sails shone bright in the silver light of the moon. She wished she could sail a ship across the seas, beyond the world's end.

– We're in deep water, now, she said.

They looked at her, a tad apprehensive.

– Everybody must seek deep water, in order to learn to swim, she stated, in her intense manner, – and we have done so, and we're already thriving, out here far at sea.

More smiles reached her and warmed her, and made her nod and chuckle in the deep, deep night.

The youths left their home to go dancing, at night, the way youths do. They danced the night away. Cold, dead emotions dominated here, as it did in similar places. They had fun because they were together. That included those of them who hadn't danced a step in their entire life. They surfed and sailed to the best of their ability. Fifteen days flew away. They kept going, as if they were still teenagers, but they were not. Ten years of acquired knowledge separated them from the real adolescence.

Their time was filled with such joy that they refrained from thinking about the future. They lived many hot days, and even hotter nights. They walked deep on the shore of life. Wherever they went they were noticed. Because they walked any place as if they owned it, as a light in the blackest night, as if they didn't care shit about anything seen as so important in the world. They passed military and police with their head held high, even though it reminded them of everything, everything they didn't need to be reminded of. Like the heavy, poisonous mist pretending to be air blanketing Las Palmas.

– The poison is everywhere these days, isn't it? Karine coughed. – It used to cover only cities and urbane areas. Now it's prevalent everywhere, whether one finds oneself in New York, in the Polar Regions or in general wilderness. It may not be as visible in forests and mountains, but it has infected the farthest areas of the globe.

Shouts of agreement and anger accompanied her passionate words.

Judith and Sivert danced on the tables in an establishment somewhere.

– To *freedom,* they howled, and toasted with each their pint of Guinness.

No one attempted to halt their proud stance, their wild dance, their quiet joy. She wanted him and knew it showed. And within her remained only a slight contempt.

There were no more places to hide. Still, they had no idea where the strength to break up and away from this place, from the pervasive life and joy came from. They would always have each other, all of them. That would have to do. Fifteen days and nights. And they didn't sleep much, didn't need to. It was like… they, during this brief moment in their self-made paradise… lived their entire life.

++++++++++++++++++++++++++++

She looked out through the window, through the narrow chink between the curtains. They were close to the harbor, to the coast. A ray of reflected sunlight faded in the east. Now, before the day's final light vanished she imagined she could glimpse the indistinct silhouette of the nuclear power plant Barsebäck on the Swedish side of the sound. But intellectually she knew that the coastland and the buildings in the east were covered by shadows and mist.

The cold wind blew outside, at the fifteen people in the small apartment inside. Curtains covered all windows. The only lights consisted of five candles, one in each of the room's four corners, and one at its center. The table had no legs and was no more than a few centimeters tall. Around it the fifteen, eight women and seven men gathered. They sat on the floor with their legs crossed.

How many groups like ours have there been? Judith wondered. Since history before history?

– We're gathered here in secret. Anya stretched out her arms, embracing them all. – But we will soon announce our existence to the world. Tonight is midwinter night, the solstice, the longest night, the true, natural New Year's Eve. Tonight is renewal, the time for life's dance to begin anew.

She looked quite alien then. This was to a certain degree caused by how she dressed, and the way she wore her dark hair, and her features that was clearly «Black Irish», but there was more.

There was the mood she created, with words, sounds and signs.

And More.

– Too many out there are content at being numb and suppressed, Kimberly stated intensely.

– We must change that, Kurt said. – Give them more than a taste of reality. Force them to abandon their Ivory Tower.

Judith sat there with a strange distance to it all. She looked to the side, half through the window, through the narrow chink. The Stone Desert waited out there, a hard and ruthless world. Now, they were finally prepared for it.

Everyone present was approximately thirty, give or take a few years. This wasn't exactly how she had visualized the Fight when as a seventeen-year-old girl she had been given the first push in the right direction, the first towards a different, independent mind. Nobody throwing themselves into the storm could predict what direction it would throw them. This was true with all of them. And as teenagers they had known even less. Knowledge, wisdom and a stronger wrath had been beaten into them throughout the years, with sledgehammers of iron and rust. It was no coincidence that the debut age for terrorists was around thirty.

I'm a bit more impatient then, she thought cheerfully/grimly.

Her own voice penetrated the initial hazy mind.

– We'll make people take a good, hard look at what's going on, take it two, three, twenty, thirty times. Make them see the writing on the wall. Burn it into their consciousness, their core. What they're suppressing and destroying.

Thirty years… After knocking the head against the wall for that long one either caved… or exploded.

– It's hard, she continued. – It will be hard tomorrow and all the mornings thereafter. The rings in the water will spread and will eventually reach the shores, but not necessarily in our lifetime. We are in this for life. We can take the occasional break, but we can never quit. Those of you having problems accepting this may leave now. I mean it.

No one moved. There was no hesitation in their eyes and body language.

– Don't presume you need to convince us, Kimberly stated calmly, with a taint of agitation below the pleasant, modulated voice.

– We have crossed our Rubicon, Sivert snorted. – There's no turning back, and that's the way we want it.

– When you start from scratch you've got nothing to loose, Jemma said.

– We must stop fooling ourselves, Kathy said, a bit bitchy. – The establishment's representatives will never voluntarily give up their privileges.

– The way I see it we have two true options, Renni said laconically. – Either we commit ourselves with everything we've got, or we find a place with very soft sand to stick our heads into.

Everybody had come from far away, if not in Space, then in Time and Spirit. In their soul, even when standing still they had made a Journey big as a universe. They had become hardened warriors, through strife, fire and darkness. In their might they were more than the sum of the parts. Beware be the might aligned against them.

– Let's do it together, Silverhair said.
Kimberly rose as if on cue. Into the farthest corner behind one of the candles there was a small sack and an oblong linen package. Kimberly fetched it. She handed the sack to Anya and the package to
– Silverhair, she said in a low, but not muted voice.
Supple and strong hands accepted it and unbound it. A smooth, oily metal surfaced in the candles' glow. Silverhair pulled out the sword and lifted it high for everybody to see. It flickered and flashed. The woman rose, while locking eyes with each and every one of them.
– He or she who lives by the sword shall die by the sword, she said. – Thus the saying goes. There is some truth in this. But something essential is left out. Nothing is said about what happens to those who don't live by the sword…
She turned its point down and grabbed the hilt with both hands. She pushed it straight down, in a hard and firm move. The point went through the table and into the floor beneath.
Without being asked everybody reached forward and touched the blade with both hands. It was an extremely powerful moment. Eyes and metal flashed in an eerie, undetermined rhythm.
– The sword is old, I've known of it for a long time. A bit out of breath Anya stopped. – I know it isn't the first time it has been used for something like this. Tonight it will help unite us forever, throughout eternity.
– Blood shall unite us, Silverhair said softly. – And tonight we shall create something lasting.
Anya opened the small sack, clearly of an old design, worn, well used. She emptied the content on the table. On the floor was revealed a big cup and many green rings, resembling armbands, made of rope. Anya pulled herself up and in on the low table, crossing her feet around the sword. It had stopped shaking. The woman pushed one wrist at the sliver sharp edge. She looked at Judith. Silverhair nodded. It happened surprisingly easy. A bit of extra pressure, a pull, and Anya cut her wrist. She held the cup under the bloody hand while the blood flowed freely. Kimberly bandaged her wound. The white cloth instantly turned red.
– One of my great grandparents knew a brew that makes a wound close faster, Anya said. – I never learned what he knew. He died just after my birth.
Kimberly cut herself on the blade. Her blood mixed with Anya's, on the metal, and in the cup. She bandaged herself. Her eyes sought Sivert, her face covered by an expressionless mask. She handed him another white cloth. He reached out a hand and cut himself. They all did. Some, like Jemma did so without discernible emotion. Others, like Dorte and Kees bit

their lips. But nobody hesitated. Silverhair was the last. The deep cup was almost full. The blood flowed from both sides of the double-edged sword and at the table. They exchanged the red fluid, gave and took of its gifts in equal measure. Long ago this had been a fairly common thing to do. Now, these days it had become an extremely risky pursuit. The risk, to those gathered this night had become an important part of the ritual. But more than that, the way they had come to see it, there was no true risk. Not to them. Not anymore.

Judith touched Anya lightly below the jaw with her non-injured hand.

– You're the Carrier of Knowledge.

– No, Anya protested weakly under the other's penetrating stare. She realized what it implied. – Please, I don't want to… Please don't ask me that.

– You're the Carrier of Knowledge, Silverhair repeated, – and contrary to your great granddaddy you will live to pass it on.

The Carrier bowed her head. Silverhair nodded and sat down. Anya grabbed the cup and drank, drank deep. She passed it on. One by one they all drank deep of the cup handed to them. She had pushed one of the green armbands far up her arm. She gave one to each of the others after they had consumed the blood. They noticed there were exactly fifteen bands.

– You will always carry one. Smell it. It's impregnated with special herbs. No one can copy it. Defend it with your lives. It is you, your life. I have more of them, and can make more, but we start with fifteen. We shouldn't need more, but we will.

They understood.

– They caught the Red Brigades in Italy, Silverhair said. – They killed Ulrike Meinhof and a score of others in the guise of suicide. All over Europe the resistance is reduced to insignificance. Following that, the methods of those who came before us can't be ours. They will be similar, inevitably, but we will do More. And more to stand against the counterattack we know will come.

– We've talked through it all, everything probable and not, Anya chanted. – We're prepared beyond anybody before us.

Rushes of cold trickles jumped down their spine. But all uttered weaker and stronger declarations of agreement.

– We won't hit randomly, Silverhair said. – No children if we can avoid it. Let's delay Death for as long as possible. But when the time comes, when it does become inevitable, we won't back down. We shall build a foundation so strong that it won't vanish if we do. We will become a family, spreading like wildfire in dry fields, a self-propagating process impossible to stop.

– I can't help fear that we do exactly what they expect us to, Yvonne whispered.

– To a certain degree, perhaps, but not exceedingly so, Silverhair said. – Not so much that it's important and far from it being crucial. We will move beyond their expectations, their imposed boundaries and propaganda, *in all things*. Drastic problems require drastic solutions. But the end never justifies the means. We must never believe that. Then we won't merely resemble the enemy, we will become the enemy.

They wrote their names on a large piece of paper. They wrote them in blood. Anya splashed a fluid on the paper. She closed her fist around it and made it into a ball, losing it in the cup. Just a little blood remained at its bottom. She lit it, and the flame licked the ceiling. The paper and the blood dissolved in ashes.

Anya Kerien
Dorte Kelser
Giovanni Rossi
Jemma Elvir
Karine Lie
Kathy Fuller
Kees Loeser
Kimberly Russel
Kurt Mørch
Morten Falck
Renni Halgrimson
Ole Sivert Olsen
Silverhair - Judith Breen
Wilhelm Otterman
Yvonne Bastian

Judith stood by the window. She pulled aside the curtains and looked outside. Sivert approached her from behind.

– What do you see? He asked.

– I'm dreaming, she said dreamily. – I see distant times, and us, as we once were. I stand on a mountaintop, and below me there are endless green plains and deep forests.

CHAPTER SEVEN

She hung alone in a dark room.

Her wrists didn't hurt anymore. She had been hanging in the ropes for so very long. So long that she could no longer feel the ropes that had once felt so tight. She had no longer any idea how long she had hung here, in this place. In her clouded mind there was only a vague idea of where «here» was. The darkness had just grown and grown, sweeping her defenseless self and surrounded it on all sides, isolating her from the world that might exist outside. She couldn't say how long she had been alone, or whether or not she was alone. There could be the lot of them standing around her this moment. She had no way of knowing. She didn't know how long she had been a prisoner. One hour, one day. To her there was no longer any difference. Sometimes they took her down and dragged her to her cell, and left her there, tied up. An impossible to measure time later they dragged her back and hung her up again, hung her to dry. They never took her down when she needed to shit or pie, but just spread her weak thighs and put a bucket under her. The black mask was never removed, not even during feeding. They fed her food and fluid through a tiny hole before the mouth. When they let their presence be known they constantly scorned her and spat questions she wasn't supposed to answer - yet. They alternated between threats and punishment. She never felt safe. At any time, without warning they could whip her with one of their belts. It hurt, it hurt so much. And they *touched* her, touched her defenseless body. They could t-touch all they wanted. She was… h-helpless. The only way she could postpone anything was to give them what they wanted, stop defying them. But she wouldn't beg. She still had her inner self intact.

A sting and she felt the pain of a sudden whipping at her naked butt. She cried out. She jumped more every time it happened, not less. In her dull, ever more one track minded thoughts she wondered if she would ever feel safe again. A cascade of scornful, vicious laughter reigned down on her. Everyone was present, the entire group. Hands touched her, both brutally and arousing, both methods making her miserable. They screwed with her body, but what they wanted was her mind.

– *Ready for a new round of hot cock, cunt*. She recognized the rough voice. She had never before imagined it this rough.

– Her husband wasn't strict enough with her. Kimberly spoke vehemently. – She still lacks respect for her betters.

A stinging whipping on her butt followed the poisonous words. Judith felt how the mask turned wet around her eyes. Salty tears flowed into her mouth. The group had kept this going for quite some time, now. She was the last being tested. The others had all suffered through the sick parts of her imagination and were eager to return it, with interest. She made the same discovery they had done. The fact that friends were behind the torture, made it all worse. Psychological torture was the worst and compensated for things they couldn't do, like pulling nails, chop off fingers and toes, things like that…

They needed to strengthen themselves, but did it have to be this hard?

– Oh, I wouldn't judge her too hard. She heard a distorted, horrible version of Jemma's voice. – I'll bet she loved his strictness, and played the rebel just to make him punish her that much harder. When push comes to shove she did nothing to get away, but celebrated their lives instead.

– She celebrated a lot, Sivert said, very pleased and very vicious.

She smelled the liquor. It tore her nose like acid. They smeared her lips with it. Earlier they had forced her to swallow it.

– Lick it up. A hissing voice. – Or we give you another round of well-deserved beating.

No. She licked for what it was worth, and when they put the bottle before her, she knew she would drink. She feared it. She waited. Nothing happened. She released a howl of despair and the only reply was a scornful laughter, coming from everywhere.

The dreams, the visions started. She had worked hard to keep them away, succeeding for a while in keeping them locked up, in the darkest corners of her consciousness. Now, they could no longer be imprisoned, and she whimpered.

This was the final test of many they had set for themselves. They weren't meant to succeed. None of the others had… But that didn't mean she couldn't.

Smoke, lights in the air. It was easy to lose oneself in the mist, and in the glimpses of it. You can look at the patterns forever. You can learn much, but you may also disappear in the infinite and eternal. Lights blink and the smoke rises from the ashes. Lights blink anew. No beginning, no end. There is one simple rule: Energy can't be created or disappear, merely transformed.

Images grew out of the air for her inner eye. She saw Olav and she saw herself. She saw them dance in the ballroom at the Brevik Mansion, only the two of them. Dressed up people, among them Olav's father stood in a circle around them, applauding. Everybody had two big horns on their forehead. And as she watched two grew on Olav's forehead, too. They passed by the huge hall mirror. She looked into it, and saw the first growths on her own sweaty skin.

What a silly dream. She was evidently still confined in a jewish-christian tradition.

It hurt so much inside. She fought to keep the images away, but was helpless. They cut ever deeper and her defenses had totally crumbled.

– Poor thing. Scornful. – She's shaking.

– Caused by lack of nourishment, I reckon.

– Or she's perhaps just an old woman.

– But not a very wise one.

She sensed lips against her own, softly, comforting. She reached for the emotion that created in her, hungered for it.

– And now Silverhair's thirst will be stilled, Anya said patronizing.

– N-n-o, she hissed with a desert dry throat.

A slap in the face, and she obediently opened her mouth, giving room for the bottle. The fluid laughed at her, like an insane mountain pond, and she swallowed and kept swallowing.

– Such a good girl. And now you will be even more so, telling us everything we want to know.

– NO, she desperately cried.

A prolonged silence followed after that, one she experienced as close to eternal, and started feeling hopeful… when the first stroke fell on her unprotected tits. She heard steps in all directions, and from all directions painful strokes fell, strokes done with belts and sticks, and she no longer knew what.

They left her shaking and gasping, hanging in the dark. She heard the door close with a bang. But… what guarantee did she have that they were gone?

A snarling whip hit her thigh, and she howled in utter despair.

– Don't mind that, Kimberly laughed. – We'll be back shortly.

How could they be so cruel? She had had no idea they could be like that. They were so cruel. She began to wonder if they would ever let her go.

She had hanged here alone forever. The alcohol seemed to mute the senses and the tortured mind, and perhaps it did - for a while. The darkness kept growing, terrifying, without limit. She started longing for the torturers' return. The darkness had grown so big that she could no longer see any lights beyond herself. For that she had to go within, and what she saw there made her want to shrink from everything and everyone.

She was just a girl again. Back where she grew up. In the urban sprawl of Loddefjord, in the city of Bergen, Norway. She walked between the huge nests (the tall blocks of flats) to school. Little Judy (that was certainly not little) could be everything from ten to her early teens. But most of all she remembered herself as tiny and defenseless.

Such a fine day. Spring came earlier every year. The remains of the winter snow had melted, and the soil, what soil there was, was softening daily. She wanted to sing. She did, a bit before looking anxiously around her and she stopped before she began. There was joy inside of her, closed in, like sardines in a box. There was no joy in this world.

Wind blew towards her through the gate and lifted her hip-length hair. She didn't want to cut it, no matter what they said and did. And she knew it wasn't the cause for all the ugly things they did to her, anyway. She had long since realized it was just a pretext. If it hadn't been her special hair color, it would have been something else, anything else. But it didn't make it hurt any less. She knew that it had, in a backwards kind of way helped her later in life, by hardening her, making her stronger, better equipped to deal with the even harder life as an adult. But it also made her more insensitive, made it harder for her to get close to other people.

The young girl stepped into the schoolyard. Every day she came here of her own, free will, and that made it worse, what she saw as her own, sickening submission. She wondered what would happen today. They would either ignore her completely, deliberately. Or they would STARE, and turn towards her as a crowd, becoming one, indistinct entity and shout:

– SILVERHAIRSILVERHAIROLDSILVERHAIRWISEOLD WIFE

The powerfully built, supple body started shaking where it hung limp in the ropes in the dark room. Judith heard the voices. They had grown, stronger, mature, but had retained their cruel, vicious nature. She whimpered like a very young girl.

– SILVERHAIR, OLD WISE WIFE, they choired.

– You're just a pathetic traitor. Anya pinched her hard. – You would have sold us all out for a few, shiny diamonds.

– You will *confess,* tell us everything you know.

She received an elbow in her abdomen, so she almost forgot to breathe.

– ROTTEN SILVERHAIR. ROTTEN SILVERHAIR.

YES, I'LL TELL, she screamed heartbreaking. Body straightened, before collapsing, and her head fell to the chest. – I'll tell everything.

– P-please… s-stop, s t o p, she whispered, she begged. She choked and gasped while desperately, more or less distinct, and often unintelligible attempting to communicate her woes, her total and unconditional surrender. – … g-good. I'll be good, a good girl, very good.

She received two stinging slaps on her cheeks. That shut her up. Then they pulled off her mask, and put a strong light in her face. She desperately wanted to look away, but they held her head steady.

– Keep your eyes open, you worthless cunt, before we skin you alive again. Fucking worthless bitch, do we have to tell you everything?

She remembered after a gym class. She had deliberately arrived late to the showers, the dressing room, after everybody else had left. Her pent up rage had been released. In a red mist of savagery she had attacked the lockers, smashed and destroyed everything in her way. She had sworn there and then that they would never reach her, never touch her inner Self. She would laugh, but never cry. Laugh at those who weren't any better than hens in a henhouse.

She remembered when she left home, and she traveled east with Jonas Bergli. «You won't lose face by cutting your hair short», he had told her softly. «It's only in your own eyes you can lose face. What others say about you is basically inconsequential».

«Besides», he had cheerfully added. «It will come in the way during the training, where you will rediscover yourself».

– NAMES. Everyone you know. Yes, I mean ALL!

She recited, almost without hearing herself. Everything just flowed out of her.

– Repeat after me: Our nation is a true democracy.

– *Our nation is a true democracy.*

– With freedom and justice, equal opportunity for all.

– *With freedom and justice, equal opportunity for all.*

– Good, but not good enough.

Another slap.

– Hideouts, future plans, Willy hissed.

They cut her loose, as she was reciting everything she carried inside, while begging for mercy in her bottomless despair and humiliation.

Legs felt so weak she was certain they would collapse from beneath her. But they caught her and supported her. A tiny light was lit behind her, casting a soft, red glow. She kept shaking, but felt a certain comfort in their smiling faces. They weren't threatening any longer. She saw their bruises and tried on her own first, tentative smile.

More lights were lit. The room brightened, slowly and considerate, and her eyes didn't hurt that much. Yvonne carefully patted her face.

– Jeez, you look worse than any of us. And you haven't even started swelling properly yet.

Judith felt numb, only numb. She looked cautious and carefully around. The room seemed pleasant enough in this light. She had known that all along, had just forgotten. They led her to the couch. A thick down comforter covered it. They pushed her carefully down on it. Her face twisted in pain the moment her back touched the soft fabric. Arms, wrists and hands were rubbed, but it didn't stop the pain from escalating when fresh blood rushed back, all the way to the fingertips. Anya put ointment on every single piece of her body. She did so with care and skill. It still hurt.

Sivert's face appeared above her. There was an impossible to interpret expression in it. She didn't know what it meant, but feared the worst. The hand appearing held a bottle of Scotch.

– NO! She sat up and almost forgot the pain. – *No!*

– Take it, he insisted.

The bruised body pulled away, almost in mindless panic, to the end of the couch. Until the shaking ended, ended after a timeless time, and everything quieted.

She grabbed the bottle… And put it calmly away on the floor. Sivert waited a bit, deliberately, before removing it.

She finally sensed the closeness and love flow through her. It felt wonderful. Everybody embraced her, one by one. They did so very carefully, in fear of causing her even more pain. The physical touches and the very air, the thick air seemed to explode in their presence. The test was done. She had failed, like the rest of them. She was only human. Everybody could be broken.

– Damn me, I'm glad we're done with this shit, Giovanni exclaimed. – It takes so much out of you… It's really taxing, if you know what I mean.

– I agree, Willy shook his head, – it's heavy shit.

Judith wasn't certain he knew what Gio meant. She did. When she had seen the world from the other side, and the helpless victim had hanged from her hands, she had carefully measured her reactions. *She had felt all-powerful. Those hanging there had been like puppets, dancing to her tune.* As had been the case the time before she ran away from Olav, when she first became conscious of the monster lurking within her, pushing to get out, never giving her any peace. It had enjoyed every single sadistic act she had performed. No, self-deception was the worst kind. She had learned that. The monster wasn't something separate, but a part of her. Perhaps more so, than an ear, a toe or a cunt… *She* had enjoyed what she had done to her friends and loved ones.

Because she, in a black, denied part of herself didn't have any friends, nobody wishing her well. And by all tyrants, she would use this insane hatred to ruin the world.

The eyes cleared. Mind and brain fixed itself in a way. Those who had their eyes on her practically observed how she pulled herself back together and grew before their eyes. She once more became Silverhair, War Chief.

– We've liberated ourselves from the past, she said slowly, confidently. – We've been crushed to pieces, and rebuilt ourselves. We've given ourselves a certain resistance if we should ever be… captured. The intelligence doesn't use methods like these until they have to. We have also gained a healthy paranoia, which is good. We'll go out in the big, wonderful dangerous world and do our best according to our ability and potential. Well prepared is half done, they say. We've been given ample proof that we're human and not gods, and only according to that we can be «judged».

She rose, straightened on the bed, towering above them, a brief moment.

– Everybody should shift their attention, their viewpoint occasionally, several, countless times during life, she said pondering. – Look at the world with new eyes.

Willy and Anya placed themselves by her side. He dressed her in a robe reaching to her knees. Anya handed her the sword.

– Bergli said he didn't know how old it is, Anya said. – It feels ancient.

Silverhair received it, accepted it, and raised it high.

– We're warriors, she stated. – We've chosen to fight on the Thunder Road. That is no easy decision to make. But it is necessary. And right. We all sense it. Not in our outer, indifferent form. But in the depth of our being where we all see the world as it is.

They gathered behind her, by her side, and around her.

– We all feel the truth of your words, Anya said softly. – They are our own. We know that the attempt alone is sufficient, especially against the seemingly all-powerful enemy we face. Even if we happen to fail a thousand times, a thousand times more than we already have.

– So say we all, Kimberly said.

– SO SAY WE ALL! Everybody choired.

Hands sought hands, hands clutching at the center of the circle, confirming what had been said, what they already knew to be true, echoing far more than a thousand times in their battered consciousness, in the place within where the fire burned stronger than any cold and wet spot.

++

With the heat the cold wind from the east finally faded. In Copenhagen and in Europe as a whole people danced euphoric in the streets. Spring and summer came, and confirmed the course of earlier years. Even the worst hawks of the western lands, teeth gritting, had to admit one by one that Prince Mikhail, the marked man, had led on in the path away from the long cold. Nothing had truly changed. The rich and power mad continued their mad reign. But bright sunshine had punched a hole in the dark night. Perhaps the enemy wasn't invincible. Perhaps only courage and very sharp steel was needed to vanquish the insanity.

These were the days the legend of the Green Rose started growing, slowly at first, then like a crescendo. The sound of countless feet, a million shadows.

– I had almost stopped believing the world could change overnight, Judith Breen told her warriors. – Now, that hope has been rekindled, at least to a point.

She shrugged.

– The remaining tyrants, the true power behind the throne of the world won't willingly give up their hard-held position, of course. We have to make them, remove it from their cold hands. Generation by generation those inhuman bastards keep human beings from their birthright of unbound freedom. That will stop! *We* will stop it!

The nascent warriors looked at her, listened to her and sensed the Burning deep below. She kept inspiring her fellow tribe members, aiding them in the intense process of inspiring themselves.

The fifteen confidantes walked out one morning. They had the same goal, but no one walked together. They went to fifteen different parts of town. In each of those places a group of five persons awaited them. Silverhair met her group by the roundabout tower on the way to Kastrup, Copenhagen International Airport. Through her photographic memory she could easily place all five waiting for her. Three had frequented the Inn. Steve Cockrum had often helped out behind the counter. One was a refugee. The third had spent the last six months behind bars. The two remaining were the girl and boy Judith had encountered her last evening in Manning's Hamburger Hell. She walked up to them with her hands in the pockets.

– A fine day to fly, she greeted them cheerfully.

– Too bad we're so busy, Steve complained, after pausing a bit.

Everything was all right.

Without dallying they started walking. Everybody stayed silent for a while, each and every one of them busy with their own thoughts.

– I don't know, the young boy said, – I have doubts about what we've set out to do today. How much will we truly achieve?

– It's a statement, Judith replied. – Perhaps nothing. You never know. But I agree with Wendy Woods telling us all to put as much pressure on the South African government as humanly possible. Then we'll see. No stones should be unturned. This is true in all areas, especially in our line of work… In my opinion the belief that the impossible is possible is the most important there is. Without that nothing would ever be changed.

– Of course. He threw her an admiring glance.

She sighed. Perhaps he one day would learn to think for himself. She hoped he would. That was what it was all about. That people would be able to think and act independently. Otherwise everything would be in vain.

The air was sharp and clear this morning. Sharp in spite of the hot wind and clear because of it. Silverhair drew breath deeply. The four powerful winds made the air in that particular moment worth breathing.

From close and far away they came, to this intersection of open rebellion, on their feet, with bus, train and plane. Some had stayed in the city for a while, others only a few days. They had a common goal. The sun rose to a point close to the center of the sky as the growing crowd met hundred meters from the South African embassy. The crowd moved forward instantly, without visible hesitation. All the feet moved simultaneously, and there was hardly a sound. Random onlookers passing by, observing the silent gathering thought there was something extremely dynamic about their motion. They sensed, like the members of the gathering themselves did, the pulsating aggression in the air.

Judith made the signal and everybody pulled their mask on, covering their head completely. And then… then it began. They quite simply ran through the open door and spread out inside the building in front of visitors and the astonished embassy personnel.

– Out, Morten shouted in English. – Every single one. Get the hell out of here.

They obeyed. There was some hesitation, but everybody got really fast on their feet when he directed his Uzi at the ceiling and fired a short burst. He couldn't resist the temptation…

The intruders started the wanton destruction. They attacked loose and fastened furniture and decorations with an unbridled enthusiasm. Judith, followed by five others, ran straight to the ambassador's office. They were met by a locked door. She kicked it in. The ambassador sat behind his desk and shouted into the phone.

– Police? Yes, you're the third person I'm speaking to. Yes, we're being invaded this very mo…

Yvonne shot the phone to pieces. The man froze in his chair.

– This is monstrous, he exclaimed in a high-pitched tone, – this is South African territory.

– Not anymore, Judith said. – It has belonged to the South African apartheid regime, which has represented their people even less than others of their kind. Now it belongs to us.

– You are hereby persona non grata in this place, this country, and the world outside your tiny pond, Giovanni said. – In your own language, you're considered *banned*. You are unwanted everywhere, and won't find rest anywhere. You will be persecuted all over Europe. Bring that to your superiors.

– And soon you will get your just reward at home, too, Kees snarled. – Like all tyrants.

Judith didn't believe tyrants got any just reward, except what they did to themselves, by choosing their inhuman path, by becoming what they had become. She held her tongue.

They started to systematically destroy everything in their path. Throughout the building they broke and smashed furniture, walls and windows.

– Two minutes, Sivert told them through the bullhorn.

The portrait of Fredrik DeClerk was perforated by bullets. This was one of the few times shots were fired during the operation. Portraits of Biko and Mandela were put up everywhere.

The parts of the walls still somewhat whole, lacking major holes were sprayed with red paint:

ANC

– Four minutes, children, Sivert cried. – Let's blow this joint.

Less than a minute later everybody had left the building. While leaving in all possible directions they distributed all the written material they hadn't left inside to all the people they met. The very revealing documents they had removed from the archives would be copied extensively and shared with the world later.

Employees, visitors, and many spectators stared astonished at the streets surrounding them. One minute they were filled with masked people, the next completely empty.

Afterwards witnesses reckoned that from the point they had entered the building, and until their departure approximately five minutes had passed. Not much happened after that. Not for quite some time. People didn't know what to do. Whether or not they should go home or remain, in their frozen positions. It took a while, but after fifteen minutes the police finally showed up. They arrived with sirens howling and lights flashing, and as one guy told it to the journalists, «in one hell of rush». Breaks squealed in pain when the cars pulled to a stop. Vehicles and men filled the sidewalk. Some spectators enjoyed it all, while others felt rage or a need for a shoulder to cry on. The uniformed, with their sour disposition didn't invite open scorn.

The journalists chased their tail. They just managed to take a few pictures before the entire area was hermetically sealed. But the newshounds got the grateful job of interviewing hundreds of witnesses, so everything was okay with the world. They got many more of the facts from them, than they would have from official representatives anyway.

WE SUFFER A SLEEP OF REASON
PRODUCING MONSTERS. WAKE UP,
HUMANITY, FROM THE LONG
SLEEP, BEFORE IT'S TOO LATE,

a note from the raiders said. Down on the sheet had been drawn a rose, a colorless rose. In the streets there were roses of all colors, though.

– Why roses? One wondered.

– Roses have thorns, too, a colleague reminded him.

The police raged on inside the embassy. They felt strangely ill when observing the calamity. A few because they enjoyed seeing the South Africans get some. Most because they rarely had been faced with such… thoroughness. None of them had seen or participated in anything remotely similar. The «house searches» they had done seemed like peanuts in comparison. They felt a definite envy.

During the day and night several persons of prominence arrived at the scene. The assembly of bystanders and international journalists recognized some of them, but not everyone. There was the Chief of the Anti Terror Squad, Erland Jostedt and Doctor Tor Kaspersen, professor in behavior psychology at the University of Oslo.

– He must have caught the first plane, a journalist said ironically, while taking pictures wholesale. He had his pockets full of rolls.

More or less public officials appeared and disappeared. Some gained access to the building, others didn't. Politicians came and showed off in the limelight, but there were surprisingly few of them. They probably feared they would be forced to take a stand for or against something substantial.

The Attorney General, or rather the Minister of Justice, (the Scandinavian equivalent) appeared and disappeared in a blur of motion. She mumbled unintelligibly about «vigilante activities», and that one couldn't accept that no matter the cause. «And let's not forget that we're talking about an embassy here».

Late at night a black car with one-way windows appeared. Those inside could see out, but nobody could glance or even glimpse anything inside. It drove to the entrance. The men and women from the Anti Terror Squad placed themselves in the line of sight when the door opened, closing it off for curious glances and camera lenses. The figure leaving the car, probably a man wore a hat and dark glasses, and he had his collar turned, to cover the neck. His extensive clothing habits appeared in an even stranger light in the hot summer night. They got a glimpse, that was all, before he disappeared inside.

– This isn't the first terrorist act on Danish soil, Jostedt said at the press conference, shaking in anger, – but it will be the last. International rabble will be kept outside our borders.

– Yes, we have for some time, now, expected the European terrorism to spread to Scandinavia, Professor Kaspersen stated, beginning his speech. – We should have done thorough preparations in that regard long ago. Yes, this is an international group, but there were Danish members, and in all probability also Swedish and Norwegian. These are people setting themselves outside any law and order. Their ideas have been allowed to develop in asocial minds and the only thing they understand is power.

That's the only thing we don't understand, Sivert thought, as he raised his hand along with a host of eager journalists.

He still had his press card. He wouldn't have gained access if the guards hadn't been given strict orders to grant it to him. They knew he wrote for «The Green Rose» now. All his old contacts had let him down. They hadn't wanted to let him in, but it would have looked bad for the illusion of the freedom of the press they attempted to uphold if they hadn't.

The world was filled with illusions. Sivert had eventually become very aware of that fact. It was remarkable how fast they vanished when one used the brain to think with.

Sivert didn't spot Dark Coat, he merely sensed him. He had heard so much about this man. From Yvonne, who had recognized him from the photographs, from others, known and unknown, whispering to him over the years. It didn't have to be the same guy, of course, but Sivert believed so. The rumors about him and others fit in a close to uncanny way. It was whispered the world over, about troubleshooters, taking care of both overt and potential troublemakers, about groups of provocateurs, a kind of assassins… the wildest rumors, about the fate of those daring to give voice to their curiosity.

Sivert had looked at these men in the shadows as a kind of boogeyman for adults, something similar to what was used to keep children from walking into the darkness at night. Now, he was no longer so sure.

Time crawled. He started growing bored. His eyes sought frequently the clock on the wall. It was a few minutes late. He looked at his own watch. Twelve, the bell had tolled twelve. A cynical smile replaced the thoughtful expression. He and the others still had time.

At twelve o'clock precisely a Shell gasoline station was blown to bits. The people working that shift were found bound and gagged about hundred meters away from the burning ruin, a safe distance… with about ten meters to spare. The huge storage thank filled with gasoline had made the explosion extremely powerful.

During the next hour four more Shell stations were blown up.

When the hour that according to old traditions belonged to the dead had passed that night, everything had changed.

CHAPTER EIGHT

The blocks of flats on the fields outside Copenhagen resembled blocks of flats everywhere, gray, with an undeniable sadness, more than a touch of despair. The areas beyond and between each block were gray, with the same undeniable sadness and despair. Sunset was breathtaking, especially from the top floor. The dust and particles from the heavy pollution did that, and those on the top floor had the best view. Thirteen floors towards heaven, and there they were, stuck, with no chances of ever getting higher. Down below the darkness descended quickly, making even the green grass gray. The exhaust from the many poison-breathing engines didn't instantly appear. What one didn't see descended on the ground, on the Earth, poisoning plants and four-legged and two-legged animals. Not the least humans, at the top of the food chain.

Four-wheeled vehicles slowed to a crawl on their way from the central parts of the city. Bicycles were faster transport, but the bikers coughed and strived virtually the entire stretch. The lines seemed endless. They were. They felt like it. They were not. The actual distance didn't cover much land. It just felt that way. If anything confirmed that viewpoint, subjective opinion governed the perception of reality, it had to be this.

A woman turned from the highway to the inhabited area. She glanced at the people waiting at the bus stop. Many a shrunken figure dismounted the bus there, after yet another uninspired day at work. Wind tumbled at her when she approached the blocks. She didn't mind. Her heavy set of clothing was essential to her not being easily recognized, but otherwise quite impractical in this temperature. For every year, now, the heat lasted longer in the fall.

The shadow of the block was badly lit. There were some streetlights, but they didn't really illuminate the air and the ground much. Silverhair pushed her bike the last few meters to the entrance. She stopped for a heartbeat or two, looking stealthily behind her. The area looked empty. Just then there were no people visible in her entire range of vision. Nobody followed her. She placed the bike under the stairs in the cellar and walked back up to the ground floor, and knocked hard, once, on the closest door. After that she unlocked the door and let herself in. The door closed behind her. She walked into the living room. Kimberly sat on the couch. She held the boy in her lap, feeding him. He sucked milk for all it was worth, filled with life's hunger.

Judith sat down on a chair by the dinner table a bit away from him.

– He is cute, she admitted.

Mist rose from her eyes and clouded her vision for just a moment.
– Yes, isn't he adorable? Kimberly brightened. Her white row of teeth was exposed in all their glory. Then, instantly her features sobered. – I must give him away soon, right?
– They don't know who we are, yet, but they will. Silverhair nodded. – It's… inevitable.
– I understand that. How many know where I am?
– Only I… and Willy, of course…
– And Anya.
– And Anya, was the reply. – She knows everything.
Kimberly slipped from the deep couch, and met her friend halfway. She offered the boy. Judith took him, reverently. She had held Dorte's child, but that wasn't the same.
– I bore him, but he belongs to me as little or as much as you and the others. He's born from the soul of us all.
Judith waved her hand in front of him. He yawned unimpressed. Both women giggled in worship. The small man blinked sleepily.
– I'll put him to bed, Kimberly whispered.
– Do that. Judith returned him to his mother. – I need to exercise.
Silverhair was alone in the room. She removed the hat and the long coat. The clothes underneath were thin and light. She stood there unmoving for a while preparing, concentrating. Then she began. She slowly lifted one foot straight out from the body, until she could grab it in outstretched hands. She then repeated the exercise with the other foot. The first few minutes she did little else but warming up, making the body supple to the best of its current ability. Speed increased slowly to the point where everything grew faster and fiercer. She kicked the concrete wall, the concrete wall covered with hardly more than a thin layer of wallpaper. On the other side nothing but air. The hard, well directed kick didn't made much sound, even though one might hear a feather hit the floor several floors below in these blocks. The concrete itself easily absorbed the hardest kicks from humans.
She used the wall as a sandbag, until sweat started flowing from her brow and all over the body. It hurt, but it was supposed to. She had hardened herself for years and years… and it would never be enough. After having continued with gymnastics for a while she finished with a series of ever faster and ever fiercer strikes and kicks in the air. She concentrated about coming as close as possible to furniture and exhibited objects without touching them. It was a revelation Kimberly watched with somber admiration. She realized she would never be able to match or even approach Silverhair's savagery and cruelty.

Judith slipped cheerfully and easily down on a stool, having crossed the floor in just a few steps. Body was tired, but the green eyes twinkled in satisfaction. She stretched the arms above her head, and cooled down at a pleasant pace, everything thoroughly, wonderfully tacky. Then she whimpered a bit, touching her neck.

– Allow me, Kimberly said attentively.

She slipped behind her and started massaging the tender neck.

– Such a relaxing touch…

Judith closed her eyes. She got the same sense of bliss as she remembered from floating in the ocean and being brought toward the shore by a soft wave. The shore and pleasant waters in Las Palmas came to mind. She was good at calling forth sensations like this. It made her frown and open her eyes. She had always had the ability to see through illusions. It rarely brought her joy.

The sense of floating persisted for a while. Kimberly's touch was soft and pleasant, and Judith did enjoy it, or tried to, deliberately closing her eyes.

The touch slowly changed character, turning demanding. Kimberly kissed her in the neck, a prolonged, sultry tongue kiss.

– Do you, too, want to suck my tits? An excited whisper by the ear. – I know you do.

Judith opened her eyes.

– You're such a cute pet, little Kim.

Kimberly let go, and pulled away. Judith rose from the stool, walking to the table. She grabbed a grape from the fruit tray, and ate it with an indifferent expression painted on her face. It was sweet and juicy, but there was a pebble in it. Kimberly pushed herself against the wall. Her back tightened. Her entire posture spoke of an unbalanced mind.

– *Do you hate me?* She asked, clearly hurt and bewildered.

– No, Judith replied, slightly irritated. – I don't hate you. Of course not.

– You have to, saying what you just s-said.

Judith reached out with her hand and touched her cheek. She attempted to pull further away, sliding sideways on the wall, but Judith caught her and pulled her tight. She fell sobbing into the bigger woman's arms. Judith petted her on her head.

– I'm just so rude sometimes, Judith said softly. – You know me.

We're told lies from birth, she thought bitterly. Something will always remain, no matter how liberated and rebellious a person is.

– Every good deed is merely a hope of love, Kim sniffed and apologized.

– I do love you. Silverhair kissed her. – But not the way you want me to. Sometimes I think I can never love anybody… properly.

There was silence, brief but pleasant, where she once again could hear the sound of the Las Palmas waves hitting the shore.

– I can return to you guys soon, Kim said abruptly. – Do you know that Anya has a daughter in Ireland? The kid's father is looking after her. Anya is registered as our child's mother, too. She will soon take him there. She has named a Eurasian as the father. Little Will will be safe.

– That's good, Breen said a bit muted, too muted. – That's great.

Night descended on them and what they saw from that point on was just brief glimmers of day. Judith writhed in bed during her entire less than restful sleep. Kimberly had insisted on sleeping on the small, uncomfortable couch. She was still asleep when Judith was fully dressed, and ready to go, a few poor hours later. The silver hair was gathered under the hat, the coat well buttoned. She looked into the mirror. The face would be hidden in shadow in the glare of the streetlights.

Strength, it was simply a matter of strength, not to serve insensitivity, but to hold out. The smile in the mirror was not a grimace. She was alive. She would remain alive. Both she and her warriors would. It was… important. Through each other's closeness and love they all found strength to do what had to be done.

+++++++++++

Karine sat there, balancing on a chair. She had her long, shapely legs on the table, a table big enough for all fifteen to sit around it, the group once more complete, up to full strength. Kimberly had rejoined them, and Anya returned from her short trip to Ireland. Karine read a newspaper a month old:

SOUTH AFRICA'S ENEMIES ARE OUR FRIENDS. SOUTH AFRICA'S FRIENDS ARE OUR ENEMIES. FRIENDS OF SOUTH AFRICA'S FRIENDS ARE OUR ENEMIES.

The front-page picture was in color, the words spread-painted on the wall with green paint, a wall not far away from a once proud, no longer proud Shell station.

– This bottle contains sleeping gas. Giovanni held it up for all to see. – Completely harmless. One push of the lever into a face and the poor guy or gal won't awaken until an hour later… with a skull-cleaving headache.

Quick as lightning he twisted his wrist and sprayed a cloud of gas in Karine's face. She coughed. The chair turned over and she fell to the floor. She remained there, unmoving. The gas drifted and spread across the room. It didn't affect Gio. He held his breath and used two fingers to keep his nostrils shut. Around the table the assembly yawned and coughed, and fell asleep, as if on cue. Except for Gio there were only Silverhair, Anya and Renni who were still on their feet.

Judith calmly left the table and opened the windows. Air flowed in. She shook her head in quite a telling way.

– The gas is quickly dissolved in air, the Italian said well over an hour later to the eleven gathered once more around the table. – But not instantly.

– Now he chooses to enlighten us, Sivert complained, holding his head.

– I rather thought you would say exactly *that,* Kimberly scowled.

Since Gio and Sivert sat on the same side of the table, close to each other the others couldn't be certain who she was talking to… or aiming at.

– Quite a fitting remark. Anya sent her a cheerful grin. Most of those present didn't quite get what she hinted at either.

Kimberly jumped up from her chair. Judith cleared her throat. Kimberly reddened and returned quite docile to the chair.

– Okay, people, siesta is done, time to get going. Judith stood relaxed by the end of the table. – Let me first give thanks to Gio for his excellent demonstration. I trust that its significance wasn't lost on anyone?

– Will you please tell us next time you want to teach us a lesson leading to a day's worth of headache, dear Judy? Yvonne said pointedly.

– Certainly not, Silverhair snorted. – It was the surprise that made it all into such a glorious event.

– She didn't know, Gio interjected, looking a bit nervous. – I… uh… decided to do it on a whim.

The eleven looked stunned at him.

– And a fortuitous decision it was, Renni said softly. – If this had been a real life operation we would've had to carry you all from there or left you behind. A premature day of headache is certainly preferable to that.

They felt even more crushed than they looked, and they wondered how they looked.

– Desist. Silverhair smiled blindingly to them all. – We've seen ample demonstration of the advantages and disadvantages of this procedure. We've gained a weapon making it easier for us to not injure or kill anybody, one that can eliminate an opponent temporarily. We must be ever vigilant and cautious, though, so it won't make us careless, make us take unnecessary risks. We're still inexperienced. We may meet opponents who are not. Then we better make sure we have other advantages going for us.

It was amazing this, this ability she had to make them listen, to make all people listen. That's what made her so dangerous. Willy shook his head. She was a Martin Luther King, John Lennon, Che Guevara, Stephen Biko, King Arthur, Roland Vallens, Chai Ling, Ulrike Meinhof and many more squared. She could have been a Peder or Olav Brevik, Adolf Hitler, Margaret Thatcher, Vicki Frost and many more, but wasn't.

– All the world's governments are at war with their own people, she said. – There has never been a war fought against another country declared by the people. We've gone to war against those who hunger for power. They will remain thirsty in their barren lands.

– Our dear Judith's poetry is like murder, Anya joked lightly and fondly. – She says it with flowers, but she speaks for us all.

– There are more than sufficient thorns as counterweight to the flowers, Jemma gave rare praise.

Judith did speak for them all. This was a conclusion, an observation every one of them shared. Judith nodded pleased. She led a harmonic group, in spite of sporadic disagreement and tension.

The fleeting smile faded and the sober expression returned. They found themselves in a minority, at a constant disadvantage against the legions supporting and propagating a world full of poison, imbalance and injustice.

– We need every advantage, every thorn and flower we may have, she said. – The immense and cruel forces set against us will only be growing in number and strength.

They looked at her some more and nodded, with even more determination and prevailing catching in the throat.

The group was for the time being hiding out in an abandoned warehouse by Europe Road 47 a bit north of Copenhagen. A spacious and even partly refurbished place, with as much privacy they would ever desire. When they left the «conference room» they spread out across the entire building. Some chose the company of others, some to be alone, or alone together. Most of them sought solitude now and then, to reflect and strengthen resolve, to harden body and mind. No matter how many one fought with, every human being had to confront the Moment of Truth alone. They knew this.

They turned more one-track minded. They felt it. It was a natural effect of the isolation they imposed upon themselves, as a group. They occasionally did leave for short, solitary trips to town. Except for that they didn't do much as individuals between each operation. They strived for variation within the confines of their lives.

– It feels strange and a bit depressing to not be a part of the refreshing and vigorous surroundings of the Green Rose anymore, Judith told Anya in a moment of solitude.

– Our departure from it was both compulsory and voluntarily, Anya replied.

There was no one else close to them. They heard the whispers of the dust in the deserted hallway.

– Regimentation means spiritual deficiency, Judith said. – It must never happen to us… like it has with so many before us.

Anya nodded somberly. The two old friends clasped hands, deliberately allowing the catching in the throat, the pain of memory and awareness to grow.

– Warrior sisters forever, Anya said.

– Forever! Silverhair replied.

Nights continued to follow nights, as they always did. An autumn storm raged outside, while they kept up with their daily, extensive exercise. Included were speed, endurance and weapons training. They had to be fanatical about stuff like this, with the life they had chosen to live. Everyone was present, except Willy. He had gone to town to gather food and supplies - and to them - other necessities.

Silverhair and Anya kept it going longer than the rest, like they almost always did. They were sparring against each other, and as was usually the case they only avoided injuring each other with a hair's breath.

Anya did a murderous kick. Judith failed in her defense and didn't pull back fast enough. She was hit in the abdomen and stumbled back until she fell on her back on the mattress. The big body did several uncontrolled rolls before stopping. She crouched there, shaking her head. Anya reached out a hand and helped her up.

They had several new bruises when they decided they were too tired to continue.

– Time to hit the shower?

– You go, Judith said. – I'll be right with you.

She stood behind the curtains. A tiny flicker was open in the middle, allowing her to look outside. The streetlights pulsated in the smog. It was gray and sad out there, harsh and ruthless. The world drained her, but it could be wonderful, too. She sort of enjoyed the desolation displayed before her.

Willy rode the bicycle in a wide arch across the field towards her. He turned towards the building and entered it at its end, where he was least visible from the road. She waited, knowing he would come straight to her. Not long afterwards she heard him come through the door to this room. She realized he was agitated about something, heard it on the sound of his steps. They embraced. He kissed her like a sister.

– They've started tearing down Liberty City, he said without introduction.

– Oh, no, she exclaimed.

– I was there, he confirmed. – As close as they allowed spectators and witnesses to come. There's nothing we can do. They're using huge numbers of policemen and units from the army. It's a madhouse. I've never seen anything... like it.

She turned from her position by the window. They had all seen it come the last few days, weeks, years... The decision to drop Liberty City's special status had been taken some time ago, in triumph, after many years of trying. The people living there had taken it to court, followed the case up and down in the system, fought with every legal alternative at their disposal. Yesterday the final Supreme Court decision had been made, the way everyone knew it would be. The decision to transform the area to business purposes could be put in effect. Fully aware of how the world worked thousands of supporters and likeminded people had arrived Christiania the last few weeks, helping build walls and defenses using old cars, wheels, concrete and everything they could carry in their hands. As a last resort the defenders had used themselves. Judith could see it, as lively as if she had experienced it personally. What would be shown on TV, and everything that wouldn't.

– It's good for us, she finally said, with a controlled voice. – In a backwards kind of way. There will be no lack of recruits. The problem will be what to do with them all.

– You don't need to play ice princess with me, he said softly. – We've known each other for a long time, you know.

– I don't understand what you're yapping about. She half turned to him, with a clear, penetrating look.

– Forget it, he said embarrassed, lowering his eyes, not taking her up on her challenge. – You know you can always talk to me. You've always been there for the rest of us.

– Anya will be meeting with a contact tonight, she said, preoccupied already, discarding him, rejecting his attempt at comforting her. – Would you make sure she gets double escort?

– Of course, he nodded.

He turned in the door. She stood with her back to him, turned towards the window, staring at the desolation outside.

++++++++++++++++++++++++++++++++

The «cleaning up» of Liberty City kept going for days and days. Some of the people chose passive resistance. They were carried off. Not with their legs first, but nonetheless many ended up in hospital. Then there were those who fought with hands and feet. A few of them ended up in the morgue, the rest in hospital or in prison cells. Those who fought with guns ended up in the morgue or they retreated after a long and hard struggle, dispersing for the four winds. A huge number of policemen and soldiers were killed, and the mood within their ranks afterwards was rather foul.

Colonel Buhl-Jensen asked for martial law on October 13th and the «request» was met on the 15th. Then the unrest had spread to the rest of the city. Every captured foreigner was imprisoned, most of them from some minority or another. Almost none of the foreigners who went into hiding were captured. The martial law lasted only twenty-five days, but nothing would ever be the same.

In other Danish, Scandinavian and European cities spontaneous protests erupted everywhere. A flower… opened. It would never stop opening. Protesters attacked police stations with everything they had and could find. Servicemen stood and watched bitterly at the wanton destruction. Someone higher up had for once used their head. The uniformed thugs had been given strict orders not to interfere, to abstain from the usual provocations.

They who had merely wandered the streets carrying protest signs returned home after the protests. The others were forced to lay low in the coming weeks, when the defenders of Law and Order extracted a terrible revenge.

But more than one human being who thirsted for justice had opened their eyes. And the thirst increased. It didn't dissipate, as was usually the case.

The Copenhagen Mayor offered «adequate new buildings and locales» as residences and homes, to those who signed a declaration «not to use violent methods in the execution of their politics».

In an open letter signed by thousands of Danes he was told, «to go straight to hell». In a less nice call to a christmas radio program that year Judith presented herself with her full name. This was ten days after she had been put on the police wanted list as a member of the Green Rose.

– But what do you *want?* The newscaster sounded desperate.

– We want people not to forget. We will remind them how unfree they are and how they allow themselves to be pushed and oppressed every day and night of their lives, how humanity slowly is strangling itself and its spirit. Those in charge give us merely pieces of what we're entitled to. Accepting that stops *now*. For every injustice and horror they visit upon us all, for everything they have done, do and will do we'll give them tenfold in return. We're the nightmares that will haunt everybody's dreams, until we all wake up.

Amazingly fast, no more than fifteen minutes' later «a government representative» called in.

– People believing that she, an unstable, erratic alcoholic has something sensible to say should really have their head examined. The lady obviously has major problems, but the public can rest assured that we won't allow her and her equally misadjusted cult members to take them out on society.

A few days before that, somewhere in Copenhagen the man had met with another in a room with muted lighting and heavy, pulled down curtains.

– We finally got the plague-infested hole cleaned up, one of them said exasperated. – One would assume that would give us some room. But it has been weeks, and there are still idiots screaming and supporting the terrorists and drug addicts. Doesn't anything help against these… these bugs?

– We must realize that it will merely lead to faster and more extensive… hatching, the other, the short one said. – We can turn this to our advantage in the sense that it will make it easier to isolate them. It's always useful to have scapegoats… during introduction of new, unpopular laws, right? We're never out of options. We should expect certain unexpected problems with this new group because of its… uncanny popularity, though.

– That popularity will be impossible to handle, too, in the short run. It's not one created by the media, but on the damn ground floor. Damn idiots don't know what's best for them. We've tried to find out who those fucking roses are, too, even gone to such lengths as to vacuum-clean various bins for information. We have still no more than rumors to go on, nothing solid. But we will… And the sheep will turn their backs on them. They always do.

– In another matter… I guess we can't count on getting our friends the Mayor and the Prime Minister reelected?

Both shook their head, though without displaying any major sadness or distress.

– Not that it matters much. We've got more than enough friends in key positions that can replace them. We always have.

– Excellently put, the tall one chuckled. – Excellent…

CHAPTER NINE

The Green Rose robbed a bank far away from Copenhagen. Or rather: three banks. Three banks in one, all under the same roof, in a busy mall, and it happened right during the worst christmas rush.

People moved, kind off, hardly more than sardines in a can, bewildered and scared.

– EVERYBODY OUT, Yvonne howled. She had fired a salvo at the ceiling, and she had silent and attentive listeners. – We're closed.

The consumers left the bank, the entire shopping mall remarkably fast. Or perhaps not that remarkable. Customers were used to and very good at following orders. With a frightening dull and distant expression in their unmoving faces they followed the last given order, and stumbled the short distance outside.

Some remained, for some reason or another. Some hateful, some paralyzed, some with eyes glowing with various kinds of curiosity.

The banks were relieved of paper money. They brushed thick mounds of cash into plastic bags and hurried towards the exit in three different groups. A customer remained by the cash register in one of the grocery stores. He held a steak in his hand.

– Whatever you do don't take that thing home with you, Sivert told him in passing, and in a very polite manner, – It's overflowing with growth hormones. If your children eat a lot of that shit they will most certainly be accepted into the Guinness Book of Records or something and for all the wrong reasons.

They laughed a lot about this afterwards.

– «Whatever you do, sir», Jemma mimicked in an unusually good mood.

Sivert laughed most of all, and struck his thigh so hard that it hurt.

The hours before midnight New Year's Eve they spent on the beach by the city of Roskilde. There were several bonfires there. Theirs burned tall and great. Judith stared into the fire. Green eyes followed the embers as they rose into the night sky.

The night was warm. They didn't know the exact temperature, but they virtually saw how the grass grew fresh and green. If it hadn't been for the cold water and the withered trees it could have been any time of the year. The Earth's atmosphere had long since started glowing because of the human-created climate change, the global warming making its presence known everywhere.

And that wasn't even the biggest problem. The progressively expanding holes in the Ozone layer, the layer protecting life on the planet against cosmic radiation were a far bigger threat. The reason for the holes was CFC's, Chlorofluorocarbons, and other human made organic compounds threatening all life on Earth. Judith wished it was an exaggeration, that the increased radiation, from Space, from artificial nuclear splicing, along with *major* amounts of other human-created chemical poisons didn't break down humans' (and the animals and plants) immune system, organisms' defense against diseases, knowing beyond knowing that it did.

Silverhair rose and brushed the sand off her clothes. Without the physical pollution there would still be the injustice, lack of freedom, oppression and inequality everywhere in the world, if this by some miracle shouldn't lead to physical poisoning. But it was connected, of course, like everything was connected.

Everybody rose when she did. They joined hands around the fire, holding hands in the eternity surrounding, embracing them.

– We've been lucky so far. Gio took the talking stick. – It won't last.

– We've always known that, Anya said. – Our awareness serves us well. Most people shrink from it, but we don't.

Her eyes, often looking as black as her hair twinkled in the light from the fire, twinkled at them all. She was dressed in her fortuneteller costume, but perhaps it most of all reminded them of something worn by a medicine woman, a witch from ancient times. One thing they didn't need to convince themselves of: She knew what she was talking about. What she had expressed in words was something they had always known deep within.

The wind came, in thrusts and pulls, hot and cold. The fire stretched from the ground. The waves pushed at the shore. They pulled back and left no more than a film of humidity, a memory of tears. The top of the bigger waves glowed white in the moonlight. The water seemed black, but wasn't. It was supposed to be transparent, but wasn't.

The poisoning wasn't evident in and around their camp. But evident most other places around here, to those who knew what to look for. A few miles out was a factory, Albrekt Chemicals, a typical industrial poison production facility. Judith sat with a flyer in her hand, reading it again in the light of the fire.

ALBREKT CHEMICALS

is producing Zinc-Chromate, a poisonous corrosion resistant agent. It has acid properties and by inhaling it, it may cause major wounds on the throat and lungs. Breathing it repeatedly causes lung cancer after only limited exposure. The workers can't avoid the exposure. Respirators are just partial protection. The compound can be found in heaps across the seabed. It ends up in the air and on the ground at and around the factory. Very few have made any issue of it, and those who have haven't received much support. The various public environmental protective agencies supposed to take care of such things, in various countries have mostly supported the polluters, as usual. The requirements of the law on the industry are insufficient, at best, the pressure from the capitalistic society to stop polluting practically non-existent.

The pressure to *go on* polluting, however, from that same society is very present and ongoing.

Release and production of dangerous compounds has to be stopped cold. And since all human-created chemicals are inherently dangerous, often lethal the only way to stop it is to stop all production, not pussyfooting around the issue. Everything is connected. A bit further down the beach the sand is polluted by spilled oil, also partly from Albrekt Chemicals, and added to that is constant oil spills from tankers and boats. Only a major spill makes people pay attention, and then not for long. Nothing is truly done to change anything. And in the name of profit, of the «bottom line», of «upholding our ways of life» the use of older ships and older *wrecks* is increasing, not stopped. This is present day society in a rotten nutshell. Nothing will be done until we do it, and no longer trust our health and lives to corrupt and power-hungry politicians and officials and money-grabbing «entrepreneurs».

WAKE UP PEOPLE

– This is good, Judith told Sivert. – It doesn't smell of polishing and politicians' evasiveness. Perhaps some people will even take it to heart.
– Thank you, Sivert said dryly, - if nothing else it will serve to remind people of the immensity of the task at hand, telling them it isn't just about «cleaning up a little».
– We will also be releasing fact-sheets, of course, Kimberly said, - where we describe in detail the bad things happening to human beings, to all life subjected to this shit.
– Of course, Sivert said casually, slightly unnerved when glancing at the fellow warrior across the fire.
– I will never understand people doing this to the rest of us, to themselves, and to all life, Kurt said, shaking his head in distress. – I mean, I understand it intellectually, the mechanisms behind it, but I don't *understand* it. The entire line of thought behind their «reasoning» is so… bleak.
They looked at him with humor and fondness in their heart, as his words made them nod in solemn agreement.
– Someone is coming, Anya said muted.
– Your masks, Judith ordered.
She pulled on her own, golden facial mask. She had decided to wait as long as possible to hide her hair color. As it was now, it flowed around her head and down her back like a waterfall. She saw the others' eyes through the trick-or-treat masks. There was the muted cocking of triggers under the clothes.
– I told you, it is Silverhair.
They heard an eager voice through the darkness. It was hard to decide whether or not it sounded supportive or judgmental.
Four figures appeared in the midnight fire's light, two of each sex. They carefully approached the threatening creatures by the bonfire, the ancient fire.
– You are Silverhair, right? One of the boys stated, excited and full of joy.
– I am, she replied.
The four consisted of two couples. They held more than hard enough around each other.
– We were there when you robbed the banks, one of the girls said shyly, with sensation in her eyes, and a light Judith had learned to recognize. The girl had the wild heart, which would give her much joy and much grief through life. – We even picked up some of your roses. Everybody believes you've flown far away.

Not just a few are impressed with the ease in which we're robbing banks, Judith thought cynically.

– We strive to do the unexpected. Sivert winked to him, smiling behind the mask. – Besides, we haven't finished our tasks here yet…

– I KNEW it, one of them exclaimed, – you're gonna do the factory. The robbery was just a diversion.

– A very profitable diversion, Jemma said sarcastically.

Sivert threw an ugly glance in her direction.

– More like two birds with one stone, Kimberly said kindly.

One of the boys had stood there ready to jump for a long time, before daring it.

– Can we… r-ride with y-you? He stuttered.

As one being the fifteen turned towards him and his friends.

– Why? Kees asked it point-blank, but interested.

– The many generations before us have made a mess out of everything, the boy who had taken the plunge said eagerly and passionately. – We wish to support the struggle to set humanity straight again.

What refreshing confidence, Judith thought cheerfully.

– We can always use more recruits, Silverhair said. – The question is on what «level». *We* have no use for children.

She deliberately chose a harsh, patronizing voice. The youths shrank under her stare. A place inside her shrunk, too, but she ignored that, as she had forced herself to do for so long.

– Kurt, she snapped, while freezing in her tracks.

Kurt crouched a bit while quickly pulling the gun from under his coat. A blink of a moment later he had it ready and had pulled the trigger. The bullet scratched the golden mask, making a tear in it. Judith kept still.

The children gaped. The tear wasn't deep, but it was visible.

– The way we have decided to fight isn't for you. You're too young. We know ourselves so well that we know we're able to make hard choices, to use harsh means, if necessary. You aren't ready for that.

– You haven't killed anyone yet, one of the girls said weakly.

– Not yet, Silverhair said sharply. – But it's merely a matter of time before that happens. To believe otherwise is to cast spells of illusions at ourselves, and we're aiming to leave illusion behind us. We've chosen a life of danger, and sooner or later we will enter a situation where we will be forced to kill or be killed.

– What about the factory, the boy asked aggressively. – We visited the damn place in class and know the security is lousy. We would love to come with you… one single time.

– One single time, the girl by his side repeated softly.

– What do you say, chief? Sivert butted in. – Some early experience is just an advantage, right?

She could glimpse the devil-may-care smile of his under the mask.

– Done, she said. – You're hereby appointed babysitter. No fun for you tonight.

The suggestion of laughter faded in the wind.

– Don't take her seriously, she heard on the way to the factory. – I can assure you that her bite is worse than her words…

The building seemed even uglier and more unnatural in the dark than in revealing daylight. Sivert didn't ponder this contradiction. He had encountered quite a few in his life. While Silverhair sent Kurt, Jemma, Gio and Anya ahead he focused on instructing the teenagers.

– Here, we have some masks left. You stay close to me at all times. You will not go anywhere alone. Not until we say so. Then you will leave us, and head home. Understood?

They nodded, clearly touched by the seriousness of the moment, even as blood boiled in their veins.

– One more thing, Sivert said after having completed a short discussion with himself. – You can, if you want to, at any time join the part of the Green Rose striving for «peaceful» struggle. It can be dangerous enough in itself. Our membership is growing, and for every new member the terror against us grows as well. We have, for obvious reasons put in place a fairly intricate system of recruitment to the groups where the fight takes a more… drastic approach. We get ever more such groups. One day may come, perhaps many years from now, when you will be angry enough, desperate enough to know that all other paths are closed to you. Do you understand?

– Y-yes. They nodded.

– Then you should put an ad under the *personals* in Ekstrabladet. Three words: PHOENIX GREEN EARTH. And added to that the name of a place of your own choosing. Then our wheels will be put in motion. Somebody will be there the next three months. To the person you meet you say one of the three words, and he or she will say the two others. If he or she doesn't walk away calm and firm.

– What if Ekstrabladet isn't published anymore?

– The Independent in London or New York Times, Sivert said, nodding pleased. – Almost any major English speaking paper will do. P-H-O-E-N-I-X, like in old Latin, get it?

The youths looked at each other behind the masks. Sivert left them for a few minutes to speak to Judith. They started speaking excitedly to each other.

– Fantastic, one of the girls cried, – they're not treating us like irresponsible children, but on the contrary like we actually have something in our heads, and are able to help. That gives us something to live up to, doesn't it?

– I know that for my part, one of the others said, – I will never forget this, even if I should live to be a hundred years old.

They had been big-eyed when approaching the fire and their eyes didn't exactly shrink now. Judith and Sivert threw worried glances at them.

– They're idolizing us, he said. – Perhaps a bit too much.

– We can't do much about that, Silverhair replied. – They must be allowed to make their own mistakes.

A high fence surrounded the factory. They imagined the layer of ugly barbed wire at the top was actually growing as they watched. By the main gate there was a line of streetlights. They illuminated the colorless ground and the building's dirty walls. Even the light itself seemed gray.

– Phone lines handled, Jemma reported.

They prepared themselves. Gio gave the signal. Anya and Kurt started cutting the fence. It clicked when they unchecked the safety of their weapons. The Green Rose set forward in one fluid motion.

The group jumped two and two through the big hole, the torn fence they could just about make out in the weak light. The factory towered above them, equal to that of an invincible death machine. And there were many such machines. There was one single, giant one.

– Door looks solid, Sivert mumbled. – It's a good thing we've brought a lot of Willy's master mixtures.

– We need to save as much as possible of that till later. Willy lifted his modified PVRK Bazooka and pointed it against the door. – This little wonder makes a nicer hole, too.

Judith raised her hand in an averting motion. Everybody stopped in their tracks. She walked to the perceived giant blocking their way and pushed down the metal handle. The door slid open. The others stopped, gazing incredulous at each other.

– After you, she bowed and jumped inside first.

– I'll be damned, Sivert sniffed. – Security stinks in this place.

– You sound cheated, Judith laughed. – Absolutely priceless. What I wouldn't give to see your faces…

She laughed louder, unable to stop.

They stormed into the office. Two guards sat there, drinking coffee. They froze in their chairs. There was a third cup on the table, empty.

– Search. Judith commanded, all but commanding.

They spread out, two and two. Only the leader and the four children remained.

– The alarm is over there. One of the girls pointed.

– I know. Silverhair nodded. – Go and see if it is activated.

The girl opened the closet door. She nodded, clearly contradicting herself, but the leader saw that everything was in order.

Poor girl, Judith thought good-natured. Her communication skills during pressure aren't quite there, yet.

Judith held her gun at hip level, but it pointed steadily at the two men. They sat still and silent. She heard whistling, the pre-arranged signal. The warriors returned. Anya and Gio had captured the third guard, a woman. All the three uniformed people were bound and gagged.

– The Green Rose has taken possession of this locale, she declared good-humored, a little self-consciously, fighting against the good mood, but she had to give in, and crouched in front of them. – Sorry, I'm quite aware that the situation doesn't warrant a cheery mood, but what is the world without it?

She pulled off her mask and dried sweat from her forehead. The three on the floor turned visibly nervous. They clearly feared for their lives.

– Sometimes it's nice to be recognized. Masks can be such a bother, can't they? To keep wearing mine served no useful purpose, since you've already made me. You may relax. The people you will speak to in a couple of hours also know who I am. I've always known I would be a media darling sooner or later. Now, when it has happened, I don't mind. It makes it easier to say what I want to say, easier to spread the message we will be sending out at the beginning of the new, false year…

They placed Willy's «cookies» in seven pairs, at key locations around the factory. Everything was connected to one central primer. The timer was set to midnight. No one doubted it would work. They had seen Willy do his thing several times. His ability to make bombs and blow them up was in no way any less than his more accepted drink-mixing skills.

– Tonight Roskilde will experience fireworks its population will never forget, Gio grinned. – Something quite different from the lousy entertainment the rock festival has turned into…

There were no more than minutes left when they carried the guards off and left the property. They left bold and relaxed through the main gate. Karine threw roses everywhere and also tied some to the guards' uniforms.

The first rockets rose in the sky. The Roskilde night was filled with glittering lights, while time raced towards midnight, and the old ways were torn apart.

– The future begins tonight, Anya said. – Finally it begins. There has been such a slow buildup, but that ends tonight.

They left the guards by the road. The three of them would not suffer any lasting ill effects there, even if they shouldn't be found for a while.

– Tell your masters they should take this warning for what it is. Silverhair spoke in a hard and accentuated voice now. – Everybody should take it seriously. We are the future.

The big car was parked a short run away, parked in the shadows where no one ventured close. The still young humans wasted no time and threw themselves inside, in the driver's seat and the spacious room in the back. Before setting off they said a brief farewell to their teenage supporters.

– Go home and stay there the rest of the night, Judith admonished them. – Don't do anything unusual besides that. Not tonight, and not for the foreseeable future.

The car started rolling slowly.

The factory exploded. It happened hundreds of meters from their position, but the fireworks illuminated the entire area, and the ground shook below people's feet all the way to the city.

– Jeez, one of the girls exclaimed.

She stood frozen, as if time stood still for her. The other three dragged her off. She was unable to take her eyes off the additional fireworks.

Car doors closed with a collective bang, and the vehicle reached the highway. It disappeared in the dark and deep night. Renni struck the wall in excitement.

– Happy New Year, he shouted.

Judith sat in the back of the car. She stared out of the window, back towards the night's fire. She thought about the roses they had left behind, their brand, their mark. This time…

This time the roses had been green…

Part two: DREAMS IN TWILIGHT

«Loneliness isn't a need for company, but a longing for kindred souls».
Marilyn French

CHAPTER TEN

Olav and Judith got married shortly after Jonas Bergli brought them together. Less than a year later Judith gave birth to their daughter Lene. They were… happy then.

They lived with Bergli's five other chosen and other youths in an abandoned building in Sandviken, in the Norwegian city of Bergen's northern central parts. Judith rested in a bed on the upper floor and enjoyed the view of the ocean in the west. The baby distracted her beautifully by being very active in her arms. The tiny mouth sucked milk energetically. Judith Breen smiled with all her youthful enthusiasm and it felt wonderful.

Lene had been born with the silver hair and if she had it like her mother it would never change color. Even this early it was clear that she had inherited the most prominent traits of both parents. She had her father's black eyes and that gave the notion of being in the presence of a tiny elf or some kind of supernatural being or another even stronger impetus.

Anya rushed into the room, ahead of a bunch of noisy congratulants. Olav entered last, his face frozen in an unusually silly grin. Everybody had been present throughout the birth. Anya had chased them off afterwards. The birth itself hadn't been too hard, but the new mother had still been too exhausted to stand a bunch of playful (and noisy) buddies for a while.

The seven of them had stayed together the entire year. Nascent friendship had grown into something more. They saw themselves as siblings, just as natural as if they had been born that way. The other six, Olav, Anya, Willy, Isadora, Nelson and Tanya embraced her first. After them there were about twenty more.

– Look at the little demon, Nelson said, speaking his characteristic «Aussie»-dialect. – I swear she has grown big already.

– Hell, she'll be just as big as her mother, Olav swore.

When does it hurt? Judith reflected, asked herself. Only when I laugh.

She and Willy cast each other the occasional glance. Aside from that everything was great.

– May I pet her? A little boy drowning in the crowd asked.

– Of course, Emmett, Judith replied good-humored. – Just be careful, okay. This little devil may be slightly bigger, but not as robust as the cats you have such fun with.

The boy was so careful when he touched the little ogre that Judith almost felt embarrassed. She relaxed. There was something of a relaxing, close to hypnotizing calming quality to Emmet's behavior. Even when he was raging around the house at his wildest he encouraged harmonic emotions. He seemed so immediate, so «genuine», even more so than other children.

Anya had to chase everybody off again. Judith protested and stated they could stay as far as she was concerned. «I'm fine», she claimed. «There's no reason for them to leave». Anya grinned at her, ironically. Not long after that Judith's eyelids turned heavy, and she felt how fatigue overwhelmed her. She drifted into a dreamless sleep.

She rose after an unusually short time in bed. There was no purpose in remaining there the way she felt. The others saw it, too. It wasn't just something she imagined. She seemed to burst with strength and vitality. Anya conceded to her leaving after forcing her to consume a strengthening potion.

– So the Celt can more than her Hail Mary's?

– It doesn't bother you? Anya asked with a strangely haunted look.

– *Bother me,* are you crazy? Judith kissed her friend on the lips in pure joy. – I think it's *great!*

A few days later they did Lene's informal, very informal baptizing. New life had been born to the tribe and they celebrated. Anya did the baptizing. She lit the torch, the fire, and the little ogre breathed in its vapors, and the infant didn't cry, but kept looking steady at everybody with her black eyes. There were cheers and many a toast. After emptying her third or fourth glass Judith started, as was her habit her toasting to the revolution. She couldn't recall later how many times she had done so, but it was probably at least one too many… since she awoke the next morning with a splitting headache. Horrible moments, minutes, hours, lightyears passed while she waited in vain for it to knock her out. The whimper or hysterical cackle (she couldn't decide which) rose from her sore throat.

Anya, fresh and spirited as ever had remedies ready for anybody (everybody) who desired, thirsted, hungered for it.

– Perhaps I should make a habit of letting you suffer an hour or so longer, she threatened. Perhaps that will make you a bit more moderate in your thirst next time. Or the time after that…

Judith scowled at her. Even that demanded something resembling a force of will.

– I will NEVER drink *again,* Nelson wailed, while writhing in bed and looking for the axe he knew was about to cleave his skull and quite simply had to be somewhere above him.

Judith slurped the herbs like one about to die of thirst.

– Hallowed sorceress, please tell me what the future will bring, what's in store for thy humble servant

Giggling she fell to her knees before Anya.

– I can’t, was the somber reply. – When you throw the dice, the result may by anything from 1 to 6.

And the dice, the probability was forever collapsing, forever rolling. They were doing it. While people sat in their deep, comfortable chairs, on their fat asses, accepting the world, its horror as it was. They did not throw the dice, and nothing came up. Judith lit up. She had had revelations in her drunkenness before, but never before during a hangover. A new experience for sure.

Giggle.

That very evening she danced on the stage in the big hall. Bam bam… bam bam BAM BAM

She waved to Anya, calling her to her. A sting of irritation, a touch of melancholy briefly touched Judith, blown away by the dance. She let herself be swallowed by the greedy mouth, surrendering to the whirlwind. It made her drift away, into the shadows of the old building, of far older structures.

Long after that, apparently she found herself staring out of a dirty window. She had made repeated attempts to clean it, without success. She followed Emmett Terrill with her eyes as he ran through the backyard. A while later she heard his energetic running inside. It wasn’t hard to see that he was quite different from the other kids, from what was seen as normal… even here, in this place celebrating variety. She froze down her spine, on his behalf.

Time - it ran like wildfire in forests and fields free of life-giving water. And it was in these days the river of time became a roaring waterfall. In the time after moving in and the birth of Lene they felt a kind of satisfaction and peace in the abandoned house. Silverhair had returned to Bergen, the city of her birth and childhood, and her allies moved with her. The seven had started to make their mark on the city from the very start. The strange, poignant part was that they hadn’t done so deliberately. Not really. They had only done what they wanted to do.

When they moved into the derelict public building, a considerable number of other colorful people moved in with them. Punks, homeless, riff raff, losers, people with jobs, people without «steady employment», anarchists and all in all a true manifold of people.

And more joined daily. What really pissed off the power elite was the number of bright students and prospective well adapted citizens that sought out the place. The squatters knew it was only a matter of time before the city’s influential and righteous citizens started their crusade against them. Jonas Bergli had taught them thoroughly about a corrupt society’s defense mechanisms.

And it happened. As if it was preordained.
They eventually started a number of activities. Some had public approval. Most didn't. Some were carried out within the four walls - others in the city at large.
It happened while the British pollution minister visited the city that the thorn the youths were became a beam in the eyes of the mighty. The line of protesters reached far and long, through streets and squares, many times the number inhabiting the abandoned house. But for some reason only the fact that *they* had participated deserved attention in the established media in the coming days.
Just like Jonas Bergli had told them it would be. Things had evidently not changed much since his youth. The admiration they felt for his sharp observational skills did not diminish. They had been prepared, and they told the other occupants that much every opportunity they got, even though they saw they didn't really quite get it. The seven grew angry, not discouraged, not like what they saw in the others, the absolute beginners, those being more vulnerable to government propaganda and manipulation.
Judith and Anya stood on the roof one stormy afternoon. It didn't rain, but black clouds covered the sky. The wind caught them, and lifted them up. It didn't make them fall.
– That which does not kill us and turns us into zombies makes us stronger, Judith said with a raised fist.
Anya nodded, downtrodden, strangely encouraged, clasping Judith's hand in a sisterly embrace.
– Look at this garbage. Judith held up a newspaper.
– I've seen it.
Anya had learned basic Norwegian amazingly fast, grasping its essentials like she did anything.
The headline said in large typefaces:

SQUATTERS ATTACKING POLICE

– A few unarmed kids attacking policemen in armor? Judith swallowed hard. – Very funny.
– Bergli warned us, Anya said muted.
– He did indeed, but we didn't really believe him, did we now? I guess that's the way it is with everybody, until they experience it in person, and some not even then. Media is the fourth, *supporting* estate, not the corrective that most like to think it is. Many are fooled, even those who have more than a ghost of an independent viewpoint. It's unnerving how most fuckers are fooled all the time.

They hadn't really sought the attention, but they made good use of it. Their growing anger pushed them forward, made them dare more than they would have done otherwise. Everything they did was prominently displayed in the headlines. The attention came from the journalists, the police, the politicians and not the least the youths in town. Most of it covered their participation in «illegal and violent protests», of course, but not everything. There were those «easily fooled and wayward souls», who actually listened to what they had to say, and decided to take a closer look at the activities they eventually started in the house.

The house had a large annex they used as a storage room, where they also had built the stage, one as large and fine as imagination allowed. They built set pieces totally out of their own head, according to what was needed, not what was expected. They called it the Hall and used it as a true variation of performances, meetings and gatherings. Other parts of the Green Lodge, as it in time was called were used to organize inexpensive offers like hairdressing, bookstore, video rental and cafeteria. Outside the combined book and film room they had written on a poster:

IF YOU ARE A SUPPORTER OF CENSORSHIP
YOU'RE IN THE WRONG PLACE
WE'RE NOT SQUEAMISH HERE
BY ALTERNATIVE WE MEAN JUST THAT
IF YOU'RE A GOOD, PATRIOTIC NORWEGIAN
THERE IS LIMITED ACCESS
NONE ABOVE THE AGE OF THREE IS ADMITTED
(WHERE THREE IS YOUR APPROXIMATE IQ, YES, YOURS)
WE THINK THAT IS ONLY FAIR
TO THE REST OF YOU:
HERE YOU WILL ENCOUNTER
ALL THE WORLD'S SIN AND MISCHIEF

Something unintelligible was scribbled below, but with a minimum of imagination it wasn't hard to understand.

Their jigsaw puzzle of a Shakespeare performance was shown for two nights, before being stopped by the police. The play was a fabulous mix between old Billy and their own obscure and insane inventions. During the twenty-four hour period since the first show the rumors spread over land and sea. People came from other cities just to experience it. The jungle telegraph beat with infamous pride the fastest invented technical communication. Gossip was something universal, at least on Earth.

A bright spring day people flocked to the place, and filled the Hall to the last available seat. People even had to stand or sit on the floor. But they didn't care. The majority of those present looked forward to what would happen.

On the wall outside someone had placed a huge white cloths banner. It had a message written in green ink:

THE HOUSE IS OURS

Below on the wall there was a line of additional text:

LEAVE ALL HOPE BEHIND YE WHO ENTER HERE

The stage lingered quiet and empty and dark before the expectant audience. They waited for the lights to be lit there. Instead the lights were turned off in the entire hall. It happened simultaneously everywhere and suddenly everybody sat there in complete darkness. Even after what seemed like minutes, when people's eyes had adapted to the new circumstances, those present were unable to spot their own hand in front of them. It was absolutely, completely dark. A few lit their lighters, or looked at watches with embedded light. A brief look, before being chastised by someone in the adjacent seat.

Light flooded the stage. But everybody would afterwards be willing to swear that there was no one on it then. At its center, fully in the open a geyser of smoke rose in the air, and when the gray fog vanished Anya Kerien stood there, dressed in black from head to toe. During the entire presentation and later performance, against the diffuse, dim background her white face was the only part of her body they saw.

– Good evening, brothers and sisters, jewel rattlers, respected citizens, she greeted them. – I am Gaia. I am everything alive on this globe. I speak to you through the spirit rising up the four winds. I am always where you are. Today you've come here. You won't like what you hear. But if you're one of those who only want to hear what you enjoy hearing you should reconsider immediately. There's no advancement without change and without change there's no true growth. You're free, you can do what you want. Do thy *true* will and enjoy yourself, children.

She vanished in a cone of smoke. They saw her in short glimpses in Helios' glow, led down from the roof through an intricate setup of mirrors. The result was… astounding, in a way they couldn't name. They were shivering with expectation, from fear and the ice and fire embracing all things.

The Gray Fog
(excerpt)

(Gaia's face bathed in Helios' rays).

GAIA: We're the same stuff that stars are made of. Those with imagination and creativity change what they observe.

The stage came to life around her. First a psychedelic landscape of heat and moisture. On a canvas at the back wall it boiled and flowed from volcanoes and cracks in the brittle Earth crust. The image shifted to flashes, sound shifted to thunder, darkness, eternal night, rain, sulfur rain, gases, Methane and Nitrogen instead of Oxygen.

Bright orbs with tails of dust fell from the night sky, from the stars. They stretched, landed and rose on their two legs, fighting themselves forward, towards Gaia. Massive barriers rose in their path. She was an island in this Sea of Eternity. They swam to her through tall waves. One of them won the race and her favor a few drops of water ahead of the rest. More attempted to get close to her, but she had erected a hard shell around her and their seed fell flat on the rock.

Flashes flared. Gaia and her mate pushed their hands, their bodies at each other, and they joined in the darkness. Her face shone happily, before that, too, disappeared. Once more everything turned pitch black. A loud scream and a bit of light returned. It turned brighter at a slow, dreamy pace, until the Sun shone from a blue sky, with a few, milky white clouds. Landscape was green and stretched on as far as it was possible to imagine, and that was many times forever. A blue ocean, bursting with life revealed itself. At first there were no animals on land, but they finally arrived and eventually land, too, crawled with life. Humanity arrived last, sixty-five million years after a group of animals no one currently alive had ever seen.

Mankind had existed in merely a fraction of the planet's history. Perhaps that was why they elevated themselves as masters, instead of allies? Minor coincidences in genetics and surroundings had given them a choice. The dice had still not stopped rolling.

But it was about to.

The three witches circled their cauldron and stirred their brew.

THE WITCHES: In ancient times the wise and those for which time was no limit predicted that buildings of rock and sand should rise towards the heavens. That they would spread across the Earth as a disease in a body. And only when man's time drew near it would be decided whether or not the disease would be defeated.

More words, echoes like chants flowed from the nondescript darkness.

Times are dark. Dark times are coming.

Soldiers charge forward and take the three wise with them. Huge, ugly buildings rise towards the sky and cover the sun, the moon. The Witches' brew is thrown away, landing on rock. Their power fades in the gray fog, in the time the wise call The Machine Age, the age of imbalance.

Witchfire and the ashes of burned witches reach into the heavens. The King steps forward with his scepter and his crown.

THE KING: Even the fiercest beast feels a bit of pity, but I feel no pity, for no beast am I.

The witches' death cry was heard across the world, creating boundless havoc and desolation. Romeo and Juliet fucked while writhing in death-throes, never truly living, killing each other time and time again. Sweat flowed while they gave each other their best, and then sucked dry their inner fire, devoured everything they had that was valuable.

The King, with the skull in his right hand turned to an altar bathed in light, where a man in white looked down at him from above.

THE KING: I besiege thee, Jehovah, to smite the worms in my kingdom.

Thunder rolled as the man in white smiled and grinned. The King turned and walked away with a happy smile on his face.

But then he frowned and with the skull in his left hand he returned to the throne, the throne now bathing in dark red light, where a man looked wily at him from below.

THE KING: I besiege thee, Satan, help me cleanse my kingdom of worms.

Thunder rolled as the man in red smiled and grinned.

THE SKULL (grinning): To be or not to be, that isn't the question.

THE KING: Spirit, like flesh is my slave. The King is God's emissary on Earth. I am the master of all I survey.

A gray mist hung over the landscape. In it humans moved, stone cold dead, even though they walked around and occasionally breathed, no more alive than the fortress of forged rock they had raised as a defense against the jungle, the wilderness they had found so merciless.

GAIA: Technology is pulling us away from the beast inside. We're forcing ourselves to tame our wild spirit, to exist in surroundings hostile to life. And the pain is tearing at us, tearing us apart. The pain doesn't go away. We do our best to bury it a place where we can't feel it. It's no use. It will always express itself, one way or another. Always…

A mushroom cloud reached towards the heavens. It shook of repressed anger and pure, crystalline wrath.

In the fortresses humans built there was more violence and greater danger than ever existed before. The wilderness returned with a vengeance.

But like a lover humanity's wild heart was seduced by the false voices of safety and reason.

THE STRANGER: They who sacrifice freedom for safety deserve neither freedom nor safety.

The End came, brutal and inevitable as eternity. It wasn't clear if it happened suddenly, with a bang, or slowly and painfully, with a whimper. It didn't matter. The sea boiled and rose. The wind raged ever stronger and rode across the Earth, and took life, instead of giving it. The land turned inhospitable and fire surrounded the world.

GAIA (sad but defiant and challenging until the end): My Journey is to the Sun, where all borders disappear.

She stretched out her arms and rose in the air, levitating towards the light. This wasn't the end, just one end. Everything passed in cycles. Life would get another chance. It might take a long time or it could happen tomorrow. A river could be delayed, not stopped on its journey towards the ocean.

Gaia rose ever higher, eventually flying like Icarus into Helios' glowing embrace. The light grew, blinding and all-embracing. On Earth one could, if lucky glance the first new green fields.

HIPPOLYTA: I never heard so musical a discord, such sweet thunder.

It turned dark as coal. Devil's Thrill by Guiseppe Tartini thundered from the speakers. It sent shivers down the audience's spines. This was also true in those who didn't know it and/or its significance/origin. Many had long since become quite upset with the play, but just as many applauded enthusiastically. No one remained untouched.

Judith, standing in the back of the theater smiled close to ecstatic and wondered why the play hadn't been stopped in its infancy or at least well before its end. A delay in the system, perhaps. Or pure luck. And skill. They had foreseen where in the play a certain part of the audience would be likely to commit their acts of disturbance. Every time, just before it happened there was an overwhelming roar from the speakers, drowning any loud boos. Beside the fact that it contributed to the show's «weirdness» it shut the fuck up everybody who wanted to disrupt the performance. The seven and also some others had placed themselves in different parts of the hall, and could testify to the tactic's effectiveness. Many of the hooligans and thugs among the audience left the place in frustration. They failed to create any of the trouble they had come to create.

Wild applause erupted when the stage light was lit and Judith and the others stood there in their costumes. They felt good inside, because of the honest recognition.

It lasted a while before the improvised «press conference» started. He who had played Jehovah/Mephisto stepped forward.

– Why are you all here? He asked the journalists. – We would like to have a reply or two for our paper «Teargas»…

– Why in the world are you calling it *Teargas?* One with pen and paper asked sardonically.

– Because that's what they throw in our face every time we want to exercise our right to free expression, a girl replied.

– And this is supposed to be theater? A reviewer stated undignified. – It turned more and more into a black mass the longer it lasted, didn't it?

– A so-called Black Mass? Silverhair thundered. – So what? Let's say we buy into your view that «black» is a negative word: That's what the current world is. Everything negative and destructive is encouraged in our society.

– Old William would have turned in his grave.

– He has definitely done so countless times already, both before and after his death, the lightning flared. – Because of the dull way his plays have been done. We don't give a shit about the cultural gatekeepers accusing us of sacrilege. Shakespeare himself meant that his work had to be kept alive. When he felt it had become a part of establishment he wrecked his office. Symbolically speaking he destroyed his art and never wrote another word as long as he lived.

– Who has a single right to define what art is or should be? Any takers?

With sour dispositions the before mentioned cultural gatekeepers and snobs, not dominating this scene wisely kept their mouth shut. They knew they could get their licks in, in tomorrow's edition of their paper or media later that night.

– We will bury those elevating themselves to mind police, and those enjoying forming others in their image, Anya said sweet and sour. – They're so self-centered that they want all people to join them in their grave, making the world their own, private burial ground.

– When William, himself did his plays it was in dirty rooms, with the common man and the poor as audience, Tanya interjected. – Not much luxury and golden champagne labels there.

– And no failed writers, a cheerful guy cried from the audience.

The reviewers reddened further. They weren't that dumb. They did know the remark was meant for them.

– Isn't it about time you all stop acting like stubborn, irresponsible children, now? A man jumped up, clearly angry and irritated. – Isn't it about time you grew up?
– My fervent hope is that we will always act like «stubborn, irresponsible children», Judith replied cheerfully, giving him the stare. – And my definition of being an «adult» is that one is able and willing to think and act independently, not merely passively and constantly repeating the words and actions of others.
– Very well put, Olav supported her.
– But what about the lovemaking and *nudity* on stage? A reporter wondered, a bit friendlier. – And didn't you imply a strong support of drug abuse? And the play is brimming with *blasphemy*.
– Taboos, Olav said thoughtfully. – We're talking about taboos.
He straightened himself slightly before continuing.
– I'm gonna speak about the drugs, the «illegal substances». I choose to do that, both because I want to, and because it is the only somewhat serious subject you mentioned.
Judith kept her eyes on him. She was so proud of him that day.
– *One:* Humans have always used intoxicating chemicals. And more, I would claim it is an integral part of our lives. They are used to search and to Travel. Which of those chemicals that are legal or not, in any part of the world today is merely a complete coincidence. Alcohol and nicotine are rather more damaging and more addictive than the less available illegal substances. And the so-called mind-altering drugs are not dangerous at all, except for the tyrants that is scared shitless that people will open their eyes and smell the stinking coffee. No, this is something depending on circumstances and the individual user. It is usually drugs new to any given society that become illegal. *Two:* I'm not saying that these ingested chemicals are totally harmless. They might damage the user, because we have a just as unnatural attitude towards them as we have to everything else. Therefore prohibition is certainly not the solution. Forbidden fruit is preferred by many, for good reasons. We're desperately seeking our roots, in all possible and impossible ways. That is a truth ever more evident in our taboo society. *Three:* It is the abuse that must stop. Curiously enough we all agree on that. In our suicidal, excess society we're abusing *food*. We eat too much. Nobody is talking about prohibiting the consumption of sheep or sugar or butter, even though they kill far more people than those pesky illegal substances. No, when we discuss prohibition of drugs we touch upon key elements about the way we live. *Four:* Drug «abuse», «crime», despondency and abuse of power are merely symptoms of the disease. Our society has a long history of attacking the symptoms and not

the disease itself. Virtually all despondency today arises because we live far from our roots. In the time before the planet's first cities, before *civilization* we lived in harmony with nature. Many of our problems would be solved by a return to that state. It's so simple - and so hard. Nature and technology may possibly coexist, but it has to be done completely, totally on nature's terms. The pollution slowly, surely breaking down, destroying all life on the globe is just another symptom. The spiritual breakdown, the black despair, and the fact that we act ever more like vultures and ever less like human beings is far worse. All these things, the tailspin, suicide run we're all a part of and participating in, make everything clear… The disease is society itself.

There was a rush throughout the hall. Judith and Anya looked at each other and nodded. The applause started in the back before Olav had finished speaking. Some reporters just looked at each other, while others wrote eagerly. It was hard to fathom that the man up there on the stage still hadn't turned twenty.

– We must create a society people would want to live in, not run away from.

And nothing more needed to be said.

++++++++++++++++++++++++++

The grand decision-makers finally found an excuse to clear the Green Lodge. All lice and vermin were removed and nothing remained. The youths had participated in a protest against the grand polluter and mass murderer Waardahl Chemicals, and when they returned the guards they had left behind the barricades had been removed and the police had placed themselves in an iron circle around the building, the entire block actually, refusing everybody admittance.

During the next days and weeks the foreigners among the Green Lodge residents were traced and arrested one by one, and deported on the spot, thrown out of a country without warmth or tolerance. Judith and Olav moved to the suburb of Loddefjord, into the house she had grown up in. It had been empty for a long time. Her parents had evidently moved out, disappeared during the time she had been away. A neighbor had taken care of the keys. She would have discovered this before if she had visited them, but she hadn't. She eventually discovered and realized that her father and mother had vanished into thin air. Nobody heard anything more from them, ever that she heard of. Neither did she. She never found out where they had gone or what had happened to them. Little or nothing felt right. Everything in her turned inside out. She stood at the airport with Olav and a few others, saying farewell to her friends.

It was «goodbye» because it started to dawn on these young, optimistic people how uncertain the future truly was.

Judith waved frenetically to everybody as they walked through the security check. They hadn't been allowed to exchange more than a few words in the departure section. She felt exhausted and empty, vacant of will and joy. Olav held her in a protective embrace.

– We can manage without them, he assured her.

– I doubt that, she said muted, with her head resting against his chest. – We're supposed to stay together. I know that… And can they manage without us?

Anya wasn't among the deported. They wondered about that, but shrugged it off as the usual bureaucratic mess, and rejoiced when they convinced themselves that she had truly escaped the authorities' attention. It muted a bit of the pain they felt, now, when the original group of seven had been cut in half.

Judith allowed, without considering it the few from the Green Lodge who wanted to, to move into the new house, but it was never the same. She strived to uphold the old enthusiasm. It was quickly evident that the old response was sorely lacking. They had already too many scars in their struggle against city hall. Factors like the prolonged distance to central Bergen also clearly mattered. Perhaps that said quite a lot about how serious the many former occupants had been in their struggle.

A few of them stood and watched silently while their old haunts, their home was demolished. What would come there instead? She wondered. Another shopping mall, probably, perhaps absolutely nothing? She would never know.

Not that it really felt important to her.

It was raining outside. It was always raining. She sat with her head between her knees in a gray room in the attic, staring out the window, at the unavoidable rain.

She usually enjoyed sitting like this, high up, for a different viewpoint and lookout. It usually made her think, inspired her to act. Lately it was as if she had fallen into a black hole, becoming ever more depressed. She wanted nothing more than to go back to bed, and remain there… for the rest of the day.

Door opened and closed. She recognized the steps. His strong arms sneaked over her shoulders and embraced her softly, in a way well suited for inciting a sense of well being.

– Your lord and master is here, Olav said lightly. – There's no reason to sit here unmoving anymore.

– Where should I be unmoving then, in your opinion?

She leaned backwards, bending her head backwards, so she could kiss him, show him how much she loved him.

– Everything will be ready downstairs, he assured her. – I did the first part of your chores and Anya is doing the rest. There's no need for you to work yourself up.

– Thank you, she mumbled.

He was so kind. When she was tired he always took care of things. He always took care of her.

– How do you avoid the rain? She wondered. – Do you run between the raindrops? Is the only recourse to stay indoors, to never feel the wind and water in your face?

– The rain can't touch us, he mumbled against the skin of her neck. – You know that, right? We can walk wherever we desire and not get wet.

– You silly bastard, she giggled, turning half around and slapped him playfully on the cheek.

Her thoughts drifted again, her attention pulled outside, at the wet and gloomy world.

His moves intensified and his touch turned… insistent.

– Not now, she begged him. – I don't feel like it.

– Yes, you do, he corrected her. – You always feel like it.

He didn't hurry. He touched her thoroughly in one spot, before moving on to the next. He unbuttoned her blouse and exposed her shoulders, kissed and patted them. She tried to wrest herself out of his grip, but he held her firmly and her resistance was wavering anyway. She sensed how every spot he touched on her body started to burn in a low flame. When he finally reached her breasts and after that the inside of her thighs she had already surrendered. She sighed in her heat. He was right. She did feel like it. He always got her where he wanted.

The strong hands bent her forward until she was kneeling on all fours. Suddenly he grabbed her pants and pulled them far down her thighs. The surprise made her blood flow and made her completely ready for him. She was very conscious of her bare ass and how the cool breeze moved across her skin, the burning skin. Moisture flowed between her thighs. She felt the hot drops there, uncannily keen. He grabbed her buttocks then, taking her as his.

They descended the stairs to the living room, arm in arm. None of those waiting could mistake the reason for her misty eyes.

– Why the satisfied grin, Olav? Anya asked with a sting. – You look like a cat that has just devoured a very fat mouse.

Judith saw worry in the look her friend sent her and that confused her. Anya couldn't be worried on her behalf, could she? She had been down for a while, that's true. She was better now.

They fought such a hopeless struggle. That was ever more evident to them. Even if the method of combat they used wasn't *wrong,* it wasn't right either. They placed themselves too much in the line of fire of the ruling elite's schemes. Everything, even what was right was wrong in this world. But they fought on, since they didn't have any choice.

They heard about and from their four brothers and sisters from time to time. Isadora was killed in an ETA-raid in The Bask country on the Spanish side of the border. Nelson slowly but surely turned into the most wanted man in Australia. Tanya returned to the Soviet Union. Willy relocated to Copenhagen after a short, hectic stay in Germany. He lived in Christiania with a friend. All seven wrote to each other, but this was and remained unsatisfactory. The final letter they received from Isadora wasn't pleasant. They were unable to enjoy good news. This was also rare, and the bad… felt beyond worse. Tanya was imprisoned the last few years before Mikhail the Marked Man was named Tsar, and they didn't hear shit from her during all that time. Long after all of the seven had left Bergen for good Judith received a letter from her, one fairly optimistic. She had joined the People's Front and been elected to the People's Congress, found a purpose in life. Judith lived in Oslo then and never replied.

Judith stood at the top of Fløien, one of the mountains surrounding the city, looking down at the many tall buildings down there. It was spring. She tied her hands into fists and knots.

– There is a bond between us all, she said aloud, she insisted. Olav and Anya stood by her side, listening to the words. – One day we will reunite, those of us able and willing.

One bright day.

– Today is a fine day, Olav admitted, a bit down, but mostly cheerful.

They pulled away from the abyss, the edge of the mountain, and walked east, into the mountain moors, walking many paths, seeking unknown lands. Judith and Anya looked at each other, fearing they were lost. Olav smiled self assured and confident at them.

The Sun set in the ocean in the west. They still saw, glimpsed the city, without that helping much. The smooth mountain wall kept them from returning directly to the streets below.

– Perhaps we should ask the next person we meet, Judith said pointedly, sarcastically to Olav. – If we're lucky it will eventually happen… in an hour or two, or three…

– I'll find a way, he insisted, strangely irritated.

So unlike him, she thought. She noticed how Anya kept her eyes on him and how she avoided meeting his eyes when he looked at her.

It didn't happen easily, but really painlessly, logically. As soon as they realized they were lost, instinct took over. By following the occasionally distinct trail along the edge over rocks and countless hurdles they eventually found their point of departure.

– I'm tired, Judith mumbled while they stood upright and waited for the train back down.

– Lean on me, Olav said in a commanding way. The order tempted her, it did.

Instead the cheerful/infamous fire, both irritating and pleasing to him lit up her eyes.

– I think… She revealed her fangs, – … considering the great way our dear guide has, well… guided us today he absolutely deserves a coach for himself.

– Are you serious? He asked while she dragged Anya with her into a coach and waved to him. – You are serious.

Judith sat down in the coach, one they had completely to themselves. Anya didn't say anything, until the train had put on speed.

– I must leave, she said quickly, nervously, with the same evasive eyes so unlike her. – I've already bought the ticket. I'm leaving tonight.

Judith had known the entire day that something was bothering her, but not the extent of it. Silverhair felt as if her heart was torn from her chest.

None of them spoke, in a time span they experienced like an eternity, but was just a few seconds. A relieved smile touched Judith's face.

– You just say this because you have slept with Olav, she said with a nervous shriek of laughter. Her friend's brows vibrated slightly, telling. – I thought so. But you're overreacting, my dear, to say the least. I know Olav does it with others. So do I. That doesn't matter, as long as we're together and love each other.

– It does concern Olav, Anya said in obvious pain, – But… you see… I don't like him.

– You can't mean that, Judith cried stunned. – Why in heaven's name not?

– I know you like him… a lot. The reply came in a painful whisper. – I did, too, at first, but now… I dislike him. I must go. Please understand.

– Don't go, Judith begged.

Her head hung, and eyes were lowered, directed at the floor.

– I must go. The train slowed its descent and stopped.

When Judith looked up Anya was gone. Olav stood in the doorway, looking inquisitive at her.

– She has left. It came out as a pitiful whisper, hardly audible. – She's gone.
– To hell with her, then, he said brutally. – We can go it alone.
– Yes, she cried out, running into his arms. – Yes!
They returned to the house. Just a few lived there now, except for them, and they wouldn't stay for much longer. Her eyes turned hard.
– Look at them, she snarled. – They've already returned to their eight to four jobs, to the former lives they've never truly given up. They aren't willing to do what it takes, to realize what has to be done, what the stakes are. Damn them!
She sought more of Olav's touch, the comfort of his strong arms.
A short note awaited her on her night shelf. She read it without delay.
«Remember that desire is hunger, and that hunger can devour. Forgive me».
Anya's writing was easily recognizable. Judith crushed the paper in her hand. She opened and closed the hand several times.
– May you be cursed, she hissed. – CURSED, DO YOU HEAR ME! TO THE BLACKEST HELL WITH YOU ALL. I CAN MANAGE ALONE.
– *Alone,* she whispered, falling on her knees.
When Olav came she held on to him when he carried her to bed, like a ship to an anchor. Far on its way to a bottomless, black hole.
The parents came and fetched Emmet one late evening.
– Since we can't get you to see reason we must use harsher measures, the mother said pointedly.
– We will never deny him, Judith said.
– That is no longer of any consequence what so ever, the father bristled. – We're taking him away from this city, far away from you. You will not have the chance to corrupt him anymore.
– You think you can achieve anything by imprisoning him, Olav said, with a look burning them. – You'll only make him hate you even more.
Emmet was dragged away, howling. They never saw him again.
Judith was arrested for public intoxication the night after that. She spent the night in a naked cell. The following week she was arrested for throwing a brick through the window of a fur shop. The fine was never paid.
Some moons passed, before they were evicted. The excuse this time was unpaid property tax. Money was a very good excuse in this world. They couldn't do anything this time either. Not a tiny shred of what was necessary. They never saw any of the money for the forced sale. She was told she didn't own the house, that it belonged to her parents and that it would take years to sort out the countless legal concerns.

– So helpless, so helpless, Silverhair mumbled, swollen around the eyes. – I'm getting tired of it, *tired* of it.

She and Olav moved into an old, tiny attic apartment in the Nordnes district. The four upper floors didn't have stairs, but just ladders. There were six floors.

There was cold and hot water… if one was lucky. Judith was actually shocked by the fact that people lived like this - and worse - in a so-called affluent society. She had heard rumors, but the difference between hearing and actually seeing was dramatic. Of course it was. It strengthened her in her resolve, for a while.

– How can people live like this, she cried, – like rats in a cage?

That remark cost her quite a bit initial goodwill with the other tenants, but she didn't care.

«It's so frustrating» she wrote to Willy. «Those around us see the revolutionary needed Change as nothing but a hobby, an intellectual exercise, something to do when they aren't doing what they see as important. But *forty thousand* children are starving to death every day in this fantasy world of theirs. And that's just the tip of the iceberg. The number of homeless is rising in all Scandinavian countries. Suffering is everywhere, also among the so-called successful. I wish… wish humanity in its ignorance had the blinds before their eyes torn off… torn off so hard that it *hurts*».

They adapted eventually, as much as they needed.

Every time they had to climb and descend the ladders brought new problems. To carry Lene up and down was in no way easy. They made a kind of harness for her, so they could carry her on the back or front, and discovered that that worked better than any accepted method anyway.

Both took casual work, did so as often as they could get any. The most underpaid shit available. The adaptation was in the practical area. They feared they would do anything in practical terms. So much that it would corrupt their emotions, their core, what they strived so hard to keep unchanged.

On rare occasions, when they both got work the neighbors, eventually warming up to them, took care of Lene. The tenants had a kind of community kindergarten on the second floor and it worked fairly well. Judith discovered there was room for some heart even in the worst of conditions, but mostly it was sad, sad as hell.

She fed Lene with what she knew was the special distant look in her eyes, her eyes staring through the plastic functioning as windows at the other derelict buildings. The house sharks had had profitable conditions before, too, but after the deregulation of the housing market they could truly thrive. Both in Bergen and Oslo they made a fortune and increased their power over the poor beggars screaming for a roof over their head. And she and Olav weren't really that much different from the rest of them, were they? The effort of procuring hard earned funds haunted their every aware moment. It was a constant struggle. They were both active in the underground markets in town and every single possible place they could earn a few bucks. But not all of it put together brought them sufficient nickels and dimes. Not when they were a family.

One autumn day Olav returned home earlier than what had been common the last few weeks. She heard him curse as he made his way up the ladders. He stopped just before he reached their floor.

– Close your eyes, she heard his cheerful voice. – I have a surprise.

– Oh, what kind? Her voice was hoarse, as it had been since the prolonged coughing that had bothered her the last month had started up.

– Don't be *silly,* he said exasperated. – If I told you it wouldn't be a surprise, would it.

She smiled and closed her eyes hard. She didn't want to cheat.

– I like your hair short, he said appreciative. She heard him crawl across the floor towards her, until she could sense his aura in front of her. – And even if everybody else returning from Tone's boudoir looks like scarecrows, you're always like an angel.

Tone lived below. She served the entire ruin in the matter of hair. Her minor effort contributed to the easing of the burden for everybody in the building. Everyone had their specialty.

Judith enjoyed the fact that she had gotten used to having short hair. It could have been worse. Her smile widened.

– It makes you look young and sweet, he said.

– You rascal, you will be sent to the retirement home far ahead of me.

She didn't feel young and sweet anymore.

– It's okay, you can open your eyes, now.

Her eyes slid open by themselves. A fat wad of bills revealed itself.

– Inspired by you I was fired from my job, he said quickly. – This heap is acquired from liqueur sale on the horserace track. You won't believe how many thirsty suckers there are out there. More than one wanted whole cases by the next track day. I refused, of course. But I turned a nice profit without the bigger risk.

– You seem to have some mysterious, inborn skill for this, she said lazily. – How come you can sell so much more than me?

– An Amazon like you? He grinned. – They expect you to charge them with a sword, not cases of booze. My own considerable bulk just makes the negotiations go smoother. The world is as it is, sweetie.

That night they went out and celebrated for the first time in a long time. When they danced his intense eyes warmed her once more. She had been waning indoors this autumn. Now, she was waxing anew, and he with her.

Perhaps they had celebrated more than over the top. They had been damn lucky to return to the closet in one piece. The closet, the sardine-box. Judith giggled. Tone had to carry Lene up for them. Or they would clearly have fallen.

She sat in the dark, rocking on her beloved. She didn't know whether or not it was a dream. Just that it was good, that it was wonderful…

She awoke early the next morning, with a sharp light in her face. Eyes were too dry for tears. Her entire body seemed dehydrated. And then there was the hammer thundering in her skull… She writhed in pain. How she managed to rise remained a mystery. She shivered in the cold, in the powerful draft from the plastic windows and quickly slipped a sweater over her head and pulled pants up her legs. Hands shook when she tapped a glass of water. Sometimes there was water, sometimes not. This time it flowed into the glass and she drank, feeling the cold against her lips, the fluid running down her throat. She slowly, painfully felt better.

Her eyes fell on Olav's wallet. It had slipped out of the pants and down on the chair. Later she wondered how everything would have turned out if it had fallen on the floor. Then she would never have been able to bend down and pick it up.

Hands shaking even more opened the wallet and counted the money. She never really knew what had caused her to twitch her nose and keep up the search. That was something she would have never done earlier, in her blind trust.

She stood there with a credit card in her hand. She didn't need to think about it. The fog lifted from her mind, a mind suddenly crystal clear.

She turned towards the man in the bed. He sat there, looking at her.

– This money comes from your father, she said tonelessly, – most of it anyway.

– He wants us to stay with him, he conveyed to her in a direct, convincing way. – I think it can be a good move for us. We can do it on our own terms, Judy.

– We can…? She took a pack of smoked ham from the fridge. She started eating and chewing meticulously.

– Come here, Judy…

– DON'T CALL ME, JUDY, she shouted and threw the wallet at him. It hit him hard in the head. He jumped up.

– What the HELL are we supposed to do, then? He shouted back. – I'm tired of going hungry day and night. I will never do it again.

Lene started screaming. Judith snarled at her.

– Shut the FUCK up!

Lene was so astonished that she stopped screaming, looking at her mother with curious eyes. Mother had never screamed at her before.

In the locker there was one bottle of Finlandia Vodka. She grabbed it, tore off the lid, and started drinking. They had no clean glasses anyway. Everything suddenly felt black as a coal cellar. She needed the encouragement. She did, damn it. It did no good. The depression merely intensified.

– I don't give a fuck, she sniveled. – Not a damn fuck.

The stupor returned, deep, all encompassing, pleasant. The fog spread and she welcomed it.

Room was fading before her eyes. The asshole was fading. It felt so lovely just to sit there, without thinking, without needing to think. She swallowed another major sip.

++++++++++++++++++++++

Bam, bam, bam. Bam, bam, bam. Rockety, rockety, rock. Bam, bam, bam. Bam, bam, bam.

The train puffed (there was no puffing) in pleasant speed through the eastern Norwegian forests, speeding up, keeping an even speed. Landscape slipped by, slipped away. The train passed Hønefoss without stopping. She didn't see the station sign, not even the station, she didn't even look out of the window. She just knew they had to have passed it somewhere. The eastern urban Norwegian landscape started appearing on the indistinct window painting. She sat in her chair with open eyes, with the back of her head touching the head support. Lene slept with the head against her shoulder. She held her hard. She, Judith Brevik. Olav had his arm around her, around them both. They crouched in the seats.

They would quite soon arrive at Oslo Central Station, where they would stop. Lene sniffed in her sleep. She was hungry. Judith coughed as silently as she could. She didn't feel the hunger anymore. She saw sparks every time she moved her eyes. She saw yellow leaves leave room for ever more major buildings. Everything was monotony. The Gray Fog grew like dead trees around them.

Where were the three witches stirring the pot? Judith Brevik wondered and it hurt, hurt her terribly.

She had always perceived a train coach as silent and always hated that. She wanted to tear the silence apart, but it was so hard. In this rain and this cold everything wasn't just gray, it was an endless, pale nothing. They sat there in frozen silence the last few stretches to the end station.

TEN YEARS LATER - GOTHENBURG

CHAPTER ELEVEN

Judith Breen had seen many photographs and films of the enormous traffic complex between Oakland and San Francisco in the state of California, United States, by far the world's busiest and most crowded. Lanes intersected in something resembling an infinite tailspin. During the most recent earthquake there in 1989 the majority of the deceased were on the roads, killed when the freeway overpasses and stacked lanes fell on the road below, filled with cars. The entire system was long since overtaxed and had quite simply collapsed years ago, and now the authorities had, at least seemingly, finally realized that there was no use building more roads, overpasses and stacked lanes. It was no longer possible to build much more of anything resembling roads. They had started the work of constructing a local railway network. And it turned out to be a success. By keeping the prices low they earned more than by keeping them high. The old law about supply and demand was actually working for once, at least in this new and improved version.

The roads leading to Gothenburg looked similar to those between Oakland and San Francisco. They were in no way that extensive, of course, but there were major similarities. If one was lost, strayed from a given direction, one ran the risk of truly becoming lost. Judith had learned to navigate here, in and around the city, after much aggravation.

In the early sixties the authorities had made some seemingly very sensible choices. They had constructed a road system at least twenty years ahead of its time. While people in other Scandinavian cities were stuck in traffic jams and endless lines people in and around Gothenburg had a rather pleasant time driving. Now time had long since caught up with them. They hadn't realized what dawned on ever more people: that no matter how big the roads, there would always be enough cars to fill them.

Judith had learned to drive during the years she had lived on the Brevik estate, in the hope of having more room for herself. It hadn't worked. But now she didn't regret it. She had never bothered to get a license. She had always disliked formalities. A conviction that had merely increased in strength as the years had raged on.

She drove within the city now, its central parts, through the park, towards Gøtakanalen, the Gøta Canal. Clouds covered the sky and the Sun had vanished. The light in the air turned even grayer. The streetlights started dominating the gray city landscape. People had left their jobs a few hours ago by now, and breathed the poisonous air with the tiny energy their short-lived freedom gave them. They managed little else before going to bed, fearing the tomorrow that might never come.

In the intersection leading to the Nordstan shopping mall she had to stop for the red light. Two uniformed cops crossed the street in front of her. She studied almost subconsciously herself in the mirror, satisfied with the dark hair and the stranger's face. The face in the mirror didn't bear the slightest similarity to that of Judith Breen, and she relaxed. But she kept her eyes on the policemen. Instinct and experience told her that they were up to something. They had hardly crossed the street when they grabbed what was clearly a young minority adult accidentally crossing their path. The man, probably of Pakistani origin was asked, asked very nicely, she gathered, about his ID. Judith sighed. The more things changed the more they stayed the same. She was unable to do anything about it, *now*.

Fortunately for the dark skinned guy he carried his papers on his body. An increasing number of people were smart enough to do that, as incidents like this became ever more normal in the streets. Silverhair was professional enough to not be carried away by such incidents. Perhaps she should have been, perhaps she should have jumped out of the car and shot the two pigs…

Lights changed to green. The two pushed the man away in contempt, a push so hard that only skill or experience kept him from falling. Long time experience probably. She turned and drove along the canal's left side, passing Palladium Cinema Theater. On her right, somewhere between her and the canal was Nordstan, an enormous shopping mall. While driving she took in her surroundings, observed and digested impressions. That hadn't changed. She discovered nothing making the alarm go off. The waterway, the canal wasn't visible to her while she headed for the harbor, but she knew it widened, until large ships could sail on it. She knew this city fairly well, now. They had had Gothenburg as their base of operations for some time. She was unable to recall exactly how long. The past turned more and more indistinct to her as time raged by.

To be on the safe side she drove a few extra circles around the blocks, and used the mirrors quite eagerly for a while. Sivert sat in a staircase, looking totally indifferent, masked to the point of being unrecognizable to most people. She wouldn't have any problems recognizing him anyway, but he was there and dressed the way he was supposed to. Everything was all right. She turned into an abandoned storage area. There were no streetlights, not as far as she could see. A while ahead there was a dark, derelict building. The door to the garage was, simply put, gone. Potential investors had long since stopped being interested in this place and it had fallen into a prolonged state of disrepair.

There were no lights inside. Moonlight would have lit up the place, but there wasn't any. Good. A part of the wall, seemingly inseparable from the rest, slid aside. She drove into the hole, the hole in the wall, turned off the lights, and the engine, and sat there, suddenly in stark darkness. The wall slid back, closing her off from the world outside. Then, finally lights were lit, only a narrow line under a door, but there. The door opened, and she was flooded in light. Judith left the car. Anya stood behind her in the darkness. She had been completely invisible. Kimberly rushed into Judith's arms from the room inside, greeting her with a kiss on the lips. Everybody present met her with a kiss, and she returned it, bittersweet like a rose… and a thorn.

She felt, as always it was funny to see Kimberly with black hair. Kimberly stood out less from the crowd by pretending to be fully Asian. Far less people looked at her while she walked down the street.

Judith looked around her with ambiguous feelings. The room was fairly big. It had no windows and candles lit the shadows. She looked at the three and they returned her look, smiling and expectant. The group would be five when Sivert returned. They had with them a new recruit, Corbin McLeod. One of the five they had added the last few months. The complete group consisted of twenty, now, spread around in the four hideouts across town. In addition to Corbin there were Elan Russel, Heike Messner, Helene Valin and Jan Walter.

– You arrived just in time to catch the news, Kimberly said.

Something in her voice, a hardly detectable excitement told Judith that something significant had happened.

They used a small, portable TV, and a pocket radio. Judith sat down in a chair fairly close to the monitor. It wasn't turned on yet. She produced a pocket mirror with support and put it on the table in front of her, making sure she could see her face, her borrowed face. Hands sought under the jaw until she found the edge, an edge virtually impossible to discover by sight alone. She grabbed hold and pulled the mask up and off. Hair remained black, but except for remains of the mask and make up it was her own face that appeared in the mirror. She saw her own face.

– What a great natural mask, she marveled. – Too bad it can only be used once.

– Or twice, in a pinch, Kimberly added helpfully.

Judith started cleaning her face, while *Rapport* (Report), the Swedish half past seven news was broadcast.

– … tonight's headlines: A new Storm, a hurricane ravaged north western Germany today. In Great Britain several lower level villages on the west coast have been flooded by a spring tide, larger than ever before measured… And outside Lyon in France, less than an hour ago the almost completed Phoenix-reactor exploded. Pieces of it have been found miles away. Officials have now confirmed that it was indeed sabotage. The terrorist organization The Green Rose has accepted responsibility for the explosion, which has already created a strongly negative response. Our associates are on their way to the scene. In the mean time we're sending other news and news related to… to the incident. Again: The hurricane Hilbert rages on…

They saw flooded streets, destroyed buildings, a large passenger jet blown off the runway.

After fairly short intermissions the stage returned to what was now a useless ruin, an even more so than it had been.

– The first cargo from Dounray to Lyon should have commenced three short months from now. Peaceful environmental groups and small numbers or the general population have fought against both the Scot reprocessing plant and the now… ruined nuclear power plant for years, in vain. There's unrest in several European cities. Former British Prime Minister Margaret Thatcher states, in a comment, that she's «deeply shocked», both over the widespread presence of the «criminal element», and «citizens' irresponsibility». Instead of celebrating a petty crime, she persists, people should support and respect «democratic institutions and decisions». If not, the street mob would rule in a very short time…

And on the radio they heard pirate broadcasts:

– Spontaneous celebrations have appeared all over Europe. Strangely positive remarks are countering the total official condemnation. And official media is slipping, quoting Maggie about «citizens' irresponsibility», but not saying anything about what form it takes. Old Maggie is going ballistic. This in spite of, as rumors will have it that she can't find her way to the toilet on her own these days…

– HURRAY for Steve and his noble human beings, Kimberly cried. – Give me FIVE!

She and Anya struck each other's hands in a fluid, united effort. Everybody joined in.

They smiled joyfully and embraced for a while, because of what had succeeded so well. That didn't happen often, but on the contrary, quite rarely, in their experience. Even their victories usually turned to defeat… to ashes. Thus was reality, in today's hollow society.

Judith stopped smiling first. The others joined her when they saw her do it.

– Let us take this as a sign, she said. – It's about time we end our little break. The blade is dulled when not used. *We* are dulled and we can't afford to be.

– Stockholm - what happened there - wasn't your fault, Corbin stated, after a prolonged silence, looking at them all. – No one could have predicted what happened. You're not to blame.

– Always expect the unexpected, Judith emphasized, staring at the wall, her head bowed.

She walked alone, into the cool darkness. The river, the dark water slipped silently by. Distant lights were faintly mirrored and spreading in its streams. She stood at the edge of the quay, listening, probing for the heartbeats of the gods.

She heard Sivert approach, heard his distinct steps.

– The night is beautiful, isn't it? She said, with longing in her voice.

– Yes, he replied, clearly surprised. Had he finally reached her?

– Too bad the horrors are obvious in the light of day, she said curtly.

He stopped behind her. Raised hands fell down.

– We're dust drifting through the Universe, they heard Anya. They turned abruptly. The voice grew out of the darkness. – Earth's consciousness. When it suffers, we suffer. When we and other animals suffer in captivity, it suffers. We're all raised and killed in captivity, until we *make it stop*. We must do so!

– We can hope, Sivert said.

– Yes, hope, Judith breathed. – Never stop hoping.

++

All twenty gathered in a remote house by the airport. They had quite simply moved in there not long ago, used it for what it was worth. The owner was abroad and would stay there for weeks. And even better: He was an Enemy, high in the hierarchy of the European Atomic Energy Commission. This place was among a considerable number of houses where he brought his non-marital relations. Elan had told them this. He knew about it because he had often brought his father's slaves here. He had reluctantly obeyed Victor Russel's orders, until they had stuck like a ball in his throat. Victor had an iron justice in this matter, as he had in all. But Elan had followed Kimberly's star and liberated himself.

Elan had a lot to add, to what Kimberly previously had recounted. Even for the members of The Green Rose it was like penetrating a world they had major difficulties imagining. It dawned on them that they were largely innocents, after all.

The lights had a special glow, like when every time the owner had his special parties there. The glow, the dirty glow could be seen from far away. Judith experienced a kind of unreality when stepping over the huge and «tasteful» living room threshold. No expenses had been spared. The best materials, the most exclusive designs had been used. The cost of every single piece of furniture in the house could feed an ordinary family indefinitely. Judith suddenly felt an overwhelming nausea.

– This is a good place to meet, she said aloud.

Those who heard her weren't confused. They knew what she meant.

After a while they had completed the exploring, filled with both contempt and youthful curiosity. There was, after all a well of varied emotions stored here, a few good as well as the many bad. Perhaps that was the main reason they had picked it.

– Okay, children. Judith clapped her hands. – Let's get on with it.

All sensed eagerness deep within. It felt good this, throwing away the last vestiges of fear of authorities. And they did, now, undeniably. They didn't *fear* the police and similar any longer. The false respect and obedience beaten into them since birth, was long gone. They knew, beyond doubt, they were exploding. And this line of thought created immeasurable joy in them.

– We're gathered once more. Silverhair started up with her usual penetrating eyes, eyes seemingly resting on each and every one of them. – It's *time,* time to shake the boat on the endless stormy sea.

Cries of agreement and eagerness.

– Well, this will be *some* shake up. As you know I, Gio and Kathy, with Helene have done certain field studies lately, in and around Barsebäck…

There was no need for her to look at Gio or say his name.

– As you know the plant is situated just north of Malmö. He got on with it without introduction. – Some progressive liberals and those with correct political attitudes will definitely disagree with this claim. Fortunately there are none in this assembly…

They stared stunned at him. He had learned to joke. Laughter filled the room. To be able to laugh felt so good, also being able to laugh at oneself. There had been too little laughter in their lives lately.

– It's straight across the sound from Copenhagen. During just one minor spill, under the *right* conditions the entire city of Copenhagen will be transformed into a ghost town. Of this there's no doubt. In addition to the long-term damages across the globe this power plant can kill a million people, and during a few afternoon hours doom others to a long and painful death.

– We took a look around and feel we have put together a useful course of action on how to deal with this. If all goes well the plant will be out for months and hopefully longer, and we will have directed a powerful symbolic blow against the entire industry.

The table stretched wide and far. They had gathered around it in the safe assumption it had been used extensively for *conferences*. They focused on the photos in front of them and the subsequent extensive explanations, knowing their astuteness in this and other matters could mean the difference between life and death.

Stockholm… The city's name kept returning to Judith's immediate consciousness and rocked it, rocked her. She touched her head. It hurt. The memories hurt. Mostly those from a while back, though. It was strange, wasn't it? One fought one's entire life to liberate oneself from the past. And bad turned worse. It was no use. One couldn't count the bridges crossing the raging river.

She had chosen this, chosen to dance to a different drum, knowing fully well its final, ultimate implications. They all had. On some occasions coincidence and fate had intervened. Often the path wasn't clear to a human being. But the final, decisive choice they had made themselves.

Stockholm. It happened during a bank robbery they had planned and prepared meticulously. The bank had, unknown to them changed the schedules slightly, not instantly noticeable the day before the robbery. The van with the armed guards coming for the money had arrived too early. In a critical moment, an unwatched clerk behind the counter activated the alarm. They had to fire shots on their way out. No one was killed, but one of the guards, and Karine and Renni had been hit. They got away with the money, but it had nearly cost them dearly.

A while after that it had turned hot for them. The reward offered for their capture had increased quite substantially. Ever more of them were identified and got their cute mugs placed on the world's walls, electronic and actual.

– It doesn't do me justice, Kimberly had stated once, after tearing one sheet down.

There were dozens of them, all over the board on the wall.

Images and faces turned indistinct to Judith. There were so many, impressions from many lives, and she had them all burned into her memory. Sometimes it was too much.

– It's impossible to bring heavy weaponry inside. She breathed hard. – But that will hardly matter. There's more than enough to go around inside. We will kill many flies with one stone. In addition to the other advantages we will be securing new, top modern weapons - for free.

– I've said it before, Sivert commented, shaking his head, – you're one hell of a sly she-devil.

She kissed him. He always made her laugh.

– So why don't we burn this place to the ground? Jan asked when they were ready to depart, expressing the desire burning in them all.

– It is so *small,* Anya replied calmly. – And then we won't be able to use it anymore. There is just no sensible purpose in tearing down this modest house. The building we want to leave in ruins is so much larger. Its feet are clay, but it is so big and extensive that it seems invulnerable.

They ended up leaving it as they had found it, without any physical proof of their visit, at least not any revealing itself without a thorough forensic check.

– I see the giant house in twilight fall like a rotten tree, Anya mused. – The question is in which direction, and how many it will crush when it hits the ground.

The others nodded in acknowledgment. Who could say for certain? One could only hope and do one's worst.

CHAPTER TWELVE

Ulf Erlander was abruptly and brutally roused from his slumber, and discovered that he couldn't move. The second after that he discovered that he had no desire to do so, anyway. He was kept in bed by many hands and a knife pressed at his throat. The blade flashed in the narrow line of light from the hall. He glimpsed the faces closest to him in the dark.

– Your wife and children are sleeping heavily in their beds. An ice-cold female voice cut through him. – All the servants as well. Sleeping like the dead. No one will wake up for quite a while. We will still prefer you don't scream for help, thereby establishing your desire for cooperation at an early stage.

The hand holding his hair and all hands holding his body down let go. All lamps in the room were lit simultaneously. Lights weren't bright, but the transition from stark darkness was so abrupt that he had to cover his eyes.

– Who the hell are you? He asked hoarsely. – I demand…

– We're the Green Rose, Ulf. I'm positive you've heard about us.

He was about to give a snarling reply, but wondered. Didn't he know… that voice?

She placed herself directly in his line of sight and he couldn't avoid recognizing her.

– Helene, he gasped.

– The Rose recruited me before I started working for you, the woman said hotly. – I've waited a long time for this.

– To answer your next question, I can indeed confirm that we want to get inside your little pride and joy, Morten said formally. – Today Helene was, prompted by you supposed to bring a gang of potential hustlers inside and given them the scenic tour. That will be us instead, and you will be by our side all the time.

He studied them all. They had dressed up and looked very much like young up and coming law and business students.

The suspiciously tall china girl handed him photographs, one by one. There was no need for him to look at any of them to realize the obvious. He threw them away, not bothering to hide his irritation.

– Okay, you've got me by the balls. A shrug. – How do I know you won't kill me afterwards, or quite simply blow up both me and yourselves?

– You don't, the Ice Princess told him - he recognized her, but only on a purely physical, exterior level. She played with the knife. – You don't believe your own propaganda, though. You know we haven't killed anybody - yet. If it is up to us we go there, we turn the entire plant useless for five thousand years and leave the place without even fucking up anybody's hairdo. If you don't cooperate we will kill you now. We can achieve a lot with that, too. But clearly not as much as we would want. Alive you've got a chance. That is logical, is it not?

– One thing… Kimberly Russel stood relaxed in front of him, displaying herself. Judith Breen had pulled back a little. – We know we can't get guns inside. We don't need any to put an end to you.

The black hair and the golden skin turned indistinct in one single flowing movement. The hand moved forward, quick as lightning, hit the wall and left a major hole in it.

– I've seen better, Erlander said harshly, – but I gather it will do. May I be allowed to dress before we leave?

His ice-cold indifference touched them not. They merely returned it shrapnel by shrapnel.

The air outside felt clear and crisp, even though it wasn't. The bus engine started up on the road ahead. With the exception of the driver, Yvonne, it was empty. They had planned being early. The students waiting at the school wouldn't grow impatient until The Green Rose was «safely» within the power plant's gates. They had planned well, reduced the possible, always possible, unpredictable to a minimum.

– Hello, Ulf! Yvonne greeted cheerfully. – The way you keep it up it isn't so strange that you and the wife have separate bedrooms. You have nothing left to give her.

The last sentence was delivered with a considerable amount of venom.

– Leave him alone, Karine said good-natured. – He will have a lot to worry about for the next months and years.

The coach was a luxury model, as was fitting for the people usually using it. Like today. Helene had picked the right students, those with the right opinions, as Erlander had instructed her to do. She grinned. She felt she had gone above and beyond the call of duty.

– You've planned this for a long time, haven't you? He scowled bitterly at her. – They must have brainwashed you. You were such a star pupil. I handpicked you myself, introduced you into the right circles…

– From the very beginning, she replied proudly, bitterly. – What you recognized as fanatical ambitions in me wasn't quite the «qualities» you were searching for. I sought them out, offered my services. I waited for years for a chance to start the fight against you and everything you represent. I suffered through school, through everything… to get as high as possible in the hierarchy, high enough to really hurt you all.

They placed him in the middle section of the bus and surrounded him on all fronts. Yvonne put the vehicle expertly in motion. They were on their way.

– And she succeeded brilliantly, don't you think? Silverhair had her eyes locked on him. He imagined he almost sensed the silver hair, even though it had been dyed black, sensed it like an aura surrounding her head. She was a completely different person, now; compared to the cowed princess he had met in Oslo many years ago. – Think of the dedication, the fanaticism needed to live with such a pretense, year out and year in. To this point she has been a symbol, hasn't she? Of the best the technological democracy, the technocracy can produce? I'm so pleased to state that she will indeed create confusion with this. What do you think the idol-seeking established media will write now? When she turns her back on the growth bubble wonder, exposing it for what it truly is?

– Sniveling brats, he tried, threw at them in contempt. – You're hopelessly naïve, and we will break you, like we've done with your kind so many times before. You're weak and won't offer much resistance.

– Perhaps we should kill him afterwards, Jemma said. – He's dangerous.

– No! Judith waved her hand decisively. – We can never procure enough bullets to kill people like him. Our job is to wake people up, so they'll understand what's going on.

– People don't want to be awake, Erlander cried out contemptuously. – Don't you think they know, know what's going on? But they wish to be sheltered, be told what to do. They're like sheep needing guidance, always with their watery eyes locked on the current Shepherd.

– He's right! Sivert said.

– That just makes our task even more important, Silverhair stated firmly. – We will wake up everybody. We will do it so *thoroughly* they will never fall asleep again. They won't even be tempted.

She hoped they didn't see her doubt, what wasn't noticeable in her voice. «Never» and «always» were huge words, really too huge to use. They were another modern contradiction in terms. Nothing lasted forever.

– We have the power, she stated. – Everybody does, if they so choose.

The road's artificial lights slipped slowly into morning and day, a day darkened by a prevailing haze. The twenty rebels and outsiders attempted to relax and not care that the road crawled with cars in both directions. No one saw through the tinted windows. The elite traveled in the comfort and obscurity they chose. Traffic moved slowly, but they had started early, very early. No unforeseen difficulties had turned up yet.

Heike and Dorte sat in front of the bus, keeping Yvonne company. The three women kept silent, kept their thoughts private for a long time before speaking.

– Are you nervous? Dorte touched Heike under the jaw.

– I guess, Heike laughed a bit. – Everything is worse the first time, right?

– We're all attempting to shape up more than a bit today. Dorte smiled. – There's always the danger that prolonged periods of inactivity make us rusty.

Yvonne looked at her. Dorte had undoubtedly changed most of them all since the early days in Copenhagen. There was very little left of the shy, unsophisticated girl from way back then.

– It's dulling our senses, inevitably, Yvonne said, quickly directing her attention back to the road ahead. – We can't let that happen anymore. If we stay away from the fire and the heat too long, we lose the edge we need to survive.

They imagined the characteristic buildings long before they actually saw them. They sensed the smoke flowing into the air. The death and nothing created by concrete, glass and metal. They caught the first actual glimpses of it and turned even more pissed. Several layers of tall, barbed wired fences surrounded the property, a ghost in a bottle wanting to lock all irritating demons out.

Eyes sought Copenhagen, the big city on the other side of the salty water, so close that they felt they could touch all the ugly buildings.

They shrugged. Copenhagen was behind them. It no longer mattered.

Everything seemed to move in slow motion to the gate. Four guards there. Six more spread across the property. Two in the control room. Everything was registered from there, with eyes and on film. They were not usually armed. The weapons, hyper modern automatic and semi automatic military ordinance were locked away in a large storage room. The Chief of security had one of the keys, Helene the other. They trusted her unconditionally. This was the woman who had been praised as the «young executive of the year» in Sweden the year before. Judith had doubts about her, but she kept it to herself. Helene was a self-taught phenomenal actor. One couldn't help but doubt her a little.

– I'm looking forward to seeing all the good stuff, Kurt said, unable to hide his expectations.

He was more than a little eager where weapons were concerned. He had always been.

It was hard to believe sometimes, that he had never even fired a gun before walking inside the Green Rose that time in Liberty City. Judith had to smile.

– You won’t be disappointed, Helene assured him, and had to smile, too.
Sweat started to turn the armpits into moist, stinky caves (damn those ineffective antiperspirants…). Something they could do little about. Fortunately it was hot as hell today. No one would be suspicious if they smelled a little sweat.
Yvonne halted the bus softly just the right distance from the gate. It slid open, slowly, so slowly. Two guards appeared from the booth. One remained there. Yvonne glimpsed guns under the coat. One stopped in front of the door, the other on her side.
– Isn’t it a great day? Yvonne spoke the local dialect well and smiled generously out of the open window.
Kimberly had taught her the language. The deceit she had learned on her own.
– Hello, the man greeted them sourly. – We would like to take a look inside. Do you mind?
– Not at all, she chirped lightly. – Uniforms always make an impression on me.
She hated them, but he would discover that soon enough.
She opened the door. The other guard, a woman entered. She had the smile in place above the uniform, but her eyes were cold when she surveyed the insides of the bus. She nodded to Erlander and Helene before turning back to Yvonne.
– Drive to the closest parking lot and stop. She pointed.
Yvonne did as she was told, drove through the gate and parked straight inside, calm and pleasant. This was common procedure, what they had all drilled into their mind and instincts the last few days.
Everybody departed the bus, stretched their limbs, and looked around. Only Erlander looked bad-tempered, but then again, according to Helene he always did.
– There will be people taking us inside soon, she told the hopeful future movers and shakers. – In the meantime it is unfortunately necessary for the guards to search you all and the bus. One can never be too cautious in this day and age.
– You’re right, one of the guards grinned, – but personally I don’t see the point. Even an army of foot soldiers couldn’t avoid major losses by attacking this place.
Everybody was thoroughly searched, except Erlander and Helene. Once again, nervous and cranky, for the millionth time Judith measured the distance to the main building. It would be near impossible to reach it during a crisis.

While they were searched two always kept close to Erlander. He was dangerous, they knew that, cold and resourceful as he was. It seemed like they had judged him correctly, though. He realized that they meant what they had said and he put his own life higher than the plant's «well-being». Besides, his sly, almost invisible smile told them that he didn't truly believe they could cause any major damage. Just like they had counted on. Not without melting the core, and that he was convinced they wouldn't do.

Nerve-cracking minutes passed while they awaited approval. They were *thoroughly* searched. They feared they would be told to open their mouth widely or spread their legs. Everything was taken out of their bags and put nicely back in place. Helene looked at her watch and then apprehensive at Judith. Silverhair just smiled. Her outward composure calmed them all.

Finally the guard signaled their approval to those studying it all behind the dark windows. In less than a minute two more unyielding and grim people showed themselves and met the guests halfway.

– Guys and gals, Helene said. – Let me introduce you to Lee Travis, the chief of security on these premises.

They knew him already. She had already introduced him, through images, clippings and highly disturbing personal accounts.

– So these are my future bosses, he puffed, with the cigar in his mouth. – Pathetic!

They laughed, a bit uncertain, quite in tune with the role they had chosen.

The first hall inside met them with its cold and might. They froze inevitably in their tracks, forcing their feet to keep moving.

Mortar had loosened from the wall, and a thin film of it covered the floor. Travis frowned a moment when Helene sent him a displeased look. He hid the abrupt and violent anger under the fake smile. Helene approached him discreetly the way a young, smart executive would do.

The two of them speeded up, so they walked a considerable distance ahead of the others.

– What is this? She asked the question in a pleasant but clearly venomous manner. – I did instruct a cleaning, didn't I, well in advance of our arrival?

– I have no explanation… yet, he replied curtly, clearly embarrassed. – The cleaners have arrived. I'll look into it. It won't happen again.

– Good, she nodded. – That was what I wanted to hear.

They exchanged mutual nods before parting, two people seemingly understanding each other perfectly.

Helene shook imperceptibly when leading the «yuppies» into the adjacent hall. Everything was cold in here. She had played her role to perfection for so many years, now, and she had started to wonder if this was how she truly was. Today it was done, one way or the other. She had felt so alone, so long that the upcoming joy was stuck in her throat. It was just as well. The trick was to remain cold. She longed to cry, though, and feared there would be many opportunities for that later on.

She knew too many who wanted to do good, but whose existence turned into a matter of survival, and nothing more.

Yvonne separated from the group, and joined the guards, in the cafeteria. Helene noted the small, encouraging sign from her. She brought it with her, as a source of both irritation and encouragement.

– Know that you're welcome, she told her friends and fellow warriors, – to the belly of the beast.

The control section was split into two rooms, one for controlling the plant itself, the other for surveillance. They surveyed all of it from behind the thick reinforced glass in the visitors' room.

The businesswoman Helene Valin spoke to eager and attentive listeners.

– ... and as you know we're inside one of the world's most secure and modern nuclear power plants, one of the world's best and secure suppliers of electricity. We, the company are pleased. The consumers are pleased. We're looking forward to getting our license renewed in 2010. The majority of the Swedish people is in favor of that...

True, she thought frosty.

– The possibilities are endless, as the world is eventually opening their eyes to the promise of nuclear energy. I'm sure you agree...

She smiled professionally.

– Questions?

Sivert raised his hand in a well-mannered manner, a critical look. She acknowledged him with a critical nod.

– What about the abnormally high concentrations of cancer cases in the surrounding area? I've heard...

– Researchers not tied to any radical environmental organizations have done research here since opening day, without finding dangerous levels of radioactivity. We take our task as public servants seriously and have an entire team on hand to follow up on leaks and accidents if they should occur. Next, please.

– What about the statistics showing an increase in cancer cases of several hundred times the previous levels the world over since the first atomic bomb explosion in 1945 and the start of the gross chemical industry in the early sixties, an industry you also have vested interests in?

Karine just started talking and she didn't raise her hand. She played the vamp and the without-bite-liberal today.

– I believe we're all critical towards such uncritical, unscientific methods, Miss Larsen. In my opinion there's little data supporting such and similar claims. The industry, generally speaking does what it can to avoid unnecessary pollution. We aren't really the Big Bad Wolf we're made out to be. Now, everything will soon be ready in the kitchen, if you'll all follow me…

– What about your arsenal? Kurt raised his hand in an eager and boyish manner. – We've heard so much about it, so I was thinking…

– I don't know… Helene looked at Travis, clearly concerned.

Judith started sweating heavily, abruptly and painfully. She knew that she and almost all the others could pull the guns hidden in rectum out very fast. Pull down the pants, fall sideways, push the hand inside and pull it out. They had practiced it until they got both sore and slightly worried. She just didn't know if it would be fast enough.

Travis had stood there, quiet all the time. Now, he was actually visibly smiling, a strange and disturbing sight.

– I believe it can be arranged, he drawled. – Boys will be boys, eh?

The door was close, only ten steps down the hall. He and Helene walked there, trailed by the eager and nervous guests. The two of them stuck their keys into the locks, and turned them simultaneously. There was a distinct click. The heavy door swung open by itself, very slow, very fast.

Kurt entered the weapon storage room with a special look in his eyes.

– As you know all the weapons are ready and loaded, Travis stated, in a fairly excited, but cold way. He was deadly. Helene knew that. The rest of her fellow warriors knew it, too, intellectually, but also on a deeper level. They had learned to trust their instincts. – No rebel scumbags have a chance in hell here.

– With due respect, Lee, Helene, now completely soaked under the arms said with a modulated voice. – I don't believe everybody here is that interested in this male testosterone thing. I will bring a couple of our dear visitors and start preparing the lecture in Surveillance.

He shrugged. Helene left the room with Willy and Anya. They walked fast, but not too fast, filled with purpose through the corridors, between the walls closing in on them.

Kurt rushed from shelf to shelf in something akin to true excitement.

– Jeez, he exclaimed, to amused laughter, both from brothers and sisters - and Travis. – An M-16A2 with an M-305 grenade launcher. Do you know that this shit can be used to fire virtually anything? It's made for buckshots, smoke, high explosives, ordinary automatic rounds, and absolutely… Jeez, there are more of them here.

– This is among the best stuff available, Travis said smugly. – And everything is ready for use on a moment's notice. If a busload of terrorists crashed through the main gate right now, they would hardly have reached the building before being eradicated from the face of the Earth.

– There's more, Kurt mumbled. – An M-60E2, a light machinegun. Heckler & Koch MP5, Heckler & Koch G-3 - a NATO sharpshooter weapon, Smith & Wesson 45 automatic… Desert Eagle 357 automatic…

Helene and the two following her stood in front of the camera in the fortified entrance to the control section. Helene hit the number code on the panel, and placed the right hand on the glass plate. It glowed while the computer read her print. The glow faded as a mechanical voice was heard:

– Valin, Helene. Security code 058348. Identity confirmed. Welcome.

The wall slid aside, and they had access to the entire control section. Helene felt expectation flow through her, and like she stepped over the red line for the first time.

The wall slid back in place. There were now, all in all ten individuals in the room.

– Little Helene is late today, one of the guards sang. He sat in a chair, in front of a video monitor with a set of headphones on his head.

– Do you have anything for me, Tomas? She asked sourly.

– Yeah, actually there is a phone call for you right now… He frowned. – We were just about to give you a call over the intercom. You seem to have lost some of the students. I don't know…

– That can't be right, she said irritated. – We can't be responsible for those not showing up in time.

She picked up the phone.

– *Where are you?* She heard an agitated voice. – *We've been waiting for over an hour. I talked to one of your subordinates, but he didn't really know anything...*

– We've had a minor accident, she replied amiably. – We will come as soon as the bus is functional. The program will be delayed, of course, but I assure you it won't be shortened. You won't suffer for our mistakes. Now, if you will excuse me…

– Eh, certainly…

Helene put the phone down. Out of the corner of her eye she saw the confusion increase in Tomas, and the first glimpse of fear in his eyes. She pushed her hand inside her specially made jacket and pulled out the Luger. She pointed the gun at him.

– Don't move, Tomas! NOBODY MOVES! I'll shoot if I have to.

Tomas stared at the alarm button on the consol five steps away, but he didn't move a hair. One in the other room took one step forward. There was a crack, and the bullet struck the floor right in front of his toes. He froze on the spot.

– Everybody in here, quickly, Anya commanded. They obeyed, sending her frightened looks. – That's good. Lie down on your belly.

– Cuffs? Willy snarled.

– In the l-locker. One guy pointed carefully, very carefully.

– Good, Anya praised him, patting Helene on the shoulder.

Helene shook lightly, before recovering, the stench of the fired bullet sticking in her nose.

Yvonne drank scolding hot coffee, cooling her overheated system.

– Now, how does it feel to be the whipping girl of a bunch of young bozos? One of four guards present in the cafeteria asked her in a patronizing voice that would have irritated a real bus driver to no end.

– It has its advantages, she shrugged.

Kimberly was striving a bit with the «cocking» of the M-60E2.

– Hi, little one, Travis said brusquely. – Let me help.

She cocked it quickly, while giving him her most exquisite smile.

Judith kept her eyes on the surveillance camera. They had no chance of knowing what happened in there. A shot wouldn't be heard through the insulation. She considered signing Sivert to go to the window to check, but didn't have to. The red light above the camera went out as they watched. There were three red blinks, and she knew the road was clear.

– *Freeze!* She and Gio covered Travis and the other guard with their Desert Eagle.

Travis had already jumped. Silverhair shot him in the thigh. Blood splashed weapons and those standing closest to him. He clenched his teeth in pain when he landed, but not after that. He didn't move.

– You're Breen! He snarled. Now many weapons covered him. – I knew I had heard your voice before. Fuck it!

His raven eyes sought Ulf Erlander.

– So they made you pee your pants.

– Valin has been one of them for years. The hatred in Erlander's eyes was, if possible even stronger now, two hardly visible chinks. – You certainly don't have any reason to brag. You've let yourself be fooled by a gang of amateurs.

– Amateurs… no longer, Travis gasped. – They learn day by day. They must be taken care of, before becoming truly *dangerous*. Satan's spawn!

Sivert had walked to the reinforced window. Blood covered his face. He saw it flow down his cheek in the mirror image in the glass. Hands, his own hands brushed his face. It was no use. No matter how much he brushed the skin he couldn't keep the blood out of his mouth. He hurried back, returned to his brothers and sisters in arms.

– They have full control in there, he reported. – They are standing. Everybody else is on the floor, hands cuffed.

Judith touched his cheek a bit, before turning to give orders.

– Gio, Kimberly, Kees, Renni, Dorte and Kathy, you do the sweep and roundup. The weapons room will be empty and we will use that as our prison, as our poetic justice. Put all the guards and unnecessary personnel here, except Travis. I want him where we can keep an eye on him. We will reassemble in the control room.

They set off. Those remaining started to carry off the weapons, weapons they would confiscate and bring with them, away from this place. Free weapons. A win, win situation for sure…

– This is all military equipment, Kurt said. – We could have asked ourselves where they got them from… if we were very, very stupid.

Renni and Dorte strolled into the cafeteria, weapons in hand.

– Nobody moves, Renni ordered, very authoritative.

When one of the guards did just that Yvonne struck him down in two rapid and easy moves.

– Any problems? Dorte inquired.

– None I couldn't handle. Yvonne eloquently caught the gun the other woman threw to her.

Half an hour passed, until everything was ready. The six sweepers and Yvonne reported back to Silverhair. The computers whirred and hummed around them all.

– Premises secured, Gio greeted her wild and triumphant. – We're masters over all we survey.

Silverhair nodded to the silent ovation she received from her friends.

– We've taken over here, she told the still gawking technicians. – This place now belongs to the Green Rose.

Lee Travis sat on a stool, pale and drawn. A tight bandage had been tied around his thigh. The white cloth had turned red.

– We should kill him, Helene stated. – If we don't, he will come after us. I know him.

– Perhaps we should, Judith replied. – But, no, let's wait until the next time. Give him *one* more chance to think it through.

And that way they would keep Death's cold hand off a bit longer, one more second in the endless day.

– As I have emphasized… Helene had placed herself by the controls. They were ready to go. – The process towards full stop will need to be slow and steady. Each of the squares on the wall represents various functions and operations. That they are blinking white only means they're operational. If they should happen to blink red… you get it. That's why we have the manager and the technicians with us. There have been a number of red blinks during my time here. The crew and the security measures have usually managed to deal with it so far. They've had to release the occasional cloud of radioactive gas to handle it, but who cares about that...

– Your aim is to... *dump* the rods into the core, then? The manager exclaimed. – You can't be serious. That will mean delays and loss of huge amounts of energy and money... It will take weeks before we're fully operational again. It's... *monstrous*.

– You've always been an arrogant asshole, Bjørnson, Helene grinned. – I assure you, this particular plant will *never* produce anything anymore.

– Do we have sufficient amounts of plastique? Judith sheepishly inquired. – To really do it?

– We don't need more than one-tenth of everything stored here, Willy replied, not without solemnity. – We could have destroyed it many times. The only thing lacking to start World War 3 here is the firing pin for The Bomb.

– And long-range ballistic missiles, Sivert grinned.

– Completely ballistic, Kimberly nodded.

– I'm confident they could have had them flown in, Kurt contributed, – if the need arose.

– That's enough. Judith raised her hands in a divergent gesture. And then, in a perfect imitation of John Wayne: – We've got a job to do.

– I think I've found where and how to set off the explosives without exposing the core or damaging the rods, Willy said. – I'm not sure.

Cracked plutonium fuel rods in one single plant could, during a worst case scenario kill all humans on Earth.

– We agreed to take that chance, Anya pointed out, unusually agitated. – The important thing is that the rods can't be recovered from the core, and they have to build a completely new «facility». At least for a while it will be one monstrosity less on the face of the Earth.

Helene and Kees carefully started the meticulous process. It would take time and the chances of being discovered from the outside would increase exponentially. Willy and his team pulled on the protective suits and gear, to be better suited to penetrate the deadly territories in the monster's belly. They couldn't penetrate very far, without committing suicide, but hopefully far enough. They had decided not to take unnecessary risks. If the radiation grew too strong they would turn back. Naturally.

There was a risk by merely being here. The reactor rods would have to be lowered faster than the regulations stated. They couldn't spend days here. Very ironic, since everybody felt that today's regulations were not rigid enough. But if the core melted they would at least have made a valid point, Morten the lawyer thought grimly…

– A good thing we shan't start up the beastie rector. It was stated with a sweaty face. – That would have been hard indeed.

– Shut up, Sivert! Judith shouted it a bit louder than she had meant to.

The work proceeded far more slowly than if the technicians had done it, but they didn't dare let them get their hands on anything. There was always the possibility that one would make a misunderstood heroic attempt. He or she could trigger one of the many silent alarms automatically notifying outside forces. Another possibility was that the individual in question could, in a panic, or deliberately, expose the core and cause the China Syndrome.

Helene had learned the entire process in her time here, listened to the eager technicians explain everything time and time again to the young executive, gone over the specs in many a lonely night. She had spent her time here well.

The phone rang. Everybody froze. While the lights blinked and blinked.

Helene walked fast to the consol to take it. She wondered how steady her feet and hands were, how they could be this steady, when all her insides felt like jelly. The hand grabbing the phone and lifting it to her ear was steady as a rock.

– This is Valin, she replied. Throat was dry.

– This is Carola. Where is Tomas?

The hand clutched the phone, undeniably. The first name was today's codeword in a security check.

– He had something very important to do, in a certain rather secluded place, she joked. – May I help you *girls* with anything?

– All clear, Helene, the voice replied. *– Next word is MEN, got it?*

– All clear, Helene confirmed.

– Goodbye. The connection was broken from the other end.

Goodbye, Helene said in a very remote tone of voice.

There was no turning back, now.

And it pleased her.

Time crawled to a halt. She realized she hadn't known what that expression entailed until today. The day they couldn't see, except through the video screens. Everything was pallid, bleached. They thought about the humans who «enjoyed» sitting in front of screens like this, watching, studying and governing others, unseen, hidden behind one-way mirrors. And they shuddered. Because these people dominated the present day world. No matter the geography or what the political system called itself. All the twenty of the Green Rose had felt this, skin and bone and soul.

Willy and his team returned from their task. Everybody had showered.

– It's worse than we feared. He shook his head. – We couldn't even enter the outer chamber without fear of irreparable contamination. We had to place all the plastique on the outside hull. Nobody survives many minutes on the inside. How it is possible to do maintenance and controls in this place is beyond me.

– We've had people inside regularly, the manager replied automatically. – And it didn't do them any harm.

– That's a lie, Lennart, Helene countered calmly. He stared at her with his mouth open. – You had a group of poor suckers there one single time. You never dared repeating it. You had too much work keeping the horrible diseases they developed out of the media and the public eye.

– How could you guys do it? Anya asked enraged and incredulous. – You and your bosses knew what you imposed on them. How *can* you?

– I didn't know, one said despairing. – I knew nothing.

They didn't know whether or not they should take him seriously.

– Fools, Travis raged. – Only power counts in the world. They who have power can do anything. Crawl back into your holes and stay there.

– We have power enough, Willy said, with a rage unusual for him. – Power enough for others not to be able to touch us. Not even your masters.

Travis laughed. It hurt, but he still did it.

– They can never touch our souls, Will continued. – Our thoughts are free. We are free. No matter what happens we have liberated ourselves from the brainwashing instigated by the professed masters of the world. They have touched us, touched us with their inhumanity, but never our depths, our core.

The laughter stopped, changing into the intense hatred exposed in the eyes of the shell of a man sitting there.

Black clouds passed by outside and were captured by the monitors. They stretched an infinite distance towards the horizon, reminding those watching them of the enormity in the task ahead of them.

The phone rang again. Helene took it this time, too. The others listened with their ears cocked.

– … a minor problem, we're handling it, Judith heard Helene handle it.

Judith pulled back a bit, out in the smaller corridor.

The dark glass was a mirror in the reflection from all the lamps. She stared at the alien face. The hair color didn't matter and the face was the same old one. But… in a way she had a hard time defining… it was different.

She stood there with bowed head, leaning at the glass with hands curled into fists.

– Judith… She glimpsed Willy in the reflection. – Is anything wrong?

– Nothing, something, everything… She raised her head, but otherwise she remained in the same position, with her back to him. – Nothing important.

He said no more. His hands, the soft hands shuffled hair in her neck, exposing naked skin, giving her a comforting kiss. He waited patiently. She turned, with dry tears in her eyes.

– Travis, he… Voice cracked by lack of energy. – He's just an empty shell and nothing but. There are no emotions left in him, if there ever were any… makes me *sick*. Am I weak when I won't exterminate a plague like him?

– No, you're human. Willy was solemn mood, mixed with humor, as was often the case. – And tactical. Not the least that. You're using the inside of the head, like you often do. As you said, there will be other occasions. There are both pros and cons concerning the choice you've made. And let me go on record and say I support your decision.

– We're not good enough if he should come after us.

– We will be when he's released from hospital, if he ever is. Willy smiled then. – And to quote the well-known Silverhair: It's better with an enemy you know than one you don't.

She embraced him.

– *You sly devil,* she whispered into his ear.

They were all watching while the bottleneck was sealed and the evil spirit imprisoned. It was done so thoroughly that the spirit would never more come this way. But they knew all of them that it had many more outlets from where it could send its wrath into the unsuspecting world. They knew it too well.

Just before they were ready to go the phone rang for the third time. Helen picked it up.

– Marc & Spencer, she replied.

What the fuck is happening, Valin? It was the District Manager this time. – *Production is dropping like a stone. If this continues for much longer you won't be able to produce more energy than a falling snowflake.*

Helene glanced at Judith. Silverhair grinned and made the V-sign.

– Take it easy! Helene Valin said admonishing, as if speaking to a child. – We've called in an expert. She will explain everything.

– *What expert? Who has authorized this? Have you gone crazy, Valin?*

– Completely bonkers, she sang, handing the phone to Judith.

– This be Judy Silverhair, was said cheerfully. – I be spirit hunter, coming all the way from America to battle the evil spirit. It be not very angry now.

– *What's your name and security code?* It was barked with all the authority the man could muster, which, as it turned out wasn't much. – *If things don't improve very soon I swear heads will roll.*

– I wouldn't be too quick to offer promises if I were you…

– WAIT A MINUTE… He broke himself off. It was almost as if they were able to see his eyes expand at the other end.

– You're Judith Breen, he finally managed. – I'll g-get you for this. You will pay!

– Promises, promises. She lifted the M-16A2, and shot the consol to pieces. – It was such a silly conversation, anyway…

The prisoners were released and herded out of the building. Two of them carried Travis on a stretcher. He was sweating and writhing, but the ice-cold look never faded. He had perhaps started out as a cynic, but had turned into something far worse.

The difference between a cynic and a realist is hair thin, Olav used to say. Judith was freezing.

The wind caught the hair of everybody outside. It had started to blow, blow hard. Silverhair turned towards the employees, a bunch of still stunned and timid people pulling close in a cluster.

– If I were you I would abandon these premises, now, she said kindly. – Run through the gate and get as big a distance between yourselves and the baby behind us as possible.

– Why not let us take the cars? The ex-manager said angrily.

– Because, as of now the car option… is no longer viable.

She fired the grenade launcher at the parking lot, where one expensive luxury liner after another was lined up. The grenade hit dead on, and exploded right between them. Wreckage flew all over the place.

Kurt took photos of all the well-dressed people while they fled through the gate. Renni looked curiously at him.

– Why do that?

– This way we have proof they carried Travis out of here, if they should happen to leave him behind.

They entered the bus quickly and efficiently, carrying guns, ammunition and explosives. They were getting good at this.

– Shite, we almost forgot the roses. Kimberly bent down and picked up a box. – They're our start and new beginning, our strength and our life.

She returned outside for a short while, throwing some of the roses on the tarmac. The rest of them she saved for the first kilometer of the road, irregularly letting go of one by one, until there was none left.

The rumble in the ground, the upcoming, sharp as a whip crack through the air made them look at each other, made them worry, made them rejoice.

– Hey. Heike exclaimed, breaking the silence. – We didn't have to use the reserves, not expose our secret weapons.

– Fuck, Jan moaned, very ironic. – I truly enjoyed the extra weight in the ass.

– I don't mind being a bit backseat heavy myself, Dorte said exuberant.

– You don't, honey? Kathy remarked coldly, pointedly. – I would think you had more than enough there already.

– You say that, needing both more fodder and weight, Dorte sniffed.

– Ladies… Kurt raised his hands in a divergent manner. – Know that we love you no matter the look or weight. I mean…

And he stopped before getting himself in even deeper.

They cackled loud and wild, falling around each other's neck. Judith shook in her laughter and tears were flowing, bittersweet, as the thought sneaked in on her afterwards. Was it a strength this, to be able to laugh in death's presence?

Yes, it was a strength.

Meters, kilometers ran away. They spotted no one chasing them, nobody close. They switched busses while police frequencies were buzzing wildly, drowning in angry shouts, more so every minute. By the time the roadblocks started appearing they were far away.

They reached the old, abandoned farm, their temporary hideout, without incidents of any kind, one more home on the long way home.

– We did it! Helene clapped her hands. – I feel such need to rejoice.

– Do it! Anya told her hotly. – Nothing stays your hand anymore.

She had felt numb when they drove through the gate, numb when witnessing the explosion. Now, she let go, laughed and cried, clapped her hands like a little girl. The others followed her lead, danced with her, howled in joy, as she did.

Candles flickered in the twilight. Some burned out, while others were lit and burned in the eternal night. They danced the night away, and the only lights they saw were nature's own fire. Another confirmation of the bond between them, and a bittersweet reminder of everything they shared.

– It was easy. Heike fought astonishment to put her feelings into words.

– Yes, Elan, who were not at all used to things being easy, agreed. – We gambled everything on our passion and won.

Judith glimpsed out of the corner of her eyes Anya moving closer to Kurt. Judith realized she was dancing tight to Sivert, and that he was virtually clinging to her. What was said made her both warm and cold.

Judith Breen and her dancing partner Ole Sivert Olsen ended up, in a way they didn't care to ponder in a small room in the attic. The day's first twilight was just about visible outside. This was Death's Hour, when many people in bed surrendered their spirit. It was at this moment of Eternity they gave themselves fully and totally to Life.

She stood with her back to him. The room was completely dark and seemed infinitely large, but she knew.

– Sivert, she said slowly. – Am I cynical?

He smiled. She didn't ask for his opinion, but about the facts. How typical of her.

– No, he replied dryly. – You're a realist, and that's an advantage in this world, as long as it isn't overdone.

He understood. She turned warm all over. This was what he had always tried to convince her of, but he hadn't been convincing

until now.

Her strong arm reached out a hand and his was there. Which one had done what first was impossible to tell, and it was unimportant. Perhaps it had happened simultaneously. They felt it that way. Hungry and soon to be swollen lips sought each other time and time again. In youthful strength they had both started the run against the wind, and since then just increased their speed. Like their hands seeking and finding their way in the darkness. It was so easy, now, they felt, to remove all clothes, all boundaries between them.

Someone, somewhere played an instrument, enhancing the strains of joy they already felt. He lifted her up. It pleased her to be in his arms. He was taller than her, but when she met him he had been skinny, and also carried too much fat on his body. He would never have been able to lift her as he did now. Now, the body was as well trained as the brain. An obvious necessity, the way they went at it. He put her down on the mattress with a difficulty they both experienced as… fun. They chuckled in small ways, body against body. Bodies pushed against each other without effort. They didn't use a blanket, didn't want to cover themselves in any way. Minor caresses were sufficient. They turned hotter than any heat around them. Both were already in more than tangible heat. He was hard, and she was wet down below. But they held back, allowed the heat to rise slowly.

He kissed her on the earlobe. She gasped, had never imagined it that sensitive. She licked his nipples and they turned just as hard, if not as big as her own. They hurried slowly, allowed everything to happen by itself, not forcing anything. She whispered something in his ear. He couldn't tell what. The conscious part of him didn't. He felt a catching in his throat when he attempted to speak.

Both were lonely a windy night. They glimpsed the stars in their eyes, so distant, deep in their souls. Longing for… longing, like all others. They had this night. There was no tomorrow, and it might never come. They clutched the other shadow in the Storm.

– The Wind of Change has blown for a long time, now. Perhaps we will experience it at its full force, blowing wild.

– Yes, she whispered. – Yes…

She rested on him. A droplet of sweat ran down her nose. He sat up. They sat tight, mouth to mouth. A droplet ran down his nose, too. Their noses and droplets met. The fluid gathered in one droplet, falling into their lair. He grabbed her muscular butt with both hands, as he placed himself on his knees. Hands clutched her hips, and with a sudden pull he had turned her around. The air rushed at the previous unexposed skin. Suddenly she found herself on all fours, turned away from him. She laughed and gasped indignant simultaneously. Always expect the unexpected from Sivert. She wanted to turn her head to give him an excited kiss, but he stopped all her conscious thoughts when he pushed a hand in between her thighs. She shook her head impatiently back and forth when he pushed and pulled his lips up and down her back. It made him so hard that it almost hurt. He turned a bit too eager and missed with his first thrust, but the second time everything happened instinctively, and he slipped easily inside her. He stretched above her while his longer arms reached along hers and down on the mattress. She tilted her head slightly close to his, and they overwhelmed each other with long, sultry kisses. And there were many more caresses, and each and every one was registered in their hazy minds. There was the beyond close contact they had experienced all too seldom in their lives. The heat from the hot Sun embraced them high on the mountain. He gasped for air, convinced he would never get enough. She didn't get enough as he embraced her both within and without. Her warm water collided with his heat, on its way in, on its way out. They stretched on the beach in the warm light and turned joyfully wet.

They rested there, front-to-front, exhausted, content. The caresses faded slowly, in frequency and intensity. She rubbed fingers across his weeklong beard. Fairly subconsciously his hand touched her distinct face.

– I didn't realize it, he said, – but with dark hair you look like an American Indian. You're totally changed. It's absolutely amazing.

– I guess I have native blood in me. She shrugged. – Most «pure» Americans are of mixed heritage. That's one of the things we've got going for us. It just remains for most to admit to that fact. I have a vague notion that such an admission would be an important step forward, don't you agree?

– Wise Squaw, he declared, he flattered her.

The hand she kept on his belly started moving towards his tight, wet hairy jungle. Playful fingers grabbed his small, soft thing. Skin was pulled back. She pushed it tenderly forward.

– Warrior Squaw makes it good for her warrior, she mumbled, with her lips tightening around him. He realized he was holding his breath. She added something, not very loud: – C'mon, you were sooo big earlier.

It twitched in the corners of his mouth. He grew and hardened in her mouth, in one single push. She pulled back a little to admire the result of her work.

– Oh, boy, she said impressed, overwhelmed by lust, biting herself in the lip. – I'm evidently a better flatterer than the other one present.

– I believe that's because you're… a bit more… *direct,* he managed. – Yes, that's definitely the reason.

The lips parted in a hardly audible moan. She swayed back and forth above him. The head, the upper body descended on him, ever closer, until mouth and breasts teasingly touched him. She couldn't believe how brave she behaved. For so long she had feared Olav had killed all *play* in her. Powerful arms clutched her, and momentarily the fear returned. Until she was comforted by Sivert's familiar, good-natured, wild features, until she had assured herself it was him. Her own smile turned huge and hot.

– You don't need to worry anymore, he whispered. – You can reduce him to shreds now, and most others, too.

A pointed look. He smiled, apologizing and teasingly, and she melted completely. She slipped down between his thighs, down on his raised sword, and it slipped through her shield. She opened and shut her mouth, while her eyes opened and closed. The eyes turned clear and misty. She moaned in savage, delirious need, welcoming the sweet pain. He grabbed hard around the firm body and echoed his mate's moans. They abandoned all traces of upbringing and civilization and didn't miss it. *This* was what they had missed their entire life, a chance to let life explode in all its colors. *Uninhibited.*

CHAPTER THIRTEEN

Uninhibited.

Non-enforced. Like a rose growing outside the seemingly endless gray fog.

The Sun had passed its highest point on the sky before they opened their eyes and managed to leave the bed. Judith stepped over the threshold and into the daylight dressed in simple clothes, covered in no more than a single white shirt, its edge flickering on her thighs. She stretched her body, embraced the summer air, the heat, the scent of the flowers, trees, the grass. She watched others do the same. Virtually everybody had awakened late, as had been their habit years ago.

She spotted Willy. He stood by an old lime-tree, scouting the horizon. He was singing. She couldn't make out the words, until she walked closer.

– «Your eyes sparkle with Life, this moment, as they did long ago, in a faraway time».

That sentence stuck. Then - and forever. He had a great voice, powerful and sensitive, filled with life. The song was rich with emotion, passion, glow, joy, and all the strings he played in her. She couldn't stop smiling, broadly and without reservations, and discovered that she didn't want to.

He had turned towards her. She made a pirouette, not just for him, but for the world.

– Isn't it a beautiful day? She cried out in joy.

– Beautiful indeed, he said innocently to the air. – Beautiful weather.

They looked at their surroundings. It seemed like the morning mist had yet to let go. It drifted above both water and land, lingering in the increasingly stronger sunlight. The indistinct painting, filled with light and shadow provoked all kinds of emotion and inspiration in them both.

He watched her while she stepped closer, danced on naked feet through the tall grass. Every time she drew breath she felt the heat in the air, the warm moisture that could hardly be measured, but had to be experienced. She felt like a young girl again, one dancing barefooted through the grass without fear of sharp rocks.

– Now, Druid? She snickered. – Does this woman find pity for thy sharp eyes?

– She does indeed, he declared. He found his voice hoarse and ragged. He had never been able to deal with her more or less obvious approaches and come-ons.

– Yours is a sight everyone must fine pleasing, Madame.

– Thank you so much, My Lord. She curtseyed deeply.

They stood there alone in silence for a while, feeling the wind, watching the sky. Everybody heard the waves on the beach. She knew that before she reached out with her senses to her fellow warriors and travelers.

Dandelion, in the Sun's soft color covered the field. They all spoke to her. Those who desired their own, private order in the Universe saw it as weed. Its many seeds spread wide and long, one example of nature's phenomenal adaptation ability. Nature struck back, in a thousand ways at those who attempted to destroy it. A minority of humans was also a part of this, fighting the current majority of their own species. Judith wanted to blow the dandelion seeds over land and sea, and rock-hard ground, helping it grow.

To this point she hadn't blown hard enough.

– Life can be great.

She sighed content.

– To know that is a strength in itself.

– Yeah, isn't it? She grinned so wide that he was convinced she would get hair in her mouth. – Too bad it's gotta be the world's best kept secret.

– Life in general is hard, he said, filled with melancholy.

– Yes, now, at present day, she stated, not at all melancholic. – But nothing says it will remain that way. Nothing at all says that!

She grabbed a gray dandelion, and blew it. The very air turned gray and colorful.

– It pleases me to see you… happy, sister, he said. – You need to be.

– I haven't been that bad, have I, now? She returned jokingly.

He turned to her, hesitatingly, pain in his eyes.

– Many people die long before the heart stops, he said, striving to keep a light tone. – I've seen it happen many times. Life is slowly, but surely, ripped apart, and turned meaningless. We are, in spite of our awareness of such dangers, especially vulnerable to them. And you're so important, to us all.

– Flatterer. She kissed him on the cheek. – Don't worry, I'll never *allow* that to happen to me.

It started small. They didn't know what caused it, but suddenly they started laughing, started laughing again. He had to hold on to himself for his life, that much he laughed. He was so pretty when he laughed. Not everybody was. Especially not when the laughter turned loud and noisy. But he was special. She joined his loudness, his cackling. When he was about to stop he started laughing again because of her. They kept it going like this for a while, nourishing each other's laughter.

A good one, only slightly bittersweet. Free, bubbling, and free of malice. Tears flowed freely.

They sat there, a while later with their backs to the tree. Happy. Exhausted. They had fun keeping eye contact, even through their eyes, their sparkling eyes at the back of their head. She smiled, turned thoughtful and smiled again. She shook in laughter and it was carried far off in the wind, along with the Dandelion seeds.

– Okay, people, she said in a menacing manner half an hour later to eighteen eager listeners. She balanced a football in her hand. – Listen up. We'll play rough, but no breaking of bones, okay? We'll do without a referee. Such an entity contributes nothing sensible to the game, anyway. We've handled weapons long enough, for the time being. It's about time for some R & R and modest theoretical insight. This game, in spite of its blatant idiocy, can teach valuable lessons. It's stating that offense is the best defense. It's also important to read the opponent's play, predict the next move, especially when the opponent has the ball, and as we all know, our opponent has the ball almost all the time.

– Silverhair and I have already picked our teams, Willy grinned wildly. – May the slyest win.

They were all dressed in white shoes, white shorts and white shirts. The reason, as Silverhair pointed out was to stress the dangers of conformity, to get dirty, and to learn to recognize each other in a… *tight* position.

Besides, it wouldn't be quite that hot in the searing Sun.

– Where did you get the suits? Heike wondered.

– In Denmark a couple of years ago, Kimberly grinned. – We stole two teams' entire supply of suits, just before the match, just before the teams' arrival at the stadium. The match was cancelled. Both we and the rest of the country shook in laughter.

– It was a laugh riot. Morten dried tears.

– One of our more successful public relation stunts, Jemma commented dryly.

The game was afoot. They had cleaned the yard of rubbish and tall grass. In the heat and the hot wind the field was more than big enough.

Muscular legs and thighs tightened and speeded up. Breath erupted like smoke from the mouth in the humid air. Hot skin was quickly covered in greasy sweat. Judith kicked the round ball high in the air, and a bloodthirsty pack set out where they believed it would land.

Corbin reached it first. He took it eloquently on his chest and howled in triumph. The second after that he was tackled and fell hard. The ball was kicked away. Dust and grass whirled in the air as the horde chased it.

The teams kept up with each other through the tussle. A lead hardly lasted more than a few minutes. After they had played an hour under the burning sun Corbin eloquently passed Helene, but he never got any further, not with the ball. She crouched and snapped the ball with her hands, rolled away from him, jumped up and ran off in a flash. Just before she was knocked down she threw the ball to Gio. He caught it and threw it in the goal, beyond a charging, lethal Kimberly. Everybody laughed themselves silly.

– An excellent score. Judith applauded.

– That wasn't a score, Corbin protested. – They broke all rules.

– What rules? Judith asked softly.

They played a kind of handball a while after that. But since it didn't give any of the teams any advantage they returned to playing soccer. But nobody knew when anyone would once more grab the ball and it happened occasionally, though not always with the same successful result as the first time.

The heat kept increasing, and their brains felt like cauldrons. They started throwing hopeful, begging glances at Silverhair. She kept running them ruthlessly. Cramps overtook ever more of them. That resulted in short breaks while they were taken care of. Very short. Silverhair herded them quickly back on their feet and back on the field.

– C'mon, you slobs. Give me some fire. *Die* for me!

When she finally nodded well pleased and ordered them to the water, they feared she had something even worse on her mind. Her devious smile made them fear the worst. Instead she just slipped silently into the water and started swimming with slow, lazy strokes. They followed her, and the cool, balm water closed around them.

They moved independently of her, like individuals, doing their best to move silently because of what they saw at the water's center. A flock of birds rested there. The humans floated under and above the water surface, enjoying the peace. And when the silence was broken, when birds rose in the air that, too, felt like a great experience.

They rested on the beach and floated in the water in lazy excitement. The water, after the intense effort in the scolding heat gave them a vitality in body and mind they hardly dared believe, one that they expressed full of life and energy, in spite of them being virtually exhausted after the physical hardship. They stretched in the water, naked and free.

– Now, *this* is what I call recreation…

Corbin sighed, a content smile playing on his lips.

Most of them were used to being naked together. Helene, for whom the experience was new and fresh, thought it was interesting to notice how… *natural* it felt. She was sexually aroused by it, inevitably, but right now it just felt good and right now that was enough. There was no shame anymore.

Subconsciously her hand sought the green rope armband and she sensed the pleasant warmth inside. The future was here, now, no matter what may come.

They had digested her blood and she had theirs. Afterwards Anya had pushed the armband up her arm, the symbol of the bond between them. No outsiders knew about them. They usually carried them on the upper arm, under the clothes. Just for identification purposes, and when they were alone together they carried them openly. She smelled the alien herbs, evoking visions of forests and plains, and it made her proud.

Judith swam under water by the reed. She studied the underwater grass as it writhed and twisted in all possible directions. It whispered to her. The narrow passageways turned and shifted constantly. You could stare at the patterns forever. She turned her head and swam deeper. It was surprisingly bright down here, even though the sunlight was far away, as she got used to the shadowy depths. She looked up. Kimberly with her full, golden body passed above her with long, strong strokes. Judith still felt desire for her. That comforted her, in a way.

Silverhair kicked at the bottom, breaking the surface like an arrow. She walked to shore and sat down on a flat rock beyond the reed, the whispering grass. After a while in relative silence her ears noticed the sound of Kimberly's virtually soundless steps.

– You heard me. The voice reached her from behind. – You always hear me.

– How did you know that I knew? Judith asked irritably.

– You curled your little finger. You're always doing that…

Soft hands touched the shoulders, even softer lips the forehead.

– How does it feel, dear *Silver?* It was said in a slightly teasing tone. – To be well over thirty, like the rest of us? You're still a defiant blackguard, I hope.

A pointed look. Judith was thirty-one.

It feels strange. Judith smiled. With the newcomers I'm no longer the class junior. As for your other question: I will always be a defiant blackguard.

She walked among the others while they sat on the ground, relaxing. Renni and Karine sat by a haycock, snuggling intensively. They looked up at her as one, single being.

– I'm just passing by, she said lightly. – Don't mind me, children. I'm just wondering how you're doing, that's all.

– We're perfectly all right. The Icelander's hard, blue eyes met hers.

– No problems? During the operation, the match or the swim? I saw you leave the water before the rest of us, but that may have other causes?

– We're fine. Karine said firmly and blushed all over her body simultaneously.
Silverhair went from there and to the shadows behind the barn. Kurt, Willy and Anya sat there, discussing weapons.
– With this you can exterminate an entire army. Kurt cuddled the M-16A2.
– With these two bottles I can either perform anesthetic on everybody in a room or kill them, Willy said. – I prefer having choices. Your cannon is pretty *final*.
Anya slipped a hand inside her medicine pouch with a certain light in her eyes. When she pulled it back out it held the neck of a little snake.
– NO! Kurt jumped up. – How many times do I have to tell you? Keep those damn reptiles away from me.
– I don't understand your attitude. She spoke with a melodic, forceful voice. – I think my pets are cute…
– CUTE? Like hell they are!
– … but in a way several of them are just as effective killing machines as your toy. Or as we are. We are the deadliest species on Earth.
– «One time to die and one to live», Judith quoted. They turned abruptly by the sound of her voice. – So, Sorceress, you didn't discover me.
– My apologies, Silverhair, Anya replied ashamed.
– We must be concerned with Death, Judith said softly. – It's the only way we can stay alive. That's a choice we made long ago. But today we have taken a break. Let's live for a short while like Kaboklos, like white natives on the Amazon River. To the degree we *can* relax, let's do so today. We can be too focused on death, you know that.
She smiled to them with eyes glowing in beauty, at least for a little while.
– I worry about Renni and Karine, she said straight out, as was her way. – How are they doing, the way you see it?
– C'mon, Willy grinned. – They got through your iron hard test.
– They're okay, Anya said calmly.
– I asked for your opinion, Silverhair snarled. – Not your dreams.
– They will be all right, Anya stated calmly. – Renni will be in pain for a long time, Karine not that long. Both will be fully combat ready shortly.
– Thank you, Judith said formally. – That was what I wanted to know.
– Good, Anya rose, breathing out. She straightened and the raven hair danced in the wind. – This place is so hot I can't remain here a moment longer.
She put the snake back in her bag, and threw Kurt an unambiguous glance.

– Come, Judith told Willy. – I need you to tell Renni and Karine they need to rest their carcasses a while.
– Hey, what about me? Kurt exclaimed unnaturally loud. – I understand more than weapons, you know.
Anya had vanished into the barn, into its deep shadow. Judith and Willy waved goodbye, very deliberately. He stared into that deep shadow, took one step forward, then another. He sensed the strength in his muscles, as the steps turned more confident. The skin's sensitivity increased dramatically and he was willing to swear that he could count the dry straws under his feet. The barn's floor felt cold and dusty with his newfound sensitivity, but the second afterwards he forgot all about it.
– It hasn't occurred to me.
He heard her dark laughter somewhere ahead. Two major steps around the corner and he forgot everything else that might pass through his head.
She stood with her back to him, with her hands on the window-frame and her thighs spread wide. The window had no glass. The wind pulled in her dark forelock. Her face was half turned towards him, half concealed, half inviting, half challenging. The hair fell down her back. For some reason he kept noticing the mole on the inside of her leg. And he noticed how he turned heavier down below. The cock wagged briefly from thigh to thigh before standing straight.
– That's good, she said hoarsely. – The heat has made me so horny that I couldn't have waited much longer. If you hadn't come I would have had to go to the beach and rolled on the ground before all the males.
– That would have created chaos. He just about managed to whisper, and wasn't sure if she had heard him, knew it didn't matter.
He saw her butt now. And an indistinct snake body writhing and wriggling. He grabbed her breasts from behind and held on. She moved impatiently. He moaned gratefully. In one single swing he pushed inside her.
She fell forward and her head, and major parts of her body ended up outside the wall. He reached for her. They rocked back and forth, like levers above a bottomless abyss. His dark hair mixed with hers. She parted her lips, joined her lips. His face pushed at hers and they both slipped in and out of the shadows.
When they rested in the hay later, with their arms around each other he strived to recall if he had been the slightest aroused before he had turned the corner and had seen her by the window, the moment everything had exploded. She had that effect on him, like a volcano, as a well of compassion. She and Judith were fairly alike here. He couldn't fathom how it was possible to be both so extremely erotic and sensitive. He had

believed it to be a contradiction in terms. But he realized that it was his limited upbringing speaking, and when one was speaking about fundamentals, shredding illusions, there were no contradictions.

– We should always be together, she said carefully, hopefully. – At least almost always.

They kissed, lips to lips. He had no desire to avoid the question, but didn't want to break the brittle mood, wanted at least to postpone the break.

– Another place, another time, perhaps. He frowned pensively, and turned even more poetic, less serious. – When I dream I dream about you.

– It pleases me that you're still dreaming, she said quietly, unusually reserved.

– Dreams can't die… he stated, – but they belong to the night.

Over the hot fields they levitated, all of them, over the stirred, cooling water, while the day was still at its brightest. Everything happened gloriously informal, even though they did feel the occasional catching in the throat, when speaking or humming, or singing. They chased each other playfully and joyfully. Their spirit hovered above the waters, on Earth and on other worlds. They allowed themselves to be kids again. Youthful, fresh, they hoped they would ever remain. The birds finally descended on the water surface and rested there, the ability to take off and fly always present within.

Judith didn't enjoy what she was about to do, but it was necessary.

She found Sivert a bit up the river.

– Once, during childhood I stood by a waterfall, he said, standing absolutely still. He had heard her. – I remember the sight of the salmons on their way up and I admired them. My grandfather told me a story, a fairy tale about a salmon swimming all the way up to die. I can't recall the specifics, only the emotions it evoked.

– It isn't like that with humans, she said softly. – For us there is always another, exciting waterfall beyond any river we might ascend.

– But I'm positive the story had a great and strong pull, she added, after pausing and pondering a bit. – And natural, not the least natural, unspoiled.

She sat down, right in front of him, crossing her legs. He made no advances, no attempt to move closer to her. They sat on a quiet, secluded spot, able to scout far and well, without being worried about interruptions of any kind. Her eyes focused on the mountains far away. It lasted well and long before they focused on him.

– I don't love you, she finally said, in her own, straightforward way. – Not like you want me to. I care about you, but not enough.

– I understand, he assured her with a strained smile. – Don't worry.

She knew he told the truth. That made everything both better and worse.
– I don't think I can love anybody… strong enough, she stated, mostly to herself. Their eyes met again.
– You can, he said in a strained voice. – I can convince you.
– Perhaps once upon a time, she dreamed, – on fields of green grass, beyond the gray fog.
She shook off the short-lived flash of melancholy. She had for a long time looked upon present day society's favoring of monogamy as ridiculous. But shreds of upbringing always remained, even within the most independent person. Everybody, including the Nightravens was a product of the society of their birth.
Night and twilight arrived. They lit a fire and gathered around it, drawn to it from whatever places they had spent their day. They arrived two and two or in groups. Their celebration of Life, begun under the Sun, exploded under the Moon. They had great fun covering themselves in war paint, headbands, feathers and loincloths, though there was a purpose behind it all. There usually was, to everything they did these days. But here, at this place it was mostly fun, or purpose-filled fun. They gambled by lighting the fire and gathering around it without posting guards. But here - now - they could be the people they most of all wanted to be.
Kimberly and Elan approached the fire, leading a figure completely wrapped in cloth. Those waiting by the dancing flames didn't know who hid beneath the cover. Most of them *had no idea*. Everybody had, after having been encouraged to do so, stared directly into the fire for a while, deliberately dulled their sharpened senses and astute skills of observation. The siblings started unwrapping the rags.
– Careful, Kimberly admonished her brother. – We used time and effort on this. Let's not screw it up.
He sent her a venomous look, clearly conveying what he felt about the necessity of her admonishing.
Eventually Anya stood there, before them all, once more nude like them, but different. She was painted more thoroughly, in more elaborate patterns, all over her body. The effect of the pattern, created by the paint and her body imposed itself on them, invaded them. The symbols moved on the skin, speaking to them, revealing and conveying vast secrets, inspiring thoughts unheard of. Eyes seemed blacker than ever in the flickering light. She started swaying, swaying, until her feet seemed to move by themselves. The entire body was… dancing. She hesitated, stumbled and stopped occasionally. It hardly lessened the experience. They witnessed how she was aware of her insecurities and improved her art for every step. Her body knew the moves and every step turned softer, more confident,

slowly, but surely, as if she had to remember something she had never forgotten.

– I've never done anything remotely similar to this before, in my life, but I can do it still. It's in my heart, my bones. I will now tell you what you already know. I want you to listen.

Her deep voice carried far. They heard her, as easily as they heard the approaching whirlwind.

– In what is called prehistoric times, before the first cities humanity lived unified with nature. We were hunters and nomads. We still are. We can no more deny our true nature than The Earth can exist without the life-giving energy it receives from the Sun. We can never recreate that time, but we can strive to recreate its spirit. It's essential, an inevitable necessity.

Morten and Yvonne approached, carrying a huge cage. Judith knelt within it. Her hands clutched and shook its bars in smoldering wrath.

– I'm many things, Anya said. – Each person is potentially many. Call me priestess, fortuneteller, sorceress or witch. Labels don't matter. Judith and William are just as much a witch as I am. First and foremost I'm a carrier of knowledge.

She reached out with her arms. Something fell into the fire and embers filled the air. Forms and figures seemed to gather in the shadows. Anya danced, more like in trance now. But they didn't see it as dance, not in a traditional sense. Or rather: In a present day sense. Not in the sense that she was performing. She was no object, not separate from them. Rhythm seemed to come from nowhere. Intellectually they knew it stemmed from Kees, from his hands hitting his handmade primitive drums, but the sounds seemed like they were originating directly from the night, from the levitating embers, the fire and night creating obscure, ghostlike shapes.

Everybody gasped. Kurt rose. He held out the medicine pouch. Their sister, whom they thought they knew so well pulled a long, slimy snake from it and let it turn and twist around her body. She turned, and the snake hissed and spat.

– This I call the Snake Dance, she spoke in a vibrant voice. They saw glimpses of an ecstatic smile. – I must admit I have practiced it ever so little.

She attacked her partner. He attacked her. Kurt looked just slightly clumsy. Both seemed instinctively to know what they were doing. They danced around the cage, rocked their heads. Bent down, straightened, bent down, and straightened at a horrible speed. Silverhair writhed and twisted inside the cage, and stretched, stretched, where she hardly should have been able to move. The bars shook.

Smoke. Smoke in the air. Everybody breathed it. It didn't rise in the night, but remained around the fire. Everybody was breathing it, cheerfully drawing it inside themselves.

It worked on them. Whatever the smoke was it made reality stretch and bend around them all. They began moaning and shouting and a low and pleased chuckle rose from their throats.

Corbin sat there, a huge smile dancing on the shadowy features.

– I'm totally fucked up! He suddenly shouted, beside himself.

– What's *happening?* Gio shook and shook his head, as if intoxicated. He cackled incredulous.

Anya suddenly stood still. They imagined they saw snakes instead of hair on her head, saw countless hissing heads stick their tongue out and reach for everybody.

– We've danced the snake dance, she said with a hollow voice. – We're writhing in clever wrath and may, if we wish to, liberate ourselves from all confines.

– *Mambo,* Jemma spat and turned to leave.

Corbin embraced her and started to kiss the dark skinned body. She struck him down.

– Don't turn your back to what's behind the veil, sister. The voice didn't come from where Anya seemed to be, but from the place in the dark where the black woman was headed. – Don't run away from yourself.

Jemma froze.

– This is absolutely FANTASTIC! Karine shouted, more than a bit delirious, completely up there. – Pray tell thy humble servant, Sorceress, how have you gone about casting your spell on us?

– I'm not completely sure, Anya admitted, and looked almost normal again. – It is from an old family recipe. I got hold of an old book I studied fairly intensively during the years before I left for Copenhagen. It seems to have… paid off… even better than I ever dreamed of, the dreams I've always had.

The ghosts and shadows almost faded, but they didn't vanish.

– Some family you've got. Gio kept shaking his head. – Didn't you tell us you didn't learn anything from your grandfather? Seems to me you learned enough to completely surpass him.

– There's no one else… They saw the smile lurking on her lips. – Not to my knowledge.

– But then…

– I never said it was my family's recipe…

Loud and carefree sounds of joy once again filled the night. They shivered in delight, allowing themselves to be carried away. The boundless lust for life lingered like an echo of the dark within and without. They had their entire attention on her, on themselves.

– We have opened wide. The vibrant speech changed into what they experienced as both gentle and rough, and they saw no contradiction in that, in that either. – We know that the Dance to Life is perceived as far more powerful in the night, and that's no coincidence, no mirage. Dreams Belong to the Night.

Drums started beating again, much louder and fuller. Kees beat his drums with closed eyes, the sound rising from his skeletal instruments seemingly spitting both thunder and lightning.

– Let's dance a dance in three, three dances in one, in nine, one or three to the eagle, the cat and the lamb. They are, like the snake dance meaningless in itself. They don't matter, beyond the questions they make us ask ourselves, what we seek. Magick isn't an object or outside effects. It moves and lives within us.

Everybody danced tight together, tight like at a disco a Saturday night, with more room than in the vast, empty forest surrounding them, the night's eagles, cats and lambs within.

– We can dream, Helene said in Renni's arms.

– We can fight, Renni said in Helene's arms.

– We can join the Kaboklo, the «white natives» on the Amazon River, Silverhair shrugged.

Dance halted for a heartbeat or two. Judith straightened outside the cage. They stared stunned at her. Nobody had seen her break out. The cage was just as whole, just as closed, just as locked. Trick or treat, reality or illusion? Perhaps neither she nor Anya could say for certain.

– My compliments, Gio applauded. He didn't shake his head anymore.

– Give in, brother. Karine reached out a hand to him. – Throw yourself into the raging current. Ask why, ask how, but don't let it keep you from anything.

Jemma picked up Corbin and gave him a smothering kiss. He returned the kiss just as wild, perhaps even a bit more violent. They melted into one being.

– Perhaps old family recipes are worthless? Judith said casually, glowing in her passion. – I've considered this quite extensively. Perhaps when push comes to shove they all are. Perhaps we're doing everything ourselves. That's quite a thought, isn't it? That all the miracles humans have witnessed throughout the ages have their origin in the human being itself.

The spirit dance began anew. Spirits reached out from sweaty bodies and ventured into the endless dark. It turned wild in a matter of seconds. Shouts and challenging howls filled the air. Embers floated in the night. Floated to such a degree that one was tempted to believe they would never land or be put out.

Will you hold me? Judith thought when meeting Sivert's eyes.

They all put their arms around each other, in ties that not even death or non-life could break. Dance quieted. All loud sounds faded in their ears. Hot bodies joined, tangled together like strains of night and fire. They writhed on the ground, floating in a cauldron of fiery embraces. They exploded in the ember rain, danced into the ebony far lands and the beyond powerful, explosive whirlwind, and nothing stayed their hand anymore.

CHAPTER FOURTEEN

– This is a Kevlar-vest, Judith said. The silver hair framed her face in the sparse light. Mere lines of light penetrated the few small and dirty windows in the limited basement storage room. – It's light body armor for protection against bullets and explosive shrapnel. As you can see Kurt is able to wear it under ordinary clothes and to move without becoming significantly disadvantaged.

Kurt made some moves and did so with such speed that he in no way looked disadvantaged. Judith signaled for him to stop. He relaxed and turned to her. She shot him in the belly. The gun had just appeared in her hand, as if from empty air. He howled. The eighteen others present gasped.

– HEY, that *hurt!* He yelped in pain and fell to the floor.

– That's good, Judith commented. – Just so we all know it. If I had shot him in the chest he would probably have broken a couple of ribs. It doesn't make us bulletproof. This improves our chances for surviving a battle without sustaining major injuries… as long as we don't let it become a crutch. This is no good against high-speed bullets, but increases the chances for us to be able to keep up the fight with just a bruise, instead of having a large hole somewhere important.

She smiled ominously. They returned their smiles, and slowly her expression softened. One hand reached for Kurt and helped him up. The other dried his forehead. She prayed she didn't show too much compassion.

– It's okay, he insisted. – At least I know how it feels, now, which is surely an advantage… if it happens even more unexpected than this. We do need to be prepared, for far more eventualities than this.

The mood brightened somewhat, even as they nodded grimfaced. Everybody nodded, even as they once more, figuratively and literally rolled their hands into fists. The knot inside would never more be completely untwined. For that it had been tied too hard, for too long.

– Next! Silverhair cried.

++++++++++++++++++

A city in Northern Europe. A room behind heavy curtains.

Ten people sat in the shadow around the table in the dark room. Only the faces of the two standing, standing very straight at the opposite end of the shadow filling most of the room had enough light on them to have somewhat recognizable features. A cold draft surged constantly through the air. The place was protected against the heat outside.

– They took Barsebäck, too. The voice came from the shadows. – Christ, that was supposed to be one of our most secure plants, the one to beat.
– They had inside help, another reminded him.
– Incidental. Many places with just as good security have also been visited. Is no measure sufficient against these larvae?
The very cross question was directed towards the brighter side of the room, demanding a well-thought answer.
– It is… difficult, sir, one of those in the light responded after several heartbeats of hesitation. – These… people are so unpredictable that they're almost predictable, constantly changing tactics, and learning, learning the game. At first they made obvious mistakes. That has changed. They're now professional, in most meanings of the word. Virtually any attempt we have made so far to stop them has just brought more larvae out of the chrysalis… sir.
– They're about to become a major pain in the ass, another, a woman, stated, her voice sharp as a whip, cutting through flesh and mind alike. – How many are identified at this point?
– The leaders, of course. Judith Brevik, Wilhelm Otterman, Kimberly Russel, Giovanni Rossi, Karine Lie, Steve Cockrum or what the hell he's calling himself these days, Ole Sivert Olsen, Sybille Xavier… They haven't exactly kept their identities secret. The movements of Brevik and Otterman, and familiars before they moved into the Green Rose are well documented. After that everything turns misty, I'm afraid.
– And Roland Vallens? One threw the name very passionately at the table.
– Vallens has stayed in Eastern Europe for ages, the reply came from somewhere in the darkness. – Forget him, for now.
– I wish he was here. I've dreamed of breaking his neck for years.
– The opposition is getting smarter, a man stated with conviction. – We must rise to the challenge. We must face the possibility that our way of life is actually threatened. Just the necessity of this meeting should be an indication of the danger.
– What about infiltration? A shadow fist cracked the table. – That should, by damn yield results.
– We have a few promising, long-term projects, sir, the man in blue suit replied. He strived to glimpse the man behind the voice, giving it up quickly, for his own sake. It should have been easier, now, when they were many, but no, the lights in the room had, as usual been masterly arranged. Just as well, curiosity killed the cat in this business. – So far our agents have been either too professional or too stupid, and been spotted easily. We've been forced to plan extremely long-term, use of recruits on teenage-

level and such. Their teaching is deliberately lacking and they've been given orders not to take any shortcuts, allow everything to happen in its own way, at its own pace. One can call this program a qualified success, since their cover has yet to be blown. They've yet to penetrate very deep into the lair of the *roses*, but when it happens each one will be able to do extensive damage. Let me add that each terrorist cell is an independent unit and has an independent structure. So even if one cell should be destroyed the others will remain fully operational. We're faced with a hydra, ladies and gentleman, a manifold of monsters and dragons.

Hot breath mingled in the air and lessened the cold draft for a moment.

– Both because of this and other factors no single solution is sufficient on its own. The man in the gray suit picked up on the other's cue. – We've taken the liberty of setting things in motion. I will give you the trimmed version.

– 1: An individually adapted protection network. Since it is difficult, to say it the least to predict their next move, we will place our selected men and women at selected locations. Their papers will show they were employed through ordinary channels of the specific factory or unit. Sooner or later our arrows *will* hit the mark.

– 2: Create a mobile unit of handpicked people not doing anything but hunting the roses. History has shown that such a method is quite effective.

– «The Wild Bunch»! One exclaimed both cheerfully and sarcastic. – The Wild West, Butch Cassidy and Sundance Kid.

Sighs surrounded them in the darkness. It was a well-known fact that this man was both a Paul Newman and Morgan Kane fan boy.

– The comparison is not unsound, Gray Suit commented with a polite smile. – Psychological profiles we've comprised say that the roses look at themselves as the Butch Cassidy, Robin Hood and Gjest Baardsen of our time, the last defenders of freedom against financial powers and authorities. Their view is that our time can easily be compared to the Wild West.

– The truly dangerous, the authoritative shadow stated harshly, contemptuously. – Worse than a loose cannon on deck. You can secure the cannons. These must be thrown off the ship.

– We've compiled a list of candidates for the strike force for your approval. You'll find descriptions and psychological profiles at the back of the files. We're also suggesting an increase and reevaluation of our various information activities. It's crucial that we give people our… version of the terrorists' motivations and deeds.

Everybody could feel each other's smile in the dark.

– That’s all then, for now? No voices were raised, contradicting the statement.

The meeting was adjourned.

++++++++++++++++++++++

THE CHOIRGIRL TURNED TERRORIST

Karine read the newspaper article with a certain pleasure visible in her eyes. She rocked humming on two of the chair’s legs, dangerously close to tipping over. Silverhair and Morten, keeping her company on the small hotel room studied the act with morbid interest.

– Now, do you find anything interesting? Morten inquired.

– It’s quite impressive, she said, shaking her head. – An obituary, really. A thorough job, to be sure, retelling my life from cradle to grave.

They had photos of her in the christian choir and the entire community around it, of her lilywhite, innocent face. Then there was documentation of her tenure as a student representative. They had covered extensively her years in and around the «Blitz» house, where at least some of the most radical groups in Oslo, Norway’s capital had gathered in the eighties. The focus was on «how negative elements» had seduced her and led her astray.

Another, similar article had a similar headline. She didn’t bother picking that paper up from the heap on the floor.

THE SEDUCTION OF A CHOIRGIRL

– They hardly deviate from the template at all, do they? She sighed. – Both or rather all articles are pretty much carbon copies of what they’ve written about Helene, describing her as a weak, dependent creature that couldn’t take responsibility for her own life and was easily swayed by the dangerous and wicked revolutionaries. And it’s an old and well oiled method. Ulrike Meinhof, among others was also portrayed as weak and indecisive.

– It’s so clever, isn’t it? Morten spoke unevenly, showing no surprise, clearly commenting on a familiar issue. – So devious and cruel. They’re lying by telling the truth, teaching generations to disregard the obvious and seek the muddled and embrace the illusion. They’re more like lawyers than lawyers, you know…

The bitter smile didn’t really brighten his face at all.

– How little they understand, or want to understand. She shook her head in dismay. – I was never content in my intolerant and limited childhood surroundings. What I basically did until the age of eighteen was to obey orders, to be a good girl, to do what I was told, live through others' expectations and needs, those of my parents, school, church and society. I suffocated and would have faded away to nothing if I hadn't escaped from all that.

She had briefly returned to Oslo after having traveled the world for years. Wilder and crazier than ever she had, through fate and circumstances met Judith, a meeting changing both their lives, changing hers more fundamentally than anything she had experienced to that moment. From that point on her life had taken a turn her old friends, also those frequenting Blitz, could only dream of.

Her eyes sought Judith's, dwelling there. There was an admiration, a respect in her eyes she hardly felt towards anyone else. Since that meeting in Oslo she had known of Judith's considerable… problems. It didn't lessen Silverhair in Karine's eyes. It just made her human.

– It's time! Judith said quietly.

Karine Lie lowered the chair quickly, safely down on all four legs. She realized she had doubts and that she always would have. There had to be doubts, Judith had said. Or one risked losing one's humanity, one's very self. As long as it didn't get in the way of resolve, the fire that was never put out, what was pushing a human being forward, no matter the odds. The society dominating today's world killed everything valuable in a human being, everything making life worth living. It had to stop, had to be stopped. No price was too high. This life, the life she was born to live felt completely natural. Karine hardly noticed she stood up and once more threw herself into the Storm, the whirlwind of all things.

– The deceased doesn't want flowers. She crumbled the newspaper in her hands and dropped it into the wastebasket.

++++++++++++++++++++++++++++++++

The cell led by Silverhair blew up the Volvo headquarters during the worst heat. It exploded in the middle of the night and no one was injured or killed. But the incident caught just as much attention as the attack on the nuclear plant had done. An attention directed at both the rebels and the big bucks. Especially because the Green Rose made sure that a lot of… compromising material about the rich and mighty was made public domain.

The evidence was overwhelming. It was no good pointing out the fact that the terrorists had published it. The information could be checked through several and various sources, and it was done. Many in positions of power and that people owed favors naturally managed to escape the consequences of their deeds becoming public knowledge. The public forgot quickly and easily. Some of the decision-makers merely had to hibernate a bit, and some didn't even have to do that. The powerful of the powerful got away, as usual. But a surprisingly high number got caught in the whirlwind. Among others a well-known Copenhagen editor had to «retire». Several politicians in Scandinavia and Germany, and the rest of Europe were forced to resign. Members of the Green Rose and their supporters were able to release a lot of pent-up frustration. They felt they had actually won a battle, but knew fully well that nothing was changed. Others, just as power hungry took the place of the fallen. The system lived its own life and wasn't dependent upon specific people.

In October they blew up a warehouse in Malmø owned by a company dumping Dioxin in the Baltic Sea. Another action followed by documentation. Dioxin was one of the most dangerous chemicals in existence and the Baltic Sea, the fish there and mother's milk in the countries surrounding it was filled to the brim with it. Since 1945 the amount of radioactivity and human-created chemicals in air, soil and water had been doubled and redoubled countless times, and the same held true for the number of cancer cases. Artificial, for some obscure reason called environmental Estrogens changed the brain, destroyed the procreation process, changed humans and animals in fundamental, destructive ways. Bacteria and viruses returned with a vengeance after humanity's attempt at eradicating them. All the myriad horrors a modern industrial and technological society created erupted from the woodwork and closets simultaneously.

A flyer shouted the message loud and clear:

IT'S ABOUT TIME
PEOPLE START
BLOWING UP POLLUTERS

Way past time, Sivert nodded.

He and the four others in his group within the group stood on a rise and admired their handiwork. The smoking ruins where a lot of worthless values had crumbled to dust. There was a lot of money in worthless and dangerous goods. Money being the key issue here, too. Sivert stared into the smoke and the fire, and wondered if he hadn't started to enjoy this a bit too much, even though he felt there was still a while left to that point. Sometimes it was difficult to say for sure. He, like his friends knew well the axiom that power corrupts.

On the Human Right's Day October 10th they carried out four independent operations in southern Sweden and eastern Norway. They posted the Human Rights' declaration everywhere.

«It's all so very funny», they wrote in an appendix. «Virtually every nation on Earth has signed the declaration, but none is doing anything to live by its words and intentions. They're not even attempting to do so».

At the end of the sheet they had written in small letters:

«We feel a bit silly because we're pointing out the obvious, but to us dummies it feels absolutely necessary».

In an unusually open hearted comment the Norwegian somewhat radical newspaper Klassekampen (Class Struggle) printed in the editorial:

«These people have kept their humor somewhat intact. That is, at least one thing in their favor».

On the United Nations Day they took part in the task of burning thousands of flags. It happened publicly, all over the world. They had the honor of burning the Norwegian, Swedish and Danish national symbol, and a couple more to boot. It happened on the Svinesund Bridge, on the border between Norway and Sweden, while teeth gritting cops were forced to watch. Kurt filmed it all with a grin that wouldn't go away for days.

– This is the LIFE! He shouted savagely, loud enough to wake the very, very dead.

Shocked spectators and some not so shocked, and some completely opposite wondered if terrorists didn't live a good life, after all.

I'm alive, Kurt thought. I'm alive!

Humanity had lost something valuable in the Machine Age. Perhaps this was one way of keeping the wild animal alive. Excitement, challenges were necessary, just as necessary as living and loving, because both were meaningless without it.

Day was warm, almost hot, with a desert dry, roasting sun, with no bite of cold at all in the air. Warm wind blew from the north. There had been many years since the last time winter had started in October in these parts. Kurt wrinkled his nose when smelling his own sweat. He hadn't washed for quite a while. His grin widened.

It had been a busy month.

Sweat was completely natural, of course, contrary to most of the smells surrounding people in modern society. One group of the most unnatural smells was all the perfumes designed to keep sweat away from human life. He shook his head and the grin widened even more.

Winter briefly visited the Gothenburg area this year. It lasted ten days with temperatures approaching a low of zero degrees Celsius. There were a few snowflakes, nothing more. The thin layer covering the ground could hardly be called a blanket or even a sheet. It was white, but that was it. After the powerful volcanic eruption in the Philippines in 1991 and the increased sunspot activity 1991/92 had led to a bit of temporary cooling, the average global temperature had now restarted its climb. The human-created climate change had been noticeable by the end of the eighties, too, but nothing compared to this. Nothing humans had ever experienced. And it happened all over the planet, impossible to explain away.

Ice melted in the Arctic and in Antarctica. Glaciers calved at an ever-increasing pace. The Sahara desert had reached Europe and moved north. Environmental refugees from the southern part of the continent no longer looked like a distant dream. North Western Europe was about to leave the temperate Zone (or the other way around). There was a progression faster than any moderate scientist had predicted and much faster than any politician in office had been willing to admit. Not so strange that. They didn't admit it now, either. People actually using their brain easily saw what was happening, both with nature and the humans living in it, how absolutely all of the world's nations and larger societies deprived human beings of what they needed to survive and thrive. And it had been thus for a long time, for a very long time.

Those who were desperate enough to do something about it weren't strong enough in numbers, not by a long shot.

– The disaster isn't on its way, Anya told Judith. – It began long ago.

The members of the Green Rose, burning with awareness were all very conscious of that fact, easily noticing the numerous and vast signs of the unnatural decay, the festering presence of devastation all over the natural world.

The day the warm weather returned with a vengeance they made their next move, all twenty of them. They returned to Denmark on the public ferry the day of the Winter Solstice.

– This day has been celebrated since prehistoric times, Anya said. – Christianity preempted it and pulled its teeth like they've done with all Pagan customs. They split it, and moved what they wanted to be the important day to the twenty-fourth, and made the new year start nine days late.

The ferry left the quay filled with people, as was the case with every sailing during daytime this day. The twenty hadn't visited Denmark in a long while, but this was the best possible time to do so. The chance of being discovered was minimal. The police couldn't run any thorough checking, either onboard or at disembarking, not without detaining the passengers, all the passengers for days. They wanted to, but one didn't do that, not in countries calling themselves democratic (or during the most hectic christmas shopping).

The storm raged on and the entire trip resembled a rollercoaster ride. The stabilizers had no noticeable effect. The ferry was thrown back and forth in the sea like it was made of paper.

It didn't sit well with most of the passengers. Some of them were close to panic.

- What *is* this? A man gritted his teeth clutching his wife and daughter. – It's bad is what it is. I've never seen it this bad.

– This is the human created Climate Change and the human enhanced Global Warming, Anya said, giving him her best smile.

He looked at her as if she wasn't very well composed, while it was he that was about to lose all composure.

– What are you fucking *talking* about?

His wife glared at him, but stayed silent and timid, pearls of cold sweat covering her forehead.

Anya tried her best to be helpful, very helpful.

– Since the emergence and start of the constant expansion of the cities after the previous Ice Age humanity has attempted to force its will on Nature, to grind it under its heel. That horrible misstep of a venture has never come even close to succeeding. And now we begin to experience the drastic inevitable results.

They approached land on the other side. The ferry made several failed attempts at docking. He looked at her, looked away, looked outside, before turning his attention back to her.

– But… look at it. He waved his hands in a rather vain attempt at illustrating the sight outside. – It's… it's…

The harbor in Helsingør was completely flooded.

She shrugged. Her brothers and sisters grinned at her with admiration in their eyes, casting patronizing glances at the more than apprehensive man.

– This is nothing compared to what will come, I'm afraid. What we see here is an extreme situation, an exception, but in a few years time there will be no need for a storm to flood lower level areas. As the average temperature on Earth increases the ice will melt and the sea level will rise dramatically all over the world, the winds will increase in strength and number. Ravaging Hurricanes, like Hugo will become commonplace fairly soon. When that happens there will be no turning back. We see it everywhere, already, really. The planet is gathering strength for an extremely hostile and durable reaction to humanity's attempt at control.

The ferry finally managed to reach the quay and remain there, as the crew secured everything with thick ropes.

The man smiled sickly and triumphant at her.

– That's just woeful exaggerations, he cried. – Humanity has everything under control, of course.

He pulled his wife and daughter with him, joined the rush towards the exit.

– Control is the biggest illusion of all, Anya stated quietly.

He heard her. They noticed how he twisted his neck. He began shaking hard.

– She's just one of those crazy environmental freaks, his wife told him. – Ignore her.

The wind threw water at the passengers as they disembarked, turning many soaking wet.

But they got off the paper boat, and reached the relative safety and comfort on land.

The train had been suspended indefinitely. The journey had to continue on buses.

They were able to continue their journey eventually, not that much delayed. The bus shook and threatened to blow off the road several times. The members of the Green Rose kept their calm here as well. Some of them just sat there, patiently waiting for the bus to reach its destination. Other glanced out the window, or attempted to, through the steamy windows and more than powerful torrential rain.

The depot in an abandoned cellar in Copenhagen was intact. They took every possible precaution before moving in, but this time it showed itself to be unnecessary.

– Not much ammunition left here, Kurt commented. – Enough for one more time of extensive use, but that's it. We should replenish as soon as possible.

– Let's hope we won't need much of it tonight. Kimberly said.

Up to this moment in time they hadn't had much need for ammunition. It wasn't something they talked much about, unnecessary and detrimental as that was.

They listened briefly to the news. The tales of the flood and storm and related events dominated every broadcast, even on christmas eve.

The sea rose. The ever more frequent winds increased in strength.

The Ozone layer above Antarctica was practically gone.

– He was scared shitless, Renni said.

– Who? Elan wondered, slightly preoccupied.

– The guy on the ferry. His fear wasn't caused by the passing danger. He knew or knew enough or at least believed in advance the realities behind Anya's *cruel* tale. There was little or no need for her to spell it out for him.

His attempt at self deception worked extremely poorly. Perhaps there is hope for him…

That caused a few smiles, but no laughter. They were all more or less tense, focusing on the immediate task ahead.

The two minibuses approached the chlorofluorocarbon factory outside the city on the evening of December 24th. It was raining, and the winds remained more like gales. They strived to listen to the silence behind the storm, which was nearly impossible, so they stopped trying. Lights were lit in the guards' room. Aside from that the area was cast in darkness. There were no streetlights.

– They could have access to infrared equipment, Kurt pondered, revealing his apprehension.

Several others glanced at him and each other, as the buses came to a halt at a spot outside the direct line of sight from the factory. Imagination ran a bit out of control tonight. The comforting darkness didn't relieve their tension. Willy shook his head cheerfully. He gave the signal and five left one of the vehicles and began the thorough work of checking out the terrain, to seek and find good observation spots and covers.

They had infrared binoculars and both the scouting party and those waiting surveyed the terrain in a constant, thorough motion.

The buses quickly turned cold. Everybody was thrice pleased a while later, after waiting in the cold night, by the fact that they were wearing light and warm clothes. Kurt signaled from a rise hundreds meter away. It was a go. Sivert and Dorte left, too, and walked, unarmed, fairly relaxed the long stretch towards the gate. There was a calling system there. They saw Dorte press the button, heard her through the radios.

– Yes? A man responded sourly and uncaring, not very polite at all. – What do you want?

– Our car broke down, Dorte sniffed, clearly distressed. – We left it up the road. May we borrow your phone, please?

A short, breathless silence.

– Okay, but be quick about it, god damn it!

The gate slipped open and closed the instant the two had passed through the narrow opening. Their friends followed them with burning eyes in the dark as they entered the building. Everything seemed normal.

– One minute, Elan noted.

Helene and Gio kept studying the terrain through the infrared binoculars.

The gate opened - wide. Sivert stepped outside first and waved, then Dorte. The buses moved forward. One of the vehicles was parked inside the gate, the other outside it. They left them in one fluid motion, spreading out in the night in a random pattern, five with their weapons in their hands and the finger on the trigger. The rest carried the explosives. Virtually every move was made economically, effectively.

– The guards are resting soundly, Dorte reported lightly and cheerfully. – But it won't be much of a rest without the additional medicine.

– Except for one of them, Sivert said in regret. – He was so good that I was forced to deal rather harshly with him. He has a minor cut in the head, but is otherwise okay.

– I expect ICI to use more money on security after this, Gio joked, a bit ambiguously. – You two aren't exactly my idea of martial arts champions.

– It was sufficient, Dorte shrugged, a little irked.

– Sufficient, Kimberly stated softly.

– This time, Judith said sharply. The others looked incredulous at her. – Let's get to work.

– Okay, Willy said, with a defusing smile. – My help has grown quite skilled lately, so it shouldn't take long to complete the armament. C'mon guys, let get to work.

He had put down the sacks of explosives. The others smiled ashamed to each other. He grabbed the sacks and was about to carry them off. Judith watched him just then, watched all the other faces, those she knew so well, and she watched his hands, the parts of him uncovered by clothes. There was a crack somewhere far away. She heard it as if through mud.

The bullet hit Willy in the chest, penetrating the thin, ineffective Kevlar protection, and they could almost hear it expanding in there, literally tearing him up inside. He was pushed hard backwards. Somebody screamed. Judith didn't know whom, just knew it wasn't her. Everybody jumped down and away, behind the bus, behind the building, behind any major and minor hideout they could find. Willy hit the tarmac with his back first. He shook in cramps a few times before he stopped moving entirely. Judith knew, with icy certainty that he was dead, but she had to be sure, absolutely sure. She crawled towards him. Towards him. To feel his heat one last time before it left him, left him, forever and ever.

Gio fired the first return salvo. What wasn't conscious thought calculated the bullet's trajectory. When the second shot was fired from the dark, far away point he saw he hadn't been completely off.

– One shooter, he shouted, – only one shooter.

Or a hail of bullets would have rained down on them by now.

Sivert threw himself down like everybody else and was floating in the air when the big caliber projectile touched him, a fact undoubtedly saving his life. The bullet just grazed his shoulder, but he was still thrown half around. More started firing at the place they had seen the rifle being fired from, while they kept moving. As if in a daze Judith crouched close to

Willy, stroking him. At the edge of consciousness she registered that Kurt and his group had also started firing at the deadly shadow out there somewhere. She put her finger at the large neck vein of the body that had kicked a few times and now no longer moved. She imagined she felt a beat, but whether or not this was correct there was no more. She clung to a corpse, clung to it in desperate anguish. His face, so peaceful…

– FORGET HIM! Jemma grabbed her and lifted her up, shook her hard. – He's DEAD!

– No, Silverhair cried. – He… is… not.

One sniper, she thought dully, only one shooter up there.

– Return to the bus, she shouted. – The operation is cancelled.

She straightened painfully. Something burned horribly somewhere inside her. She fired her gun at the invisible enemy.

Who the third bullet was meant for wasn't certain in what was now a whirling myriad of dynamic movement. No matter - it missed. It cut some of Kimberly's dancing hairs. That's all.

Silverhair felt a certain pride when observing how swiftly and effectively everything was done. Kees and Anya carried Sivert between them and were among the first inside the bus, the huge minibus seemingly so large before, so small now. It would be tight in there. Some of them had to run behind it until they reached outside the fence. Every second counted and was a threat to them. Reinforcements were on their way, they could be sure of that.

Gio raised his gun a bit. A bullet hit it. Everybody heard that, and the sound of his wrist breaking as the weapon was torn from his grip.

Somebody kicked hard at the door to the guards' room. They heard that distinctly, too, with senses insanely sharpened in the few seconds that had passed since the first shot was fired. The door was kicked open. A guard appeared with a glowing gun in his hands, his face distorted in an insane rage. Yvonne was hit in a thigh. Blood flooded the others. Judith was hit, at the side of the ribs, a few of the ribs breaking. Otherwise she was unharmed. The Kevlar vest had worked like it was designed to do. She fired at the guard. Many of the others did, too. A hail of bullets hit him, and he was pushed backwards as the door closed with a crack.

– I saw one more with a gun, Jan cried out.

– Heike! Silverhair commanded sharply. – Everybody else inside.

Heike raised her ready-to-go PVRK one-time Bazooka. She fired. The grenade shot through the night air and the entire building dissolved in a firestorm. Judith changed clips. Lights blinked and faded. It turned dark and they, too, turned into ghosts, as they should have been from the start.

She stormed to the bus door and signaled to Corbin to start the engine. He did, reaching up from the floor under the wheel.

– Dorte, Renni! Silverhair snarled.

The two fired their PVRK's at the production buildings, several huge halls, so huge that they couldn't do total damage to it all. But the explosions lit the night sky and the production would be stopped for at least a while, a fairly long while.

Silverhair was the last jumping on the bus. There hadn't been more shots from the sniper, the shithead demon. Kurt and his group had made sure of that. Judith cast one final look back at Willy's body.

His eyes… not closed. She saw the dead flare in them in the light from the natural flames, the eyes so alive such a short while ago. Her facial muscles tightened. He was dead.

– *Listen carefully,* she told them harshly, making sure everybody heard her. – We will be ghosts from now on, untouchable to everybody wanting to get to us, harder than steel to those who want to hurt us.

The wounded sat in the back of the bus. Anya and Renni tended them. Renni walked to the front and fetched Judith, bringing her back with him. She dumped down on a seat and remained there, like a doll, still like death. The fuzzy eyes sought the blood flowing from Yvonne's thigh. Anya tied a tight bandage around it. It turned red in an instant. The bus stopped. Judith noticed how pale Helene was and she wasn't physically injured. Judith knew she had the same, unhealthy skin color. But something had shaken Helene harder than any injury or death.

Kurt and others jumped on the bus, and they were all leaving.

– He escaped, he reported.

Judith managed to nod. She felt completely… disconnected.

– It was Lee Travis, Helene whispered tonelessly. Everybody heard her. – I'm positive. I saw him through the binoculars.

Everybody sensed the draft of horror, of the spiritual death.

It seems likely, Morten said, as quickly as he could. – They didn't know where we would strike, so they placed a specialist on selected places.

– He was well hidden and outside our search area, Kurt said. – He made mashed potatoes of us.

– Don't misunderstand, Gio said, just as quickly, more down than they had ever seen him. – But we were lucky as bears, getting away without major… losses.

– I think we did good, Jemma stated. – He took us with our pants down and we still got away easily. We destroyed much of the factory, too.

An ordeal, Judith thought. Jemma is correct. We did good.

She looked at Sivert. He cried quietly and the physical pain didn't really cause that. Yvonne was sweating. Both pair of eyes was misty in shock and the medication Anya had given them hadn't started working yet. She patted them on the head. The others' voices sounded farther and farther off.

So much blood, everywhere and everywhere on her. The sight of blood had never bothered her. The sight might sicken others, but not her. Never. Neither

She was nine. Little Silverhair was nine.

the time a thousand years ago, during her third year at school. Images were crystal clear to her, as if it had happened yesterday, and not twenty-four years in the past. Little Judy hadn't known much then, but she had seen and heard.

Later she learned more…

+++++++++++++++++++

Autumn 1970…

The winds of change blowing across the world for years had finally reached Norway and the city of Bergen. Bergen was nine hundred years old. It was celebrated everywhere, in the streets, at school, in all public buildings.

The Sixties, a wild and rebellious time was over and done, and the city celebrated.

Flower power and the Sixties had never quite gained a foothold in Norway. The country was too far away from important events and the people too full of themselves to notice the strange currents shown (or not) on TV. The world and Norway were changed, but it didn't dawn on most Norwegians until long afterwards. It took ten years before the local public monopoly broadcasting started playing hard rock. The music revolution passed them by, just like the attempts at doing one that was more extensive and meaningful. San Francisco, the Chicago-uprising, Paris, Mai Lai and everything were merely names to most people. In the world at large the oppressed rose in a common goal of justice, freedom and happiness, and were met with closed fists everywhere. In Norway there were just a few attempting to break the vicious circle. Most were cowed after a brief stint at verbal resistance. Some, on the other hand kept fighting…

And they paid the price.

The philosophers and rebels Lene and Ketil drove in their stolen car on the road to Loddefjord, the narrow, uneven road that would become so broad and even twenty years later. They had passed Laksevåg a while back when they sensed the bad vibes inside and heard the distant sound of sirens, a sound quickly growing in strength and importance. Vibes and fears turned to certainty.

– I was right, Ketil said bitterly. – The guy at the gas station recognized us. He was quite simply too polite under that short, pointed hair.

He increased the speed. She opened the compartment before her, revealing the guns. She looked inquisitive at him.

– We won't need them, right? He looked inquisitive back at her and flashed his teasing warm smile. – Throw them away.

They had never shot anyone, even though it had been close on occasions. She threw both weapons out of the window, into the bushes and the ditch.

– I've never been to these parts before, she noted. – Have you? Do you know where we're going?

– I've passed through here a few times, he replied. – We should be able to avoid them.

The school was just in the thick of where the huge, cold shopping mall and suburb grew and spread like cancer.

Little Judy stretched her tall and thin body in front of the blackboard. Miss Larsen, the teacher always asked, what she saw as a courtesy if the pupils wanted to sit by their desk instead of doing their written reply on the blackboard. But Judy didn't mind. The incredulity she read in Miss Larsen's eyes kept surprising her, even if she often heard what a «precocious little girl» she was, whatever that meant. In truth it didn't bother her, but she had been born with an irresistible curiosity and decided to look up the word in her dictionary at some point.

Sunrays brightened the room through the narrow chinks of the blinds. She sighed. It was such a fine day. She wondered why the teachers wanted them to hide from it. It would be too hot if the Sun shone straight through the windows, Miss Larsen had told them, and they couldn't open the windows because the wind blew from the north and smell from «some factories» in Skålevik would reach them. Judy didn't really get that either. Was it the wind or the smell there was something wrong with? She made one of her (un)usual leaps of logic, and asked why the factories weren't shut down.

Miss Larsen didn't appreciate her wit.

– That will be enough, young lady. You're confined to the hallway for the rest of the day. You may sit there and consider your words.

The adult woman stood there, red faced and more than a bit… *excited.* The kids laughed. More confused than ever, Judy wanted to ask the teacher what there was to consider, but brokenhearted and fearful in her wisdom the girl kept her mouth shut and prepared to obey, to leave the room, when they all heard it: the sound of screaming tires.

Ketil had planned on driving to a place where they could hide the car and escape into the woods, but patrol cars approached them from all sides.

When he discovered an army of them coming at them straight ahead he pushed the breaks hard and turned, practically on two wheels into the schoolyard. He stopped in front of the main building.

– Why did you choose this place? Lene asked softly. – This place… to stop?

– I… don't know, he replied hesitatingly. Then he turned towards her and took her hands. – This is it. There's no chance of escape.

– I know. She smiled. – We should never have spent the night in Kosher's house. It's strange how fate works sometimes. We didn't just piss him off, but saw far more than we were supposed to.

– Done is done, he said lightly. – I'm just sorry you became involved in it.

– Don't be silly! She reprimanded him, just as softly. – I'm not a frail flower in need of protection.

There were more screaming tires, a lot more. Cars and uniforms rushed in from all sides. Policemen charged forward with drawn guns. The two youths emerged from the vehicle with their arms above their head.

– We surrender, Ketil shouted loud and clear. – WE SURRENDER!

– THEY ARE ARMED! A man clothed in uniform screamed insanely. – SHOOT TO KILL!

– NO! Lene and Ketil screamed, turning and running automatically. They had almost reached the entrance when Lene was hit in the back.

She fell. He threw himself down by her side.

– Leave me, she insisted. – Go alone.

– Never, he said teeth gritting. – Get up!

He pulled her up and supported her, and they charged inside the building. He tore open the closest door. A teacher and an entire room of children stared at them. Lene lost her balance, and he lifted her up. He carried her to a corner and lowered her to the floor. His remaining strength faded quickly. She almost slipped from his grip the last few centimeters.

– Young man… Miss Larsen exclaimed, in spite of her probably being a bit younger than him.

She was sweating. Lene was sweating. It seemed like she was bleeding from all over her body. He could see the light fade in and out in her eyes. She was dying. He locked eyes with the teacher.

– Do you think you'll be able to keep your intolerance in check a few minutes? He begged her, snarled to her. – Make sure they won't go near her?

The woman nodded, angry and shocked. She nodded again, firmly.

– Don't leave me, Lene gasped to him. – Help me stand on my feet.

He shook his head. She understood and nodded.

He surveyed the room, meeting the eyes of some of the pupils and suddenly turned dizzy. Especially two of the little girls… He remembered… He had told Lene once:

Paths that cross, cross again. Paths that cross, will cross again.

He tore down the blinds and looked outside, pushed open the window. No cops in sight. Good. He smiled and smiled to the skinny rascals standing by the desk he was standing on.

– This is for you. He handed her his black, flat-brimmed hat.

Judy accepted it, wide-eyed. A swift move, a swing of his body, and he was gone. He had jumped. There was a long way down and he landed hard, but managed to stay on his feet. Judy leaned forward, well out of the open window, and followed him with her eyes as he ran, ran like the wind.

Miss Larsen tore off her jacket and turned it into a pillow under Lene's head. Lene gasped and gasped, striving to breathe.

– He… won't be b-back. We both know that. I've always admired him for his… clear thinking.

Judith sat on the floor in the bus, patting Yvonne's head. Eyes didn't blink. Not once. Was this life? Death? Suffering and mutilation? Memory showed her crystal clear images from the moment she had witnessed death for the first time.

Judy saw red color (like in the butcher shop) erupt from the body of the big boy. He kept running. It cracked many times. He fell to his knees. The cops lined up around him and took aim.

NO! She couldn't tell if it was he or she who shouted it or shouted it in the mind.

He dressed strangely, she thought. She liked it, in a way. It was cute. His eyes were sad, but the spirit in them wasn't broken, not in any way, and not in death. She would remember those eyes… or rather the expression in them?

She would remember… forever.

Tears flowed down the child's cheeks. In the days and weeks to come they were told that the boy and the girl had been very bad and had threatened to hurt them all.

– NO! She shouted. – The policemen are bad. Very bad!

STUPID SILVERHAIR STUPID SILVERHAIR

In the months and years to come the cries had increased, both in strength and number.

– Stupid Silverhair. Stupid Silverhair. Stupid Silverhair.

STUPID SILVERHAIR STUPID SILVERHAIR

CHAPTER FIFTEEN

She saw the cops take aim and shoot him to pieces. She saw it time and time again. The first time she saw death. There had been more times since.

She awoke with a sharp pull. Eyes opened wide.

Yvonne held her arm hard. Yvonne… sat by her side on the train, on the train to… On the other side of the table sat Kees and Corbin.

– Are we there soon?

– We'll be arriving Central Station in Amsterdam in… five minutes, Kees replied dryly.

Judith dried the film of cold sweat from her skin. There were no tears. Only fluid from her tear canals when she was yawning extra hard and she did so rarely.

The truth, as it had been explained to her by parents/teachers and police/authorities hadn't appealed to little, innocent Judy. The real truth she hadn't heard until long afterwards by a close friend of Lene and Ketil, a teacher and friend both: Jonas Bergli. She had up to that point been digging and asking questions on her own, and received nothing but evasive answers.

She had asked in class what punishment the bad men butchering the boy and girl would receive. She used the word «butcher» because she had been to a farm and seen it being done there. She hadn't enjoyed it then either and screamed like hell. Then they had patiently explained to her that animals were animals and that this wasn't done to humans. The other kids had cackled wildly while she had presented her thorough reasoning. Miss Larsen had laughed, too, but then she had smiled and given the correct interpretation.

Judy hadn't quite realized what «butchered» or «killed» or especially «dead» entailed then, but understanding came later, with the ruthless teasing and bullying. She had always been different, but hadn't turned less «strange» from what the entire school should have been able to se.

She grew up in Loddefjord's concrete hell, a place with hard and sharp edges, turning increasingly worse as everybody looked away. The feeble attempts at improvement just made things worse. Bushes of blocks made by concrete and glass rose towards the distant sky in the local suburb. People moved into tiny boxes and fooled themselves into believing they were living a good life. They said nothing aloud, but deep within they knew it was Death. The sneaky sort, allowing people to move and breathe long after the decay had started in their core.

During adolescence she had had some contact with Beate, a girl who had also been present the day Lene and Ketil had stumbled into the classroom.

But Beate's parents had moved away, and taken her with them.

Judith met Jonas Bergli the year she turned fifteen, two years before he returned and «fetched» her. She visited a café with a bunch of punk rockers, and heard him speak about Lene and Ketil with someone by the neighboring tables.

«You chose yourselves», Bergli had told his seven students after one of the many times they had asked him why *them?* They had chosen themselves by reacting strongly against the world's injustice and bondage.

She looked down at her hands, raised her head once again. Willy was dead. Gone! Life went on. It wasn't a matter of what he would have wanted or not. The decision was hers. She felt relaxed, ready to whatever might come, whatever she might choose.

Kurt met them at the station. She hardly recognized him. He had become so damn good at disguising himself that she occasionally doubted he recognized himself.

– May I tempt you with the scenic tour?

He revealed his fangs. His sense of humor had been deeply buried for a while, but now it slowly reemerged.

They left the station, walking outside, into the afternoon city, the darkness and the neon lights. Central Amsterdam was small compared to the actual size of the city and that of other major cities. Everything was sort of packed tight. This was both good and bad, as far as they were concerned. The many narrow alleys, packed with people made it an easy task to hide, but more difficult to keep watch. Judith easily spotted Gio and Karine on the opposite sidewalk, but not when they were a bit ahead or behind. The city was a cauldron. There was vitality here one usually only experienced in London or Berlin. It had within its borders both the worst and best, and most of what was in-between, of humanity. The sense of freedom was so pervasive that it was almost visible in the air. Censorship was an unfamiliar if not unknown concept here, even though money ruled, also in this particular stone desert. Everything was offered for sale and measured, appraised. Everything was just business. Many things not negative in itself were used and exploited.

– By damn, I do believe they sell illegal substances on every street corner, Judith exclaimed. – Great!

– It becomes ever harder for the establishment in other places to claim that Amsterdam has a drug problem, Kurt stated empathically. – If there are any problems at all they are far less than in other cities, in spite of the far greater availability.

Corbin made a face, a grin only a little bittersweet, embracing his surroundings with outstretched hands.

– There is freedom here, but corrupted by the thoroughly corrupt society it exists within. Everything turns sour when humans live far from their natural surroundings, far from… life.

– True! Yvonne sniffed. – Poetic, but true.

They laughed and reaffirmed yet again within themselves, dwelling on the bittersweet moment… how good it was to live.

Judith and her fellow travelers penetrated deeper into Red Light District, passing the crimson glow in the windows and those hanging above the canals. In the windows the living dolls sat on display, exhibiting their values. The majority was forced to sit there and the rest sat there under some kind of duress, «voluntary forced». The prostitutes making money, those at least partly independent weren't here, but worked in exclusive clubs and locales far more tempting then this.

Ten years ago Silverhair might have reacted more harshly and immediate to what she saw, but she was tempered now, stronger. She was able to hold herself back, allowing the rage to grow, saving it for an unspecified future moment.

The smell of food lingered in the air. The scent of spices, along with far easier to identify aromas flowed through every street. They walked across the bowed bridge and returned along the canal with red lights dancing above the water. They were in no way the only people walking in circles in this place, and drew no attention whatsoever to themselves. There were a majority of males here, but a surprisingly large female continent. Elsewhere in the city, like in the area around Central Station the number of the sexes was fairly equal.

By the end of a main street a group of christians had taken possession of a major area, really making a spectacle of themselves. Three young women and one young man accompanied two older, stern men.

– Turn your back to Sin, one of the women cried in a loud, clear voice. – Don't let it gain on you.

– Why not? Silverhair asked her. They stopped just in front of the stall. – What's wrong with breaking christianity and religion's narrow morality?

– What do you… mean?

The woman looked stunned at her.

– You know very well what I mean, honey. A forceful voice cut through them all. – You know that the freedom here isn't wrong, that it is, on the contrary, natural and right. You want to attack what is destroying what is natural and right. What you perhaps haven't fully realized is that you, by your deeds are supporting what is destroying and corrupting, that religion and society keep going, greasing what is wrong also in this place. You're merely attacking one symptom of many, while the disease itself is spreading.

Silverhair saw the doubt she had sensed in the innocent eyes. The woman froze in her tracks. She blinked once.

– What are you yapping about?

One of the other women, a bit older charged forward like a panther.

– This… Silverhair indicated her surroundings with a hand, – … is just business. The people behind it are of the opinion that everything can be bought and sold. Money isn't directly at fault. Money is also a symptom. Both things and individuals are *merchandise*. And that's the attitude we must fight.

– Like jesus in the temple, Kurt added cheerfully.

Judith smiled. Kurt understood her so well that she on occasion believed he was a mind reader.

She saw recognition in the younger woman's eyes.

– You are… you are, the blonde stuttered.

Judith sighed. Perhaps it had been a mistake to just use the black wig and a bit of make up as a disguise. She had become quite famous, or rather infamous, depending on viewpoint.

– What's your name? She asked the young girl.

– That is Silverhair, one in the crowd stated empathically. – I'm damn positive.

– Jannicke Martens, the girl whispered. – Jannicke…

– Let us get the hell away from here, Kees said, clearly worried.

– Do you want to join us, Jannicke? We can show you the sights.

Jannicke thought that sounded strange. These people were foreigners and she had grown up in this town, after all. But… in a way… there was a kind of logic to it.

– Desist, Jezebel, one of the older men thundered.

Both had stepped forward and placed themselves on both sides of the girl, protective, judgmental, forceful. Judith expected to see a garlic-stinking cross at any minute. She kept her calm and just looked at Jannicke Martens.

– I'm of legal age. The girl pushed herself through the two walls of men. – I'm free to do as I wish, right?

– Thank god, Kurt sighed. – God's will be done.

– I know you want to hold her back, Silverhair told them. – But is that truly wise… here?

– LET THEM TRY! An excited youth in the crowd howled.

Two men dressed as civilians, clearly police officers talked very excited in a radio. Kurt grinned. He waved to them.
– I'm not being kidnapped, Jannicke shouted. – Everybody present is a witness to the fact that I'm leaving of my own accord.
– If you leave, there will never again be a place for you here, the other older big man hissed hatefully.
– That's okay, she said. – I will never return. I… reproach myself for not noticing the hatred in your eyes a long time ago.
– I have always had my doubts about you. He spat his poison at her. – Sin has danced in your eyes.
She ran after Silverhair. Free. Sudden, uncompromising, inevitable. She was in good shape, but had to strive real hard to keep up with the others and that was okay. There hadn't been too much uncertainty in her life before this.
They slowed down. She had to work hard to keep the others' slow pace. She was that excited and that worried. After they had turned some corners Silverhair stopped her with a soft touch.
– I'm Judith, Silverhair said, offering her hand.
Jannicke took it.
– I know, she said with blushing cheeks.
– These four rascals are Kurt, Yvonne, Kees and Corbin…
– In here, Kurt said muted.
They moved on and rushed through dark, narrow alleys. As soon as they knew they didn't have obtrusive and close company they stopped.
– You're blond, Silverhair said. – That's good.
– What…
Judith removed her black wig and long, red hair flowed down her back. The wig she pushed down on Jannicke's head. Kurt made her eyebrows darker with a small brush. Everybody turned their jackets inside out, and the clothes suddenly had changed both color and shape. One was given to Jannicke and she put it on.
– That should do it, Kees stated somewhat pleased. – We've got time for more, but let's save it.
Less than a minute later they had reached Amstel. Judith stopped Jannicke a moment and pushed a blond lock under the wig. They kept going in the same, pleasant pace along the broad canal.
The girl took in stride the relaxed walk and the others' calm… the first, few minutes, but she turned visibly nervous after a while.
– Shouldn't you… we think about disappearing?
– You have no idea how often I have been «recognized» one place, while being far away. Judith calmed her. – If what we witnessed had been seen as

a positive identification we would have been forced to deal with a full-fledged mobilization by now.

– And the nice men on the corners would have dispersed with the wind, Corbin whispered conspiratorially.

She looked shyly at him. He was about her age and not so fearsome as the others. Then she looked carefully at the street corners, where many different kinds of people were lined up. Some smoked something, others didn't, but they laughed and joked more or less with each other. She moved her eyes from them to those she suspected ever stronger would be her companions for the rest of her life. It surprised and even to a point stunned her how long she had pondered doing what she had just done. The difficulty had been to break out of confines, her familiar surroundings. She had needed a push.

She followed them through the once so familiar streets, and she experienced a vastly different city.

It felt so incredibly strange. She wondered if her senses had turned that much sharper from one moment to the next.

– Don't your eyes hurt? She asked with both innocence and sharp irony. – I mean… the way you keep moving them…

– She's bright, isn't she? Corbin joked without sting.

The others chuckled softly.

The laughter echoed through the streets. It echoed through the room in *Tenrec,* a semi-respectable bar and restaurant on the east side, where they had their dinner. It was quiet and empty in the streets outside, but inside people filled the place to the brim. Kimberly and Kathy served there. Like the other employees they didn't look too busy. One couldn't help noticing a remarkable excess of waitresses, waitresses with clothing that wasn't very excessive at all.

– They had no problems getting… hired? Judith let her snout slide into the beer foam.

– The supervisor took one look at them. Kurt grinned, both pleased and sober. – And practically begged them to let themselves be hired.

Whatever went on here, in the tavern's dark corner the mood lingered in the air, thick and musky. The place's furniture, food and drink, its impressions and sound played their senses. The music was Bruce Springsteen's almost ten year old live box set, 1975 - 1985. Judith allowed herself to be seduced by the music, by everything, by the time machine, a portal back to the past. She knew better than most people that «the good old days» weren't really that good, that the impression was more or less caused by a selective memory, but she still drifted off, in the music and the senses, and Kim's moves. The way she danced and served simultaneously was even more gracious and hot, now, compare to how it had been during the nights inside the Green Rose. And she was warm. So warm that even the most insensitive in the room sensed *something*. Judith knew fully well that it would be wrong to claim that the violence and death hadn't done anything to Kim.

But it hadn't penetrated her core. The blood kept boiling uninhibited in her veins.

Judith attempted to swallow the catching in her throat. It seemed like it was always there, the catching. She tried to recall if it had been there right after Willy's death.

She couldn't do it.

– Why did you pick me? Jannicke asked, clearly tense. – Please, tell me!

– It was an impulse, a spur of the moment decision, Silverhair replied, shrugging deliberately indifferent. – We have learned to trust our instincts.

– I heard that one of you was killed. Jannicke stared hard at the floor. – It made me cold inside. I don't know if I can kill anyone, even to save my own life.

– Well… Silverhair spoke with a soft smile. – There are many things you can do in the world besides being a terrorist.

– Perhaps I can help with something anyway?

– You can, but you can't join us.

– I want to join you.

She spoke so sudden and impulsively that she wasn't even certain she had spoken. She knew she had decided long ago, earlier today, when she had parted with her old non-life, her old self, and had run away with the pack.

– Are you certain? Kees warned her. – We will be probing your reasons for joining, the fact that you made up your mind so fast. Our initiation is unorthodox, harsh and cruel. We must be certain you're able to kill before you can join us in *anything*. We must be certain of many things.

– We've got absolutely nothing to worry about, Silverhair said patronizingly. – Little sweet doll wants to play. The need is burning inside her.

– *Are you sure?* Kees asked.

– I understand, Jannicke said with eyes of glass. – I'm sure.

The truth was that they had followed her through trusted proxies over a considerable amount of time. They had studied her thoroughly and personally since Kurt and his group had arrived in town. Only the way they had picked her up had been impulsive. They had confidence in their instincts and methods and their initial judgment call. The five nightravens saw her as a mirror in which they could see themselves. If she wasn't the real thing they would find out soon enough.

– Do the lords and ladyships desire more beer? Kim towered above them, smiling sweetly. – If you want to be served by me you'll have to decide quickly, since I will soon be leaving the ship for the day.

With the black hair covering her brows and the Chinese dress she looked like a full-blooded East Asian. The make up enhanced those features, and except for her height hid the most visible traits she had inherited from her biological father.

– We wouldn't dream of ordering from any other than you, my beauty, Kurt stated cheerfully.

Jannicke was busy in her own mind. So many thoughts raged through her head that she could hardly hold on to any of them. These people seemed so free to her, both together and as individuals. She knew such impressions could be traitorous, but not here. Not among them.

– Dance? Corbin stood and reached out a hand to her.

– I don't know… she hesitated, casting longing looks at the wild, sensual, abandon dance.

– Come, he said playfully. As if in a dream she reached out her own hand, and let him take it. – We must all lose ourselves to find ourselves, right?

It struck her after just a few steps: he was so cautious, so overly kind to her. The movements he made her do weren't in any way… provocative, at least not compared to those made by the people whirling across the floor around them.

He treats me like china, she thought.

She threw herself impulsively, resolute at him, and kissed his lips greedily, held on to him, wouldn't let him go, wouldn't let go of anything. The dance turned wild, uncontrollable. She was like a different person, now, here, under the black wig she glimpsed in the mirrors. The surroundings slowly faded. Just parts of the lyrics and the music echoed within her, in the words he whispered in her ear.

– *We are strands of fire burning in the night. If that is pain, then let me burn. Dark secrets rule us. The more we understand, the more we burn. We are shadows spitting fire in eternity.*

– So poetic, she whispered back. A tear hit his shoulder.

The music sounded different now. Darker, mystical… Light seemed muted. It was. She was able to see the glow in his eyes and her own. Sin danced in her eyes.

– *We are the children of fire, he whispered.* She took a deep breath and opened her eyes wide. – *The fire can never be put out. Phoenix will always rise from the ashes.*

– *Little sister wants to dance. Dance all the way.*

– Are you sure? He asked uncertain.

– I'm sure. Soft, wet lips brushed his.

One single decision, a lifetime worth of consequence.

Jannicke Martens felt the fire inside, now, and for the first time it didn't frighten her. But in the small room upstairs when it grew to unimaginable, unbearable proportions she wanted nothing more than to extinguish it. But afterwards, when it was done and as it quickly progressed and grew even more, it felt so good, so great she swore she would never let it fade again.

Canals and streets passed by, so fast, so very, very fast, like in a rollercoaster. Every calm moment was just a premonition of a bigger fall. Dizziness overwhelmed her.

– I'm drunk, she giggled.

– For the first and last time in your life, Yvonne laughed.

Amsterdam had hundreds of squatted houses and buildings. If truth should be told (and it should) no one had the exact number, but it had to be close to thousand. Youths arrived here from the entire continent, the entire world, and quite simply moved in, with or without permission.

– Isn't it risky for us to stay in a house with so many unknown people? Jannicke asked, more curious than worried.

– There is a risk. Silverhair nodded. – But we run risks all the time, no matter where we are. And we see this as one of our «safe» houses.

– So, how about the Tenrec supervisor, your new boss? Kees asked Kim and Kathy. – Any problems?

– He suggested a threesome, Kathy grinned. – «To make it easier for us girls to adapt to future demands». You should have seen his face when Kim told him she didn't like men in her bed, and I reminded him he had hired us as barmaids.

– That the truth, Kim said from the back. – I not a needy girl. I not interested in a big, soft bed and lots of money.

The rain started abruptly as they parked in the yard outside the derelict office building. They rushed through the doorless doorway. Outside the torrential rain already hammered at the roof. There was a hole in the makeshift cover just inside the entrance, where water had already started flooding through.

– We've got our own little private waterfall here, Kurt said, quite unnecessary to Jannicke. – Isn't it great?

The «reception hall» had a sense of former greatness. The walls were decorated with raincoats and drawings inside glass displays, and other assorted rarities like a paper thermometer. The waterfall increasing by the second fit in well. A smiling Jannicke shook her head in bemusement.

A woman with a stern expression met them. After the greeting she cast a critical look at Jannicke.

– This is the new recruit? She said, evidently filled with righteous doubt. – Doesn't look like much.

– Reneè, this is Jannicke, Judith presented. – I'm sure Jannicke is pleased to meet you, too…

– I have a black belt in karate. Jannicke stated firmly, just slightly subdued. – I won't be a burden.

– We know we can trust you, Janni, Silverhair said. – We know a lot about you already, and soon, very soon, now, we'll know everything.

Janni stared at her. Judith was very nice and Janni liked her just as much as she had thought she would do. But sometimes… she could be downright *terrifying*.

There were leaks all over the place, leaks through the ceiling, from pipes and such. Not as extensive as in the hall, but noticeable. There were a lot of band-aids, attempting to keep the leaks from leaking, in vain. It was warm and cozy, though. Many people lived under the same roof, without it becoming impersonal. Janni felt surrounded by a bunch that all wanted to show her the sights. And they were in no way intrusive. She felt safe.

The song, the dance and the music surrounded her from all sides, and she forgot the last stray thought as well. She had stopped seeking safety the easily identifiable moment earlier that day.

– *We are eagles*. She sang with a momentary clear-sight, the words erupting from the larynx, from somewhere deep within herself. – *Floating over rugged cliff, birds flying in the dark.*

She whirled round and round with others while there were people standing in a circle around them, singing. She clapped her hands and shouted out loud in joy, hardly aware of what she was doing. She felt so welcome, and it was all true, not at all like the systematic hypocrisy she had experienced in the christian «fellowships».

Short of breath and with a hectic red in her cheeks from the great excitement she sat down and took a break.

Why me, and not one of all those other people, here and elsewhere? She asked Kim Russel in a quieter moment.

– They won't use physical violence, Kim replied. – We respect each other, at least to a point, even though we disagree on method. But that's only a part of the explanation, of course…

– Yes? Janni pressed on when the other hesitated.

Kim touched her jaw and she didn't feel intimidated by it.

– You've sought and found other places like this and they haven't satisfied you. That's no coincidence. You've got something, a restlessness lacking in others, a kind of despair and a fire that must be released. They don't hate enough, love enough, aren't desperate enough. You do, you are.

We saw the signs in you instantly. They aren't difficult to notice. Not… to us.

There was sadness underlying the kind smile. Janni understood a bit of that, she believed.

– You didn't pick me from the street at random, she stated as a fact, with just a minor shudder in her voice.

– From now on there will be nothing but complete honesty between us.

That sounded ominous as well as comforting. Like Kim certainly had meant it to be.

Then she smiled some more. She smiled a lot. Janni… liked that.

As the night darkened the air more «guests» arrived. Janni recognized Giovanni Rossi, Helene Valin, Karine Lie and a few more. The room turned quiet. Sound faded to silence. Yes, that was how she experienced it. The mood changed, to a mix of expectation and a kind of worry, echoing Janni's own thoughts.

Janni… She was Janni, now, Janni of the Green Rose. Her old life didn't exist anymore. Soon she would no longer be a stranger to these people. Soon, she would be a Stranger, like the nineteen other unified members of the Green Rose.

– We're here to welcome our latest, rough diamond. Jemma Elvir spoke. – To do our best to make her one of the few, the proud shining jewels in the dark night. Dreams belong to the night.

– DREAMS BELONG TO THE NIGHT, thundered through the air.

How many people were present? There had to be well above fifty, closer to hundred. But Janni didn't feel her shout was in any way overwhelmed. It sounded, on the contrary strong and powerful. She had heard the sentence spoken before, too, heard it thundering through the night, but this was the first time she had dared participate herself, making the entire world hear her cry.

– We're the ravens of the night, the Nightravens, Jemma stated proudly. – One part of many of the Green Rose.

Janni had heard that name, too. It didn't matter. Names meant little.

Or so much. A taken name meant far more than one given by birth, given by others.

– She has seen how the world can be, has looked at it with longing in her eyes. Silverhair rose and stood straight. It looked like she filled the room. Janni stared admiringly at her. – Janni, come here.

The girl stepped over the floor towards the waiting impatient giant.

– It's important that you get more than a passing glance of the coin's other side.

The girl shrunk under the burning look. She felt like kneeling, but remained stubbornly on her feet.

If she had knelt they wouldn't have accepted her, she was certain of that much.

– Anya.

A hooded figure with coal black hair and a body swept in a wide cloak walked through a door Janni hadn't known was there, that she still could hardly glimpse. This would be the Sorceress, a shadow, a legend within the greater legend. Around her neck she carried an Ankh, a piece of jewelry, an Egyptian, pre-christian symbol of eternal life. This would be a mystical ceremony, created with a certain goal in mind, but there was no mystery, not here. That would come later, during the initiation, she reflected.

– Our little sister standing here has chosen to live by the sword. That's both a very right and a very wrong decision. We can't do anything but support her through her life, support her as best we can, through a life filled with danger and strife. *We are the Green Rose.*

– THE GREEN ROSE

– So, do you have anything to say for yourself? Heike asked her.

– Yes, she replied quickly. Her mind was completely blank. She didn't know shit about what she was about to say, except that it erupted from her depth. – I no longer believe there is a god, any god. Perhaps I've never believed, except as a cheap convenience.

– Good. Come.

The sorceress didn't take her hand, but she still felt like she was led, led, pulled by what burned inside to the hidden hall, shuttered and dank.

Was it? Was it really? She found herself in what she felt was its center. No windows. No walls, floor or ceiling, just old, long rags hanging from somewhere. A vast space suggested itself to her. Several walls, floors and ceilings had been removed here, at some point, to make room.

One by one the few lights were put out. She stood in stark darkness. Jesus, someone here had to be an excellent production designer or something. If they had wanted to make the place scary, they had succeeded one hundred and ten percent. Suddenly everything was terrifying.

She wanted to speak, wanted it desperately, but all words had been stuck in her throat, all expression hidden within.

A light was lit. It was directed straight at her, at her eyes. She didn't dare look away. Another light was lit. She hadn't heard them enter. They stood in front of her in a cluster, the nineteen that had been twenty.

– Undress, Kurt commanded in a chilling voice.

Kurt, who always had a joke, a kind smile on hand. She gasped and obeyed. She hesitated a bit, before pulling down her panties, too. They stared at her with a blank expression, black, judgmental eyes, like an incarnation of the Spanish inquisition. She lowered her eyes, like a young farmer girl accused of witchcraft.

– Look at her, Kim hissed. – How she enjoys revealing herself.

– Sin dances in the tramp's eyes, Morten stated, very judgmental. – She is Lost.

They approached her. She glimpsed a horrible black mask, before they pushed it down her head. She felt ropes tighten around her wrists. *Tighten.* There was a final moment of light, where she in truth saw nothing but the mirror image of her own pale, sweaty face. Then the mask's collar tightened around her neck. Everything turned black. There was nothing there, nothing more. She stood rigid, alone in the black darkness.

And the screams began.

A figure, a creature sat relaxed and half dozing inside a circle of attentive listeners.

– What I felt during the… examination? I tell you, as you know it was no pleasant experience. I discovered things about myself that I hardly knew were there. And I realized what was important in my life, past, present and future… I feel that it eventually turned out to be a positive experience. Because when I found my inner strength I didn't know was there, and it was *crushed* I found more. An inexhaustible well that was only me, that will always remain.

She stood naked by the window in the gray morning light. She had no idea what morning, what day. It hurt terribly. Her body was beaten badly and skin hurt everywhere. And she felt it. Anya Kerien rubbed relieving and cooling ointments on her skin, anointing her haunted soul.

– This isn't so bad, Anya told her softly, soothing. – We've learned to limit the injuries. It used to take us almost a month to heal properly.

– I failed, the girl said with a faltering voice. – I sang like a bird.

– We all failed, Anya said. – Everybody can be broken, and now you know.

They had kept her captive in that horrible dark cellar hour by hour, year by year, and she had told them everything they wanted to know, and more. She had told them everything. Afterwards she had talked about everything on her mind, in her heart, talked for so long. And it had felt so good. The body hurt, but inside she felt like after hard exercise. She felt good. All in all she *felt* so much more. As if she had expunged a lot of… waste. Things that didn't belong there, the waste society had dumped at her most valuable spots. The bad she had experienced earlier in life seemed distant now and her resolve just increased.

– Nothing has changed, she said incredulous. – Only been enhanced. Perception is… just *phenomenal.*

She choked stunned, a marvelous, deep and uplifting experience.

– The sword has been laid bare. Now only the final touch remains.

– And what is that, the final touch?

– Nobody knows, Anya said. – It's different from person to person. But you will know when it happens.

Experienced hands removed the bloody bandage around the wrist. Janni carefully touched the cut. It didn't hurt much anymore and had already closed. It wasn't swollen. Anya lubricated the inflamed skin with herbs and put on a new bandage. Janni couldn't take her eyes off her. The dark, black-eyed woman seemed almost… almost stranger now, compared to when Janni had seen her in the shadows earlier. The fair-haired girl blushed slightly. Good. She didn't know much shame anymore. There was no way she could have brought herself to stare this way at another person before, before all this.

She lowered her eyes, raised them again with tight-woven lips.

– One of the worst things you did to me was when Corbin was… cross with me. I had come closer to him and was vulnerable to his actions. I know how kind he is, and that just made it worse.

– Clever girl. A pat on the cheek. – You'll be easy to teach.

– You will be… my teacher?

– We will all be that, but most and foremost you will be your own teacher and your own master.

Subconsciously the girl moved her hand from the white cloth around the wrist and up her arm, to the uncanny green rope encircling it.

– Is it tight? Anya asked. – Does it hurt?

– It feels good, Janni replied. She pushed her arm at that of the black Irish, and their ropes touched. Anya smiled and nodded.

– We've followed you from the cradle and will follow you to the grave, Judith had stated at some indefinite point during the eternal night.

She had received their blood, their communion, and they had received hers.

These people demanded nothing of her. Nothing she didn't demand of herself.

She stared out of the window at the horizon, where the Sun was about to break through thick clouds. Suddenly she didn't give a fuck about what day it might be.

– Isn't it a wonderful morning?

She leaned at the window. The entire wonderful and terrible world waited out there.

She blinked slowly.

– … sleepy. She felt she moved so very, very slowly when looking startled at the Druid. Cold trickled through her. – Like a vampire at sunrise.

– It's the ointment, Anya explained. She supported her to the bed and put her on it. – There wouldn't have been any pleasant sleep for you without it. You'll wake up healthy and rested. Well, as good as healthy, anyway…

Janni fell asleep with a smile and worry in her face. Anya tucked her in. The blankets embraced her on all sides.

– Youthful and with youthful optimism. That's good. That the sleeper awakens doesn't always lead to good things. Then there is a major advantage in being able to see the light from the deepest well. Your naiveté persists. But don't worry, we will rip it out of you while there is still time.

Anya watched over the girl until her breathing turned even and silent. A twitch showed in the remarkable face, while she stared at the other, at the sleeping beauty.

So innocent. There wasn't more than a twelve-year difference in age between them (not much at all), but an entire life in mentality. That difference would be lessened quickly. If little sister lived that long.

– You will sleep. The voice was deep, coarse. – You will dream and you will be transformed.

Anya bent down and kissed the pale skin on the forehead, a comforting feather-like touch. Then she left the room, so quickly and silent that the dreamer wouldn't have noticed, even if she hadn't fallen deep into sleep, hadn't levitated into distant Night.

+++++++++++++++++++

Morten and Yvonne wolfed down an early dinner at Tenrec. The place had a considerable number of visitors even at this time of day, but wasn't as hectic, as noisy as it could be during the evening and night. The two had to be constantly on guard, as always, but when the crowd was less of a crowd they allowed themselves to be less aware for a short while.

Outside on the other hand, there was clearly a higher degree of activity, now, during daylight. People chased by, chased to and from work, even from a shopping trip, totally stressed out. Morten shook his head. Those who had both time and opportunity to enjoy life didn't, while Morten and Yvonne, and brothers and sisters in peril who didn't have the time, did. It was all so very ironic.

– Perhaps it's true, he noted. – People need to live dangerously to fully enjoy life.

– I think you've got a point there, she nodded, something catching in her throat again.

He had seen them everywhere, the people to and from work. On the trains, buses, behind wheels… exhausted to the point of falling asleep every quiet moment they could find. People tired of life before they had lived at all, not really seeing what was wrong, while searching for meaning in their meaningless existence.

– Civilization destroys everything making life worth living, he said to her. – Everything valuable is devoured, by the meat grinder that never stops grinding.

– It's true! She stated it with pain in her every feature. – One can't possibly, simply put go too far in one's fight to put a *stop* to that. No way!

Kim and Kathy served thirsty customers, customers constantly thirsty. It was easy to tell these two had experience in serving. The difference was plain between them and the other «waitresses». Then again, most of them didn't earn their living by serving *beer*. Morten smiled softly. People frequenting the Green Rose would certainly have recognized Kim's eminent technical prowess.

Time passed for him. Time didn't pass, but just flew away in pleasant and interesting company. He watched her laugh, studied every nuance in her features, as the moment vanished in a puff of smoke.

He didn't have to consult his watch when the time had come for a changing of the guards. Another watch wasted.

– I like it here, Yvonne teased him. She had easily noticed his irritation. – Good food, good spirits, nice view…

He wanted to explain it to her, to explain his evident moment of anger, striving to find the words.

The Nightravens kept Tenrec under surveillance. Added to Kim and Kathy's presence at all times were two others, being present here, or in an apartment across the street. Kim and Kathy hadn't revealed, in any way their familiarity, hadn't treated their brothers and sisters different from others. The Nightravens had, all in all stuck so meticulously to plan that just coincidences could have given them away. They were getting good at this. All their considerable experience and improved instincts told them so.

Morten smiled ironically again. Careful. Overblown confidence had never led to anything good. *You should know that by now.*

He had seen Willy fall, never seen him be hit, other than in dreams. He saw it close-up, much closer to his friend than he had been in the real-life, actual event. They had all turned older and wiser during those few, critical seconds in the yard and in the dark, uneven terrain. He wondered painfully whether or not experience made a person more or less predictable. And ended up with the same conclusion he always ended up with: it depended on the person.

– Why aren't we content with good food and drink, and the view? He wondered, stunning her by taking her hand. – We've never been content with just that, have we?

– I, too, have thought about that, she admitted, glancing shyly at him, as if they had just recently met and dated for the first time. – Of course I have. I guess we all have. It doesn't have anything to do with unselfishness. I see the very word as a contradiction in terms. But I do believe a person somewhat in harmony with herself or himself is better suited to help others, *the way that person believes he or she can best help them.* I don't know… I believe there are several reasons. We're not a homogenous group, of course we aren't. That is the point, I guess, or one point. Nothing is, when push comes to shove fundamentally unselfish. No one does anything for the community, only for herself or himself. And I am convinced that is also the way it should be… but without the hypocrisy, bondage, taboos and boundless injustice and inequality humanity has surrounded itself with, in a beyond destructive stone desert society.

She turned eager, unnoticeable, inevitable, meeting his eyes.

– We Nightravens or Green Roses, or whatever we call ourselves - labels, like a lot in this superficial world don't matter - are willing to go that much further, to the farthest limit… and beyond, for what we feel is right. We refuse to be sucked into the maelstrom. Dreams mean more to us than ever at this stage, and we hope we'll live long enough to enjoy the fruits of their «labor».

He sat there, pondering, without pondering.

– Freedom is a black hole to those who have nothing left to lose.

Their eyes widened and hands clutched on the table.

– I'll rather feel alive for one single second than to exist as the living dead for a hundred years, she whispered.

Judith and Sivert walked through the door. A gust followed them from the street outside.

The moment died. She literally watched how he pulled back, retreated back into himself.

– Okay place, Morten shrugged, speaking to the air, not making sense, not even in his own mind.

– Oh, you. She kicked his leg under the table, chastising herself for her stupid grin, for not chasing the moment.

Good timing, he thought, and touched one eye to dry a tear of pain, the signal to Judith and Sivert that nothing of significance had occurred.

They did one more dance before leaving the place. He saw that her thigh was still stiff enough to hamper her movements, even if no one else did. They saw only the light and easy moves. She had run herself so hard after the wound had healed, so hard that it worried him. He had no doubt she was better equipped to take care of herself now, than she had ever been.

Later that day Judith and Sivert walked from Central Station, up Damrak Street. They had once again shifted position in the internal network. When they reached Amstel they stopped and looked at it, studied it for a moment or two. Out there, between Amsterdam and Rotterdam was the dam that had been called the Netherlands's foremost defense against the rising sea. Already in the fifties one sixth of the country had been flooded. Since then the sea had just kept rising and the Netherlands had made yet another concerted effort to protect itself against the inevitable.

Sivert talked, kept the conversation going. Judith feared, if she said too much the smoldering, uncontrolled rage would rise to the surface. Not directed at him, specifically, or anybody else. But present, existing like an independent creature within her, as it always had. Sometimes it slept, seemingly dormant, but it never left.

They walked arm in arm, like most young tourist couples. When they stopped they realized they were on a bridge. The mood of the place pleased them. He grabbed her head and kissed her on the lips. All of a sudden short of breath she responded. They stayed there for a while, snuggling some, before reluctantly disengaging. Silverhair didn't pull away, but stayed close, pleased by the fact that she could still feel something.

– We knew what we did, starting this, he said, suddenly in a much better mood, with something of his old flair. – It just hasn't dawned on us until now. All rebels have a better chance of succeeding if they have more than a good sense of the consequences of their actions. No one can challenge the old, stale powers of the world unpunished.

– As always your observations are spot on.

She spoke softly, apologizing in advance before she bent slightly forward and touched his shoulder. It didn't hurt anymore, but was still stiff. He shrugged, grimacing. The stiffness would go away. He had been lucky that the bullet hadn't crushed any bones. Lucky, period!

A tall, fair-haired man approached them from a corner. He spoke in a low, conspiratorial voice.

– Can I help you guys with anything? I am at your disposal with whatever you might want.

– What about some ID? Sivert asked curiously. – A complete set of papers?

– Sorry, man, not my department. The man held up his hands divertingly and vanished.

– It was mostly to get rid of him, Sivert said afterwards, without Judith saying anything. – But not only that. I'm not even close to being as good

with forgeries as Willy was and Helene is. If anything happens… to her we might need to think about alternative procuring methods.
– Use the time well, Judith said dryly, back to her usual aloof self.
He looked at her, probing her for a sign of compassion. There was none. They moved on. The girl smiled to him, as they walked arm in arm, like most tourist couples in love.
They met Heike and Jan at the pre-arranged place. The German girl and the Swedish boy sat tight on a bench, seemingly enjoying each other' company and close contact.
– … don't go there, Judith heard Heike warn him.
Heike pushed Jan away and rose.
– One phone call, she reported, standing straight. – They had nothing particular to report. From the home front I can report that it is the witch keeping the recruit company. No trouble reported anywhere.
Judith hid a smile. Heike was often serious, too serious. That could be just as dangerous as taking it too lightly would be. There were very often similarities there.
The phone booth was about ten steps from the bench. It wasn't in use for the moment.
– We've stayed in this city for a considerable time, now, and we got nothing to show for it, Heike said impatiently. – How much longer must we wait?
– We risk drowning in trouble very soon. The younger woman got her challenge met with a look hiding ruthlessness far superior to her own. She lowered her eyes, bared her neck.
The phone rang. All four froze for a moment, tensing further. Silverhair strolled to it and grabbed it.
– *Condor,* she replied, not without a certain sense of humor.
– *The carpet has fallen.* She heard the voice of Sybille, Sybille Xavier.
It was the «right» message. Any variation would have been synonymous with «no» and led to an end to the conversation. Silverhair sharpened her attention.
– We want to attack Dionysus this moment. He has already sent one cargo.
– When is the next? Judith rubbed her forehead.
– Not until tomorrow morning. There was a slight question mark there at the end.
– Wait until midnight. Silverhair made herself hard. – Then the cargo will have arrived, and everything been decided at this end, one way or another.
– Accepted, Condor, Sybille said goodbye. – Good dreams to you all.

– And to you. Judith heard the click at the other end before she put down the receiver.
– Dionysus? Heike wondered. She had listened in.
– Good ol' Sybille, was, is an archeologist, Judith explained cheerfully. – She referred to the Greek god of wine, food and joy, but like most wish fulfillers he's rich men's god.
– I… understand. Heike nodded.
Friday the major rush to Tenrec started early. Tired and exhausted people had worked the entire week and become even more downtrodden. They wandered endlessly around town, chasing cheap thrills. Everybody wanted to lose themselves to the abandon and had no idea the vultures didn't give a fuck where the bloody remains ended up. They just wanted to sink their teeth in then while they were still somewhat fresh.
The manager (in his boundless generosity) had given Kim and Kathy a break in the hard work. They weren't sure if they liked it much. He was clearly insincere and they knew he had ulterior motives.
Something was up tonight, that much was certain. They had spotted guests not guests. Quite a number of them. The owner, or rather the perceived owner, on one of his rare visits to the place had conversed eagerly with two giant bruisers and they hadn't bothered to hide the appreciative glances they gave the two women. Kathy and Kim knew they seemed younger then they actually were and that it worked to their «advantage». They knew something was up before the actual signal was given: that six of their fellow warriors were present in the room simultaneously.
They were taken to a room on the upper floor they had never been to before.
– What are we doing here? Kathy asked innocently. – We've told you we don't want to…
– That, sweetie, remains to be seen, the owner said unusually pleasant. – Wait here.
Kathy and Kim exchanged programmatic and worried looks with the two other girls present. They were left alone and all felt fear and insecurity.
– Perhaps the rugby-players come from a magazine, one of the other girls expressed hopefully. – Perhaps they will photograph us? Only that…
– Well, I for one don't care to remain here a minute longer. Kim yawned. *She looks so calm,* Kathy thought and sent her a glance of approval. – I must pee.
Kim sent Kathy, who really looked worried, a calm look, before leaving the room.

Kathy assumed they were being observed from the adjacent room, through the huge mirror on the wall. She worked hard not to stare straight at it.

Kim went straight to the owner's office. She and Kathy had been there briefly when they were hired, when he wanted them to be *kind* to him. She knocked on the door. There was no reply. She pushed the door open and hurried inside. Without wasting time she started searching the room and the drawers. She didn't have to look for long. These people were way too careless, unaccustomed to any true opposition. She opened the wall safe with ease, and found several contracts actually signed by Hugo Manning. They proved he had interests in both this and other, similar enterprises, as they had been fairly positive about all the time. He was one among many, but a major force behind this enterprise in Europe, the increasing trafficking. The owner did two account books, one official and one unofficial. They weren't that different, except that one showed a moderate profit, and the other a major one. Kim didn't have time to look thoroughly at them. She had seen more than enough. Everything was put meticulously back in place. She hurried back.

The feet returned her to the room she had left, led her into captivity. She had an almost unruly desire to return to the restaurant, and relate what she had found out, but that would ruin much, too much.

Two of the men waited relaxed in chairs. The three women were gone.

– Where have Ronette, Una and Atje disappeared to? She asked casually.

– We sent them along, one of them replied. – Both they and we were satisfied with the outcome of our conversation. We hope you will be, too.

– How old are you? The other, the dark one asked abruptly and brusquely.

A cheap trick, Kim thought.

– Twenty-two, she replied, at least a bit shyly.

She hoped she didn't exaggerate. These guys had considerable experience judging a person's age.

The blonde rose and placed himself a few steps behind her, in a manner definitely non-threatening to a young, naïve model to be.

– You're tall to be Asian. You're mixed, are you not?

– My mother is Swedish. She's a head taller than daddy.

– Excellent, the blonde stated. – I kinda like the racially mixed. They're very popular.

Kim didn't feel very tall just then. She had never allowed herself to be scared by any other man than her father earlier, but something about these two… made her shake inside. Something unrelated to their sex. It wouldn't have mattered if they had been women.

They radiated a pervasive, total ruthlessness. Other people were like nothing to them. They were so cold. She feared she would freeze if they touched her, freeze to stone. And they would, she knew that.

– Listen, perhaps I and Ronette should talk a bit.

She had played the stupid doll to this point. Perhaps it was time to display some basic ingenuity.

– What magazine…

She smelled the chloroform as his left arm embraced her neck. Perhaps she could have prevented what was happening, but she didn't try. The cloth smothered her nose and mouth. Silverhair and the others would… they would save her, save them all. She sent a pointed elbow at the man who held her. He took it on his hip, casually.

– Your body suggested you have trained Martial Arts, little doll. She heard the deep, friendly, emotionless voice fade. – You should have trained harder and better.

He touched her and froze her. Eyelids turned heavy. Arms fell. Froze her.

Come, Silverhair. Come!

She froze, crumbled in his ruthless grip, as she fell into the vast darkness, fully aware of the implications of his acts. They viewed her as little more than merchandize, one to display and supply to whoever could and would pay. She imagined how they displayed her in the modern desert wasteland somewhere, more a puppet than a human being.

Silverhair and Sivert had kept watch at the front of the building. Judith had almost walked back and forth to the point of their feet turning sore, when the communicator she carried on her hips buzzed. They had received a hand signal from Renni inside Tenrec that something was going down.

– Yes, she snapped.

– *The birds are headed for the cages*. She heard Kurt's calm voice. – *They were carried to a van with the two other girls by the icemen. Everything is under control. We have Elan, Anya, Jemma, Morten, Yvonne and Gio in three cars shadowing them.*

– Gathering, Judith commanded, far calmer than she felt.

The huge van waited for them further down the street. They were on their way the instant everybody had jumped inside and closed the doors. Each and every one of them immediately started preparing another set of weapons. They slipped out of the jackets and extra set of pants, and their light, functional clothing remained. The sound of weapons being checked and prepared kept echoing through the confined space and their focused, active minds.

– *They're on their way south,* they heard Yvonne. – *No, wait, they're turning north, northwest. They're driving in the airport lane*.

The big van, with Kees in the driver's seat reached, after a seemingly endless time the lane leading directly to Schipol airport. They left the half moon formed older Amsterdam and drove through the outer modern parts of the city. Janni sat in the seat beside Kees, quiet and timid.

– Kim and Kathy allowed themselves to be captured? She spoke Dutch.

– A calculated risk, Kees replied and smiled carefully at her.

Traffic moved slowly forward on the multi-lane road this night. To the hunters it was both an advantage and disadvantage. It made it almost impossible for the kidnappers to discover the three chase cars, but there was also a higher risk of the Nightravens losing sight of the car ahead.

– We have the back car with Yvonne and Gio in sight, Kees reported.

– Okay, slow down, Silverhair told him. – At this point we're precisely where we're supposed to be.

The three smaller cars exchanged position for the second time. Now Jemma and Morten were closest to the target.

– They're turning, Jemma's nervous voice sounded. *– We're on to them. We will lose eye contact after the next turn, but count on it being temporary.*

– You better not lose them, Judith mumbled.

– What was that, Condor? I didn't quite hear you…

– Private conversation, Kurt said, very softly. – Nothing important.

Nothing more was said. All their energy was focused on the task ahead of them.

The drive-off led them deep into the city's modern parts, street up and street down. Streets with less traffic, but with sufficient number of cars to make the tailing less then hopeless. It clearly turned more difficult. They had to stay a considerable distance behind and often they hardly glimpsed the back of the car as it turned around a corner. At one point they lost it in the next street and split up, a ball hard feeling like a small rock stuck in their throat, before rediscovering the target after a minute or so, the longest minute in their lives.

Time showed 9.30 when they entered into an area with several storage buildings, several derelict structures, emptied of people and goods. The rest well used and carefully locked.

– This must be it, Sivert nodded. – An ideal wasteland of city property.

Not much traffic. Minor disruptions. Minimal risk of exposure. Ideal for doing various businesses undisturbed.

Making it easy to slip away without a trace.

Suddenly the car vanished. One moment it was there, the next it wasn't. It turned a corner, and when Anya and Elan turned the same corner not ten seconds later it was like vanished into thin air.

– This is a full alert, Anya reported. – They've disappeared. There must be a hidden entrance somewhere. We keep driving to not cause suspicion and to make sure… about everything.

They circled back to where the others had parked. There was no need for words. During the next few minutes they established posts where they had the entire street, and the parallel streets on both sides in question under surveillance.

Behind every one of those walls, doors, windows there could be hiding enemies, ready to kill. Silverhair's eyes narrowed into chinks. They were ready for anything that could possibly be thrown at them. She had underestimated the danger one time before. She would never do so again. Neither would any of the others. She would make sure of that.

Even Janni was well trained in the weeks since her education began. She was as ready as she could possibly be, without having experienced the actual first baptism of fire.

– What are we waiting for? Jemma wondered.

– For the truck, Silverhair replied with a patience she in no way felt. – It might have arrived already, but we wait until 11.30. We should attack as close to Sybille's deadline as we can.

– That way, we will also know where to attack… Sivert pointed out, with his great gallows humor.

– Oh, sod off. Jemma snarled.

Time crawled, like it always did for those waiting impatiently for something. Sivert could have sworn that the numbers on his watch, the mechanism supposedly showing time, didn't move at all.

Half of them kept their attention at the buildings, the other half the other way, outwards, facing the roads in the hope of spotting a truck with Danish registration plates.

Nothing. Nothing that mattered.

– Time? Silverhair looked constantly through the binoculars.

– 11.15, Jemma helpfully enlightened her.

Silverhair swept the binoculars back and forth, up and down the street. She saw nothing in particular at first, but when she swept across the yard at the end of the street she wondered. Her attention returned to the place with a hammering heart. There. Movement. The ground started… rising. A hatch, a big one opened.

They heard a loud engine. A truck… with Danish plates appeared from the hole in the ground.

– If that is the one… why is it leaving so early?

– It's on a busy schedule, Kurt said darkly.

– Yvonne and Gio, it's headed towards you. – Silverhair sent, anxiously calm. – Follow it, but don't take any chances.

– Understood, sort of. Gio acknowledged, breaking off the connection before she managed to respond.

Judith stared at one of the five lamps on the communicator blinking red. It lasted no more than a few moments. She rose on her feet. The truck disappeared into the endless dark gray. They could just about make out the small vehicle shadowing it.

– Let's get the show on the road, she sent brusquely. – And let's make an effort not to make it too bloody, okay.

Kurt handed Janni a Desert Eagle 357 automatic. She accepted it quietly, keeping her eyes steady when she looked at him.

– Don't use it if you don't have to, he admonished her. – Do like we've shown you. Hold it up before you with both hands around the grip and pull the trigger.

– Don't worry about me, she stated.

She recalled the recoil well enough. She didn't need any reminder. Every time she had pulled the trigger she had seen a faceless human in front of her. She had been told that this was a pretty common phenomenon.

They charged forward, from corner to corner towards the building closest to where the truck had appeared. They ran in the dark gray. This was what they were born to and trained to do, confronting the enemy on their own turf, with heavy odds in their disfavor.

– This is a rare thing, isn't it? She spoke with a hardly audible voice, fearing she spoke too loud. – Not many people are able and willing to take on the establishment in such a decisive manner.

– Unfortunately not, Kurt replied, – but hopefully that is changing. There are unmistakable signs to that effect, won't you say?

– I will! She stated proudly. – I heard about it repeatedly, long before you guys made contact, how ever more people discover and open up to the green rose.

Silverhair's back hit the wall by the door. Quite an ordinary door, really, basically consisting of glass, ordinary glass. There was no problem breaking it. No howling alarm. But possibly/probably a silent one someplace. Time to get moving. She waved her seven with her. Kurt led his seven through the backdoor.

They saw no people, as they made their way through quite a few luxurious offices, seemingly not much in use. Lockers and drawers were virtually empty. It was like they had assumed: This was just a front.

Silverhair spotted Kurt and the others down the hall. She signaled for them to keep their distance. The two groups reached the center after having searched each their half. The corridor between them led to two rooms at the side of the building. Like they had strongly suspected most of the activity happened underground. Silverhair pointed Kurt in one direction. She took the lead the other.

They made every possible preparation before charging into the room, all unnecessary. The room was empty - of people.

It was filled with electronic equipment, video, monitors, computers.

The computer monitors were dark, but the surveillance monitors showed the entire block around the building. Luckily the guards were absent. Not that it would have mattered much. It would just have forced them to move faster. And they could naturally be observed on other screens this very moment, but Silverhair didn't believe they were.

– Security stinks here, Renni sniffed.

He didn't say what everybody thought: that perhaps the truck had left with everything and everybody.

– Don't get cocky, Sivert warned. – It might be an entire complex below, filled with trigger-happy people.

The others approached, dragging with them two unknown people in uniforms, one man and one woman, their uniforms in disarray. They were dressed casual to the point of ridicule. Kurt grinned big.

– They took themselves liberties, these two.

– A stroll in the wild, Karine added.

Both were thoroughly tied up.

– You're terrorists, the male exclaimed in horror. – What are you doing here?

The surprise seemed genuine.

– You've got every reason to be surprised, don't you? Anya commented. – There isn't much of interest to us here, is there?

– No, the female said weakly. – What do you want with us? Please…

– I almost believe you, Silverhair said, after a glance at Anya. – You should pray you don't know anything about what's happening here.

Kathy woke up from the drug-induced unconsciousness slowly and painfully. Everything past and present was spinning in her hazy vision, bars, scared faces, and newspaper headlines, so conceited.

GIANT FAILURE
FIRST DEATH FOR THE GREEN ROSE

If they had just written about everybody they had buried, figuratively and actually before they had finally turned to the sword. The articles and television broadcasts made the dead guards into a major issue. No article mentioned the fact that it was the first time the guerillas had ever killed anyone, while those in charge, through servants and proxies had previously killed a countless numbers of their friends. And the assassin Lee Travis was portrayed as a hero.

She blinked. That, too, happened slowly. Limbs felt heavy. She was attached to the floor like glue… to the bottom… *of a cage*. Wherever she turned her head there were bars. NO, they couldn't do this. How could they? She fought her way up on her knees. The cage was tall enough for her to stay on her knees. Tall enough for that, but not more than that. She had to rest her butt on her heels to not be forced to bow her head. It was, in general so tight that she had difficulties moving. She saw all the other cages. They were placed in a circle in the hot, humid room. Torches oozed on the walls. Kim crouched in the adjacent cage, still unconscious. Kathy saw she had been chained from wrist to wrist, ankle to ankle. Kathy discovered her own chains, tightening around her own wrists, her own ankles. She wanted desperately to scream. Somebody did, four or five cages to the right. Trembling hands clutched the bars and shook the cages, shook hard, howled and screamed, attempting to be heard above the rest. A most hopeless task, of course.

Kim had woken up. Everybody had been awake for a while now. They were sweating and suffering in the wet heat. Kathy kept her eyes shut. Not that she could stand keeping them open. She tried to think. Everybody had been allowed to keep their clothes on, both the girls and the boys. Kathy was tempted to tear off every single cloth, in the hope of making hell a bit more livable. She wondered how long time had passed. She couldn't tell. All watches had been removed. She and Kim held hands outside the cages. Where were their brothers and sisters? Perhaps they would never come.

A door was opened and closed somewhere. Kathy sensed a slight draft in that brief moment. A flash and it was gone. In spite of what her intellect told her she feared she had imagined it all. It had been quiet for a long time, now. Everybody had been so dulled by the heat and fear that they couldn't do much. Only muffled sobs occasionally interrupted the sickening silence. It was impossible to avoid hearing the heavy, ever louder steps. Someone approached with well-crafted, vicious moves.

Pull yourself together. She had to. She and Kim knew salvation was at hand. It had to be that much worse for everybody else here, paralyzed by uncertainty and fear, discovering a cruelty they had never imagined existed. Or did they have it easier, after all, because they had no idea how slim the chance was of being rescued - if it didn't happen soon?

A large woman appeared, with two even larger men in tow. The men seemed threatening in many ways, but they didn't scare the prisoners half as much as the woman. She terrified them. Not because of her clothes, the high heeled boots, the leather, the whip hitting the right boot. It was her eyes. Her eyes burned straight through them, staring at them all, even when her back was turned. They felt her presence like claws in the gut.

She wasted no time on introductions.

– You've said goodbye to your old lives, she stated, terrifyingly convincing, while walking between the cages. – It's just as well this didn't happen voluntarily. From now on you will never display any form of independence what so ever. You will do what you're told, what's expected of you, and nothing more. If you do that we may choose to reward you. Every time you disappoint us the punishment will be increasingly severe.

The woman stopped in front of Kathy's cage. The men placed themselves behind the woman, like unmoving statues.

– I like your dress, girl. It pleases me that you're used to displaying yourself. That will be required often of you from now on. *Now,* little pet, I won't you to show me your tits.

Kathy crouched with her arms and hands covering her chest, shaking her head, with eyes big and scared.

– You do it on your own, now, or these two beasts behind me will *help* you.

Kathy sniffed, and pulled down one of the shoulder straps, then the other. Pulled them far down. A pleased, sarcastic expression appeared in the woman's face. Kathy lowered her eyes.

– Excellent, pretty slave. Do you desire water, slave?

Kathy raised her head again, with fiery eyes.

– My name is…

– You HAVE no name. The whip struck the floor with a loud crack. The prisoner shook in fear. The woman pushed the whip's shaft inside the cage and touched Kathy's nudity. – You don't have a name, not unless we choose to GIVE you one. Is this understood, slave? *Now, do you want water?*

Wet eyes stared at the tiny cup appearing in the woman's hand.

– Yes, please…

– Not bad, not bad at all. It will have to do… for now.

Kathy attempted to drink slowly of the tiny cup, but the mouth was so dry. It devoured everything in an instant, so fast that the drop in the ocean was hardly noticeable. The woman outside the cage laughed sharp and scornful.

Kathy had been chosen as an example. The others obeyed faster and with less resistance. It didn't take long for the woman and her entourage to complete the turn of the circle.

– That wasn't hard, now, was it? The woman with the tight-woven hair stood in the middle of the circle, at the center of everybody's attention. – As soon as you were shown correct behavior it all went like clockwork. Basically…

Two prisoners, a boy and a girl had turned quite troublesome. Spit curses. They were dragged out on the floor and hung from the ceiling. Their clothes were torn off them. Their feet didn't touch the floor and the pain on their arms was horrendous. It showed in every line on their faces.

– You're such sweet children. She circled them while swinging the whip ruthlessly. – You will learn the punishment for disobedience. You will learn.

The whiplash struck their naked skin. Kathy sat in her cage and shook for every stroke. It was like she felt every sound physically. She had felt it before - on her own body. But that was nothing compared to how this had to be. That had, after all been light taps. Nothing equal to what the two poor bastards went through. Kathy thought that perhaps she and her fellow warriors had kept a certain naiveté, in spite of what they had experienced.

The howls echoed through air and between walls. Suffering and pain pulsed and vibrated.

Silverhair led on down the stairs. Anya, right behind her slowly stopped, with a strange, painful expression in her face. Silverhair reached the lower floor, while Anya blocked the others from descending further.

– I heard… something, Anya said startled. Then she shook her head. – Let's get moving.

They advanced down a small corridor, five and five together. Janni's heart hammered, in fear and excitement, and fear that she wouldn't be able to hack it. She succeeded in moving in the same, sneaky mode the others did, but to do that she had to concentrate hard, so hard that the sweat was flowing. To the others it had become instinctive, second nature. It would take time before she would have pulled it from her instinctive consciousness, but she would do it. She would.

– What the hell…

A man rushed out of a room with a lowered machine gun in his hands. He raised it in a fever-like move, swift and deadly. They shot him before he got there. A short salvo went into the wall.

The sixteen carried a variety of light and heavy weaponry, prepared for anything. Janni kept seeing the bloodied body of the man they had shot, shot and killed. Her lower lip quivered.

Sivert looked into the room the now dead man had come from. There were no more people there. They checked every room they passed. They met with no resistance. In one of the rooms one single man stood in the middle of the floor. He had dropped a gun by his feet and had his hands raised above his head.

– Kees, Janni, you take care of him, Silverhair barked the order, already on her way.

They reached a corner. Silverhair stuck her head out. Two guys stood twenty or so steps away with raised guns. Anya grabbed the red head and pulled her backwards, just as a hail of bullets raced by and took off a major piece of the wall. Kurt reached beyond the corner with a gun and fired, but as expected the two men had taken cover.

– No more doors, Silverhair stated. – I saw two side corridors. The two assholes are in the one farther away. Both are to the right.

Kurt and Heike steeled themselves. They were two of the five carrying M-16A2's. The enemies fired a salvo. There were still only two weapons being fired. The moment the hail of bullets stopped Kurt and Heike threw themselves at the opposite wall. They fired the grenade launcher at one target each. The explosive load hit the far wall in each of the two side corridors and exploded. Blood and smoke and remains of the wall welled into the air, and the crack echoed violently through the closed in area.

They rushed into the smoke, ready for anything. Kurt, leading the way into the near corridor easily saw that people had been standing here, too. How many, however, were no longer easily discerned…

He had once watched a movie called Stuntman. During the take of a battle scene there had been a beach full of body parts. The spectators had believed they were real and screamed themselves silly, but the «wounded» had risen from the dead, unharmed, with all their limbs in place. That wouldn't happen here. But here there weren't any spectators either.

A stretch ahead there was a large and well-lit open area. On the way there two doors, one on each end and side of the corridor. The closest explosion had blown off the hinges. There were no people in the room… anymore. There were four cups of coffee on a table, where there were also dealt four hands of poker. Vapor still rose from the cups.

The other room was luxurious to the max, just like the room on the above floor, where they had found the two guards in heated embrace. Kurt had always imagined such rooms in luxury bordellos.

– *Kurt,* Karine cried out sharply.

She stood in the doorway signaling for him to take a peek outside.

A man walked out in the bright, major hall with his hands above the head.

– WE SURRENDER, he said calmly. – THERE IS NO NEED FOR FURTHER RASH ACTIONS. MY COLLEAGUES ARE WAITING IN THE OTHER ROOM… IN PRUDENT CAUTION.

Kurt and Karine stepped cautiously into the light. They saw Judith appear through a door further down. She gave them the CLEAR signal. Sivert appeared through the same door the polite man standing before them had walked through.

– It's… all right, he said with a strangely flat voice.

They had never seen his face like this before, a study in contradicting emotions.

The Nightravens rushed into the room with the cages. The woman and the big bruisers were still there, along with four others.

– What are you doing here? The woman asked indignant. – Don't you know we're protected? Damn klutzes!

Judith pushed the already tight bound man at his colleagues. She looked around the room with an ice-cold stare, but inside she was like a small tremor before the big earthquake. She had lived like that for years, but never felt it this intense. She had major difficulties controlling herself. All parts of her boiled over.

– We are not cops.

She sounded completely relaxed.

– You're not…? The woman released the whip from her hand and it fell on the floor. For the first time signs of uncertainty showed in her face. – But what…

– It's the fucking terrorists, a man exclaimed.

Kees and Janni arrived with their prisoner between them. Janni's eyes widened, round and hard. She gasped for breath.

– I think I'm going to be sick, Dorte said.

They stared at the cages and the people inside them. Eyes locked on to the two hanging from their arms, at the marks on their bodies, the pain and the shock in the watery eyes.

Judith's eyes found Kim and Kathy through the bars.

– Get everybody out! Quickly. She finally managed to speak. The fear and the hatred had almost paralyzed her. – And put all the fun people inside instead.

Anya had already helped the whipped boy and girl. She was tending them a stretch away. The distance was necessary, if she should have any chance of freeing them from the silence and dejection threatening to strangle them. Shadows and demons danced nightmarish through their minds and darkened everything around them. Anya knew this condition well.

Kim, repeatedly choking didn't bother to have the chains removed before embracing Judith.

– They wanted to put out all lights inside me, Silverhair, and I wouldn't have been human anymore.

– You're terr… the Green Rose?
One of the freed boys spoke up, with skepticism noticeable in his voice. He pulled so hard in the chains that Sivert faced major problems in the attempt at freeing him.
– You saved us, and we're deeply grateful, another boy said, with an ugly look at he who had spoken first. – I certainly am.
The two guards from the video surveillance room were brought in, attempting thunderstruck to grasp the situation.
– We didn't know, they repeated in variations.
They spoke, muttered mostly to themselves. If they were acting they were good.
– The police will be here soon, a girl said with hope in her voice.
– Don't be stupid, another snapped. – They haven't called the police. Of course they haven't.
– This is no dream, Kathy said. – The sooner you realize that the better.
Kurt walked to one of the cages. The man inside scowled at him.
– Allow me to introduce Captain Jon Van Der Wet, a respected member of the Amsterdam police force. He's among the many either deeply involved or on their payroll.
– This is one of many «projects». Karine spat poison. – Over the entire wide world. What we've done here is so inconsequential that it's fading to virtually nothing in the whirlwind touching all things, but hopefully it will bring some limited, short-term attention.
– What are you talking about? The first girl who had spoken up shouted. – This will be major news.
– If we are lucky it will be news, Karine replied in regret. – But not for long. Haven't you noticed how even the most grotesque events are fading in people's consciousness after a while? Society has raised and formed us that way. Unpleasant and dangerous stuff shall be forgotten, shall fade after a while. They might have their uses, seen from the establishment's point of view, when it comes to short term manipulation, but if they cause people to think and act independently they become real and thereby truly dangerous.
– What will happen… to these? The girl looked at the cages, in a sudden, shivering rage.
– With this much publicity they will spend some time behind bars, Morten considered, in a very subdued, rational way, the rage buried deep in his voice. – But they will be out soon. They have powerful interests behind them.

Judith noticed a nauseas', disgusting feeling inside. She fought against it with everything she had. At the edge of her vision she observed Helene sneaking behind a wall and they all heard the sound of vomiting.

Silverhair met eyes, those of Anya, Sivert, Kurt… and eventually Kim and Kathy.

– We can't let them get away with it. He who had been whipped and tortured spoke up, painfully. – We quite simply can't. With this or what they've done to others.

– You doubt, Silverhair said. She cocked her weapon. – That's good. We all do.

– What are we *waiting* for? Jemma, beyond enraged raised a fist.

– It must be unanimous, Silverhair said firmly. – Among us who have chosen the sword. We will take the responsibility and live with it.

She turned to Janni first.

– Don't feel any pressure. She admonished their newest, youngest member. – There's just you and you alone that can make your decision.

Janni looked down, at the floor, but then she raised her eyes once more, shadow and defiance dancing in them. The Fire burned white hot inside her.

– Kill them, she said after just a short hesitation.

– Kill them, Corbin said.

– Kill them, Jemma said instantly.

Everybody had voted «aye». Only Silverhair remained.

– I'm just sorry it will be over so quickly, she stated with regret, and they could sense the fire in her, stronger than ever. – May they suffer in something resembling an eternity.

– You won't get away with this, the woman with the whip howled. – What are you thinking? You won't…

Silverhair shot her to pieces. The body crouched there, in the cage, as distorted as her face.

– I believe she felt she had the right to do what she did, Kathy said, ice numb. – What a *monster*.

Kathy shot one of the bruisers with one single bullet in the head.

The butchering kept going in what seemed like hours, but was probably just a few minutes. Some of those about to die cursed and swore, others begged for their life, all in vain.

The man and woman from the surveillance room looked at it all quietly and subdued.

– We don't know whether or not you knew what went on, Silverhair said to them. – We won't harm you.

– We wish to join you, the man said.

– Yes, the woman said.

– Wait a bit, Anya said to them. – See if you still feel the same.

– How do we find you? The woman asked.

– If the subject comes up again we will find you.

Kurt's voice had a dark undercurrent. Janni looked at him for a while before understanding hit her.

She looked at her smoking gun.

– Is it correct what is being said, that the first kill is the easiest… and that it becomes easier from there? She asked Corbin in a low, subdued voice, clearly aware of the seemingly inherent contradiction brought on by her words.

– I think there is some truth to it, he replied, as softly as possible.

No one in the cages moved, turning stone cold, like an exhibition in a carnival of death.

– Call many police stations, Anya told the still paralyzed released prisoners. – Call all the media you can think of. Here is an extended list of numbers. Everything going on here has been filmed. We found videocassettes and have copied them. You can trust us to send them around, so you don't need to be afraid of not being believed. You will face incredulity, perhaps contempt and hatred, but not disbelief, at least not that particular kind.

– Thank you. The nearest accepted the phone list. – We can never thank you enough. Never!

– Try, Kurt said, diabolically cheerful.

He was the only one waving. As if on cue the warriors left the room, setting course for the hall outside. And like a snapping of fingers… they vanished.

The female guard ran after them, but when she reached the hall there was no one in sight. Still, she knew they would always be There.

CHAPTER SIXTEEN

Clouds raced across the sky.
Waves rolled towards the shore.
While the sea kept rising.

Almost at exactly the same time Silverhair & co struck in Amsterdam the cell led by Steve and Sybille attacked estates owned or controlled by Hugo Manning in Copenhagen and Hamburg. Other groups, hundreds of enraged «non-combatants» struck all over Europe and exposed what happened in dark cellars while most people slept. With guns and fists and publicity and any tool available his life's work was ripped apart during just a few, critical hours. The subsequent day evidence continued to arrive at media headquarters. He was arrested and jailed… for exactly four hours, until a court meeting released him, to await a trial that never took place. He was never seen in public again.

During the coming year three new groups of nightravens were formed, each with their own structure and tactics. But in all the ways that counted they were all one. Worry started spreading in earnest in the corridors of power.

Judith turned more and more obsessed and desperate as the time raged. Everybody could see that. Summer felt short to them all, even though it lasted longer than any other in memory.

In July, in broad daylight they returned to Copenhagen and the factory belonging to ICI. Two weeks earlier they had issued warnings, broadcasting their intention to «eradicate the factory from the surface of the Earth». Two weeks. More than sufficient for the executives and workers to consider their options. The warning wasn't heeded. Especially not after the factory and the surrounding area was filled with cops, armed to their teeth. A few workers quit. They were threatened with blacklisting, but quit anyway. The day preceding the attack another communication was issued: «They who aren't a part of the solution are a part of the problem.»

No more quit. Production kept going unabated.

Two choppers flew low, closing in on the target. Helene and Corbin sat behind the controls. They were both experienced pilots. Corbin had basically done like Helene, cooperated with establishment in order to better fight it.

The turning of the blades above reverberated in Silverhair's head. The sunlight didn't penetrate the darkness surrounding her. She knew that and it bothered her no more. She had chosen her life, just like Helene and Corbin.

The choppers were old, rejected military models. That didn't mean they were in bad shape. The national and international armies had had an even flow of means available since the start of the second Great War. They could afford to buy new, shining models long before the old were actually useless, something creating heavenly working conditions for international gun-dealers. The market was overflowing with weapons and equipment. The choppers had been well equipped when they procured them, with nine millimeters machine guns and extra protective walls. To that they had added their own lethal stuff. The end result was two deadly war machines. Too bad they would only be able to use them once. But they couldn't carry them around, unfit as they were to their way of warfare. Besides, after today this kind of surprise attack wouldn't have any value anymore.

The afternoon sun was bathing the area, lighting ugly gray square buildings, long rebuilt after the superficial damage done to them half a year earlier, working, effective plants. The workers had been given a raise after the warning had been broadcast. They kept striving for something less than lousy wages, something that could never be anything more, with their empty eyes and faded spirit. There was nothing noble about it, but rather something the exact opposite. Silverhair sensed the rage flowing in her veins and she welcomed it. She finally welcomed it.

Uniformed men no longer bothered to hide. They filled the area surrounding the factory. It didn't take long after the battle began before they ran like rabbits.

The choppers appeared like out of thin air. One moment they weren't there, the next they were, and suddenly there were raining bullets everywhere. Yvonne and Kees the second pilots kept pulling the triggers. They watched how desperate people ran in all directions down there, as they were hit and fell, hit by bullets and shrapnel. Back in the choppers one in each of their open doors fired at everything they saw. As soon as one had emptied a clip another took his or her place. Bombs and rockets fell like hail from the sky and flattened every single building.

– We can't do this often, Karine shouted joyfully. – We could rob a bank every day, and still lack the necessary resources.

– You're crazy, Yvonne shouted from the front, marveling at her friend's devil may care attitude.

– Yeah, isn't it GREAT?

Flames licked and darkened the sky. When they flew away in triumph and dead and wounded remained everywhere, they still heard explosions. This time the factory would have to be rebuilt from scratch.

– I have some problems flying straight, Helen's voice sounded from the pilot's seat. She added bravely: – No vital parts are hit, though. We should be okay.

Silverhair fired and kept firing. When one clip was empty she switched and fired until the next one was empty as well. She pushed away those who wanted to take her place. Kim and Sivert put their hands on her shoulders and embraced her, held her gently. She slowly lowered her weapon, staring at the carnage and destruction down there.

– It's enough, now, she mumbled. – It's enough *for now*.

– We should probably lay low for a while now, right? Janni sat there, quiet and timid. – They won't be very pleased after this.

– Perhaps ICI will lay low for a while, too, after this, Corbin said, characteristically hopeful.

– Smaller companies can't take losses like this, and the increased insurance, Gio said, – but Imperial Chemical Industries can absorb the impact of several such «incidents». To truly strike at them and other multinational companies we need to go for the jugular, to attack the leaders and the owners.

– That's why we shall drown this entire, rotten world in *fire*, Silverhair said fiercely. – That way we'll catch an infinite number of flies in one swoop.

It turned quiet. She had, as usual put everything in perspective for them.

She sat there with her eyes closed. The choppers flew away from the smoke and the flames, from blood and death, to blood and death. She kept her eyes closed, allowed the images of pale light to flow behind the eyelids.

The legend of Phoenix, the bird of fire and life. It had wings so large that no one could keep it from flying. Nothing, neither storm nor rain could halt its flight. But it lived so strong and so intense that it was doomed to fall, to crash in fire and smoke. Time passed, as its ashes were spread by the winds. *And then,* it rose yet again from its own ashes.

After the previous attack on ICI they had been laying low in Denmark for a while, while things calmed down. Now they had more than a sense of that it would never do that. The same night they crossed Øresund to Sweden in speedboats. It didn't take long. They reached the other shore without encountering problems of any kind, and a few hours later they reached the relative safety in their four hideouts in and around Gothenburg.

They needed to relax and they did so. But they didn't like staying inactive for too long. It led to restlessness and worse. When Silverhair called what Kim enjoyed calling war council after just a week, they were more than pleased about it.

The council took place on an old riverboat Jan had used to traffic the Gøta Canal. It had led to many a hazardous trip.

He still owned it. He could do so quite safely. No outsider had ever connected Jan Walter to any Green Rose activities. He shared this anonymity with just a few in the room, never using his own name or face when others were present. It had turned out well so far. His guess was that it wouldn't last that much longer.

– To this point we have struck swiftly and surprisingly, and then gone underground, waiting for things to calm down… Silverhair - they thought of her ever more often as Silverhair - talked to them as she usually did during similar circumstances, with an increased hope of satisfied expectation. – That tactic did work rather well for us for a while. It will do so no longer. And soon we will be over a *hundred* green roses running around destabilizing modern society. It's time to grab the initiative, and keep it.

She met the eyes of each and every one of them. They were with her. Everybody was always with her. She read worry in Kim and Sivert's eyes, but that had no true significance. They would follow orders, they, like all the rest.

I'm the Green Rose, she thought. I'm The Phoenix.

The Phoenix must fly.

Control. Feet stamped at the naked floor, silently, wildly, soundlessly. The solid wand whirled in the air, directed at a faceless enemy or opponent somewhere ahead, or behind or to one of the sides, above or below. Precise control. But never total, never chains, in any form. The room she found herself, the space she dominated wasn't large or small. Such measures, ways of seeing things were meaningless. The human mind was *limitless*. There were no borders, only obstacles. *Adaptation*. To adapt was the little death, to die long before the heart stopped. Adaptation meant to imprison the mind and thought. Imprison the *infinite* power of life and mind.

This room. She had personally fitted it, placed all kinds of obstacles all over it. And the other nightravens moved things around between each of her sessions, so she would always encounter an unexpected and varied path. Ropes hung from the ceiling. The point, some of it anyway was that she wasn't supposed to touch any of them. Sweet poured from open pores. Muscles and limbs hurt. Her vision blurred. She kept going. The ropes moved because of the air pressure. She knew she didn't touch them.

The room had a small window. Outside was an ordinary birch. It had green leaves. It was November. Her moves increased in intensity. Thoughts rushed through synapses.

How many times had harbors in unprotected areas and towns been flooded the last year? She had lost count. How often had it happened in protected areas and harbors? She had lost count. How many millions had suffered a way too early and painful death because of the pollution and injustice so prevalent in the world? The number wasn't a number, just a unit impossible to measure. What would it take? People couldn't avoid seeing what happened right in front of their faces, their noses, their eyes. What would it take to make them *react?* SOMETHING. Something big. The ticket was to find something no one could ignore or be indifferent to - even if they should happen to be deaf, blind and mute.

Her motion turned even more intense. It was like most people lived in a dream world. One had to see the world as it was, not the way one wanted it to be. Near the end of today's trek she pushed the wand forward, pushed it hard and fast. It hit the little ball hanging there, and pulverized it.

She fell to her knees, exhausted, with fire burning body and soul. Not as strong as before. Stronger! *Vishnu and Shiva warred within her, the way they had always done*. There was no way she could be both the Preserver and Destroyer simultaneously… was there? And wouldn't she eventually be forced to choose between them?

She stood straight again, with feet steady as a rock. Fire flowed through her veins. It burned and burned. Like it would always do, she realized.

She hit the walls in precise, wild hits. It hurt, but that was… the way it should be.

When Kim entered the room she did gymnastics on the floor. Jumped up in the ropes, pulled herself up, under the ceiling. Kim waited for Silverhair to begin, to say something, anything, but she didn't. And Kim had to.

– Corbin will make it, she said with relief evident in her voice. – I got that from Anya just before she fell asleep.

– What about the arm? Silverhair asked sharply, landing softly on the floor.

– There might be problems there. Anya fears it will never be completely okay.

– No big problem, Silverhair said, more to herself. – If he can move it okay. He has always been good at using both hands.

– And Anya says Janni and Dorte will be completely recovered, if you don't run them too hard too early.

– Good, that's good. Silverhair returned to the jungle of ropes, away from the Eurasian woman.

Kim turned halfway around, set to leave the room, but stopped with a resolute expression in her face.

She joined the other in the ropes. Just as casual, supple and graceful as Silverhair. But she lacked the savagery and the violent energies.

Death was better than the little death. It didn't enclose the mind, but liberated it.

She performed for Silverhair, doing her best to be funny, and she finally got her reward, when she succeeded in making the other smile.

– Silverhair, she said after while, when both of them rested on the floor, – you must leave the path you're walking. It's a self-destructive, self-perpetuating course turning you, turning us… insane.

– I don't know what you're talking about, Silverhair said irritated.

– Yes, Kim said rigidly, – you do.

She put her hand on Judith's arm.

– Willy knew the risk, she said weakly. – We all do. He means a lot to us all. He was my mate, as much as he was yours. And what we experienced in Amsterdam must not be allowed to destroy us. Silverhair is a focal point, standing for more than pure destruction, the wanton vandalism we've been doing the last few months. Please, Silverhair. You're hope incarnated. To many… to me, since we first met. You… we can't go to war. It isn't our… function, not our wish. Silverhair… everything I've ever wanted I see in you.

She rested her head at the other woman's shoulder.

– You're such a sweet pet, little Kim.

– Don't call me that! Kim reacted instantly, backing off. – DON'T USE THAT WORD!

– Why not? Silverhair asked, in a crushing blow. – Because your dear father used it? I can actually understand him…

– STOP! Kim attacked in wrath and despair. – YOU'RE CRUEL!

She struck Judith on the cheek, struck so hard that blood flowed from both her mouth and nose. Judith had pulled her head back, and avoided the full force of the blow, and she backed just a short step. Kim kept up the attack in one furious flow of movement. Judith parried her kick and made one herself sending the other flying across the room. Judith took her time, allowing Kim to regain her footing. A wounded, hateful look, and she came and asked for more.

– You little sweet cunt!

Judith grabbed her arm, holding it in an iron grip, and sent a fist into the unguarded belly. A loud gasp, and before she could draw breath Judith struck again. Another blow would have finished the fight. But it was just a slap on the cheek. She was pushed back. Judith chased her and rained hits and kicks on her. None of them were dangerous or even physically damaging. It was just punishment, a lot of punishment. Kim gasped and begged. It was no use. Judith kept it up, merciless, unbowed.

She crouched on the floor, half unconscious. Judith stood, towered above her. Wasn't she through yet? Judith grabbed her hair and pulled her to her knees, placed her kneeling in front of herself, pulled down her pants. Kim started shaking, shaking violently.

– You're actually an irritating plague of a pet. Judith saw herself move her lips in a smile in the reflection in Kim's eyes and it was a terrifying sight. – *No more!*

A crescendo boiled in her ears, louder and louder. She saw Kim as nothing but a red scarf, and didn't hear her pleas for mercy, encircling the defenseless prey like a vulture. Ever so slowly she pulled her belt from her hips, savoring every moment.

– You're actually kneeling. Judith grinned viciously. – Like a servant, like a *slave*. How pathetic is that!

The belt hit the naked, unprotected skin. Kim screamed. Good. If she moved ever so little… She really shouldn't…

Kim sat still, quiet, as the horrible punishment continued. She hardly shook each time the belt hit her skin anymore. There was a kind of ripple on her body, from top to bottom, as if everything was soft and limbless, and no more.

Judith struck her on her butt as methodically as she had done on the rest of the body. Tears flowed from Kim's eyes while her features twisted in shock and she stared blindly, unreasoning and unfocused in front of her. In a haze of red mist the whipping turned wilder, disharmonic. They changed from being humiliating to *crushing*.

– YES, I know I've been bad, she shouted. – I'll be good, mother. I promise… P-PROMISE!

The physical punishment halted. It didn't make Kim feel any better, didn't make her feel anything. If Judith had just said something, anything… But Silverhair just turned and left. The silent, scornful laughter echoed in a room suddenly so very, very big. Kim shook in tears and remained crouched, left behind and lonely. *Broken like dry twigs in the Storm.*

Silverhair chased off, with no idea where. Air wheezed out and in between clenched teeth. The horrible inside her, what she had held in check for so long hadn't faded. How could she have believed it would be any use? To fight it, attempting to exorcise it, had only made it grow, made it worse. The blood flowed like lava in her veins and melted her from the inside, slowly and terribly.

+++++++++++++++++++

Was anyone hiding out there, waiting for him, hateful and bloodthirsty, a mix between a vampire bat and a human being?

Ole Sivert Olsen - a slight smile, there had been some time since he had thought of himself by that name (it was mostly Sivert these days) - moved with normal walking speed through the narrow Dronningens Gate (Queen's Street) in Gothenburg, moved through a night chilly and dark.

Not really that chilly. He probably just saw it that way. This evening, in the middle half of what used to be winter, was hardly any colder than an early autumn day. The cold Baltic Sea wind didn't blow anymore. Sivert had grown up in Copenhagen, where it had been blowing just about constantly in the wide streets. There, as here, it was Gone.

Not really that dark. It never turned truly dark in a city. Its inhabitants merely experienced it thus. The area between the city centre by Nordstan and the amusement park Liseberg was huge and deserted, a lot of cold office buildings. Neon lights and the occasional crowd didn't change the gray impression.

The weight of the Desert Eagle inside his jacket was a comforting constant. He knew he was able to draw it from its confines with a speed that could hardly be measured by the human eye. That was indeed comforting.

He had psyched himself to enjoy the considerable walk when he passed the enormous parking complex and Liseberg at the other side of the road sort of illuminated the gray.

Liseberg amusement park opened itself to him. Right inside he walked through the light alley, a bright passage. He smiled. It reminded him of Judith's eyes. She had kissed him wildly, passionately before he left. Corbin had looked at the wall and Kim had been in another room. Things hadn't been good between them lately - between Judith and Kim. Kim followed Silverhair with her wounded doe eyes day out and day in. Could she still be jealous? She had been in the early days. It had been more than obvious then. He had to talk to her. No, she had to know by now, like Sivert did that she had no more reason to be jealous of him than he had of her. They had to have a talk all three of them. Soon!

Anya waited for him here, somewhere. The same place he would meet Tom Rawlins.

Sivert didn't like Rawlins very much. He didn't like arms-dealers, even though he willingly conceded that that was more than a bit hypocritical. They needed weapons. Period! An even flow of guns, ammunition, and related goods. And Rawlins was the typical, atypical arms-dealer. He sold to everybody. Judith saw nothing wrong in dealing with him. Sivert had always felt she was a bit too pragmatic.

A skewed smile. Others, like Jemma and Gio, probably felt she wasn't pragmatic enough.

He crossed the park, passing the rollercoaster, the carousel and the river kayak, until he reached the playhouse. The park didn't have that many outdoor guests tonight, this weekend evening, but inside they had filled the place. Even if Gothenburg belonged to a category of one on the list of nice cities in Scandinavia, people here were also starved for experiences.

The cigarette smoke lingered in all the rooms. That was something he never got accustomed to, another thing he never wanted to get used to.

The noise from the slot machines overwhelmed any other. Old ladies puffing on cigars threw coins in them like clockwork. He saw nothing unusual. With senses and reflexes even more sharpened he moved casually and controlled upstairs. The humming sound from all sides made him unable to hear his own steps. After the long walk in relative silence, the illusion of deafness felt extremely strange and claustrophobic.

He entered the room of card tables and roulette. It had been expanded since his last visit. He walked to one of the roulettes. More than one of the women there almost touched the ceiling and could have been Anya. She wore a blond wig. Face and habits, and even body language had changed completely. He wouldn't have had a chance in hell of recognizing her, if he hadn't watched her transform herself. Still, it felt awkward. His own disguise seemed hopelessly inadequate in comparison. He had merely disguised himself. She had transformed her entire being.

He placed himself a few spots away from her. She had a nice heap of chips on the table before her, but he needed only to note that she avoided two particular numbers. Everything was okay. After five more rounds she picked up her winnings, and left. She changed the chips into cash and set course for the restaurant in the adjacent room. He played for ten minutes and won, observing how most people rushed to the tables without preparations, how they gambled and lost. During his first time here he had studied the game for half an hour, before playing anything. What he suspected early on was confirmed: The wheels were skewed. Some numbers were inevitably hit more often than others. If the house had arranged it that way, or if the wheels were old didn't matter. It didn't take long for those who used their mind to identify the lucky numbers. A game, usually with marginal profit probability, suddenly had significantly higher winning changes.

When he quit he had won two thousand Swedish kroner. The house - or the government - didn't allow high stakes here. He exchanged the small stack of hundred kroner chips with steady hands.

He drifted upstream into the restaurant. Left the room with green felt and discrete lighting, and stepped into the twilight. The only visible lights here were the candles on the tables. Good.

Rawlins sat close to the wall, but fortunately not in the deepest part of the room. Anya sat at its center, attracting a lot of attention and admiring looks. She hid by not hiding.

She okayed the stage, the room. Her sharp eyes had seen no immediate danger. «Be on guard», she signaled, quite unnecessary, as if it wasn't a matter of a danger she wasn't certain of, but merely sensed.

He sat down by Rawlins' table. There were only the two of them. The gorillas filled the three closest tables. Sivert's claustrophobia didn't exactly improve. The fact that there were no more than two by the main table pleased him.

– I see you were lucky.

The implied question mark at the end of the sentence was typical for Rawlins.

– Lady Luck granted me some of her grace. Sivert shrugged.

– My sincere compliments, Rawlins said with admiration in his voice. – You guys are taking quantum leaps in improving yourselves. I don't think I can recognize a single one of your escorts tonight. I can't even say for sure who among these pretty people it is.

– But what about you, Tom? Sivert felt a bit better. – One can be tempted to believe you've become afraid of the dark in your old days, with all the companions you're keeping.

– A minor problem. Rawlins grinned widely. – An itch to be removed. A dirty job, but someone's gotta do it. Perhaps you would like to do it for me? When push comes to shove, haven't you realized by now that the sword is mightier than the pen?

Sivert wasn't surprised that the slime recognized him, and kept up the appearance, the pretense of calm. Rawlins was infamous for his power of observation. But Sivert was still infuriated, as long as he didn't know where and how he had given himself away.

– I would say you're slipping, the former journalist said pleasantly. – You didn't need a small army to protect you in the old days.

– How is the shoulder, man? Rawlins wondered with even white teeth. – Still a bit stiff, the way I've heard it.

– Ammunition, and stuff, the usual. This was it. The conversation, if one could call it that, had lasted way too long. – And we want only new or recent produced stuff. We've had some trouble with older stuff jamming.

– Bad treatment, Rawlins said dryly.

– Bad delivery, Sivert snarled.

– Let's have a toast. Rawlins filled the glasses that to this point had been empty. – For good days and bad, for many years of profitable cooperation, past and future.

They toasted. Sivert noticed, at the edge of his vision Anya move across the floor. Something was up, and it had happened fast. He hadn't noticed that she had left her seat. She was headed for the lavatories, but the interesting part was that the phones were situated in that very direction. The two men toasted again. Sivert concentrated on drinking evenly and slowly while concentrating. Two men, Anya signaled. One is phoning in. Large probability of more.

He froze in the chair. Which one was it? It had to be someone close to her table. There were several tables with only one man.

A man appeared from the shadowy hall. That exact moment Anya tripped out of the toilet and stumbled behind the guy in a way impossible to misunderstand. She was taking a huge risk there. That proved how desperate she was. Sivert kept his eyes on Tom Rawlins. Anya's message, when given was hardly necessary: «Time to fly». Sivert turned calm, very calm. The sense of claustrophobia, bothering him since his arrival vanished. How strange. The uncertainty disappeared now, when the battle grew close.

– Nobody has followed me, he said relaxed to Rawlins. – Therefore you're the one who has failed. You're getting old.

– What…? Baggy eyes widened.

Anya acted. It happened so quickly that not even Sivert, who had expected it reacted immediately. She struck out with hands rolled into fists, fists opening as arms were straightened. Sivert closed his eyes shut. He rolled off the chair and further across the floor. The room exploded in smoke, sound, lights and colors. The absolute chaos erupted. He saw nothing more of Anya in the smoke and uproar. Many stumbled around half blind after having looked straight at the sharp lights. He was among the first to reach the stairs. People started screaming and howling everywhere, not only those who had been present in the room when it exploded in sensory overload. Panic spread like wildfire. Many exposed their bestial sides, in faces and actions, when fighting their way through the crowd in the worst ruckus. This confirmed Sivert's conviction of how fragile civilization in truth was.

Showtime, he thought, in fear mixed with joy.

He rushed down the stairs, fell the last few steps. Rolled around a few times, jumped up and set off at warp speed out of the nuthouse. Thank, goodness, he had broken no vital parts. His right arm hurt, but he had no problems moving or using it. The somewhat fresh air worked wonders on him, sort of shocked him, totally cleared his mind. He went from automatic to high alert. *Wait,* he admonished himself. *Hell on wheels*. He waited until most of the panic-trodden crowd had run past him, before throwing the grenades. These had a time delay, but were otherwise as harmless as those Anya had used.

– BOMBS, he howled. And ran.

There were thunder and lighting, smoke flowed freely behind him, and the noise surrounding him increased to a crescendo. He spotted Anya a few steps ahead. They ran side by side towards the exit.

– He called for back up, she said. – He reported «bite». Gothenburg will shortly be filled with hostile forces. At least four tailed Rawlins. I should have spotted them earlier.

– You would have to be psychic to do that, he grinned.

Strangely enough her expression turned even weirder then.

– Thanks to you we're escaping, he kept it up, – and not on our way to a shuttered and dank cell.

He stopped speaking, scowling himself. Did he have to do encouraging speeches all the time?

With the panicked crowd they rushed out through the main gate, and straight into the road. Brakes screeched when wide-eyed drivers did their best to stop. Sounds of collisions and screams of pain filled the air. Sirens grew in the night until overwhelming the rest of the spectacle. By then Anya and Sivert were well under way, through darkened streets. They had penetrated the first iron circle, the one around the amusement park, before it had been formed.

They slowed down and kept walking in a quick, but relaxed pace. There weren't many people outside tonight, but they were prepared for the fact that every person they encountered would be an enemy. Out here in the whirlwind one blast, one gust was sufficient to blow out life's light. The whirlwind… a place and a state of mind both wonderful and terrifying.

A few seconds were lost in a narrow alley. They tore off masks and removed as much of the disguise as possible, then switched jackets. It worked passably.

They navigated according to the canal. Reached it a notch north of where they had intended. Ahead there was a parking lot full of cars. They crossed it with all their senses jacked up.

– We're in trouble, Anya said, very low in volume, high in intensity.

He looked around. They had almost reached the far end of the parking lot. Two others in dark clothes, behind them moved between the first cars. Two more were up on the sidewalk. The four showed neither weapons nor appeared threatening, but their intentions were clear. They didn't bother to hide.

Anya and Sivert walked up the stairs to street level again. They speeded up slightly. The four with their expressionless eyes quickly equaled their faster walk and also moved that tiny little bit faster, closing in slowly (but surely).

The Nightravens drew their guns and turned hurricane-like - like one being. They fired like one at their four enemies. Two fell instantly. The third died with his hand inside his jacket. Only one managed to even fire once, but he was hit several times and his shot went in a totally wrong direction. He fell and didn't fire again.

The two ran, hidden in shadows, one with their surroundings.

– They had convinced themselves we wouldn't fire first, Anya stated in grim satisfaction. – Idiots!

– Too bad we're doomed to encounter wiser people eventually, Sivert replied cheerfully. – And we can't go home. They got our scent now. We must make it on our own for a while.

Eyes met. *Completely alone*. They would have to split up.

Instead of moving towards Nordstan, the shopping mall they set course for the small stone bridge. It would be suicide to return the way they had come. This was the only way, and it worried them. They set out on the bridge in swift, economic movements. Never resting eyes attempted to look at everything simultaneously. They kept the revolvers in both hands, their arms raised in front of them, pointing straight forward. People spotted them and hurried off to relative safety. Everything moved. Among the sheep were there any… any two-legged wolves? Were there any in hiding? There were so many places, so much to keep track of…

There from their side of the canal, a dark figure stepping forth from behind a corner, gun in hand. Sivert turned towards the whirling target. What happened reminded him of one of the old electronic arcade games, well into the advance sequences, when the resistance started to become high intensive and a figure, fast as lightning appeared and fired with deadly accuracy. And he reacted just as slow.

He heard the crack from Anya's gun. Right after that she was hit. He saw her tumble at the reel, the brick reel. The enemy shook as the bullet hit him. Sivert shot him again. He wanted to help Anya. He wanted it so bad. Instinctively he fell to his knees. A bullet, fired from the other side of the canal passed straight above his head. Anya fired and fired. He heard shouts of pain from the street. Sivert fired against the two enemies he could see. One of them fell. Anya was hit again. He would never forget her face, twisted in desperate concentration, lips pulled back, making the fangs stick out.

She slipped over the edge and fell with a heavy splash into the water. He rolled across the bridge while his revolver switched back and fourth between targets. He wondered a lot about this, at the back of his brain. How the weapons seemed to be alive in his hands. How both he and Anya seemed to *be* weapons. He rested at the end of the bridge and stuck his head out, reloaded in two painful motions. One of the opponents, a woman lay bleeding with her back to a truck-wheel. She lifted her gun. He shot her twice. This time she stayed put. Feverishly he looked down on the canal. The surface seemed unbroken, and the water flowed calmly. No signs of Anya. He ran off and forced himself not to look back. When he passed the post office one single shot was fired. He had seen the man a moment before that and was flying through the air when the bullet hit. It didn't stop him. The jump gained him a clear line of sight at the sniper and he hit him with so many bullets that the already dead man shook violently before collapsing like an empty sack.

Sivert got up and kept running. A hand surveyed the wound. It wasn't even close to fatal. The bullet had only marginally penetrated the body armor and rested right beneath the skin. It would be a simple task to remove it, once he got the time. He stared at the Desert Eagle revolver in his hand. The bullets fired from it easily penetrated a bulletproof vest.

These guys are nothing compared to us, in spite of all their expensive training.

Was that, because they, to this point hadn't stared death in the eye?

Careful. If in nothing else, they have the advantage of superior numbers.

There was a powerful crack. Thunder rolled across the sky, through the streets and shook the ground. Suddenly it was raining, raining a lot. Oh, excellent. He kept running, ran through the torrential rain with the certainty that there was a legion chasing Sivert tonight. He was alone. If he had only brought an UZI… or a Stengun. An oversight. If he lived through this he would never forget again. Tonight what he had in his hands would have to do.

More cracks, a prolonged salvo. He threw himself down just before the load from the machineguns passed above him, rolled into a wall, crouched and kept running. Blood trickled from small wounds in his side. He jumped into a small, confined hideout, a dark hole where he was practically invisible from the street. They had zero chance of discovering him by a casual glance alone.

They came charging, barking, an entire pack - many heavy boots, bad sense of smell. They passed him. Lightning and thunder was instantaneous.

The crack rumbled in his ears. He inhaled, exhaled, casting a cautious look in both directions. No one there. Wait. Were there voices? He slid across the smooth wall, sneaky like rain. Two of them. They had posted two guards at the end of the street. The dogs had their back turned. In case he returned the same way they thought he had fled. He sneaked up on them, heard their snarling, scornful barking.

– Here we are, in the infernal rain, one of them muttered. – Because of that Satan of a rebel, and we are not even allowed the pleasure of participating in the final hunt.

– He's probably far, far away from here by now, the other nodded. – The Captain wants him more or less to himself, so that fewer share the glory.

– I would have loved to get him alone for a few minutes. Fuck the reward. These people are scum and they don't deserve to be treated as human beings.

– *Amen.*

Thunder rolled. Sivert shot them both in the head at close range. Lightning and thunder simultaneously. Twin flashes, twin cracks, inferno. He witnessed the two falling bodies like frozen images photographed two times a second. They made a splash as they hit the street. Illusion of timelessness was broken. Sivert grabbed the machineguns before proceeding at a murderous speed. Adrenaline pumped so hard into his veins that the pain chased through his body. He heard the sound of many feet making splashes in the flood. Good. If he should die he wanted it that way, leaving fewer for the others to deal with.

He threw himself down behind a corner. They chased towards him from the end of the street. He had hidden in a badly lit, shadowy area. The streetlights made the white cream of splashes and the faceless soldiers to appear like still targets on a shooting range. He took one step out in the open and fired weapons from both hands, in a murderous salvo. Only a few, spread bullets were returned. Several of them threw away their weapons and ran off in panic from the demon confronting them.

More arrived, from all sides. He threw away the empty guns and ran once more. He should have had an M-16 with the grenade launcher. Then he should have showed them… but, no. He reneged. It was asking for too much.

He supported himself on a pole, dizzy and weak. Had they used a tranquilizer or was it caused by the loss of blood? *Unimportant*. Time to get away, far away from them, from here. Then everything would be good. He charged into a narrow alley, kept staying on his feet, kept struggling… *towards freedom.*

… had to… So silent. *Nothing*… He didn't hear the rain anymore. An arm

(he tried to lift his gun he still had it)

fell by his side, into the flowing river created by the drain. He sat, crouched with his back to a slippery wall. That was what he needed to do. Sit up, but everything was slipping, everything that kept him up.

… sit here for a while. He had hidden his body well. They wouldn't find him. Millions of feet trampled at him. He rejected the sound as more of his very active imagination. *You're imagining things*. He would just sit here a little while, sit still, enjoying the silence, until it once again would be safe to return to the world.

++++++++++++++++

Judith thought for one moment she was unable to hear her own steps on the floor, but couldn't say for sure. Kim and Corbin sat on the couch, holding around each other. Judith didn't want to do that, sit down. The steps were measured, calm. One found no signs of worry in the walk. One might confuse it with daily walks people made in the park. She wouldn't sit down. Then the other two would definitely turn mushy, and she couldn't stand that.

It was still raining outside, and the storm seemed unstoppable. Lightning flared and thunder rolled between the walls, shaking them hard. Pictures flickered across the TV-screen. Judith looked at it occasionally, and her eyes were cold. The show tonight was in its entirety broadcast from the Gothenburg streets. Nothing much happened really, but the reporter looked very tense, and babbled into the microphone. He *howled* into the microphone in an attempt to eradicate the Storm. The camera showed the turn leading to Nordstan. Behind the reporter the bridge, canal and post office were visible.

– We have, as stated an amateur photograph of Ole Sivert Olsen and an unidentified woman, with her back to the camera. Behind me divers are looking for just this woman, but the chance of finding her - dead or alive - isn't very high. As you have seen the police and other government representatives have closed off major sections of central Gothenburg. As reported there have been extensive gunfights here tonight, and it may still not be over. Witnesses have confirmed heavy casualties. There are no bodies anywhere. They have all been removed. We can state this with absolute certainty. With our viewers we will take a closer look at our surroundings. We will observe blood on walls and in the water flowing in the streets…

Judith followed Corbin with her eyes as he rose abruptly, rushed to the television set and turned it off with a heavy fist on the OFF-button. She didn't allow it to faze her. He had always been more than a bit tense, unbalanced.

– It's the uncertainty that is the worst, he said embarrassed. – The certainty that we can do no more than sit here and wait.

– We don't have to leave here for a couple of hours, Judith stated stoically. They listened for signs of emotion in her voice, in vain. – If they are captured they will hold out for days before breaking.

Three hours now, since they were supposed to return. Long. Too long. It was time to leave this place, leave it permanently. Under the influence of what was called truth serum, even if it took time the two could come to reveal the position of this and all other hideouts they knew. The two, like all of them were trained to resist the serum's effect. And to obtain precise, valuable information during such conditions was often very difficult, like a puzzle. The information would have to be gathered and assessed over time to get anything sensible out of it. Often it would have to be straight out interpreted. During the first, critical phase, before they had broken the prisoners they would certainly prefer more *direct* methods.

All this under the assumption that they were taken alive and in secret. If the public was given proof they were taken they couldn't be tortured, of course. Then the subtle tyrants would have to be content with throwing them in jail and throwing away the key.

She asked herself how she could behave so calm, so indifferent when two of the people she cared most about in the world were perhaps dead, or thrown into a dark room awaiting torture and worse. She wanted to howl, to shout her grief to her friends and show them that she cared. But the scream from her depths never reached the surface and fell instead ever deeper in the mud.

Kim and Corbin dozed off on the couch. Not completely awake, not completely sleeping, but writhing constantly. Judith couldn't understand how they were even able to close their eyes.

She closed her eyes and it made her wish she hadn't. The induced memory was a pleasant one, but still painful. But again, Corbin was correct. The uncertainty was what really bothered her. She recalled once she and Sivert had been together. One of the few occasions she had allowed herself to be vulnerable after Willy's death. That vulnerability was always there after she had made love to Sivert. He had spoken to her in his usual teasing, devil-may-care voice, not certain if she was really listening.

«I'm not afraid to die. That would be foolish. Everybody dies. Fundamentally it's selfish, I guess. I can live without me. To live without you is quite another matter».

Another memory: Just as painful, now, as when it actually happened, seemingly a thousand years ago, and still it was crystal clear to her. It could have happened earlier today. Events of the day returned at night, often stronger then. The school, the shots, the *murders*. She had lost her innocence in those short, hectic moments. Something she hadn't realized at the time, of course. It had just hurt. It had happened decades ago and she had had ample opportunity to ponder it since then.

And she had seen, sensed something the moment the defenseless young boy had died, something she had never quite understood. In that very micro-cosmos of time a series of images had flickered for her inner eye, the images of an old man riding a horse through the desert, along a highway, and where several cars had passed until one stopped. A man from the car had approached the rider.

That part of the story she had never shared with anyone.

Something touched her consciousness, had done so for so very long… Something… If only she could grab hold of it…

An indistinct sound from the outside distracted her, alarmed her and rocked her world. She lifted her head. Something unmistakable once more faded away, burying itself in her subconscious mind. She was irritated beyond words. Now, she had almost caught the fleeting notion roaming the depths of her Self. More sounds reached her and this time there was no doubt that they were close. They could no longer be mistaken for random groaning of walls or similar. She had an AK 47 in her hands a moment afterwards. Kim and Corbin, too. They cocked their ears, but heard no steps. This sounded more like… someone dragging oneself over the concrete floor. Silverhair signed to them, making them rush into position, becoming battle ready.

Then they heard the distinct scratching at the upper parts of the door.

– It's me, they heard a hardly recognizable voice.

With two of them directing their weapons at the sound, Corbin opened the door, pulled it open a bit less cautious than he would otherwise have done. Anya practically fell into the room. They lowered the weapons and dropped them right there, on the floor and stared paralyzed at her. She was wet with water and blood. Skin looked transparent. They were shocked by seeing her like this, this reduced. They had never seen her… in such a miserable condition before.

When lifting her they feared one horrible moment she would fall apart in their hands, fragile and shredded as she seemed. Shaking hands lowered her carefully down on the bed. A few seconds passed. Kim found scissors and everybody got on with everything they needed to get on with. They cut off her clothes. The vest was actually easiest to remove. Their first impression was that it was shot to pieces. Anya moved nothing by herself, and for some time her breathing was so shallow that they feared she was gone for good. She had kept her eyes closed. Now she opened them by a supreme force of will, opened eyes bloodshot and withered.

In their depths they saw the same, indomitable will.

She was clearly exhausted, completely drained of energy. They could hardly believe it. Before Corbin closed the door he got a short, unwelcome glimpse of the blood trail over the floor in the old building. She had clearly dragged herself the remaining distance to the door. They wondered how far she had dragged herself.

– We must get away from here, she gasped painfully.

– No way! Judith decided.

– Just wanted to warn you… get here…

She spoke half delirious while they worked with her.

– You will get much further than here, do you *hear me*. Judith had to fight herself to not shake her, shake her hard. – Find her brew, her witch's pouch. She needs something strong and strengthening.

– Okay, Anya nodded, to herself more than them, suddenly that much clearer. – Take the white bottle. Its contents will strengthen me and make the wounds close faster. First priority is to close the leaks. I've given enough blood this month.

The mood brightened by her pragmatic approach. They forced themselves to act in a relaxed manner. After they had washed off her blood and bandaged the wounds their hope increased considerably. It had looked far worse than it was. She gave them instructions about what she hadn't taught them before with a clear, firm voice. They warmed her brew, cooking without heat, and gave it to her, surrounded her in warm blankets. She started sweating, and then freezing, and sweating again. They had removed some of the bullets. A few they didn't dare touch remained.

Judith sent Kim and Corbin to make necessary phone calls. She was tempted to say some mollifying words to Kim before she sent her off, but didn't. The wall between them couldn't be removed with a gesture, and she wasn't certain she was willing to do much more.

Not even now.

Especially not now.

– Don't fret, Anya said. – There's minimal risk for something to happen to them. Whatever has happened to Sivert, one way or another he has certainly removed the enemy's soldiers from this part of town.

– I don't fret, Judith said coldly. – Concern yourself with yourself.

Anya managed to force a teasing smile. She clutched Judith's hand, surprisingly strong.

– But if you don't stop using Kim like your personal punching bag you will lose her anyhow. In her own way she's just as proud as you, and she won't put up with your behavior much longer. Nobody will, except Gio and Jemma, and perhaps a few more.

– So you're using the opportunity, now, when you know you won't be punished, Judith exclaimed enraged. – Do you dare oppose my will?

– You know perfectly well what's happening with you and hate it. Anya's smile paled. – Everything turns self-perpetuating. Your self-contempt causes you to treat others even more contemptuously. You know this, know the pattern well. I don't really need to draw a picture, do I? But I'll do it anyway, to make sure.

– You shouldn't strain yourself. Judith tried softly.

The hard knot inside turned even harder.

– You're… pushing too hard, way too hard. Anya kept it up vigorously. – Yourself, those who love you. You… we must not lose sight of the goal. Then we will have lost even if we win.

Anya's hand fell. Eyes closed. Judith was almost overwhelmed by panic a moment, and pressed her ear at the other's chest. The heart beat strong and even. Anya had slipped into a healing sleep. Fever was down. But it wouldn't last. Unless the bullets were removed and the deadly wounds treated, she would quickly turn worse.

Silverhair watched over her carrier of knowledge. She didn't want to sleep, and thought she wasn't actually capable of it. But her eyes closed. Morpheus' shadows descended on her, as well. Long nights, hours and hours she slept and lived by her sister's side.

In a well-hidden room somewhere in town daylight slipped through blinds. Anya slept in the only bed in the room, covered in white sheets. A hypodermic needle was stuck in her arm and she had oxygen plugs in her nose. For the first time in something resembling an eternity she opened her eyes. Judith had been sitting there, looking at the lines of light. When she once again stared into the two deep wells she found it impossible to rein herself in. The face broke in a huge smile.

She attempted to say something, anything, in vain. Words turned completely insufficient. Anya attempted to say something. The lips moved without a sound. Judith raised her head, and pushed a glass of water at her numb lips. She coughed, but managed to swallow some of it. The head fell back on the pillow. It was still a shock to see her like this. The eyes were the only thing alive in the pale face. The hair looked, if possible even blacker in contrast.

– You look… tired, she said, so hoarse that it could hardly be heard.

– Very funny, Judith said sarcastically. – I would have laughed myself silly… if I hadn't been so tired.

Silverhair lowered her wings on her, carefully embracing the bedridden woman.

Kurt stuck his head inside.

– Hey, she's awake.

He managed to keep the voice volume low, but grew excited, like a flame offered fresh oxygen.

– Will someone fetch the surgeon? Judith straightened her sore body.

It was unnecessary. Susan Palmer had heard the commotion. She appeared behind the group of happy faces.

They kept their eyes on her while she examined Anya. She was known as one of the best younger physicians in Europe. She had specialized in surgery, but had a wide range of knowledge and skill, and that also included natural medicine. What very few were aware of was that she was a part of the Green Rose underground support network. She had been a student activist, but after her father had been killed by police officers during riots she had transformed into a glowing revolutionary. This was her way of fighting. She had seemingly adapted to society after her father's death, but it was just a front. To many who got to know her she would be seen as some of an enigma. Not so by the strangers embracing her. She lived her life like a strange mix of love and hatred, a state of mind everybody present knew well.

– You will be good as new, she declared to Anya. – If this bunch isn't tiring you completely and you, yourself manage to relax a few extra seconds or so.

– Thank you. Anya clutched the physician's hand.

Judith repeated it. She formed the words with her lips, but there was no sound.

She needed sleep. She realized that. Shower was first, cascades of hot water drowning her and being so pleasant and opening so many wounds. She couldn't be more tired anyway. The bed and a dreamless sleep awaited her. But before she surrendered there was something she had to do.

Kim stood by the window in the bedroom. She looked out between the curtains. There was no one else there. They had it all to themselves. Judith walked to Kim and knelt before her, bowing her head in submission. Kim remained distant, indifferent briefly. Then she smiled, and knelt, too.

Soft hands in the hair, the face, neck, on the body, it felt so good.

– I let you pay for all my problems, pay a lot, Judith said in despair. – Treated you like furniture, not a person. We all need to let out steam, occasionally, but not… like this.

– We all need to relieve the pressure inside, cleanse frustration, Kim said softly. And… comforting? – But we have challenged an entire, addled world that for millennia has hardly used any arguments but violence and threats, and we must be prepared for the consequences…

She hesitated a bit. And then shrugged and completed the line of thought.

– We are at war, she said simply. – People die in war.

Judith scowled at her. Kim smiled. They smiled cheerfully at each other and laughed a bit, a laughter carrying a hard, brittle underlying quality.

Soft hands, supple, writhing bodies. They stretched across the connecting beds and made soft, slow love. Tears flowed from Kim's eyes in joy and sorrow.

They enjoyed the peaceful silence and each other's close proximity. These were old emotions, and it was years since they had previously experienced them. But Judith didn't cry.

Not a single tear.

+++++++++++++

Darkness. He stretched out his senses. No matter how far he reached there was nothing but darkness. He wondered how long he had spent here, in this place. He had no idea. Saw nothing, heard nothing. Suddenly someone stuck nose plugs in his nostrils. They released such a horrible stench that there was hardly room for anything else. He hardly felt anything. They had beaten him senseless. He retained the capacity for taste. The taste of blood and iron never left his mouth.

He had certainly been a prisoner for quite a while. A check on his wounds… those he hardly noticed anymore confirmed that. They had stitched him up before they started taking him apart. Good, that way he would have some meaty pieces he could throw to the sleeping wolf. So it might sleep a little longer. He had a plan. Not much of one, admittedly, but sufficient to not make him give away too much about his friends. He had no longer any hope of being rescued. If there had been the slightest chance for that it would have happened already.

He wondered how long he had been sitting here, unable to move a finger. His toes moved, seemingly of their own accord, but that was all. His body had become so tied to the chair that he saw himself as part of it.

Voices far away. Steps. They hadn't blocked his hearing. They wanted him to hear the prolonged howls and cries of despair from other places, other rooms. Recordings? He didn't let them rock him. He knew well, without thinking about it much that they would never let him out of here alive. This was a place «that didn't exist» in any democracy.

Powerful lights in his face. Head was pulled up so hard that hair loosened from the scalp. He didn't give a fuck. High. They had to be high above the ground. He had sensed the building sway in the wind with the gift of the extra sharp senses his enemies had given him. If they had only known the strength… strength… how they *strengthened* him, the fuckers.

– No one knows you're here, Olsen, Gray Suit said brutally. – No one will be able to claim with certainty and authority that you've been caught. We will definitely not do so.

What building… Did it belong to SEPO, the Swedish Intelligence? No, too risky. It would be another, less official place, but official *enough*. The pussies. They had no idea how strong they made him.

– *Get it?* The word was spit at him, followed by the predictable strike.

– Go to…

Another. This pushed air from his lungs.

– … hell, God's tiny devils.

A swearing and Blue Suit broke the first toe. Perhaps he should scream a bit, give them a bit of show?

He had one hell of a show in mind, Academy Award material. But not yet. Patience. Pat…

A tight grip around his balls. He moaned like a lost soul on its way to condemnation. These guys… he knew that, but such things one accepted only grudgingly… had no humanity left to lose. Perhaps they behaved like saints somewhere, somehow in the world, were nice to children and animals, but that was just a front, an *act*. A masquerade. Insanity only had an advantage if it wasn't exposed for what it was.

Pain. He had never imagined he could experience so much pain and yet live. They were so cleaver, so beyond cleaver. They knew well that the body sanitized the places of injury, and that it took time before it truly started hurting. When the toe did start hurting they went at it for real. They turned it round and round and round. *And round*.

– I don't know if you want to hear this, Olsen. The name was emphasized, spat like a curse. – You almost look beautiful, at least compared to your friend. You've heard her howl the last few days, haven't you?

Had they captured Anya, too?

A wet hand clutched him in its grip. He fought against it and pulled himself together.

– Carla Wolf? He wondered.

They constantly attempted to trick him, to trap him. To make him talk, to betray secrets, and if he first broke he would break like a dam.

– Yes, Carla, Blue Suit said sweetly. It was incredible how nice a threatening voice could seem. – She has told us things about you that even we didn't know about. Now, you will tell us every detail you know about her. Don't fear, we'll assist you, help you remember.

And he jabbered like a peacock, incoherently, like a confession usually was.

– An address, Gray Suit spat an eternity later. – Your quarters, your last. He heh.

He mumbled the reply, hung and rocked in the chains for an age, an eternal silence after that.

They came at him with glowing fire out of the darkness. The hot point of the metal poker hit him just below the right eye, burned hole in his skin.

– Appearances deceive. He recognized the snarling voice of Gray Suit. – Carla Wolf, huh? You're a first class liar, Ole. Know that I give you deserved praise.

– Your Carla Wolf isn't registered anywhere, Blue Suit pointed out softly. – The address you provided exists, but it was abandoned and cleaned up. All the rats had left. You will have to do better than that, little Ole.

Sivert gathered strength, and spat a giant clot of blood through the air. Teeth and skin accompanied it. It hit Blue Suit perfectly on the nose tip, and splashed across the entire broad face. The man blew his nose like a bull and used his hands, drying it with his sleeve. In savage anger he delivered his first strike during this performance, and his second, and his third, only slowly regaining his composure. It was more than sufficient to knock Sivert unconscious. And Sivert welcomed it.

A bucket of water, another sharp smell in the nostrils. Eyes slipped open.

He saw nothing, only the white light everywhere.

– You will tell us everything, you pathetic worm, even if there is nothing more than the tongue and lips left of you.

A female voice. He recognized it, recognized her, easily. Elsa Andersen.

His vision cleared somewhat, and he glimpsed three distorted faces. Holy, it *hurt*. He steeled himself once again, used all the resources he had, enabling him to steel himself, one last force of will. It wouldn't be long, now. Thoughts wavered. He wasn't fatally injured. They could keep him alive until they had squeezed every last drop of juice out of him. Turned did his thoughts, as did he, above deep, eternally dark wells. Bottomless pits. This was the world as it was, hard and ruthless, true blood and violence. He hungered in the dark, and discovered then that he, in spite of everything very much, so very much wanted to live, wanted to fly through endless Space, without cages, without boundaries.

They started on the rest of the toes and fingers, mashed them to pieces, ruining them, attacked his hands, smashed them bone by bone, slowly but surely to red dust.

– Time for the dentist, Andersen ordered maliciously.

Good, she was impatient.

And the dentist arrived, with his mouth cloth and instruments. The man smiled pleasantly beneath his mouth cloth. Sivert imagined it that way anyway. He thought the guy would start the treatment without assistance when Andersen pushed the table with all the equipment into the light.

– Let's see… Yes, there is indeed much work needed here.

He sounded like a kindergarten teacher. Andersen smiled as well.

– There's no need to worry, she assured him. – I have considerable in-service training.

She placed a pinch in his mouth, pushing it wide-open. The drill appeared out of nowhere in the dentist's hand. The nice kindergarten teacher went to work without hesitation. The drill quickly penetrated the tooth, forced itself deep into it, into the root canal. Sivert howled. He didn't have to strain to sound louder than the drill. *Horrible…* he had to take it… *Just a little bit longer*. A hidden, indifferent part of him realized he was about to go into shock. Good. He would fade again soon. Fade, *fall into darkness*.

He floated in a warm, pleasant darkness. Not long, now, until he could fly on the wings of night. He heard voices, distant, insignificant.

– *He can't take much more…* a voice floating in and out of his awareness.

– *He can take it for days, and that will be more than sufficient*.

– Damn, we need him to sing *now*. It has been too long already.

When his eyes once more slipped open his attention was drawn to his right hand. Elsa Andersen held a sharp butcher knife in her hands. He had no doubt she was fully capable of using it.

– Okay, this is it, Sivert. We will cut off fingers and pull out teeth and then tear off limb by limb, and we will do so without anesthetics, until you sing, and sing beautifully. And believe me, you will be alive. Our physicians have assured us that you're still strong as a bull. We can administer lethal injuries, but it will take you a long time to die. Have you seen a man without arms and legs? Our surgeons are very skilled. I assure you…

He turned it off, wanted them to get going. He wanted to tell her something all right, something very far from what she desired. It didn't matter. His mouth was so swollen that he could hardly move it without major pain. Instead he conserved his remaining energies. Not much, now, not much longer.

His little finger was already standing out at an impossible angle. They removed it slowly and gleefully. The next finger they sawed off, rather than cut.

– STOP, MERCY… talkI'lltalkTALK.

Words came unintelligible and from deep down his throat.
– What was that? Gray Suit grinned. – We didn't quite hear that.
– Must see ight, light, please. *Lighttalk.*
– Keep sawing, Andersen said, totally uncaring.
She had given the blade to Gray Suit and had pulled back a little, to survey it all.
The middle finger vanished in howls and a piercing sound.
– TalkightalkAHHHH
– Eanie, meanie, Blue Suit scorned.
They proceeded in a more random fashion, a toe there, a finger there.
A hand pulled the hair, making even more of the scalp loosen. Ole Sivert Olsen was filled with gratitude towards Silverhair, beloved Judith, who had had foresight enough to at least be close to imagining what awaited them if they should be captured in secret.
– Now, shithead?
Without the interrogation/torture training they had completed he would have sung like a peacock, and perhaps been condemned to live like this caricature of a human being.
– … lightlightlightlightlughtlught, he babbled, and babbled, and babbled…
– SATAN! Elsa stamped her foot at the floor.
– This isn't an unknown… phenomenon, Blue Suit (or Gray Suit) commented. An excellent soccer game, the way he referred it. He he. – We could use the serum, but it's an uncertain method. He might snap completely. To minimize that risk he needs at least a couple of days' *rest.* If we take him to a place with daylight he might break completely and give us all the help we ask for. I've seen it happen before.
– Okay, let's grant his last wish. Elsa shrugged, her body language telling him she wasn't really shrugging at all. – We're talking about an excellent tradition here, are we not?
They untied the cadaver of a body from the chair and pulled him on his feet, but kept the chains on. They let go of him, and he fell to the floor like an empty sack.
– On your feet, potato-face,
The whip they had used when softening him, through the initial stages of the treatment was now returned to the honorable spot.
Yes, he had to regain his strength, in the legs. Had to! But he couldn't show them how much strength, how much infinite hatred he retained. Miracles! He could stand. Since the chain was so short, he hardly managed to put one foot in front of the other. But it worked. He stumbled and subbed between the monsters calling themselves human beings.

The torture was, after all mostly in the mind. They hadn't touched his innermost being. Because he had, long ago realized he had nothing more left to lose.

The curtain fell. Previously Silverhair had led the way through darkness. Now he would have to manage on his own.

The twilight land awaited him. Perhaps there was nothing there, or quite a lot. He had never feared the unknown, and he had no intention of starting now. He was ready.

An office appeared before his watery eyes, spacey and fashionable, so chilled and pleasant. A man sat there. Sivert didn't know him. He felt strongly that he knew of him. Or others like him.

– Now, Herr Olsen, you've got something to tell us?

The disfigured creature lifted his chained hands. They shook as he reached for the light. Were the windows, too, fake, or was there air, pure, clear air behind them? His thoughts wandered to the salmon swimming up the steepest waterfall, a stray thought turning into that selfsame waterfall of blood, one that dominated every single weave in him.

After a nod from the man behind the desk Blue Suit rearranged the blinds, and light flooded the room.

Ole Sivert Olsen crouched like he was about to collapse. He felt how his muscles were filled with power. He retained the wild fear that his body, that he would fail in the critical moment. Fail

as he jumped. He jumped up on the desk, almost too far, and almost landed in the fat man's lap. He laughed out aloud, overwhelming their alarmed shouts. Two supple legs jumped, took off from the edge of the desk. There was just a step to the broad and high window.

(what if the glass was unbreakableNO)

The jump had such power that he broke the window and ended far away from the swaying building before he finally started falling. He saw the ground clearly down there, in the distance. His thoughts touched, touched, touched upon the story of the salmon. Later it was hard to interpret his expression, twisted as it clearly was, in joy and wild *triumph*. The whirlwind caught him and blew him away… while he flew one, final time.

++

The entire wall was covered in TV-screens. The vast majority covered the same «news». All of Europe's stations and channels were represented. Tom Rawlins sat in a chair at the center of the room. The room at large consisted of naked, sterile furniture. No sounds were heard. Not outside, not inside. He nipped to a filled glass, attempting a kind of overview, striving to look at all the images simultaneously. Got fed up and turned on the cacophony of sound. A Babel Tower of languages filled the empty air.

Images and words started penetrating his skull and invaded his brain. He sighed, had already seen the recordings a few times. His thumb touched a new button. The wall turned into one single patched image, into that of the American news-channel CNN. They had never had this many correspondents in Sweden and Scandinavia before. Northern Europe had been seen as one of the world's quiet and peaceful corners.

A man holding a microphone stood in front of a tall building. The sharp-eyed among the audience couldn't avoid seeing the broken window up there.

– ... and it was from this building, belonging to the Swedish Secret Service, SEPO Ole Sivert Olsen jumped to his death. The building wasn't known to be a SEPO hold out, but the connection has now been proven beyond doubt. Added to many other exposures, members, prominent members of SEPO and ESF, the new European Security Force have been observed leaving and entering the place. Under the Defense of the Realm security act they attempted to keep the entire incident under wraps. But when several articles were published in Eastern European media the news broke like a dam. Everything started when Roland Vallens, the notorious outlaw «tipped off» newspapers and television stations. No one knows where he gets his information, but his tips have proven very reliable in the past. Ole Sivert Olsen's last flight was covered extensively. Nothing is covered up or added. Officials deserve praise for one thing: They never attempted to claim the missing fingers and toes were caused by the fall. They are not that stupid or confident. Marks from burns and lashes also speak plainly about what was happening inside. Heads have rolled and will keep rolling over this, probably not because of the acts themselves, but because they were exposed. Ole Sivert Olsen made sure of that... The events have caused some worry in the general population in many countries, and questions are being asked about the justification behind the very existence of the secret services. It is claimed that their activities are not really directed at foreign countries and spies at all, but on the contrary against a given country's own population. The belief in the innocence of western democracies has been damaged significantly, perhaps beyond repair. Huge numbers of protesters are now filling the streets for the third week in a row, and for the moment their activity shows no sign of abating. This is Neal Conan from Gothenburg - a city seething in rage.

The newscasters in the studio pulled themselves together. One of them eventually started speaking.

– Yes, even here in the united states there are demands of an impartial scrutiny of the intelligence community and that the paragraphs concerning the Defense of the Realm and similar are removed from law. President

Clinton, however, is considering sending American «experts» supporting the newly created ESF «dealing with the new wave of terrorism in Europe».

A man, an intruder had opened the only door to the room with the many screens, and walked inside, and done so with impunity. Rawlins reached with a concealed hand for the gun he hid under the chair, but decided against it when he spotted the gun in the intruder's hand.

– Rawlins, the man greeted him, presenting a calm surface.

– Vallens. Rawlins concentrated hard in holding on to his mask, his frozen features.

– I've come to your residence on a special errand. Vallens placed himself by the wall, slightly crouched. – I'm sure you realize that I didn't much care for what happened to Ole Sivert Olsen, that I, in fact didn't care for it at all.

– I didn't have anything to do with that, you know I didn't. Rawlins' voice turned a bit more agitated. – But I can tell you that the incident revealed several serious gaps in my organization's security. I can assure you that they have now been dealt with.

He studied the young face thoroughly, in the hope of learning anything, in vain. Vallens was in his middle twenties by now. Several years had passed since they had last met. If possible the man had become even more shrouded in mystery. He played with the gun and Rawlins inevitably smelled sweat in his armpits. Suddenly, as if by magic the gun vanished.

– Sorry about the gun. Vallens smiled. – I thought you would be fairly nervous these days, and better safe than sorry, right? A great piece of work this place of yours. I don't always have access to recent news. There is a great uproar these days, isn't there?

– It won't last, Rawlins mumbled. – The sheep are taught to follow the shepherd - all the way to the precipice.

– We can always hope, Vallens said with a big smile.

The way Rawlins saw it there wasn't much optimism in the other's voice.

– Seen enough news already? The arms-dealer inquired. Vallens had turned to go, and didn't seem to care about the scorn. – I have more than enough room. You could write a poem or a song?

– Do you know what I think, Tommy? Vallens didn't turn around. – You *are* growing old. ESF in its inception must have followed you around on several of your meetings previous to the one with Sivert, before scoring. Perhaps you should retire?

Rawlins turned off the TV, doing so with a tightly woven fist. Only the light through the open door illuminated parts of the room. The rigid features on the sitting man's face were lit, juxtaposed by the otherwise dark surroundings.

– Cut the bullshit, he said harshly. – I assume your special errand has paid off?

– You're still on my list of recommended contacts, Vallens calmly confirmed. – If you're lucky you can keep bartering helplessness and worthless paper until being totally covered in moss.

– I'll have flowers ready for your grave.

– We don't have more to say to each other. That fact should please you.

The intruder left. He had reached the doorway when Rawlins stopped him.

– My men, they are dead?

Vallens turned his head.

– Dead as doornails. My apologies if this sadden you.

Rolland Vallens would soon be gone, returned to the shadow world he had come from.

– Not that they will soon be worm food. Rawlins took care to show his extra rough smile. – Just the fact that they were overpaid.

CHAPTER SEVENTEEN

They crossed the English Channel with the night ferry from Oostende, not completely clear on why they chose that route, instead of the Chunnel train from Brussels. The explanation they were somewhat content with was that they were following their instincts and whims, to be more unpredictable. Besides, they enjoyed it. They saw themselves as a nomadic tribe, and a nomadic life contained few ordered elements.

Some slept and twisted on the floor in the public quarters, while others, wide-awake hardly closed an eye. Other passengers also slept on the floor and other possible and impossible places, but they hadn't traveled far, like the Nightravens. It was just life breaking them. Silverhair and those following her had long since learned to fight with indomitable will against towering despair.

London in spring was a city bubbling with life. It was almost too much for them, who constantly lived strongly, on the edge. They danced through the streets, danced in the parks and fed on every possible sensation. One thing they had learned about good moments in life was to enjoy them, short and fleeting as they were.

The group reached the end of Tottenham Court Road, continuing further south on Charing Cross Road, passing Centre Point. From the Underground station or from the Subway, where many homeless lived they heard the sound of a bagpipe, wailing, filled with longing. They imagined actually seeing the musician in their line of sight. Silverhair felt like she was immersed in the music, as if in tears, joy, sorrow, rage.

Doves rose at Trafalgar Square. Laughing children ran between the water fountains. The Sun warmed Silverhair in the face through the mask. They hit a spot, and sat down close to each other, on walls and benches, all nineteen together now. There were so many people wandering through this city's streets at any time that even larger groups vanished in the crowd. They were just one group of many. One could truly disappear in this town, and hide in its wonderful murky depths forever.

The bagpipe, one single tone echoed in Silverhair's mind. The dreams she had carried in her youth, were they gone now? She could, when listening still hear them, like distant echoes from green fields, from the deep forest, the heartbeat of the gods. The first time she had visited this town Jonas Bergli had brought her. Shown the seventeen-year old girl another reality, shown her that existence could be different from constant sadness, boredom and despair. She had come here a few times after that, and each time the visits worked at relieving the pressure she always felt.

In addition to the undeniable sense of freedom the city inspired, the inspiration to keep looking, there were many fantastic radical environments here, places of true freedom to run to, for all the persecuted from the entire big bad world. These places had grown quite a bit the last six months… to shrink once again.

– It's the same here. Kurt spoke muted, sadness and rage evident in his voice. – Not as bad and evident as elsewhere, but tangible. The rebellion isn't *visible* anymore.

– It is said an elephant never forgets, Elan spat. – But instead of having the memory of the elephant, people's attention is diverted as easily as a well-fed cat on the prowl.

Laughter. Kim petted her brother on the back.

– It's the way we're all raised, Gio said in despair. They could sense that despair, his desperate rage as something physical, tangible. – People are trained, encouraged to have the attention span of a fly. It serves to keep people in line. Fortunately there are people raising and educating themselves.

– It's like they live in a totally different world, Judith said passionately. – A closed circuit, isolated from their surroundings, from nature. What we must do is something nobody can possibly ignore or isolate themselves from, be indifferent to. Something they will never forget. *Not even after a thousand years*.

– I know what you're thinking. Kim put her hand on her shoulder. – Please don't.

Silverhair squeezed the smaller hand in a calming grip, sent her a smile without sting. What she had in mind wasn't on the agenda - yet.

They walked to Covent Garden. The original market had been moved south of the river years ago, but against the government's wishes the area had kept much of its distinctiveness, its alternativeness. The pack arrived from the south, up through a narrow alley from Strand. Once, not long ago there had been prolonged ongoing construction work here. A horribly ugly building was the result of all the hard work. But the area's distinctive mark endured.

One of the first sights meeting them within the car-free zone was a group dancing «Kacha», a special technique mixing nature dance and gymnastics. It was supposed to be done in wild nature, but it worked anywhere. Anya glanced hopefully at Judith. Silverhair nodded merciful and also irritated. Anya would ask permission for anything. She behaved annoyingly obedient sometimes.

She lit up and reached out her hands to Kurt. He smiled, shaking his head. She insisted. He lit up, too, and he followed her. They whirled off, joining the people dancing unrestrained on the hot cobblestones. They shook and moved to the ancient rhythms and tones, to the gracious, but wild moves. Joy, the conviction that they were alive and thriving was written in each and every one of them during their unrestrained moves, in a unity of mind and body working independent of old injuries. Anya jumped high up, landed on Kurt's shoulders, and balanced on them. The other dancers gathered around the two. She danced on their shoulders, too, as sure on her feet as if she was on the ground. Soft flesh and bones had become her floor. A sea of faces flooded her consciousness every time she looked down.

Afterwards she stood there with blushing cheeks and accepted the applause from what had grown to a considerable audience.

The thoughtful, partly confused expression didn't leave her for a while.

– What's on your mind? Kurt wondered.

– I don't know… When I moved there, among the other dancers I had a sense of the buildings… disappearing around us. The cobblestone turned to dirt, and we were out in the wilderness somewhere.

They looked at each other. Everybody had «seen» the same. Not in such a distinct way as Anya, perhaps, more like an indistinct illusion, but clear enough.

Suddenly a figure appeared in the street right in front of them. To them it was like the old woman dressed in rags materialized out of thin air. The madness lit up her windows to her inner self.

– *What you saw was real. This is the illusion.*

She struck out her arms, embracing everything they could see.

– Here is some money, Miss. Kurt gave her some bills. – Do what you want with it.

– Many thanks, My Lord. She curtseyed in something that couldn't even be called a caricature, an ironic act. – Live long and prosper.

She left them while putting every single bill in her mouth and chewing them thoroughly.

The group headed north and the streets turned narrow, congested, the alleys and sidewalks resembling a labyrinth instead of streets. There were shops with green roses painted on windows and doors. In a hidden cellar they found a stage play they enjoyed and they remained there until their stomachs started screaming for food. There were major signs of joyous underground activity everywhere. By Seven Dials they were «forced» to choose between many great non-expensive, non-poisonous dining places. All the countless food cosmetics people were poisoned by on a daily basis shone in their absence. The group felt… at home here.

The owners of the place they finally decided upon started seriously brightening when the huge, wild pack stumbled through the door. Small tables were joined to one big. A few minutes later the Nightravens ate and drank in joyous celebration.

They had stayed a while when a loud sneeze sounded at the far end away from the flower stands. Karine didn't enjoy herself quite as much as the others. Fluid flowed constantly from her nose and tightened by the second. She had patiently waited for it to happen, like a stoker for the train to leave.

– The allergy again? Renni wondered, not without compassion, while cheering with Corbin on the other side.

– Djes. She blew her nose, turning red on the neck where the mask didn't reach, striving to keep her nostrils open. – One or more of the flower species around here definitely has the right wrong type of pjollen. Hjell, pollen.

She heard a tearing sound. Her mask. The sound was so loud that she convinced herself that everybody in the room had heard it. Nobody reacted, except for Renni and Heike, the two sitting closest to her.

– Am gjoing to cjool djown a ljittle, she sniveled.

Heike and Renni nodded. They would quietly notify the others, if necessary.

Tall people had, in general, a shitty deal when doorframes were concerned. This upper frame was lower than most and she knocked her head on it when stumbling through the opening to the toilet, almost fell in her rampant dizziness. Tears flowed and she didn't see shit. She tore her mask to pieces to gain proper access to her nostrils. A hand fumbled in a pocket and finally found the small spray. She sprayed her nostrils in two quick moves. A horrible moment she was almost overwhelmed by the thought that the medicine would not work or not work until she had choked to death.

Her airways cleared slowly. She filled a palm with water from the tap, put a tablet in her mouth and swallowed it with lots of water. The cool water flowed down her dry throat. She sighed relieved, having fixed herself for a few hours. By then they would be gone from here, and she wouldn't need more medicine, at least not until next time. The damn pollution! It fucked up the body's immune defense system. Fucked up the body, period! Any body. Made humans, animals, plants vulnerable to diseases they would have dealt with easily in a poison free environment, one clean before, during and after conception. A boy she had known had asthma. A physician had told him that the disease would never have emerged if it hadn't been for the pollution.

She removed the remains of the mask, kept the wig. Normal color returned to a face just slightly paler than usual.

A man stuck his head inside. An unknown. She reached inside her jacket, and sensed the shape and cold of the gun.

– I'm quite harmless, he assured her. He started talking quickly, nervously. – It's true, compared to you, at least.

– What do you want?

She didn't relax. The years had taught her caution.

– When I see the sleeve tightening around your arm I see something that might be an armband. Please, don't be embarrassed, it's just a minor detail. I wouldn't have noticed if not for the other minor details and my fervent interest. May I see it, please?

Details. They lived and died by details. No thought, only a driven, instinctive consciousness.

Her first thought was to tell him to go to an even warmer place. But… something about him, the imploring attitude, the curiosity and enthusiasm convinced her. He resembled them all a few years back. One could never be safe from deceit, but…

– Only those who take chances are truly alive, she sighed.

She pulled up her sleeve even further. The green rope armband appeared.

– I knew it! He exclaimed. – You *are* Karine Lie.

She held back another sigh. It had for quite some time been a source of joy, anxiety and embarrassment to her that she was one of the better-known members of the Green Rose.

– I am! She replied proudly.

– Jason Edwards, he presented himself. – I've read all your books. I am especially fond of your traveling diary Blood and Flowers: the Limitations of Pacifism. And the horror story The Undead Politician. *Great* stuff!

She smiled in spite of herself. Gallows humor always made her high spirited. But the enemy would know that. She had to be careful not to like the guy too much, too early.

– You're one of them, he said, more somber. – To just have met you is certainly cause for celebration in itself, and then the entire group sits out here. Radical!

– You haven't answered my initial question, she said mildly reproaching him.

He blushed but caught himself fast enough.

– I wish to join you.

– We will come back to you, if things check out, she just said, and added: – It's procedure.

– I realize that, he nodded calmly. – Security must come before everything else. I don't mind. My life has been an open book, to this point.

Kim stuck her head inside.

– Kimberly Russel, right? He gave her hesitatingly his hand, while attempting to be a bit more a man for his hat. – My name is Jason Edwards. A pleasure!

– It's all right, Karine said cheerfully. – Under the benefit of the doubt tag.

A roguish flash was lit in Karine's eyes. She decided to throw caution to the wind - for a short while. Then she had to laugh at the irony of her own thoughts. For a short while? Ridiculous! They had thrown all caution to the Storm years ago. That was both advantageous and disadvantageous. Beyond all it had given them long flashes of their own mortality… and convinced them beyond doubt how great it was to be alive.

She made no attempt at hiding her face when rejoining the table.

– Our new recruit, she presented Jason. – Another idiot burning to have his head blown off.

Jason had a wonderful day, evening and night. After they parted it took a long while until he saw them again. But this wonderful day, evening and night he would always recall with fondness. Most famous - or infamous - people didn't do justice to their reputation, but these guys surpassed it. They were - in more ways than one - bigger than death. And yet they were living, breathing people, with faults and shortcomings. He fought with himself to keep a minimum of sobriety and neutrality, but it was hard. He had to improve himself. They wouldn't want a fanatic without critical judgment. That was a lot of what was wrong with today's society. Too many were good sheep, and followed orders blindly.

Familiar streets he had walked his entire life were like *transformed*. He got thoroughly blitzed, but that wasn't exactly new. He led on down Shaftesbury Avenue and imagined he walked on another planet. The flame had been lit inside him, and it burned away the poison in his system. The whirlwind made him sober virtually in an instant. He turned like that very wind, but they were gone like shadows before the Sun. Karine had touched his shoulder and after that he had neither seen nor heard of her. They vanished unnoticed one by one, and Karine and the few who had kept him company a few more minutes had probably beaten it at the last corner, by Wardour Street.

He smiled sheepishly, looked towards Piccadilly Circus, and felt better than ever before. Something swelled within, stronger, hotter. A weak ember, transformed to an ever-burning fire. They might be gone, but they had given him something he had been lacking and subconsciously longed for:

A direction, a purpose in life.

++++++++++++++++++++++

Two days after that they blew up the ICI's headquarter. It happened late at night, while there were only board members in the building. Those very board members attended a meeting where also several representatives for the ESF were present. Many birds were killed with one stone.

This was seen as so big that the public was convinced it had to be the Nightravens' operation in the United Kingdom. When none of the members were captured during the most massive watch of the borders, the coastline and the channel in history sarcastic remarks from political commentators stated they had once again slipped through the grid. Rumors even told they had taken the trip across the Atlantic to the united states to prepare operations there. All of this was

An excellent diversion, Silverhair thought. Or several fat birds with that stone.

The wind was blowing heavily through the old ruin that had once been a new, proud hangar. There was still one wrecked plane there, rusty and missing a wing. But the runway was still in use, and was more than sufficient for the two planes they had brought here.

The group had set up shop at this remote spot, just a bit north of the infamous Sellafield nuclear power plant, re-christened from its original name *Windscale* in the early sixties, in a desperate attempt by the authorities to alleviate people's more than validated fear. This time, with this one place they had failed. Or had they? This construction of fear and arrogance was still operational, more than thirty years after the re-christening.

The distance, even directly through air was considerable, but the planes had double tanks and could fly back and forth easily. They could have flown one way, to the Norwegian coast, if necessary.

The entire vast surrounding estate was owned by a dummy corporation called New Silicon Valley, a computer firm in the early stages of its existence, a useful, temporary façade for the Green Rose. The other cell used it as storage facility of weapons and explosives.

The planes had originally been constructed with four seats. The two backseats had been removed, making room for a lot of bombs. The force flying to Sellafield was Corbin, Helene, Yvonne and Kees.

– I'm so looking forward to fly, Yvonne exclaimed cheerfully. – I could have flown all the way, you know.

– Yeah, as soon you have learned take off and landing, Morten commented dryly.

– That isn't hard, Yvonne rebutted. – I've become such a great pilot, haven't I Corb?

– Taking off is hard. Landing is not hard at all…

With that line he managed to draw attention from his red face. Everybody laughed heartedly.

They had turned quite fond of gallows humor lately.

The Sun set on the hills in the west. Because they drove on the highway in that direction, the Sun set slower, and they could enjoy it longer. They drove a first class tourist bus, rented through the New Silicon Valley project…

This operation was coordinated with the other cell, and the biggest since the attack on Hugo Manning and partners. Earlier they had attacked targets from either aerial or ground position. Now, they would do both simultaneously. Their task was to flatten Sellafield, to destroy it utterly. Steve and Sybille lead their group against another target, one supposed to be officially opened tomorrow, the reprocessing plant in Dounray.

Conversation halted slowly. They never spoke much the final hours before an operation. The jokes descending on Gio in the driver's seat, because of his correct, very formal attire stopped coming.

Most of them carried their anxiety openly. It was natural, and to some, a necessity, before an attack. But Silverhair had kept an eye on Anya before and after they had entered the bus. With her sharper power of observation she noticed what the others didn't. Anya had displayed small, but visible signs of worry all day, and it had turned worse the closer they came to the target. Now Judith actually spotted a pale flair in the suntanned face. Eyes flickered and she had them locked at a point on the window. It could be a kind of battle fright. It was, after all fairly common among people who had been injured in a fight. But it had been six months, and Anya had participated in several gunfights since then without breaking stride.

Anya sat in front, with Gio. She stared out through the windshield. Silverhair sat down by her side. Gio turned off from the highway. They were getting close. At this moment the other group of Nightravens crossed the farmland approaching the plant in Dounray. Everything turned dark, tight and heavy. The narrow line in the horizon had no bearing on their situation, good or bad. Judith embraced herself, realizing she was cold. Good. As long as it kept her focused that was good.

The road stretched infinitely in front of them. But the lights lit only a small area, of the infinite distance ahead.

– Time to call air-support, Gio stated. Judith nodded.

Gio followed their preset route. The first phone booth they passed was taken. It didn't matter. The next was just a few hundred meters away. No sweat.

– Stop, Judith ordered calmly.

– What's the matter with you? Kurt had joined them in front. Anya stared at him with wild eyes.

– STOP, she howled. – STOOOP!

Gio had started to slow down. Now he shook, and stepped on the break. The bus swerved and halted abruptly. Everybody was thrown forward. Only Judith managed to somewhat stay in her seat. Kurt held hard around Anya.

– The DRAGONS are waiting for us with their fiery *mouths,* she whispered. – Waiting for us, waiting for them…

Judith ripped off a seat, found a gun with a silencer and put it in her pocket.

– Turn around, she told Gio. And to Kurt: – Hold her. Tie her up if necessary.

Kim ran forward to help. Anya writhed in their grip like a snake. Judith threw a rope to them. Gio didn't need to be told to open the door. Silverhair put her hands in her pockets and jumped outside. The woman in the phone booth was suddenly busy dialing a number. Silverhair stopped by an imaginary line, like she would have done on a firing range. The booth was ten meters off. Silverhair shot the woman in the head. The phone slipped out of the weak grip. The body slipped to the floor.

The bus returned to the night from which it had come.

Jemma tied Anya with a thick rope. It took some time for the black Irish to calm down so much that it was possible to get some sense from her.

– Call the hangar, Judith ordered curtly.

Jan, sitting there with the radio looked at her.

– What about the people there?

– They're on their own.

Jan said one single word into the microphone, before turning off the radio.

– I was afraid of saying anything, wasn't certain, Anya mumbled with fever hot eyes. – Then… I saw so much, saw *blood and death* everywhere.

– You should have said something. Judith affectionately petted her cheek. – Instead of being worried we wouldn't believe you… fortuneteller.

– You're right. I didn't want to admit… what I am…

– Untie her. Judith retreated to the back of the bus. – And turn on the news.

Gio hesitated with a finger on the button. It was strange seeing him like this. Judith sat down in the middle of the backseat, sat down in the Lotus Position, and started a meditation deepening in seconds. They feared what she feared. The voices in the speakers slowly penetrated the haze of their mind. The news was quite ordinary at first, pretty much the same as the day before or the day before that, and before that, and before that… The tense situation between the nuclear powers Pakistan and India had taken a turn for the worse. Hurricane number six thousand and one assaulted the american mainland. The Maldives sent their protest letter number ten thousand to the UN. Or was that ten thousand and one? The only reason it was mentioned this time was the fact that the entire delegation to the UN had jumped off a pier and into the New York Harbor. An american delegate had told them to do just that… and they had taken him up on it. Perhaps they had interpreted his words a bit too literal, since they had jumped with heavy concrete blocks around their feet. They had long since drowned when the rescue team reached them. Commentators speculated quite a bit on why they had gone to such extreme measures to get their points across.

Kurt started laughing. Eventually he laughed so hard that his face was wet with tears.

– The fourth, *supporting* estate never fails to amaze…

Then, towards the end of the news, when they were about to repeat the headlines:

– We're getting a message, now… it's from… Yes, we're now receiving a report from our correspondent at the nuclear reprocessing plant in Dounray.

Ken Carnevale, the reporter (yes, that was indeed his name) was breathing heavily into the microphone. It took two or three try-outs before there were any words.

– I'm now standing in a field about hundred meters from the plant itself. The lights don't quite reach out here, so one does not see the color of the grass, one doesn't see that it is colored red in several places. There are literally bodies everywhere and that's only *half* of it. What has happened at this remote, windy place on the Scottish coast is indeed a startling development. In a dramatic battle less than an hour ago an entire cell of the terrorist organization the Green Rose was eradicated. With us here we have one of the heroes of the day, the plant's chief of security, Scott Lobdell, and we ask him: What happens now with the long planned opening tomorrow?

– I can assure you and your audience that it will happen on schedule. As you know; Ken, these prospective vandals and murderers didn't even get inside the gates.

– Scott, were many of your men injured or killed?

– Not many, Ken. We surprised the bastards. I have to say we gave them every chance to surrender, but they started the shooting before we had finished the first sentence. It must be admitted they're some nasty creeps... but they can't compete with true soldiers.

– What can you tell us about security here at the plant?

– We have the best protection money can buy... and more. I can't disclosure details, of course, but as you've seen security is top notch. We have the best men, the newest technology. It won't be long until the video cameras will be able to catch the movement of a fly crossing the perimeter. *Nobody* is allowed inside the safety zone without proper authorization. We are protected against attack from the air... even if that wasn't important tonight. They had two planes ready, but we *stopped* them before they could depart. But I will say one thing: They're getting better and acquiring better equipment the longer they are at it. There are more of those ingrates, and they are getting more and more dangerous for every passing day. The threat must be dealt with, decisively, all over Europe. No expenses must be spared...

– A poet, Kurt sniffed and giggled. – Can you believe it?

After a moment in time, one that could just as well be an eternity of nights, they arrived at one of their «safe» houses, just outside the city of Birmingham. Walls, floor and ceiling felt cold, insensitive. Everybody's eyes burned hard, in something transcending pain.

– It was said that everybody is dead, Janni said hesitatingly.

– At least one is alive, Gio said from the door. He hadn't sat down. – Unless they made a horrible mistake somewhere. That one can be very valuable to them in the years to come, depending on whom it is.

– He or she can start counting days, Dorte put simply, and uncommonly intense.

– I agree, Judith said. – Without us repeating the old vengeance/blood oath garbage, that is.

It didn't start any argument. They were too exhausted for that.

Anya fell asleep first. She seemed totally wasted. Some joined her voluntarily, others by necessity. Weariness cut and dulled them all. Judith remained awake, with a few others, on guard duty. She had had trouble sleeping lately. She couldn't tell if it was an advantage or not, if it was good or bad. Perhaps it would have been wrong if she had been able to sleep. Jemma and Gio slept soundly, but lightly, and did so every night. She would never want to be as heartless as them.

They held a wake, and waited for Corbin, Yvonne, Helene and Kees. No one showed up. They waited for signs of life. None appeared. Rigid eyes looked at the door that never opened.

Thick morning fog framed the forest glen. Judith, Kurt, Kim and Morten did a different kind of wake. The four of them had hardly closed an eye during the night. Anya stood before them, fresh as a lemon, impossible to read. She had colored her hair and face white. Not with an ordinary bleaching agent or paint, but rather natural colors, they assumed. She had drawn a vertical red line, from the hairline, over the forehead, the nose, and to the jaw. Green circles around black eyes, three lines of green from the eyes and to the ears, swept a black cloak around her body. Not a single piece of bare skin was visible. The result was stunning and enticing. They felt like they faced one of her druid ancestors: But they quickly realized that that impression was wrong or incomplete. She was timeless.

– There's something I must do, she said quietly. – I don't know how long it will be. Wait here. Let no one into the forest.

A whirl of movements, and she vanished between the trees.

– Why? Judith cried after her. – What's so important?

– I must find out who I am, they heard the wind, the forest breathe.

As if she had become the wind, become the forest.

They held the wake where the forest began. Occasionally, in glimpses they saw She Who Dances in the Forest deep therein. A rough, rocky dance Anya Kerien had learned nowhere.

– The Bewitched Forest, Kurt sang cheerfully.

Dots of mist in the air created forms, seemed to create forms, they reminded themselves. Images started forming. Some dark. Some bright. Dark clouds no sunlight could penetrate, but still did. Not just fog, but smoke, too, from a campfire. A campfire She Who Dances in the Forest encircled, humming and mumbling. Or she sat close by, and inhaled smoke from. She disappeared in the cloud of smoke, appeared from behind a tree and disappeared again in front of a bush. The Spirit Dance continued for days, weeks and months. The smoke made Judith cough. She dived deeper into it. Eyes started flowing. Thoughts raged on. What was time other than timely hooks and crannies for reality to cling to? Silverhair had always seen existence as a net. Between the threads there was nothing but emptiness.

Silverhair shook her head hard, as if to clear her mind. The Sun warmed her face. She and Anya, just the two of them sunbathed on the terrace.

– I spoke with great granddaddy today, Anya said abruptly, pausing a bit before proceeding. – He told me I was born with the mark of the Witch, a mole on the leg. I rested in the baby stroller. Mother had taken me to his house in the forest. He grabbed my leg. I remember it crystal clear. Mother left us alone, for a long time. He taught his craft that afternoon, because he knew that I one day would remember.

Judith turned her chair so she could look at the other all the time. Anya did the same, for the same reason. Gradually Judith, too, glimpsed what waited behind the veil.

– It's time for me to leave.

Judith nodded slowly, realizing the decision had been made, but not giving in by immediately condoning it.

– A more reasonable explanation would do well here.

– You don't need it, Anya, slightly numb replied. – You made me the Carrier of Knowledge. I'm pumped up again. This moment is just as good as any other. It's time, Silverhair.

To this point the conversation had taken place in calm, even sleepy ways. Suddenly Judith's voice changed to a weak, almost pleading quality.

– Why did you leave, leave the first time?

The reply came abruptly, and tore into her like knives. After all the time since it had happened it still hurt, like a stone stuck in the stomach one was unable to push from the bowels.

– Olav… raped me, Anya pushed out, – and he made it clear that he enjoyed it. And I'm certain he knew I enjoyed it, too. Or that he could teach me to enjoy it. His knowing smile told me how much he would enjoy relating it all, his version to you.

– W-what? Judith's voice faltered. – Why didn't you *tell* me? Are you aware of what it would have meant? If I had known…

Anya's expression revealed that she was indeed aware of it. That she had been aware of it every second since it happened.

– I… couldn't. You were so trusting, so naïve and innocent. I don't know… Just then the thought of crushing your dream felt worse than what had happened to me. And I was afraid you would… blame me. Can you imagine the depth of his deed? He wanted to get rid of me, and he did, just as effective as if… He could just as well have k-killed me. I blamed myself. I hated you. I hated myself, the moment I left, and in all the lonely years since.

– I should have told you everything instantly, but I was young, insecure and stupid.

Anya rose. She slipped into her jacket, let it hang loosely over her shoulders. She didn't carry more than the clothes on her body.

– I'm leaving. I have everything I need. Today or tomorrow I will be in Ireland. A new phase starts in my life.

They both clutched each other's hands and kissed each other's cheek.

– I will always be with you, Anya said to Judith.

– I will always be with you, Judith said to Anya.

The curtains flickered. The lights flickered between the cracks. Silverhair returned alone to the living room.

There was knocking on the entrance door, the correct signal. They took no chances, and cocked their weapons under their coats. Heike and Elan entered with Kees and Helene. The reunion brought great joy, and they embraced. But the two couldn't embrace the joy.

– Is everybody present? Kees asked.

– Yes, Silverhair replied.

– Where is Anya? Helene wondered.

– She will always be with us, wherever we go. We will always be with her, wherever she goes.

Kurt's eyes widened, but then he nodded, as if he understood.

– I don't know… don't know quite how to say this, Helene began hesitatingly, – but we don't believe Yvonne and Corbin will be returning either.

– They gassed us with the spray, Kees said curtly. – When we woke up both they and the planes were gone. They left a recorded message.

He held up a cassette. Everybody stared at the small, flat thing in their friend's hand. Kees put it in a player, and pushed «play», and they listened to every word. It was unnecessary, really. They knew in their depths what it was about.

– *Yvonne here. I will just say that I was the one who came up with the idea. I do it with doubt, but willingly. I feel it just has to be done, that there are things in the world that just have to be done. It's my fault. Don't be angry with Corbin. I love you all. Until we meet again.*

– *I will strive to explain.* They heard Corbin's voice. *We redirected the cargo. Everything is connected, and can be armed with a single grip. Yvonne asked me when we were alone… we had heard the news… if take off truly was that difficult. I repeated what she already knew, that it was the landing that was the truly difficult part…*

– He doesn't have to say it, Morten stated. – He doesn't.

– *Yvonne's reply was that it didn't matter. We have decided to do the trip north. I can't do it alone. I wish I could. Take off went well, or you would have known… Yvonne will follow my instructions the entire flight. It shouldn't present major problems. I reckon we will reach our destination... our target sometimes tomorrow. Well, I guess this is it, folks. Until we meet again.*

– Turn on the TV, Judith said tonelessly.

Renni sat in a chair, juggling with the controller. He didn't have to be told what channel to choose.

Desolate, even occasionally untouched nature filled the front of the square box, a coastline and huge fields. The main camera swept over the farms, and zoomed in on the nuclear plant in the background. The official opening ceremony began. The area's population that had acquired, with a high price attached, a substantial number of new jobs applauded for the woman on the dais - without even wanting to know what deal they had made with the devil. In a few years, with the outbreak of an abnormally high amount of cancer cases they might finally react, but by then it would be too late for many of them. They hadn't listened when people had told them what danger the plant represented for all of Europe. They hadn't listened all the times they had been told about the danger it represented to them. They applauded the director when she stepped closer to the microphone. They applauded the security forces hiding outside the selective choosing of the cameras. Guards demonstrated the cannons on the roof, and the applause increased even more. The ongoing protests in all major European cities were hardly mentioned.

People are fed up, Judith thought. They talk the talk, doing so loud and clear. But that isn't sufficient. They must act as well and act decisively.

The situation was more than bad, even without this additional mass of radioactive material being transported on roads all over the world, on all the seven seas.

– Dear friends, the woman greeted people she had never before met. She spoke faultless Oxford English. – Many have attempted to shut us down, both inside and outside our own country, shamefully interfering with the democratic process. They didn't really have any chance, of course. Progress can't be stopped. We have a plant here, fully capable and willing to accept nuclear waste from all over Europe. Transport, reception and reprocessing, all processing is done under the strictest security measures, and is completely safe. No one has any reason to be worried, and no decent, law-abiding citizen is. Decent people don't listen to radical fantasies, to the radicals set to destroy everything we have strived to build. We are here, dear friends, and here we'll remain.

And so on…

Judith closed her eyes, and rubbed her fingertips on her forehead.

– … and I hereby declare the Dounray Reprocessing Plant for OPENED. She cut the line in front of the entrance with large, artistically made scissors. – With our excellent defense against attack and sabotage it will certainly stand forever.

Applause (more applause), horns, marches. The cameras covered the happy event. One followed the director into the main building, into the control-room. The plant had been run on a trial basis for weeks, and was now brought to full capacity.

The director frowned. One saw it, saw that the harmony was rocked. Those who could read the body's movements, its language discovered clear signs of worry. She turned to an assistant running towards her. Anybody could easily see he fought to stay calm. But his expression exposed him.

– *Stop recording,* the director ordered, in a voice not accepting disobedience.

The image changed to an outward scene again. Everything seemed calm there, by a superficial look, until one discovered the fact that ever more people looked up and pointed at the sky. A camera with a telescopic lens was directed upwards. Then everybody saw it. Two small planes appeared from the south. No one had permission to fly within a wide range around the plant. Everybody knew that.

– Remain calm, remain ordered, the security chief shouted into the microphone. – We will stop them long before they even come close.

People howled and screamed, and ran in panic in all directions.

– They fly too high, he grunted satisfied, forgetting the sheep running away. – They must turn and fly back. Prepare to fire.

Everybody stared at the planes, even the very busy bees. The birds of prey were almost directly above the plant now. But… weren't they… bigger? YES! *They were on their way down.* The first plane dived. The other slipped in its stream. The security chief cursed insanely. Shocked, white skinned faces surrounded him on all sides.

– Fire, he shouted. – FIRE!

They must break out of the dive soon, a soldier mumbled and mumbled in a vain attempt to comfort himself. – If not it will soon be too late. They can't… They can't be thinking of…

The cannons were raised as high as possible. It screeched in nails and attachments as they were pushed to the limits. Repetitive salvos were fired at the descending birds. It finally dawned on many that the planes had no intention of breaking the dive. They stared at the metal beasts, in a useless attempt to discover movements in the cockpits. Was there anybody inside, anybody at all? Was it really only fire and life, a force of nature executing vengeance on mankind?

Inside the small house by the forest nobody took their eyes off the screen. The tiny square seemed to explode and expand all over the room.

A grenade exploded near the wing of the first plane, causing no substantial damage. The deathbirds continued their journey. Only survey images were transmitted by now. Nobody operated any camera anymore. The planes appeared in the picture just a few moments before the big bang. Both hit the target, the roof of the plant, close to simultaneously. The enormous explosions made the ground shake for miles and miles. Geysers of fire reached high into the air, and were seen far, far away. In the subsequent inferno remains flew to all sides. Smoke, flames, heat smothered the ground, lighting grass and air. It seemed like it would never stop - a rage not waning at all, but rather waxing - and Death spread with the winds.

CHAPTER EIGHTEEN

People gathered on a small soccer stadium, a place in western Norway, on the evening of June 21st, Midsummer Night. The long years stretched far ahead, like the Milky Way Galaxy in the night.

The Sun had not yet set when people started to fill the pitch. The hot evening brought clear air. There were no clouds in the sky. The stadium was at the top of a mountain range. Several roads and paths led to it. People rushed to the place from the entire district and also from the world at large. Groups of guards, heavily armed, were posted on all access points and also in the terrain. Not merely one bonfire, but many rose in the sky. People danced around them. Sounds of many hands hitting drums filled the air. There was singing, clapping and shaking, flashes of understanding in hungry eyes. Many had waited for something like this for a very long time, waited for *this*.

The rather simple stand space covered just half of one side of the pitch. It was built on the rock itself, like giant steps on a natural range. A group of twenty-two people, Silverhair and those following her appeared at its top and made their way downwards. The cry of recognition and myriad of other emotional nuances rose towards them. The Nightravens halted on the broad, lower step. Silverhair put the bullhorn she held in her left hand before her mouth. There was one last excited cry, then expectant silence.

– Present day society does one thing in particular wrong. Judith's voice was loud and powerful, after many years of crying against the Storm. – It treats the symptoms of what's wrong, not the actual disease. It's easy to understand why, of course…

Her infamous skewed smile turned very distinct.

– … since the disease is society itself.

The mumbling cheer turned to a rush of heated air rising, blowing the cover off the steaming kettle.

– Pollution is just another symptom. Like «crime», drug «abuse», devolving, alienation, passivity… There are people who just want to clean up a little and be content with that, and continue their misunderstood life in the same, tedious track. Those people are worse than our worst enemies, because they are legitimizing everything the establishment is doing. They who are not a part of the solution are part of the problem. As Freire said: «Washing one's hands of the conflict between the powerful and the powerless means to side with the powerful, not to be neutral». The illusions must be exposed. The world must be turned downside up, in a process going far beyond current expectations. Perhaps everything must *go,* before we can start over. We have nothing left to lose, no time left to lose. No single group or person has or will ever have a single right to the truth. Life is death and blood, and nothing besides. And I also mean that in a positive way. I won't lie to you. The struggle is hard and ruthless, and will turn ever rougher and bloodier in the many years to come. I admit that I have thought of giving up, giving in. But I tell myself, my rage tells me, that the *dream* is always worth chasing, the dream about freedom and justice for *all,* without exceptions, in a softer, but yet rougher and wilder world. A world we can live the life we're born to live, not the insane existence we exist in today. The dream, not the nightmare is, whether we like it or not bigger than us all, than we can ever be. According to an old saying there is one time for love, and one for war. Now, more than ever it is time for both.

Jason Edwards stood in the midst of the seething human cauldron. Like many of those present he shivered both in cold and heat simultaneously. Like so many others he wanted to be up there with the twenty-two, be among the new five. But he did accept that they hadn't chosen him, accepted that he would have to wait a little bit longer. He knew it wouldn't be long.

– Radical, huh? One at his side wondered in excitement. – There must be thousands here. Surely such a ruckus can't remain unnoticed? The power elite or some of their lackeys have to know about this. Perhaps they don't dare to even approach. By damn, I believe virtually everybody here is carrying some sort of weapon. They need an army to «clean up» this place.

– We in the front line have had the pleasure of meeting quite a few of you throughout the years, Silverhair continued. – It can continue no longer. That we show up at these gatherings has become too dangerous, both for you and for us. We've become too well known and too big a threat to the power elite. After tonight we will break all contact and isolate ourselves. We've come here… to say goodbye. From this moment on, we'll fight even harder and the countermeasures will increase in both quantity and quality. If we are not true outlaws at this time we will be, soon. We are the new Spartans. We fight until reinforcements arrive. After us there will be five new groups, and from each of them five new. And thus we'll grow until we're overrunning the planet, unbeatable. We'll win… or die by the sword.

She spoke and they listened to every word, and then they formed their own opinion of what was said. Spontaneous applause and cheers often interrupted her. Some shook their heads, some left, and some of those who had come here out of curiosity started listening.

A guard carrying a machinegun on a strap around his shoulder ran to the group. He stopped by Silverhair and whispered in her ear. She smiled and sent him off again.

– We will have guests shortly, she shouted. – Six police cars, four in *disguise* and two patrol cars are on their way. They're stuffed with cops. Let's receive them in a calm and reasoned manner. They might be persuaded to leave here without anybody getting hurt. We must give them a chance to behave like human beings.

Those who stood closest to the edge had a clear view of the valley below. The cars swerved in the turns as they advanced up the road. Not long after that they skidded, one by one into the parking lot behind one of the goals. Before they had managed to stop properly they were surrounded and covered by a thousand guns. The guards had pulled back a little, but had placed themselves more than close enough. The thirty police officers dismounted the cars with guns in their hands. They had sense enough to let the barrels point downwards, at the ground.

Karine stepped forth from the crowd, surveying them in a cold manner.

– Leave, she ordered them firmly. – You're not wanted here.

– You say *we* are not wanted here? The Chief said, even paler in his increased rage. – *You dare.*

– Take a good look around you, Karine encouraged him. – Who do you think has the power here?

– You're Karine Lie, he snarled. – You're under arrest.

– I'm giving you a fair warning, Karine said relaxed. – Those of you making a single wrong move will be taken care of.

– GRAB HER!

None of the officers moved. That would have been an insane act, with all the weapons directed at them.

– You're not very high on your horse, now, are you? Karine scorned them. – When you don't have all the advantages on your side. Drop your weapons. You don't need them, do you?

The Chief's eyes bulged, to the point of threatening to leave the sockets. The facial skin expanded and approached breaking point. Slowly, only slowly he cooled down, and managed to get his blood pressure down.

He raised his weapon and threw himself at Karine. Several guns were fired to his right. He was shot asunder, and was dead before he hit the ground.

His colleagues and subordinates let go of their weapons and made no sudden moves.

– We can kill you, like *this*. Silverhair snapped her fingers. – But our cause is better served by letting you live, humiliating you. Everybody here now knows how easily cops can be successfully opposed, when the odds are not on their side. Get going now, before we lose our cool.

They rushed back into their cars. The scornful laughter haunted them.

– This isn't over, one of them howled before turning the key.

– You can bet it isn't, Morten replied, seething. – For your own sake you better pray we never meet again. You've gained a bit more time, to think your life through. Don't spoil that, do you hear?

A boy and a girl sprayed one of the cars with a stylized E and following letters: *Enemy*.

The cars left, with an even greater speed than they had arrived. The unbound, to them nightmarish laughter haunted them.

– Bergen isn't far away, Silverhair nodded. – We must assume that reinforcements are already well under way.

– The party is over, folks, Kurt cried. – One of those short, but hectic things we read about…

They walked from fire to fire, clasped every hand offered to them. Smoke rose from the flames, and gathered high in the air, on the winds of wings. Silence reigned, both in terms of wind and people. No voices broke the silence when the twenty-two men and women ascended the stand, ascended time and time again, as if everything kept repeating itself. It was so strange.

Silence reigned. In spite of this they heard the sound of the Storm.

– Speak to the Spartans. Kurt waved.

Judith Breen stopped at the top of the stand, while her siblings and fellow warriors disappeared behind the hill. She stood there, with her arms down, her hands rolled into fists. Her hair seemed red in the glow of all the fires.

– We may return, she cried. – We may not. Whichever… Remember us.

– Always, Nightravens, Jason said. – Always.

++++++++++++++++++++++++++++++++++

Clouds flew across the sky. The waves rolled at the shore, while the sea kept rising.

I can't remember any point in my life I didn't struggle.

Days flowed like weeks, weeks like days. A new month began with every full moon. Time was measured by the growth in the boys' faces, the shit in the girls' tired mugs. Seasons came and went. It was so difficult to think, especially during the active struggle, and they seemed to be in that state, or close to it, ever more often. All… experiences, thoughts mixed. Night and day mixed into one united whole.

– JUDITH! Helene screamed at the top of her lungs.

The warning reached her in time. Silverhair threw herself down just before a hail of bullets blew right above her. Gio fired from the front of the van. She jumped in behind just as Helene pushed her foot (and the gas pedal) through the floor. Judith landed safely in Karel and Janni's arms. Karel shut the door just as the van turned the corner. They rushed through the concrete jungle's nannies and crannies. They saw no signs of pursuers, even though they heard them from time to time.

They had waltzed into a bank. They had cleaned the place, relieved it of money, and destroyed just about everything, setting fires everywhere. Archives had been emptied and burned. Data files deleted. They had believed they had all guards covered. The mistake could have cost them.

– We were lucky, Celeste said. She bandaged Karel's arm.

– That's right, Judith said. – Our blunder didn't cost us. It isn't easy knowing when an extra security guard shows up on his day off, and goes to the john during a critical juncture, but we should have checked it anyway. There will always be a broad range of unpredictable things happening, and we should be able to predict most of them. This wouldn't even have qualified for membership in Fake Fortuneteller's Union.

Strained laughter.

– We must stop the velvet glove treatment, Gio argued passionately. He turned serious first. – If people fear us they will also listen. I, for one am sick and tired of burying friends.

You're not alone there, damn you. Judith kept her eyes closed. Was Gio right? Would doing it his way help stay Death's hand… or simply make the losses easier to bear?

– What our actions do to others isn't the most important part. She smiled, recreating Anya's face and voice within. – What they do to us is.

The six switched cars, switched faces, pulled masks over their natural masks and removed the overalls. After driving for a while on the narrow band of gray fog, they simply stopped by a tavern, and had a meal.

No one talked much during the meal. Somebody played dark, moody music from a cassette player somewhere in the room. Judith studied Janni cautiously. The girl had cried her heart out after her lover's death. And even after all this time Judith saw it in her moves and her features. For several days after Corbin had crashed his plane into the poisonous Dounray Reprocessing Plant and left it in ruins, her behavior had alternated between hysterical and erratic.

– Cry, Judith had told her. – Get it out.

– Grieve, Gio had said. – But not too long. Let the grief turn into something else.

Let the grief turn into something else. Silverhair looked down at her short, well groomed nails.

Janni sat course towards the toilet, just after she had finished eating. Judith waited a bit, before following her. A stream of steam and scents drifted in the intersection between the dining area and the lavatories, the waste area. Perfume and so-called good smells penetrated the air. The rooms were huge, clean and spacey, made of new, expensive materials. The owner made good money. Everything seemed more like a hotel than a roadhouse. There was spared no expenses. The owner probably had a score of these. Perhaps it would be worth the effort of relieving him of some money.

Janni stood in front of the mirror, but didn't look into it. Judith assumed she was afraid of what she would see. The girl had hardened, as had they all. Was the worry there, because there was too much or too little hatred in her? Judith stopped inside the door, uncertain if she had a task here.

– You? What are you doing here? Janni turned a dry, but distorted face at the intruder. – Go, I wish to be alone.

– Yelping pup. It came in a low, scornful voice. In a moment Judith's face had changed into the hate-filled, mocking expression she hated so much. – Poor little puppy. Why don't you crawl back into your hole and stay there?

There were flashes in the young woman's round eyes. She straightened.

– I'm sorry, she said rigidly. – Listen to me… Everything seems so meaningless. It just seems so meaningless to go on.

– No, you listen to me, Silverhair said low and enraged. – Don't talk to me about meaninglessness. I have lost most of what gives life meaning. We all have. Life *is* meaningless. What did we teach you? What have we all learned? Why do we fight? We know our own value, we know it is there. We know that the flame burning inside… the fire driving us… is worth any pain.

She saw Janni lift her head high, and keep it there, saw herself in the younger woman, a fighting heart refusing to stop beating. Janni smiled bravely. She would be okay.

Back in the dining room Janni sought to the dancing floor, and danced to the dark, moody music, in slow, swaying moves. Light shifted constantly in the locale. She danced in and out of the shadows. An unnatural mist distorting the senses entered the place… from nowhere.

Judith blinked. She thought she had had Janni in her line of sight forever. But it wasn't Janni, but Laura, Laura and Emmanuel, two of the new and inexperienced. They had gained little practical experience, and had exposed themselves in a critical moment. They had been blown to bits, blown to bits in the Storm, grains of sand slipping through the fingers.

The three other recruits, Karel, Celeste and Jim had made it long enough to increase their chances significantly. Karel had lot of experience from the civil wars in the former Yugoslavia.

The Mists of Time… They had brought Anya back, so she could listen to her Great Grandfather, to her own Total Recall.

Another Storm raged. In what seemed like an endless row this year. A night like this the Nightravens had killed the first of the individuals pulling the strings behind European Security Force. And the endless wind turned to a Storm. They closed in on the persons in the shadows, slowly, but surely, usually one by one. Five had been identified and five were dead, killed from roofs, in streets, in their homes. And after every assassination compromising information appeared in the media and alternative media the subsequent days, about the role the deceased had played in life. Or some of the enlightening info also had to be published in advance occasionally, since these five had been a close-knit group. The fact that a couple of them had been given advance warning hadn't saved them.

Tanya Kirbuk walked through Brandenburger Tor on her way east. Berlin's streets were flooded and the wind blew with such ferocity that the water almost stayed in the air. The umbrella was turned inside out so many times that it had been totally wrecked. She threw the useless thing away. In spite of the weather and the otherwise very bad conditions, she was in a fairly good mood. Every time she spotted the Green Rose graffiti she felt sort of encouraged, without being able to say why. She had lived in the city the last three years, and during that time she had seen an increasing number of the same or similar symbols. On walls, train stations, toilets… She giggled. She had seen the symbol everywhere, in all the towns she had lived in and visited. In Moscow, Riga, Prague, Budapest, Hamburg, during broadcasts everywhere. It pleased her, pleased her so much.

Everybody needs encouragement in life, she thought.

Berlin had, during the last few years become the place to be for those on the run from something (and there was a score of them). The city could practically make a person disappear, in good and bad ways, physically and mentally. After the fall of the Wall people had rushed to the town, to its western parts, where they had always visited, but especially to the countless abandoned and remote buildings to the east.

She lived in a small loft studio a few blocks from Unter Den Linden. The studio was spacious enough for her. She also liked to live high up, to more easily see beyond the horizon. The many squatter buildings had tempted her for some time, and she considered moving in. The decision had been postponed quite a few times by now. She liked it here.

And then, a seemingly unmotivated thought: There was even an escape staircase, running from top to bottom at the back of the apartments, where a person could leave and enter without being noticed.

Tanya used the main entrance. People she met in the stairs didn't greet her, and she didn't greet them. What a cold, cold world. The moisture invaded her and chilled her as she made her way upstairs.

Something cut and shook her when she opened the door, like a dull saw that hadn't been sharp for years. The room within sighed. She sensed a cold draft, a gust or a refreshing wind. Heart beat faster, both in fear and expectation. She reached inside the wet coat and pulled out her gun. She crouched a bit and found the switch on the wall. Ready for anything she pushed it.

She noticed the open window, and the wet wreck of an almost unrecognizable creature crouching beneath it.

– My apologies if I've ruined your carpet.

Tanya hardly recognized the rough voice either.

The water from the open window showered the woman crouching there.

Judith.

– The carpet…?

Tanya looked empty-eyed and disoriented ahead of her for a moment. Then she rushed forward, and knelt right there in the waterfall. She grabbed and held, and carefully pulled Judith away from there, to the couch. Bloodshot eyes opened and closed, opened and closed. Tanya opened and closed her mouth without being able to say a word, and had no idea what to do next.

– It's okay, Judith said. – I'm okay. I just need to… rest a bit.

But she recognized the indomitable will. Tanya imagined she would have recognized Judith Breen anywhere, no matter the circumstances or the face.

She rushed back to close the window.

– We must dry you, she mumbled. – Bathe you and dry you, and dress you. You aren't injured?

– Not particularly. Judith managed a weak smile.

She grimaced in pain when Tanya removed her jacket.

– I think… I've broken my arm, she admitted.

Tanya managed to coax the clothes off her and put her on the couch. She wasn't critically injured, but the powerful built body, now visibly thinner, seemed like one big abrasion.

– What are you guys doing to yourselves? Tanya asked shocked.

– This isn't in any way… representative. Judith laughed a bit and coughed. – We've got one wounded, Dorte, and I played decoy, luring the pursuers after me, giving the others a chance to get away with her. That was… What date is this?

– The first.

– … nine days ago… outside Munich. I've had them after me since. Last night they captured me, or thought they did.

– Good fucking Goddess! Tanya exclaimed.

She had to say something, had to get some of the shock and paralysis out of her body, her mind.

– They threw me in a cell, but forgot to check me… inside. Their celebration, about to become major, by the look of it, was rudely interrupted. I think I shook them off fairly quickly after that… I think so, but I'm not sure. I'm sorry I had to come here, but I had no other places to go.

– I'm just relieved you managed to find me. How did you?

– I did get your address about a year ago, and I'm quite familiar with this neighborhood, this little corner of Europe. It wasn't hard.

– You're exhausted! Tanya exclaimed passionately. – How you have managed to move at all the last few days is beyond me.

– Drawn on my reserves, Judith whispered. – Eating what I found in garbage cans, haven't slept much really. Couldn't. You should try it. Quite an interesting experience, actually. It's amazing what we human beings can do. When we have to…

Voice weakened, until it faded completely. Tanya managed to wash her somehow and oil her. It was hard to say if she was sleeping or unconscious or not during the process. She opened her mouth and swallowed when Tanya put spoons of soup at her lips. She was tucked in in blankets, and when her head was lowered on the soft pillow she made no move.

Tanya glanced at the big revolver sticking out of the jacket. She took it and lifted it up, chose it before her own. It was fully loaded, superior to hers, deadlier, better in all ways. She turned off all the lights, and with both hands around the weapon she sat down with her eyes locked at the door.

Judith slept for twelve hours. She woke up and didn't blink. Her eyes locked on even sharper than the Russian woman remembered. Not so strange. She hadn't been hunted then, and less haunted.

Judith dived up and down in the water, enjoying herself, and it boiled and bubbled in the bathtub around her. Her left arm impeded her movements. It was broken. She had jumped from a pedestrian bridge and landed wrong.

She stood on the carpet. Tanya frothed her with a big towel.

– Dry a bit more there, she grinned.

– Give me a break, Tanya replied embarrassed.

The night before the girl had been completely exhausted. Now, after two light meals and a bath she already seemed good as new. There were yet bags under her eyes, but the way Tanya saw it she jumped around, spry as a foal. Tanya bandaged the arm a bit breathless. This was what she had the biggest trouble dealing with, how fast Silverhair regained her good mood.

Tanya had always thought of her as Silverhair.

They had dinner at dusk. There wasn't really any dusk to speak of, only the air and ground mixing and changing from gray to dark gray. The Storm raged on.

– Fifteen years, right? Tanya let the fork rest in the air. – Since we last saw each other. Jesus, it feels like yesterday, so long and so short a time.

Why haven't I forgotten? Why do I remember it as if it was yesterday?

– You live alone?

That astute…

– How is it? Tanya asked impulsively, her anger vanishing as quickly as it had appeared.

– Out there, in the whirlwind? Judith's eyes grew distant. – It's both… wonderful and terrifying. You feel like you can't live without it, even though you know there's no longer any way out of it, and that one single wrong step may be enough to finish it. Dorte didn't do any overt mistakes. It just wasn't her day. The odds are bad and getting worse these days. They're hitting us hard, also by going after our supporters. Most of our old safehouses are gone. Resistance increases proportionately with our skill.

The haunted look, something like a shadow crossed her features.

They laughed a bit reminiscing about the old days, as the twinkle of the candles added to the mist in the air.

– Do you recall the speech Olav held in that old house? Tanya wondered rhetorically. – I do. I recall every word. I can still see people's faces.

– I can see it before my eyes, Judith said dreamily.

– What happened between you two?

– He… adapted, Judith replied curtly.

– I'm sorry…

– It's all right. I don't mind talking about it. It has happened and can't be undone. Everything is useful talking about… occasionally.

She frowned. Tanya waited and the vulnerability she felt stopped her from saying anything. Fifteen years… Nothing. A flash in eternal fire, everlasting hunger.

– The pain… the losses we have to live with… aren't felt in the moment. It returns later. Not strong, but more like sadness. It never goes away.

They cleared the table.

– Hey, I got a letter, a christmas greeting from Nelson, Tanya exclaimed and lit up in her eagerness. – He complained over the fact that I was the only one of us with a fixed address. I burned the letter after I had read it. I recall everything anyway. He wrote that he was tired of being the most wanted man in Australia, that he could just as well be wanted here. Perhaps we can meet… we who remain.

The four of us, Judith thought. And then there were just four…

– I know why Nelson wants to come here, she said. Laughter fought to express itself. – Too much free time on his hands. He must have robbed every single bank both in Australia and New Zealand… at least once.

Tanya walked to the locker in the corner, finding a bottle of wine.

– Chateau Lascombes Margaux 1981, she said. – I've had it in the locker for a long time, waiting for the occasion.

Judith couldn't find the resolve in her heart to say no. Besides, she needed the break, no matter how short, any break, from the world as it was.

– The boycott has lasted long enough. Kirbuk shrugged. – It doesn't serve any purpose anymore, and it never did.

They cheered.

– To old days, Judith said. And then cheerfully: – To the revolution.

– To mankind, Tanya smiled. – May it rise from its own ashes.

Judith knew her «visit» brightened Tanya's existence, but she was perhaps not aware of how it went both ways. It had been a long time since Judith had had the opportunity to speak to anybody outside the tribe, her tribe of warriors, forced to isolate themselves in an unrelenting struggle. In solitude, even group solitude one ran the risk of turning singled-minded. To have access to another viewpoint was… refreshing.

Dorte… the crossfire bullets had torn her up outside and inside. She had still been alive when Judith had last seen her, ten days ago. She was now either out of immediate danger or dead. Judith's head dipped. She hadn't been drunk since before she had left Olav. It had usually been bad every time. She had never been able to stomach much. But she recalled positive experiences in that regard, as well. It dulled the senses, a lullaby, a fog covering the thoughts. It drugged her, and she needed to be drugged, just for a little while. One last while.

++++++++++++++++++++++++

Four of her siblings had carried Dorte Kelser on a stretcher the remaining distance to Susan Palmer's care.

– Lee Travis was there, Helene insisted. – I saw him. I'm positive it was him.

– Jeez, you do have a problem with that guy, don't you? Janni looked big-eyed at her.

– He's dangerous, Helene said shifty-eyed. – I had him close to me for years. We know he is highly placed in ESF, and he certainly doesn't need any excuse to hunt us. I can't help it. He gives me *goose bumps*.

Kurt could only use his left arm. The right hung straight down, bloody and torn. Kees limped heavily. He started to feel the pain in the leg more like a murmur than an irritable disturbance.

– I can handle it, he replied to Helene's worried look.

Susan's eyes opened wide when she appeared in the hall, and spotted them, dirty and downtrodden as they all were.

– I'm sorry to say we couldn't avoid being seen on our way here, Kurt said. – We had no choice.

– Follow me, Susan said, with a brief hesitation, but no malice, barking orders into her communicator.

They carried Dorte to one of the operating halls. There were already several physicians and nurses there, waiting for them, looking at them with the usual wide eyes. They were used to that, used to so much. Dorte was put on the table under the bright lamps. Susan shook her head.

– Start the prepping, she barked. – Start this instant.

She brought the four to her office. Kees just made it to a chair, before his leg failed.

– Why are you doing this to yourselves? The surgeon wondered in despair.

– We have to, Kees replied. He didn't change expression while she treated his leg. – The world is in free fall. Somebody must stop all the horrible… We must try…

Susan removed the bullets from Kees and Kurt's bodies and dropped the small metal pieces in the sink.

– Know that we appreciate what you're doing for us, Janni said softly. – But… the time it was possible to sit on the fence or hide in a hole has passed. I want you to know that. The stakes are too high, and increasing every day.

– Dorte is as good as dead, Susan said curtly. – I can't imagine how she can still be alive. I will do everything in my power, but only a miracle can save her.

– We suspected as much, Kurt said darkly. – You will take care of her, no matter the result?

Susan nodded with bowed head.

– You should report this, Helene admonished her. – Way too many outsiders have seen us outside or inside.

– Okay.

A nod. Lips were too numb to move more.

She wished to say more, about how much they meant to her. Tell them how many who supported them, in their heart, but it felt so insufficient. There was a slight waving of hands, a nod from them as they parted outside the operation hall. Then they seemed to fade like rain a glowing hot afternoon.

The surgeon walked to the table where the warm, fragile flesh waited. So vulnerable, and in spite of this it contained a will able to move mountains. But what if thousands of mountains had to be moved, millions? Susan couldn't fathom how they could stand it, could hold out.

A hand grabbed hers in a steel grip. She looked startled at the piecemeal creature falling apart on the table.

– I know what you're thinking. Don't! Don't…

Susan couldn't be positive the bloody lips had moved or if the human being had really spoken. She and her crew kept preparing for the surgery, kept moving dull flesh and bones.

– They say there are no colors in the night, but that's wrong, so wrong. The night is filled with them... filled...

This time the lips did move. The vocal chords did vibrate and the words, at least until the final syllable were spoken loud and firm.

Then the body rested once more, but it wasn't done. It kept breathing. The chest kept moving up and down.

The surgeons shook their head in bewilderment, in a horror, an amazement deeper than any conscious thought.

Two hours later Susan Palmer leaned against the closest wall, exhausted, and with an overwhelming need to lie down and rest and never rise again. What was really the point, the point of living, fighting on in the gray hopelessness? One of the assistants lowered the blanket over the body and head on the table. Susan hated every moment of the wake. She hated, oh, how she hated. Could this… dark monster be pulled from the deep, help her to fight, achieve something?

All the bright colors had been turned off. The warm, vulnerable body slowly turned cold.

Dorte Kelser was dead.

+++++++++++++++++

Indistinct mirror images echoed in display windows, drifting by in an endless row, an infinite number of houses. Peaceful moments were fewer and shorter. Reduced to nineteen again they had been reinforced in their choice of not accepting more recruits. The game had grown too dangerous, too cruel for young, inexperienced warriors. The risk was too great. The enemy could permit itself the use of cannon fodder, but they would only lose by doing it.

The enemy used a lot of cannon fodder. Parading them, hoping the shark would bite, like they had done with the Baader-Meinhof gang and the Red Brigades twenty years earlier. They placed juicy targets in shopping centers, public buildings, schools. But the Nightravens did little more than sniffing the bait. Like similar movements in the seventies the Green Rose argued that no one who had lived a while was innocent, but they didn't kill indiscriminately. When they blew something up there were rarely passive combatants present. It was quite impossible to avoid it completely, of course, but they had gained a reputation as rebels that first and foremost wanted to strike at the powerful. And when the enemy hadn't succeeded in tainting them in the eyes of their supporters it wasn't because they hadn't tried. Silverhair couldn't do anything but gloat a bit over that fact.

One evening they decided to have some fun, indulge in nostalgia, and during less than five hours they blew up three Shell gas stations. It took longer than expected, since they hadn't planned anything. They weren't even close to being in any danger, though, and they had a great time. Nobody guarded gas stations anymore…

The day after they made sure to remind the public about Shell's long rap sheet, in South Africa, Nigeria and countless other places around the globe.

It cheered them up this, reminded them of the fire burning inside. It failed to improve upon their long-term mood.

Only at night did they feel they could be fully themselves. The night was their home. If they had one at all it would have to be the forest of shadows and flickering lights.

Dreams Belong to the Night.

She repeated it often, like a mantra. In her features she saw lines that hadn't been there a few months ago, and certainly not a year ago. Gio, the oldest had lines of gray in the long and smooth hair. Kathy, typically enough, looked ever more often at herself in her little pocket mirror. Kimberly could no longer be mistaken for a twenty-two year old. None of them could. Not even like indistinct images in display windows.

Janni, still the youngest of the Nightravens had a rigid expression in her face that normally was associated with far older people. When Judith on rare occasions allowed herself to think about this, she didn't find it strange. The life they lived, in constant danger, and what they did to themselves, had to leave traces.

Fire burning in the wind burns shorter, but stronger.

Hamburg was located right in the bottleneck between Scandinavia and the rest of the European continent. They drove from the north sometime during the early days of the new year 1997. Grass was still green. It would still take a while before most growth would grow and flower, but this was clearly spring, not winter. To the left of the Autobahn was the bridge stretching across the city, a landmark just as visible as the TV tower, at least when arriving from the north.

The tall, round tower was very visible over most of the inner city. At close range, and towards the night sky it appeared overwhelming.

And this was, naturally the way its makers wanted people to think.

Manfred Klein did one of his usual surveys of the town, his town, from his well equipped office, with the latest in Internet and computer technology. From here he controlled the town, and from the town he reached out into the world. He enjoyed comparing himself with the old feudal lords. The power was less obvious these days, but just as real. And today one achieved more easily power outside one's local turf.

He left the office with quick, measured steps. Day turned to night.

The bodyguards waited for him in the reception, as they had done the entire day.

– You may go, he told his secretary.

She left everything on the desk, grabbed fearfully her purse and coat, and hurried out of the room. Good, she had learned obedience. She knew the risk of irritating him. Something she would do if she didn't obey in a swift and detailed manner. It was expected of his people that they would perform to the utmost of their abilities. And obedience was certainly one of the qualities he expected of them.

The bodyguards closed and locked the doors. Two more waited in the hallway. The four formed a square around Klein. They constantly kept a meter away from him, on all sides. The elevator was for his use only, and couldn't take more than five people.

TV-cameras covered the walls, and showed pictures from the parking lot, and the area outside. Everything was in order. In the garage there was no sign that the elevator arrived or that there was any elevator at all, before the wall slid aside. The Limousine had received the signal, and approached from the far side. It would stop in front of the elevator precisely one second after Klein had stepped out in the open.

The car stopped. Ten meters away.

The bodyguards stiffened. Klein calmly lifted a hand, stopping them from taking action.

The car remained on the spot, threatening, like a hearse, one raging through the night, collecting the souls of the condemned. Klein enjoyed that thought. He knew what it was about.

The four doors opened simultaneously. He instantly recognized the five leaving the car. They were all unmasked. Judith Brevik, Kurt Mørch,

Kimberly Russel, Giovanni Rossi and Karine Lie - the most famous members of the Green Rose. None of them had drawn weapons.

– Guests? He said in what resembled stunned surprise. – Perhaps you should have waited for an invitation?

– We don't need any, Kurt said cheerfully. – We love surprise parties.

– But you have given us many invitations, Manfred, Karine pointed out. – We have given you many chances by not accepting them. You succeeded in your efforts eventually, though. Temptation was too great. When you sent the ignorant Turkish group of workers into the Grausvald-reactor you succeeded admirably.

– It also helped that you are a leading force behind the ESF…

Silverhair had the same skewed smile he had seen on photos.

– I praise you, he cried. – You are resourceful. The countless skeletons you have managed to dig out of the closets and the fact that you're still alive show that. I can use people like you. You have caused me a lot of grief, but I can be generous.

– We have all received similar generous offers during the years and rejected them, Silverhair returned the cry. – We have rejected life as masters, rejected life as slaves. Why are you repeating it now?

– Because it is the end, is over and done. You know that, without me telling you. You're lucky if you stay alive a few more months. You have come far. I salute you. But you've come to the end of the road.

– No! Kim replied softly.

– Too bad, he mumbled, moving the arm a bit further to the side.

– Your assassins are dead. Gio laughed coldly.

The bodyguards hardly managed to move, before they, too, were dead, filled with lead fired from invisible weapons. The only loud sounds came from the ricochets whining through the garage.

Klein remained on the same spot, unhurt.

– You're one cold son of a bitch, Silverhair stated, with admiration in her voice.

– I like you, too. I will therefore give you one, last chance. You have now proved you can be extremely valuable. With my support you can go far. Join me. Throw the dream of equality and brotherhood on the garbage heap where it belongs. The strongest rules. Thus it has always been, and thus it will always be.

– A pessimist, Kurt grinned. – That I would never have guessed.

– No, he's an optimist, Karine said.

– It will improve, Judith said. – It has to.

– Why? Klein shouted, in his powerful voice. – What will be different in the future, different from now? Will you wave a magic wand, and make everything better? «If you want a picture of the future, imagine a boot stamping on a human face - forever».

The wind carried his words and enhanced them.

Silverhair drew the revolver. She walked to Klein and kept it raised. The barrel pointed at his forehead.

– Hold on now. A chink of uncertainty finally appeared in his armor. – If you kill me you're making…

– … a very big mistake. I know. Silverhair grinned without humor. – The hierarchy will start feeling seriously threatened.

She pulled the trigger. The crack echoed between and outside the walls. The bullet penetrated Klein's forehead, and blew away large chunks off the back of his head. Blood and pieces of the brain erupted into the air, and remained there, while the body fell to the ground, hit the concrete floor.

– It won't be your boot, Silverhair mumbled.

The echo of the crack was still heard, like distant thunder, not growing more distant, but growing closer fast. Newspaper pages floated on the ground, twisted in the wind. Silverhair turned and returned to the car. Everybody entered and they drove off. When they had gained speed Kim opened the door. She stood straight, and emptied a box of green roses into the night, the everlasting mist. Life - and Death's - winds caught them and carried them with it.

++++++++++++++

Europe drowned in water. Europe died in heat. The polish nation, the first nation of many received a death sentence it never recovered from. They «lived», sort of, all of them, a little while longer, before dying in convulsions and pain.

The glowing hot night burned around them. Leaves on trees green and huge danced in shimmering hot air. Nineteen light-clad men and women walked on Unter Den Linden this summer dark, this seemingly quiet tropic Storm. The bright, almost colorless hair to the woman leading the group flickered in the wind.

– Silverhair! One among the crowd shouted and whirled up a gale.

Judith smiled encouragingly, and waved back.

They had lived out here, on the border for a while, on the edge between dream and reality, where heaven and sea became one, in Berlin, a seething cauldron of many and varied brews. Everything and everybody was allowed here. To the east was no man's land. To the vest the enemy waited with its huge gap. Huge parts of the city were, in fact occupied by invading forces. The authorities had only limited control many places. People crossed borders unhampered in the European Union's market. The irony was almost too much.

Everywhere they went they were met by their special form of greeting, hands closing and opening in a random pattern. They returned it cheerfully and informally. Most places they passed through, where they were recognized, they encountered people filled with hatred and fear, crying viciously at them, but not here.

Though… almost all the people, both supporters and opponents of the ravens flying in the night, mostly saw the unbelievable cheerfulness. Not the eyes constantly moving. They wondered about the sports bags ten of the outlaws carried, or why there were only ten. Those watching had little or no knowledge of how it felt to be on the run and need to be constantly on guard, not being able to relax a second. The Nightravens knew what a single moment of inattentiveness could cost them. Rest gave them no rest.

But warmth, support assaulted them, big and small, here and many places they walked, and it strengthened them. Even though they knew their strength would have to come from the inside, and that they had only themselves to rely on.

Narrow, darker streets meant less people. It was ever thus. The few and the different were forced to hide in the dark, places outside main roads, the beaten tracks. During the brief time called Recorded History it had usually been like that. But now didn't mean forever.

Judy/silverhair/Judith/Silverhair felt the changing times. The new age would wash away the old like a Tsunami. Blood would both boil and flow. Blood was needed. It was ever thus.

Berlin's Green Rose hid in a secluded cellar. Steam drifted in the air by the entrance. A long, dank corridor led to the large, bright room, its walls mostly consisting of visible bricks. Not really that solid or nice to look at, if one looked for such things, but the place had a great atmosphere. Tables stood tight. Smoke from torches and blazes rose in the air, through the cracks in the ceiling. Mead flowed from the taps in the noise and savagery. Silverhair spotted Tanya and Nelson at the center of it all.

– Judith.

They met and embraced in a wild and warm clenching.

The ruckus faded slowly at first, before everything suddenly quieted, with just a weak, underlying buzz.

– It's them, one exclaimed. – I'm positive.

At first everybody treated the strangers almost with reverence. To Judith's relief the ice was broken fairly soon, and a great casual mood grew between those present, with just minor or no worship. Shining eyes saw them both as human beings and idols.

Silverhair circulated and made sure that the others did, too. But she stayed mostly with Tanya and Nelson. They had so very much to talk about.

She looked around, listened, sensed, but didn't really need to do that to know what was happening. She saw younger people carry pints around, enjoyed the fierce action at the bar, and listened to people speak and discuss without prejudice. And the most important of all: She saw boys and girls that thought and breathed and lived. Through fire, through night she looked back, at a place similar to this, an eternity ago. The rebels were growing younger, and far younger compared to those gathering in the first Green Rose in Copenhagen. And that was good. The earlier they realized the truth the better.

Tanya looked far better than she had been doing nine months ago. A light had been lit in her eyes. No exaggeration. She glowed with will and spirit.

Nelson had the same mug he had always had, the same attitude of defiance and devil-may-care. A face clearly showing the years, of course, and she found, when looking into his mirrors of the soul the same wounds there, as in her own.

– Judith. She heard him speak to her. – If we should win, against all odds, gain enough support for it to be done… what happens afterwards?

– *What do we want?*

– We get rid of everything giving people power over others. She discovered that the room had turned quiet, and that everybody listened. – A drastically decentralized society without any kind of border, national or otherwise, without factories, without kings, everybody or as many as possible of those who want to taking part in society. There will hopefully always be people who don't want to join the majority's more or less sensible activities. There will be no appointments, no elections. «Leadership» and organizing of tasks will be done by an extensive rotation system. No form of organizing is permanent. In a society in tune with nature nobody shall rule others, decide what others must do. It must be a flexible system, where freedom and variety are the norm. Each person gets primal needs covered without question, without harassment. And then everybody is given the opportunity to be different, to be special. This is crucial. Originality and variety… no society has true justice without it. It must not merely *accept* independent thought and action, but *encourage* it.

She spoke for half an hour, talked herself warm. When she stopped she felt exhausted, empty. She had a habit of keeping her thoughts locked in.

The applause started, spontaneous and totally without duplicity. She felt good about it, felt pride, for herself, but also for them.

Night dawned. It crept close to them. The party continued. Judith didn't drink any alcohol, but was the wildest of them all. She swallowed a huge mug of berry juice, and jumped up on a table.

– Hey, Silverhair, Renni cried, with a lot of beer foam on his upper lip. – Haven't you sipped enough of the stuff by now? Perhaps you should sleep it off?

He was joking, she knew that… But… in a horrible moment her demons broke free from their confines. Berry juice fermented, in some circumstances, everybody knew that, and she couldn't handle alcohol. Absolutely not!

Bullshit. *Bullocks!*

– Let's have *fun,* she cried. – We can all sleep when we're dead.

She jumped back down and landed softly, catlike on the floor in front of Renni. It felt good. She felt good. Life could be great. Could it be that the few good moments balanced all the bad? She grabbed the Icelander's huge body and pushed her lips at his. They danced, swayed from one end of the room to the other. She kissed him greedily.

She swayed in the fog filled with flashing lights. In the mirror-like surfaces she glimpsed herself, bits of her identity. She recalled the lyrics Willy had sung to her, about the glow, the inner glow, seen through the eyes. There was still something left. It moved within her. She saw it in the eyes she met, saw how the excitement she showed on the outside and felt inside… how contagious it was.

They had lived every day the last year as if it was the last. Perhaps it wasn't so strange then if… desperation flashed in their eyes. An unending longing to live life to the full had always been driving them. They had long since prepared for the consequences.

The wind cooled her, even though the night was hot and sultry. She stood at the top of the building, at the flat roof, and stared at the city. She stood with her back to all the stairs she had climbed.

She had jumped up on another table and raised her pint with soda. They had called her name, *Silverhair,* and it did feel good.

– To the Dream, she had cheered. – May it live forever.

– THE DREAM, they replied, in a repetition of thundering echoes.

It didn't turn weaker with repetition, but stronger, and never as a mere copycat of the original.

Never forget!

Light the fire, and make it burn forever.

Forever, that was a long time.

Judith sensed the frost. She held around herself, in an effort to stay warm, in vain. She leaned her head at the shoulder and strived to keep her eyes closed. That didn't succeed either, and that sort of pleased her.

– Silverhair…

She turned. Karine stood there, with Tom Rawlins.

– This good man has petitioned for an audience, Karine said lightly. – Where do you want me?

– Stay here. Judith blinked slowly. – There's no danger, but I want you to listen in.

Silverhair turned her attention to the arms dealer, waiting for the word. She couldn't read the ragged face. She had never been able to do that.

– Tomorrow at twelve noon, Susan Palmer will be giving a speech, a very critical speech, inside Nordstan in Gothenburg, he told her with a skewed grin. – ESF will execute her, and you will be blamed. An obvious trap, if you ask me. They know you will hear about it somehow. They plan for it.

– It doesn't matter. She shook her head. – They know we'll come, no matter what.

– I was afraid of that, he commented, suddenly very, very solemn. – Those sly fuckers.

– It's time for you to join us, she said, still impulsively. – With yours and Kurt's expertise we will have a considerable bigger chance.

– A few notches above none, you mean? No, won't do, can't do. Who will take care of your daughter when the time comes?

You sly old satan. She smiled almost admiringly. Almost.

– Escort this good gentleman on his way, Silverhair ordered preoccupied. – Organize everything, we don't have much time… And make sure I can be alone. I have a lot to think about.

She was alone. Sometimes she preferred it that way. *Dance, little sister, dance*. She imagined she saw the old, tired face of Jonas Bergli in front of her. It had turned intensely alive every time he told them to never stop dancing. And her core had agreed. Now, her dance would soon be done.

But the big rain would come, unstoppable. That was clear to her, now. It would flood everything in existence, a rain of fire no one could escape.

Where Judith Breen stood on her high mountain and stared at the old city, sending her thoughts into Time and Space, she could see Forever.

CHAPTER NINETEEN

Gothenburg, June sixth 1997.

They drove to the enormous Nordstan Mall in five low buses, having realized early the need for extensive storage capacity. The Nightravens brought tons of equipment, everything remaining of their stock in the Gothenburg area.

Everything seemed lazy, quiet outside the vehicles. There were people all around them, and almost everyone was dressed up and waving Swedish flags. The heat was extreme this day. The air conditioning in the buses worked to full capacity, without it being of much help. Celeste, driving the front bus turned and drove at the side of the tramlines. Most of the guys in the buses had taken more than a good look at this place on earlier occasions. For some reason, it had always held… a special significance to them. They had sensed that they sometime, somehow would get to use their knowledge of the place.

There was the alley of trees. Behind them Palace Restaurant, in the building Vernlandsbanken had previously occupied. The green leaves on the trees didn't move. There wasn't a single breath of wind in the air. The buses turned again, and now Palace Restaurant was to their right, and Nordstan straight ahead.

During the night, the night before dawn, they had reinforced the vehicles with steel plates, steel cables, iron pipes, and everything they could think of and had available to them, done so in front, behind, over, under and on the sides.

The front bus charged at and through the main, tall entrance, not tall enough. It smashed glass and metal under the big, red Nordstan sign.

They drove slowly through the crowd, but certainly not too slow. They passed people, who irritated or curious were pushed aside. McDonalds was to their right, the first enterprise among many. Pressbyrån to the left further in. With its thousand stores this place was filled to the brim every day. Even on a less crowded one the stress and fuss dominated. Today, even more people sought here, also because it was clearly colder than outside. Or rather; less hot. The air conditioning worked well enough for the visitors to sense the difference. The suffering was lowered from white-hot heat to just heat a certain distance from the entrance.

The Nightravens saw only «private» guards. No policemen. The police station was nearby. There it most certainly crawled with them, in all shapes and forms. In all probability they swarmed through the crowd here, too, just making an effort above the call of duty to look inconspicuous. The stage was set. Hopefully the play would end vastly different from the way the intended director wanted it to end.

Nordstan was a giant complex with two broad and long main streets crossing each other. From the center and outbound represented by four street names, among them Nordstadtorget, which, long ago had held the original market. It had grown quite large since then.

Guards in black, ironed pants and equally ironed white skirts knocked on the bus doors to make the drivers stop and turn around the unwanted vehicles. They were ignored. The guards exchanged glances. Others in the crowd did, too. Messages were exchanged through radios, and the hidden activity increased drastically. Shoppers hardly noticed shit, but the Nightravens did. Their senses had, a long time ago been sharpened way beyond any normal standard. The ordinary, unconcerned visitor didn't register the faster steps, the larynxes whispering clandestine words, at least not on the surface of their dulled consciousness. But the Nightravens did. They knew fully well what was happening.

The buses drove to the big, open crossroads and made a circle. Wide-eyed people stood frozen outside and inside the ring. The Nightravens rushed from the buses. Susan was about to enter the podium.

– What the fuck are you doing here? She asked Kathy and Helene, who charged her, in a more than frightening way.

They didn't reply, but grabbed her, and dragged her quite harshly into the nearest bus.

– There's a sniper here, somewhere, Helene hissed. – Lay still.

Perhaps, she thought.

Gio and Jemma fired at various angles in the air, avoiding the glass and the statues hanging from the ceiling. Dust fell from the bullet holes.

– EVERYBODY FREEZE. YOU WON'T GET MORE THAN THIS WARNING.

Some obeyed. Some ran. Four running were hit in the leg. Almost everybody stopped, pale and stunned, howling and whimpering in terror.

– LAY DOWN FLAT ON THE FLOOR. DON'T MOVE, UNTIL YOU ARE TOLD DIFFERENTLY.

Kim's compelling voice sounded through the bullhorn. Another salvo was fired above people's heads, and more threw themselves down. Journalists photographed with their body pushed at the ground.

Silverhair looked through binoculars and checked all the four main entrances.

– Such a huge place, Janni whistled. – Perhaps we should have brought an army?

– We are an army, Karine stated.

Silverhair observed while police cars arrived from all sides and stopped well outside the building. Good, they were wise enough to have respect for their enemies. Finally! One single car broke the line, and raged between the trees, and into the mall. Silverhair signaled quickly and Morten sent away a rocket blowing it to bits. Several people escaping were blown to pieces, too. The last of the shoppers still inside threw themselves down, completely beside themselves. Those few reaching the outside ran like scared rabbits beyond the iron blockade already forming around the place.

– You could have picked me up in my apartment, Susan said undignified. – Why come *here?*

– There wasn't time, Helene patiently explained. – We didn't find out about the assassination plans until last night. Besides, I'm willing to bet, bet hard, that your entire neighborhood would have been crawling with uniforms. Here, as you can see, we have solid cover.

– But how will you get away?

– We have a slim or rather microscopic chance. And when we go you must go with us.

– Go with you… It was said in wonder, dreamily.

– You've shown your colors, now, Kathy said. – Your only chance to survive more than a few days is to join us, *us,* the Nightravens.

People crouched flat on the floor from entrance to entrance to entrance. Some were bleeding, but most of them had no visible injuries. But meeting their eyes, one saw easily that they weren't really there, that they didn't quite believe what was happening to them.

– EVERYBODY WILL COME HERE AND SURRENDER THEMSELVES, Kim shouted. – EVERYBODY IN HIDING HAS FIVE MINUTES TO SHOW AND SURRENDER. AFTER THAT WE WILL FIRE AT ANYTHING THAT MOVES.

An order of sorts slowly established itself. The nineteen Nightravens gained a modicum of control. The first, critical phase was completed. They stood there, in their rigid flesh, breathing through the gas masks. After a while they allowed themselves to relax a bit, or to be less agitated.

– If we assume there is a sniper, where did he go? Kurt spoke to Silverhair.

– If he didn't get out he must be one of the crowd.

She studied everybody sitting by the buses. There had to be at least thousand of them. Good.

Nine warriors were sent out to do the sweep. They searched the building systematically. They secured the video-surveillance control room and started redesigning it to their own needs. They shot two people hiding, as they had said they would do. Several others surrendered. They were allowed to live.

– HELLO OUT THERE. Silverhair had taken the bullhorn. The powerful voice carried far beyond the complex itself and even the city limits. – We have a message to you and you better listen. If you make the slightest attempt at entering the building or the slightest attempt at circumventing the rules, in ANY way we start the executions instantly.

A few minutes passed. Then a lone figure appeared before the main entrance, the Chief of the city police. He didn't step a millimeter over the line.

– IF YOU LET THE HOSTAGES GO WE CAN TALK. What do you say?

The only reply was Silverhair's scornful laughter.

– WHAT DO YOU WANT? The man cried out.

His voice had a simultaneous subtext of both triumph and desperation. He didn't know what to think. He had no idea. *Good!*

– You wanted us here, Judith Breen shouted in wild cheerfulness and abandon. – We have accepted your invitation, and we like it here. We intend to stay a while.

The nine she had sent exploring returned. They brought a few more prisoners, and in addition to a few other things, a sharpshooter rifle.

– We found this, Gio said. – Somebody had left it on the upper floor, in the Femman place. From that position it's a straight shot here.

Silverhair looked up there, nodding, imagining she was up there, aiming, squeezing a trigger.

– A Heckler & Koch, she said in appreciation. – We were so lucky to get our hands on some of these. They're usually only available to NATO-personnel, to their *specialists*.

They started to carry the dead and the lethally wounded outside. Police officers crawled like ants out there. They approached from everywhere, driving, running, stumbling, adding to the circle already established, already surrounding Nordstan many times.

The Nightravens crouched slightly when moving forward, light on feet, expecting the enemy to start firing at any moment. But it didn't happen. Kurt, the last one leaving a moaning creature returned to the relative, immediate safety.

He looked at the scared faces of the humans crouching on the floor, and the unbelievably calm features of friends and fellow warriors, his brothers and sisters, his compatriots.

We're ready for the world, he though happily, sadly, enraged. Finally!

– We are the Green Rose, Silverhair said loud and clear. She didn't use the bullhorn, but everybody within Nordstan heard her. – We have come here, and we have voided the ruling law and order, all law and order. We wished to save our friend Susan, but also came here to protest against this celebration of dominance, injustice and oppression…

In a swift move she fired at the flags on the wall. Howls filled the air anew. The flags fell to the floor. Some of the bullets went so low that they made chaos inside Nordløf Shoes. Remains jumped in the air.

– The celebration of the Swedish «liberation» day isn't that sickening, really, compared to that of other countries, Judith commented, – but the Swedish nationalism is neither worse nor less pronounced than other places.

Karel and Celeste poured a highly combustible liquid on the flags and lit the heap. These weren't made of the non-flammable material that was so popular these days. The flames licked the air, for a brief moment all the way to the distant ceiling. The fire devoured the cloth in a brief, violent storm and virtually put out itself.

– «Nationalism is a childhood disease», Kurt quoted cheerfully, his teeth showing. – «It's the measles of mankind».

– You fear us, Judith stated. – With good reason. We will kill each and every one of you, if necessary. We hope it won't come to that. The most important reason for our coming here today is that we have something to say. We can only hope some of it will stick, and that you'll start thinking for yourself. You haven't done a very good job of that so far.

They felt x-rayed by the cold, green eyes.

– Remember that, Morten said, – when this is over and they run you through the gauntlet of «debriefing» and crisis therapists to get you back on track.

– The secret police wanted to kill me today. Susan stepped forward. – They didn't like what I had to say, and then they would have blamed those they call terrorists.

She drew breath, before continuing.

– The disaster has already hit the world. It's not on its way, but has been here for a long time. There is hardly the illusion of freedom left, and all humans, animals and plants will soon be ill of one thing or another. The establishment's reaction to opposition grows ever more violent. I've strived to fight this insanity with «peaceful» means. That's no longer possible or fruitful. From this moment on, I declare I am joining the warriors of the Green Rose…

Cameras clicked and hummed. Numerous recording devices caught all imagery and audio.

– You did great, Kurt told her. – I doubt anything will reach established channels, but it will spread on the Internet like wildfire, with all the rest happening here.

Under his supervision they started building the sets they had used the entire night to create in their mind everything possible to confuse and divert the opponents. Kurt had a great time. It had been a long time since he had been able to use his skills as a production designer.

He stood there, surveying the work, looking at everything, reminded of an evening in the Green Rose in Copenhagen, after one of the countless raids the police had undertaken there. The nightravens had been young then. They had met all the resistance and ruthlessness with a smile, and tried even harder. The joy… it had been like an integral part of them. He saw it as an eternity ago. Satan, was it really less than ten years? They had gone for the jugular of the gray fog, and the joy was now just a pale light in the distance.

They rendered totally harmless, immobilized little by little all their shields of flesh and bones against the vultures out there. They removed the prisoners' shoes and tied them hands and feet. It took time, but surprisingly small amounts of rope. It was so easy to chain people, but even easier to do so with these people, since they were already picturing themselves in chains, living downtrodden lives.

Half an hour had passed with quiet and intense work when the activity outside once again visibly increased. Judith placed sentinels on each of the four corners on the upper floor. Kim, Karel, Kees and Kathy had a nice view of what was happening, but they didn't really need to convey much. Everybody saw it before their inner eye.

Behind the ring of police officers long lines of soldiers marched forward. With them arrived a small group dressed in the uniforms of European Security Force. The Siege of Nordstan approached an incredible level.

– If I didn't know better, I would have claimed they're attempting to intimidate us. Judith grinned in expectation.

– I would say they have unlimited success, Karine commented cheerfully. – I mean… we're good, Judy, but this is getting ridiculous.

– Hey, you guys, Elan shouted, – do we ask them to surrender themselves?

– You are mad! A journalist cried out.

– It isn't wrong being mad in an insane world, Renni said. – But they are really nuts. They believe we have come here unprepared.

– They trust their power and huge numbers, Kurt spat. – They're underestimating us. They always do.

They heard the Prime Minister speak on the radio. He declared martial law in the city of Gothenburg, and restrictions all over the country.
– We won't let ourselves be pushed, he spat for the third time. – Our healthy, democratic system won't tolerate worms on the edges. I want to stress that the civilian administration of Gothenburg won't be put on the sidelines. But police and military forces are given a temporary permission to detain and keep detained…
– That was fast, Morten said curtly.
– A bit too fast, Jan commented. I think he slipped up more than a bit there. He behaved even more like the fool he is.
The prisoners stared wide-eyed at everything being carried out of the buses and the stores. A lot of stuff was sold in here, and the Nightravens used a lot of it. They built and enhanced their fortress there and then, a scarecrow castle against the enemy forces.
And then everything was ready, everything was set.
They could look outside, but those outside saw nothing of what happened inside.
– Pure Academy Award work, man, Jim said in high praise, patting Kurt on the back.
– The reviewers don't appreciate it. Kurt shook his head. – But who cares what they think…
He looked up, imagined he was levitating, up there, right under the ceiling. And if one desired… then the ceiling disappeared, and one could enjoy the sights above the clouds, dance between the raindrops, while the rain washed everything away.
She imagined they danced from one mountaintop to the next, the riders on the Thunder Road, on their field of roses and thorns, towards the far, far green fields. Silverhair opened and closed her eyes. Longing and enraged. Enraged and longing.
I will sleep when I am dead.
– We stand in the fire, she cried. – It is said that one who doesn't live today, never does. That's correct. We live, contrary to the living dead, dead even though they walk and breathe. People step in poison, and call it civilization, a society so steeped in regulations, laws and rules that we're taught to behave like robots. We're supposed to fit in, adapt. Children are brainwashed throughout adolescence. Perhaps they're going through a brief phase of rebellion, before adapting, before dying, before falling asleep, and never waking up. What happens is so elaborate that I, for a long time asked myself how there could be rebels at all. Until a friend liberated my mind, and pointed out that there will always be mutants and new mutants. We are the mutants. The future belongs to us. The

environment will change and we will breed like rabbits. The old tired ways will disappear. The storm is coming. It's on its way and washes everything away. Be prepared. The day is near. The present belongs to us.

The day is here, Kimberly Russel thought, *if not today, then today... or tomorrow or the day after tomorrow*. Oh, She Demon, oh, Child of the Storm, you live among us, and your wrath is *terrible*.

For a thousand years they had been here. How long had it been for the poor suckers crouching on the floor? They experienced true uncertainty for the first time in their life. They found themselves on a tightrope without a net, and were helpless to improve upon their situation. And they reacted very different from each other. The slightest breath of wind could extinguish their light, the light they had hardly acknowledged in themselves. Some shrank further in their tracks. Some shrank and hated. Some felt only numb. Others wondered and perhaps grew.

A radio squeaked. Kim started dancing to the inciting music. She stretched out her arms to her sides. On the opposite side Kees, too, started on his dance. *Dance little boy, dance. Dance little girl, dance.*

Judith shook her head, shook it in wonder. She felt more clear-thinking then she had for years and yet more confused.

I can see the path so clear before me, but I falter. Why do I falter?

Frustration. Despair. Only words. They didn't even come close to describe how she felt.

A small man had placed himself on the line at the main entrance. They let it pass. Music faded.

– I have been sent to hear your demands, he shouted.

– We want free passage out of here and a plane before twelve noon tomorrow. *Give him a bone. Give them.* Content and pleased they would grow lazy. – Unless this is met we will shoot the first hostage, and then another every hour. That's all, for now.

The man vanished. She turned to the prisoners and sent them what was supposed to be a calming smile. She suspected it didn't have the desired effect.

– Do it, she told Karel. He had come to her, without her signaling him. – Sector wise.

– *The charges will blow outward? You're certain?* A brief conversation in the night.

– *It's quite a simple matter,* he had assured her, fairly unnecessary. She knew the basic principle as well as he did. – *That isn't the problem...*

They set up and connected the enormous amounts of explosives they had brought with them on the inside of the outer wall all around the vast complex. Wires were connected with wires and an intricate combination of laser beams. If anybody tripped the wires or the laser it would all blow. And everything could also be activated by a single push of a button on the control box in Judith's hand. Technology was wonderful stuff.

Then, and only then their sense of time returned. They had been inside this place for hours, but the ticking of the clock hadn't really made sense, until now, when the countdown had begun.

Darkness entered like something expected and welcomed. It sharpened their senses further, making the green pulsing glow inside grow even stronger.

Eyes turned sore by attempting to keep track of all the various access ways. There were so many not visible from their position. Therefore there were always at least three of them on guard in the surveillance room. From there they could easily keep an eye on every nook and cranny of this overgrown monster.

– What a great setup, Jan commented cheerfully.

Kurt took a stroll down the alley of low streetlights on Nordstadtorget. He cast satisfied looks around him for a while, admiring his own work. The sets and trick mirrors would undoubtedly confuse and befuddle anybody charging in here. Anybody outside, too, making it impossible to assess the situation properly. Elan, who sat on the hood of one of the displayed cars, was really five meters away, and in a completely different direction from where he seemed to be. Nobody who hadn't participated in the setup could make sense of it.

Kurt Mørch had for so long dreamed of doing his own play, and now it finally happened. He chuckled.

The problem wasn't in here, but out there. There was a closed-in footbridge away from here and over the wide road. He saw no one on the actual footbridge, but uniforms crawled everywhere on the road itself. They did nothing to hide themselves, naturally. It would have been easy to spot them even in the shadowy light covering this place. Under all the bright lights it was a raw deal. They wanted to be seen, to scare and intimidate those inside. Perhaps it worked with some. Not so with the Nightravens. The fear they might still carry inside had nothing to do with fear of authorities and death.

Four of the ravens of the night sat with their backs to the cars and strived to relax a bit.

– If we could just have taken the train, Kathy sighed, always the practical girl.

– Perhaps we can, Celeste said with a desperate hope in her voice. – They won't expect that.

Gio shook his head.

– They control enough automatons to cover any eventuality.
– The question is whether or not they will attack tonight, Kees stated soberly.
– It will be a massacre, and they know it, Kathy said hotly. – They know we aren't bluffing.
– They want to wear us down, Gio said relaxed. – It's a good move. If the attack comes the first night it will come just before dawn. I don't believe it will. They're still exchanging pleasantries among themselves, attempting to lay blame on somebody. As always they're scared of absolutely everything, and what's scaring them the most is to be stuck with the blame.
Morten kept to himself. He preferred that. It was easy for him to ignore his fellow warriors' attempt at a conversation, and the prisoners' scared and begging eyes. He felt numb and dead most of the time, and was constantly searching for something, anything to fill the void.
– W-water, a man with a bandage on his right arm moaned.
– Shut the fuck up, Morten shouted brutally. – Don't be such a sniveling baby.
Oh, god, how he despised them, despised them all.
Silverhair brought water in a jug. She knelt down by the fever hot man and gave him water in small portions.
– We have put antipyretic plant juice in it, she said softly. She rose and spoke to all the prisoners: – Food and drink is on its way to all. There's more than enough available. The sheer logistics of it all will delay us, though. We humbly ask your forgiveness.
Laughter. Morten couldn't fathom it, how easy everything seemed to Silverhair. She had also lost people close to her, and he knew it did faze her. But she made them laugh. They were helpless prisoners, and they laughed. The Stockholm syndrome aside, it was ridiculous.
Helene rushed at them with an insane, haunted look in her eyes.
– I *saw* him. They didn't have to ask whom she had seen. – *Travis*.
Are you sure? Kathy asked lightly. Couldn't it have been a relative or a double? All great men have doubles these days, you know…
Helene turned to Silverhair, hands trembling.
– He's outside. What are we going to *do* about it?
– He's human. Silverhair held her, kept her on an arm's length. – We take him down if necessary, same as with everybody else. *Okay?*
Helene nodded with bowed head. Silverhair kissed her on the brow.
– I'll take him. He's mine. The first chance I get…
The blinding lights split the pleasant darkness and hurt the eyes.
– How much energy are they using out there?
Kim shook her head in wonder.

– So much for the energy conservation plan the government announced the other day.

Jan grinned.

Kurt turned his back on the fake light outside. How strange. He shook his head in exalted wonder. How many movies hadn't he watched, how many books hadn't he read, where the main characters had put themselves in impossible situations, and basically rejected them as unrealistic because no one could be that stupid? Now, he was there himself. Reality surpassed the imagination in all ways. Had they truly had any choice? Perhaps it was better to die with a shout than with a whisper. Humanity lived far removed from nature, from its origin, its home. It longed to return.

– Technology removes us from our true Self, Silverhair spoke to him quietly, – caging the wild animal inside. We will do anything to break out of the cage, to keep our Self alive.

He looked sharply at her. He had always wondered if she was a mind reader.

– Like Sivert pointed out countless times… getting old shouldn't be a goal, not in itself. If we can't laugh in Death's presence, what's the point?

She had disappeared again. Kurt couldn't be certain she had ever been there.

The man he fed scowled at him.

– Why are you doing this shit anyway? He asked. – Do you really believe the world can be changed, that you can change it?

– The world is changing all the time, Kurt replied cheerfully. – There have been extreme changes the last decade alone, and far more the last fifty. The question is *who* is making the changes. *We* have changed it, completely contrary to those who believed they had single rights to reality… There are now people sharing our beliefs all over the globe. That is very much thanks to our non-fatalistic viewpoint.

– What's the matter with you, anyway? The guy just kept mouthing off. – Don't you have anything sensible to do? I mean… blow up places giving people work, where is the logic… No, the world needs more than ever leaders able to knock some sense into people, reinstall some discipline and order.

Kurt pushed a spoon filled with food into the open gap. The guy got some of it stuck in the throat, and had to cough a lot before being able to continue feeding. He didn't quite care for Kurt's stare, and wisely kept his mouth from yapping during the remaining part of the meal. Kurt expected him to bleat, like a good sheep.

– You seem to have placed yourself in quite a bind here, he said nervously, after a prolonged break. – I would guess you have some sort of plan… right?

– We have several hundred sympathizers hidden all over Gothenburg, Kurt confided in him. – On our signal they will start the war, and we will leave this place. None of you prisoners will be harmed.

In spite of the cold/cheerful smile the last sentence was probably meant to be soothing, but the man who supported discipline and order didn't feel soothed. Absolutely not!

– But… a confrontation between you and the soldiers, and the police… it will be a war… your powerful weapons… the city will be left in *ruins*.

One good thing had to be said in the man's defense. He didn't seem too relieved by the fact that the people here would remain in the safest spot in town. Kurt smiled hard while standing up.

– You say that as if it is a bad thing.

He would live long on that shocked expression. He admitted that willingly to himself.

– Priceless, Silverhair whispered to Kim. The two of them stood a bit by themselves. – He hasn't lost any of his humor, even though it has turned a bit… caustic these nights.

– Too bad the stuff about the several hundred sympathizers isn't quite true, Kim said, grinning roguishly.

– Sooner or later his words will be brought to the attention of those outside and that is the important thing. Jemma had sneaked up on them. – He's good. I've always said that.

– Not always, Kim fired.

– Give it a rest, you guys, Silverhair commanded exasperated, sensing claws being sharpened.

And she added, with a catch of despair:

– Is this really the time to inflate old grievances, whatever they are?

They bowed their heads, looking ashamed at each other.

– I'm sorry. Kim took Jemma's hand. – I love you.

– I'm sorry, too, Jemma said, – so sorry, for everything. I love you.

They embraced and kissed and smothered each other in the growing dark.

Night. It seemed short now, but would soon grow long. Time is short - or long. It can't truly be measured, but it was about to run out. *Dream a dream*. Seek into the stone desert, the gray fog, and hope you can find pieces of the many colored green rose.

Stand in the fire, and you get burned. But not all burned children dislike fire. Some, the brave, the stubborn, the stupid return for more. Or perhaps the fire burns so strong in them that it can't be put out.

Silverhair joined the three in the control room. She held a microphone to her mouth. Her voice was broadcasted through all the monster complex's speakers and was heard well by the faceless outside.

– We have a demand to be met before the evening, she shouted with her clear voice. – This is non-negotiable. During the day *all* prisoners shall be released from Swedish prisons, from all chains.

– She is nuts, a female officer exclaimed.

Lee Travis, standing not far from there shook his head.

– Humans aren't animals in cages, Silverhair said. – And animals don't belong in cages either. «We» imprison everything we don't understand, everything that doesn't fit in. No creatures belong in cages. Not animals or the human beast, Homo Sapiens Sapiens. No one will any longer be allowed to keep others from the freedom road.

Messy. She put down the microphone. *But you saved yourself nicely. You're good at that*.

Karel looked attentively at her. She showed him her unmoving mask. He didn't know her, and he was also unknown to her. She could get away with it. They trusted each other. She trusted all the three new warriors, but they were in a sense strangers.

Dawn, the color of rust and blood. The Nightravens slept in shifts. They would need all their energy in the days to come, those who lived that long. Some didn't want to or couldn't sleep. So many thoughts surfaced when one looked death in the eye.

Ten o'clock. Everybody waited wide awake, while digesting the morning meal. They ate well, but didn't fill themselves. They chewed carefully. The food was well dissolved before it reached the stomach.

They focused on enjoying every possible aspect of life, as they experienced it.

– CAN YOU HEAR ME IN THERE? They heard the thunderous voice from the outside.

– We can hear you, Judith replied.

She didn't shout, but they still heard her well.

When she closed her eyes a moment she saw an infinite number of white dots of light floating in the dark.

– This is tricky. WE NEED MORE TIME.

– YOU HAVE ONE EXTRA HOUR TO AGREE ON AGREEING. One o'clock, and not a second later we'll shoot the first hostage.

Silence reigned anew. Judith remained on the same spot. Her hands rolled into fists. For once the mask cracked ever so little. She stared, stared hard at all the people on the floor, looking anxiously at her.

– You're wrong, thinking we enjoy this. She spoke with an undercurrent of desperate despair. And then partly changing a shadow of a smile spiced the intensity in the unusual face. – Well, perhaps we are enjoying it, on some level. We would have liked to do something else than to blow up stuff and shoot holes in people or be shot ourselves, though. But we're damn good at it, because we have to be, and because human beings are natural warriors. To live long isn't the most important. It's what we do while being alive, damn it.

And then she left them, left them to rot, and that was also how they felt.

– When do you think they will attack? She asked Gio right afterwards.

An unnecessary question. She knew the answer. They all did.

– Well before twelve, Gio confirmed.

She nodded. The others did, too.

So did those tied up on the floor, while observing the Nightravens while they did their final preparations. Weapons were checked, readied and checked again. Every one of the roses eventually resembled a walking arsenal. They really did. It was no exaggeration. They had dressed in several layers of light body armor. But in spite of everything they carried they moved light and supple. Only Susan Palmer was close to unarmed. She carried something that had to be an UZI, a weapon even small children could fire without major trouble. And she had a gun stuck in her belt.

She wore a solid bullet-proof vest.

Jenna wanted to spit something, but Kurt stopped her.

– We must unfortunately leave you, now, he said with a cheerful regret. – The party was short, but hectic. We're invited to a party that will be even shorter, and even more hectic. As you probably know the host is the very insistent kind. Be faithful to yourselves, all of you.

He didn't say anything about his strong need to pee. It didn't matter, really. He wasn't ashamed of being human.

– I want to join you. A man sitting there, impatiently for quite a while cried out. I'm positive.

– Me, too, two others repeated several times, attempting to shout each other down.

Shocked cries followed these statements.

– We have come… too far, Morten said categorically. – We can't take more recruits. *We* can't.

– It isn't hard to find the Green Rose, Kimberly said softly and assertively. – Through the glowing web or other ways. Our procedures are not unfamiliar. You can do anything you want, if you truly want to.

She let herself fall to her knees, and kissed the two men and the woman on their lips. People laughed hysterically. Nobody saw the cards she put in their pockets.

Outside the Sun shone from a blue sky. Erland Jostedt saw only clear air wherever he turned. He had reason to be pleased.

– What are the updated numbers on the, uh, civilian death toll? He asked his aide.

– Two hundred, conservatively speaking, the woman replied, slightly nervous.

– Well, we can't do anything about that. We've been cleared from the top and the policy of not negotiating with terrorists is well established. People will eventually blame the guerilla. They always do.

The activity persisted and even increased around them. It wouldn't be long, now, until everything was set, and everything could once again become what it had always been. Cut off the snake's head and it doesn't grow two new, but dies writhing in the mud.

The soldiers in the circle checked their weapons. They positioned themselves on the ground, on the roofs, in the apartment windows. The military, police and Special Forces waited for the attack order. They would charge inside like bulls, and destroy anything in their path. If any ravens, in spite of this were able to flee outside sharpshooters waited for them.

The poor bastards hid behind quite an elaborate scheme in there, but it wouldn't save them.

Silence lingered in the air for a prolonged moment in time, almost like a physical presence.

The explosion overwhelmed everything. Blew eardrums, blew everything. The lower walls all around Nordstan dissolved. Success! Kurt did blow all the fuses simultaneously. Virtually the entire explosion was directed outwards. Millions of fragments shot through the air at the army besieging the place and penetrated a vast majority of them. Windows far away were shattered. Dust and smoke, and smoke from grenades whirled in the air. Sight was reduced to a few meters. A few seconds, and relative order was transformed into total chaos.

The ravens of the night rushed out of the large ruin before the dust had even begun settling. They left the same place they had entered, firing short bursts into the mist, and fired the grenades in their M-16A2's. Each of them carried two of them today. Explosions kept shaking the ground. Screams of pain and horror seemed to come from everywhere. *Good!* The enemy fired, too, but certainly not at them. They spotted bloody and mangled bodies on the ground. The smoke disappeared in front of them for a moment. Three soldiers with dead eyes rushed at them with fire-breathing barrels. All three were instantly executed.

Smoke and fog, and blood rose everywhere. Death and the blood rocked everyone. Rational consciousness faded, but the senses were sharpened to an uncanny degree. People rushed back and forth around them. Guns were fired. Fire was returned. The hyper-reality hit them like a soft glow, with no impact at all. Just for a moment they saw no more soldiers and it seemed they had broken through the ring, broken completely through. Perhaps they had, too, but there were still soldiers in front of them, more cannon fodder, more revenants of a dead world. The inferno obliterated buildings, shapes, even the air itself. Everything dissolved… but not the soldiers charging them.

– TRAVIS, Helene howled. She fired at him. Missed.

He fired and hit her, fired again and hit her again. She fell.

Silverhair fired, moving her gun like a fan around the center of her body. Soldiers dropped like flies, but they kept coming. In the unreal landscape of blood and death she saw Kathy be hit and fall. She registered it - nothing more. No tears, no thoughts. Then Jim. And Renni and… was it Heike? They started dying all around her. Heike still moved, still fought. She fired and ran, fired and ran, fired until the gun ran out of bullets, changed clip, fired until the gun failed because of the heating, threw it away, changed to another weapon. Morten pulled her with him. They were hit several times, but kept firing. Only slowly, terrifyingly slow they fell, fell side by side to the ground, their faces frozen in concentration, far into death.

Travis was also hit, but nothing seemed to faze him. A grenade exploded close to the tall, skinny body. He remained on his feet, quiet as death, while his gun kept roaring.

Gio and Kees ran back to back. An enemy fell for every bullet they fired.

Silverhair was convinced she could see every moment, hear every heartbeat, every crack. Taste and smell the cordite from a thousand guns. And more. Sense everything happening from a, to that point unnoticed sense. From all sides, all angles. It was unbelievable. She had never felt anything similar. Nothing she had experienced earlier even came close.

She fired a grenade at the top of a building, zoomed in at what she in a flash saw as the biggest threat. The soldiers not being blown up fell screaming to the ground far below. Susan was hit in the arm. She lost the UZI and swayed. Kurt and Karine pulled her with them. Travis stood just as unmovable, unaffected, like a force of nature. The Nightravens cut through the few remaining soldiers not yet dead or who had thrown away their weapons in blind panic. They had completed the breakthrough now. The majority of the uniforms were behind them.

Travis kept firing. He and he alone demoralized them a bit. Nothing seemed to faze him. They fired at him in a flash of a free line of sight. He stood straight.

Helene seemed to fly to her knees. She held a revolver in both hands. Her body leaked red all over, but she fired time and time again. The bullets hit Lee Travis and pushed him backwards. One hit him right in the neck and crushed it. He fell in a gust of blood. Helene followed him the very same moment. The light died in her eyes.

Feet trampled on the ground. Silverhair heard them. Everything had happened so quickly - and so incredibly slow. She was hit. The reflected lights from the surroundings, from the indistinct, the extremely distinct surroundings exploded in colors. She stumbled and fell. *Vision shifted, turned unclear*. She sensed heat flow and leak from the wound. But it didn't hurt. It had been like a powerful, very powerful push. That was all… was all…

Jemma and Gio helped her back on her feet, supported her the first critical steps further, until she could continue on her own. Miracles! She felt no dizziness, no weakness. There was blood on her hand when she pushed it at the wound, but not… a lot. She would survive a lot worse, she knew that.

After a time they experienced as many eternities, they finally reached something resembling a cover. They threw themselves down behind corners, where the soldiers didn't have free line of sight to them. They shot down those stupid enough not to use natural cover. This was urban guerilla. This was what they had trained to do, and had lots of experience doing. They had known they would draw advantage from it. ESC had been the enemy counter move there, but the elite forces had been in the first line of attack. There weren't many - or much - left of them. Jemma's teeth flashed white while she covered the retreat of her comrades. She fired one last salvo before she ran after them. She had always been a good runner. When her fellow warriors reached another corner she had almost caught up with them already. A machinegun was fired from a window. She was hit in the neck and head, and fell dead to the ground. Her life had been extinguished abruptly and violently.

The others ignored the sniper and kept running. The area they ran through was desolate, abandoned. The security forces had long since emptied the buildings of people. To make sure no one or nothing else lurked there the guerillas used their last rockets to blow up the houses ahead. Not that it mattered, but they imagined that blood gushed from several of the explosions.

The Nightravens, those who yet lived, reached the boundary of the closed off area. As they had expected there were several curious bystanders there, and only a few guards. The guards fled or were quickly eliminated. People (no longer bystanders) ran off in panic. The many-colored green ravens mixed with them while throwing away all visible weapons. Weapons they no longer had much ammo left for, anyway. The first part of the marathon ended. Now another began, a test of endurance they couldn't see the end of.

The chaos rested eventually. It felt incredible. As they slowed down their run to a walk almost nobody looked twice at them. And those who did kept their distance. The groups of green roses still alive spread out in the gray, mixing with the bland mass of two-legged creatures.

Kurt and Karine had pulled Susan into an office in a mall, another mall.

– I can't believe it, Karine said, close to euphoric. – It succeeded. We made it. We rolled over them. We must have left hundreds of bodies. *Thousands!* It's great. *Great!* I love it, love it *wildly,* can't help it.

Her fist hit the table, in an enraged mix of triumph and sorrow.

Susan cried softly, while Kurt bandaged her arm. Not because of the arm. The physical pain was as nothing, compared to what she felt inside.

– It isn't you. Kurt held the fist up in front of her face. – In a very true sense this has or had nothing to do with you at all. We had to do it. If they had taken you out and succeeded in laying the blame on us the damage would have been far worse. Now they've been exposed in a way that has fucked up their credibility for years. They will try to put a spin on it, of course, but it will be difficult. It will take a lot for them to be believed, if they're attempting something similar the next few years. And this would have come sooner or later. In a way they did us a favor. We had to take an open fight, a full battle, while we still could. And we did. And we succeeded beyond our wildest dreams. Whatever happens next ESF is ridiculed for eons.

– Cry, Karine said harshly. – But don't let it last. Don't let yourself drown in grief. Let it become *something else*.

– Yes, Susan mumbled. Her eyes slowly dried. – *Yes!*

They pulled masks on, masks showing unrecognizable faces. The women exchanged jackets, all of it an old, well-proven method. After a short reconnaissance they returned to the streets. Life in those streets resembled that on an ordinary day. There was a strong undercurrent of excitement in the air, but on the surface everything looked normal. *It won't last long.* Karine looked at a huge wall clock. It showed one minute to twelve.

There was a soccer match playing on Nya Ullevi, the home of the city's foremost team. *And now... sports*. Karine giggled and almost fell over in laughter. Kurt looked at her. He didn't get the joke. How could he?

Today's match was for charity, one where the income went «unabridged» to a watering plant in Southern Spain, another desperate attempt to stop the desertification. So typical… and ultimately useless. Another silly EU-project.

– I suddenly recalled something from an old British television satire, she explained to the other two, while they all looked for their contact to separate from the whirling mass ahead. – «Nine o'clock news» or something. There was a nuclear war brewing and then they had sports and…

There. The signal came from

She couldn't be certain, not in this crowd. Good in a way, but the line of sight wasn't good, and she needed to see thirty meters straight ahead. In the faces of the people around her she didn't see much serious worry, but on the contrary a horrible indifference. Unbelievable! When one listened to these people and their conversations about mundane events the violence and blood close by… felt unreal. One was tempted to believe it had never happened.

the man in the gray jacket. She made way for Kurt and Susan. She blinked. Once, twice. She was forced to blink, and couldn't stop. Something… reality returned in a flash… Eyes.

Eyes.

Fuck, not now. Those flower-beds…

– Go! She ordered. – Quickly!

He heard she was sniveling and understood, hesitated, until his feet and the cold calculating reason brought him and Susan away. Just before she disappeared in the crowd he saw Karine push the spray up a nostril. Susan stared shocked at him, paralyzed by understanding. He pulled her with him, clenching his teeth. They reached the man in the gray jacket, and those with him, and vanished in their midst.

– Are you the only ones? He asked.

He and the others in the group had difficulties controlling their expressions.

– I don't know, Kurt said frustrated and restrained, – but we must assume that's the case.

– Jeez…

– They saved me, Susan said abruptly. – They showed that loyalty means something in this world, and they showed that The Nightravens, *we* nightravens are a power to be reckoned with. I can assure you we gave far more then we took. No matter, I'm eternally grateful. We all are. We have something to live up to. They showed us the standard to uphold.

Kurt looked at her in approval. They all started moving, moving slowly. Kurt looked back a few times, but not Sue. She never looked back.

Head cleared slowly. Irritatingly slow. Karine set course in the opposite direction of Kurt and Susan. If possible her senses were even more sharpened than ever before in her life, even more than during the battle a few minutes earlier. She wondered if she was just imagining the eyes in her back. No, she had learned to trust her instincts, the third eye long ago.

She saw them. Four. Four «coats» (even thought they didn't wear coats) rushing forward (or so it seemed to her) sixty degrees to the left and right, ten meters behind her. She had had them after her for a while. They kept the distance. It wouldn't surprise her if they did it with just a few centimeters variance. So predictable that it was almost embarrassing. They were not merely assholes, but boring, too. Boo.

But… something should have happened already? Her watch had been smashed by a bullet. The clock on the wall had to be insane, yes, that's it, a raving lunatic wall clock.

The ground shook below her and she cheered. The cracks thundered from all sides. A building fifty meters off seemed to split in two. People *howled.* Nerves were high strung these days. She crouched, hid in the wavering mass. There were constantly new explosions. Fireballs rose in the air. Karine Lie looked wide-eyed at it all, both fascinated and a bit shell shocked over what happened in her line of sight. Civilization was indeed fragile. And that was such a good thing.

– THE END IS NEAR, a man whimpered.

People moaned and complained. They pushed and stamped on each other, without any concern for their fellow man. Karine Lie almost found that funny. Almost.

She fought her way through the Storm, while the wreckage floated by. In smooth and concentrated moves she switched back and forth between walk and run, until she was far away from where the explosions had started. She kept walking, a tightrope between hope and desperation. She was alone now, for the first time in many years, with only herself to rely on.

They were gone, the coats, flushed away by the tall waves. She allowed herself a cautious smile and kept walking. It was necessary to get out of town before all hell started here. That thought brought another smile. The military marshal law would soon be in full effect. The question was how soon.

People around her had also slowed down, probably on their way home. They looked scared to all sides, waiting in dank fear for the lightning to strike anew. Karine, too, sensed the fearsome sensitivity, but her eyes remained measured, as they calmly kept taking in the sights.

She froze inside. The coats had braved the tall waves, and were once more behind her. Not the same as before, but there were so many of them, and she knew their type so well. So many… blackest hell. In a cellar black as coal she considered her options.

Such narrow alleys. The gray fog drifted close to her, making it hard to breathe, harder than ever.

She was alone. No one close by had any chance of helping her, even if they had wanted to. Only pure luck could help her now.

The coats hadn't drawn any weapons. Not now, either. They could easily have shot her before she had discovered them. That they had denied themselves that pleasure didn't make her feel better. Perhaps they hoped she would lead them to the others, but, no, they certainly couldn't think that? The truth dawned on her in its horror. They wanted to take her to a room without light, and have their fun with her, like they had done with Sivert.

Now they came at her from in front, too. She instantly knew how her options had shrunk to virtually none. Her mind raced. Her body raced. Thought and action turned into one. She drew the revolver and fired in one smooth move. It happened so fast, less than a second after she had caught them in her sight. It happened so fast that two fell before the others reacted. People started screaming again, freezing in their tracks, running like cattle in all directions. Karine turned abruptly and returned the way she had come. Several cows and sheep were hit by bullets close by her. The enemy cared ever less about caring. Fingers of ice seemed to clutch her heart. Temptation reared its ugly head. Perhaps her best option right now was to put a bullet through her own head. Escape seemed futile, yeah, downright impossible The coats on the scene of the crime had a ridiculous superiority of numbers on their side.

She rushed into a restaurant, suddenly able to feel the hunger, gnawing in her stomach. She drew the UZI from behind her back and fired at the ceiling, feeling the *Hunger,* the beyond powerful taste of blood in her mouth.

– EVERYBODY FREEZE, she shouted, a menace on two legs.

A man pulled a weapon from his jacket. She shot him through the head. The brain splashed on the table and the wall close by. His former female companion released a whine, slid off the chair and lay motionless on the floor.

Karine Lie saw herself with their eyes. No one within the four walls of the restaurant had ever seen a wild animal, and certainly not one pushed into a corner. When it moved it was like watching the wind. Basically one saw nothing, nothing at all.

The coats weren't so square that they attempted to follow her inside. Very good! It was so nice to be positively surprised occasionally. Too bad it happened on such rare occasions.

They knew they had blown it, and discussed how to salvage the pieces of their now, oh, so brittle strategy.

The single green rose started the preparations for what was to come, the inevitable. She found most of her remaining hand grenades, pulled out the pins, and placed them, one by one on various tables.

– W-what if they won't s-stand properly? A guest asked her, quite pale.

– Let's not hope that, she said lightly.

(And cheerfully).

She placed a bunch of *heavier* guests in front of the back doors and blocked the access ways. No one would enter there without the use of a bulldozer or something. At the front door she waited, ready to receive the upcoming guests out there.

– I would like… to make a phone call, a man said calmly. A journalist.

– You won't get any objections from me, Karine grinned.

He slowly brought a hand inside his coat, and revealed a cell phone. Unbelievably enough the network still worked. It didn't matter, but it was still a small miracle.

People started gathering outside, a considerable distance away from the beast inside. An army of journalists and photographers. Among them the remaining few of all current foreign correspondents in Gothenburg.

Karine pulled off her mask.

– Everything to please the photographers.

She took a bow, a smile playing on her lips.

The amassing choir shouted her name several times. She felt a strange detachment to it all, to her own unmasking, her own claiming of identity, while completing the job of brushing and cleaning, all the time with an ironic taint around the mouth. It was all so strange. The eyes turned distant. Except for the bruise on her wrist, where the bullet had hit the watch she was actually unharmed.

– Berglund, *Aftonbladet,* Miss Lie, the journalist said, very businesslike. – Is there anything special you wish to share with our readers?

– The media is the government's lapdog, she said teasingly. – The fourth, *supporting* estate. I don't know… Let me put it this way: I would be surprised if I was quoted at all and stunned if I was quoted correctly.

– KARINE LIE, it thundered from outside. – COME OUT UNARMED. BE SENSIBLE AND SURRENDER YOURSELF AND WE GUARANTEE FAIR TREATMENT.

– Fair, she mumbled in a biting tone. – Fair?

Then she brightened.

– FAIR! She exclaimed.

She fired a salvo. The window broke and the man with the bullhorn was felled by a hail of bullets. A shocked silence followed that moment.

– That's life's small, ruthless coincidences for you. She giggled, very loud.

– A very convincing argument, Miss Lie, Berglund commented matter-of-fact.

– Wasn't it? She held her head high.

She and the journalist sat in a corner, sat there for while, with tables, chairs and people as assurances against interference. There was clearly ongoing activity outside, but nothing of significance happened.

– I've always been fond of traveling. The voice sounded distant, but the eyes remained focused, sharp. – I learned early on that a truth isn't necessarily a truth even though it is accepted in each individual's birthplace, learned that it was important to see an issue from at least two sides. I learned independence that way. I saw, I learned, often the hard way what the world is like, what it has become. I mean… according to the logic of the pointy elbow syndrome it is clear that your value increases while others' decrease, right? It's so logical… and so wrong. People drown in poison, and call it civilization. I certainly don't want to be a part of it. Open eyes see injustice wherever a person goes, mostly organized, systematic, but also the random, unfocused encouraged by the very society where it exists. It has always made me quite pissed. One day or one night we were just fed up, I guess.

She plowed the hand not holding the gun through the unruly hair.

– We tried, we really did. We held back, were cautious and didn't go to extremes. Not at first. We followed the passive resistance's tenet about not provoking the opponent, just show him and her our existence. In hindsight I would say that worked beyond expectations, all right. We tried everything… even though it was evident from the start, really that the two-legged wolves understand nothing but power. When we realized that… beyond doubt, we realized more was needed. You don't build on a rotten foundation, not if you're somewhat sane. You tear down the foundation, and start all over… Perhaps the rain will do it for us. Rain of fire or water, it doesn't matter. Everything will be flushed clean.

The glow of madness faded from her eyes. They couldn't wait for others to do something, for something to happen. They had understood that long ago.

– Humans are nomads, she mumbled. – That's our natural state of being. We must be free as the bird, like the bird Phoenix. Or we aren't human.

She rose, pulled herself together.

– YOU! She pointed at one sitting by the door. – Tell them I will come out, come out and play.

They stared harder at her, beyond stunned and shocked, rocked to the core of their being.

He walked to the broken window, and did as he had been told.

There was a reply from the outside, a kind of confirmation.

She hadn't actually heard the words or tried to. It didn't matter. She turned her head as she headed towards the exit.

– You will never forget this, she said softly to them all.

The door opened, and Karine Lie strolled outside.

– I am Chai Ling, she cried. – Chai Ling driven too far.

Inside the restaurant the journalist was sweating hard while attempting to remove people from one of the back doors. He fought his way through it and started running. It could work. There was still time.

Karine had wondered, briefly, if she wanted them to fire, whether or not she cared at all. The moment ended. She heard clicks all around her, gunmen cocking their weapons. Like the most natural way in the world she threw herself forward. She landed softly, supple like a cat, and continued her movement across the street. The bullets hit her right after she had thrown her final hand grenades. She had pulled them out in her flight. They landed among the soldiers and blew many of them apart. She was shot to pieces. She felt it, felt herself be ripped apart. But many of the bullets missed her, and ricocheted inside the restaurant. She saw it all, so lively. People were hit in there, and panicked, tipped over the tables. The hand grenades rolled off those very tables. A fog formed in the air. She managed to smile. Her eyes burned in passionate defiance until the end.

The first of a series of explosions erupted in there. The restaurant was transformed into a ruin in seconds. The fog reached the figure all heat leaked from, the fog of dust and shit and light surrounding her. The cold surrounded Karine and she turned hot… so very hot. The human bird rose from the glowing ashes.

They traveled through a cellar dark as coal, five of them. Breen, Russel, Loeser, Rossi and Russel. The others… gone on the endless road of gray and red. Perhaps they were dead, perhaps not. They had been separated from their fellow warriors during a shootout an hour ago. Right after that they had heard a number of shots being fired, and then… nothing.

A curfew without time limit had been announced at dusk. The five hunted outlaws charged through the twilight, through deserted streets. It never truly turned dark in Scandinavia during summer, but enough for them to take advantage of the night. They moved unseen by the people crouching shivering and troubled in their beds, by those sleeping uneasily behind heavy curtains.

Slept the common man and woman did, but never more in safety, or even the illusion of safety.

Waves of fatigue washed over the five. They fought themselves forward, chased like beasts. And beasts they were, and the awareness of their precarious circumstances chased off the fatigue time and time again. A natural endurance, animal cunning, a will deeper than any night, than any day or civilization, and the hatred against the monsters hunting them kept them going.

But in their boiling insides, where everything was clarity they wondered how long they would be able to keep it up, how many times they would be able to pull themselves up by the hair.

– If they hadn't been so many, Kim exclaimed irritated, weary, beyond weary. They leaned against a cold brick wall. – They may charge us from any direction, any…

She straightened, straightened yet again, rolling hands into fists one more time.

– *Okay*. It doesn't matter. We will take them if they are a million, or hundred millions.

She loaded her UZI with the last clip she had left. The others had a few more.

– How's the wound? Kees asked Silverhair casually.

– It has reopened, she shrugged, – but there isn't much blood. It's okay.

He didn't fool her. She didn't fool him.

One of their safe houses was nearby. They circled in on it, cautiously optimistic, taking their time. Their pursuers had chased their tail for such a long time, but now it looked like they had finally shaken them off.

The green light at the end of the street, the lamp by the house' entrance was consistent with expectations and hopes. But the other sign, at the start of the street wasn't. The pottery plant was missing in the designated window.

They kept running. Lungs threatened to burst. Muscles in stiff thighs screamed for rest. Screams. STEPS. Everywhere. So loud they could hardly stand it. They heard them from all sides. Throat felt like it was burning. They kept going.

Dawn arrived early, far too early. They finally reached the suburbs. The enemy hadn't showed itself in a long time, but they all felt its presence, its truth like something physical in the air.

The block of flats turned into shadows against the horizon, instead of nightmares in the dark. Kim and Gio glanced at each other, and then at Judith, then at each other again. The pace and the run's durability clearly began affecting Judith. The wound was a «trifle», and she didn't seem bothered by it, but even she would eventually reach her limit. The will could ignore the body for a long time, but not indefinitely. It was a good thing that they had decided to stay indoors during the day. They sought inside a block, automatically reading the number on its front. The entrance door wasn't locked. They stepped into the silence, seeing no one. Gio found the key to the first apartment on the ground floor under the doormat. He opened the front door to the apartment swiftly and efficiently. The five slipped inside. Gio and Kim searched the rooms. There was no one else here. They nodded when returning to the hallway, and they were all able to relax a bit, finally. Judith collapsed then, two steps from the doorstep. Elan and Kees caught her before she fell. They carried her to a bedroom, putting the fever-hot body on a bed. Kim pulled a blanket over her. The others looked at them, worried sick over the pale woman's closed eyes. Kim checked her pulse. A bit irregular, but strong.

– She's asleep. Kim looked at the others with a mix of irritation and numb relief.

They couldn't really tell how long they had been sitting in the small living room, when Silverhair walked in.

Kim rushed to the kitchen and returned with a fuming cup.

– The herbs should take care of your fever, she said, conveying her apprehension to her friend.

I'm fine. Judith kissed her on the cheek.

She had made another, tight bandage. Still a bit pale she met their eyes with her steady gaze, the one they had learned to know and respect during the long years of struggle. A just as steady hand held the cup to the lips, and she drank.

– It is so quiet, she marveled.

She loaded her guns, her part of the storage that had awaited them here. The others had already done theirs.

It was quiet. They had fought so long on the front line that they hadn't registered the overwhelming silence.

The silence before the ever returning Storm.

And inevitably like death, it returned.

They sensed it like a series of strong pains, in thought, mind, the psyche, sensed the armies of death charging them. How many times hadn't they been sitting like this, ready, with weapons primed, considered their options, screamed at the fates, the inevitable, concentrated, while reaching out with their consciousness in the hope of sensing what was beyond the senses?

One thousand times, in this room alone.

Everybody controlled the weapons one more time. Aside from that, and thinking back they had nothing to do.

Judith saw the forest. The wind was blowing where the witches danced naked, the seven… no, six witches and a demon, one from the depths of the black hole. She clutched the blood red sword of fire and life that split the darkness. She held on to it for her life.

She stood by the wall and stared through the binoculars, out of the window. The landscape consisted of fields and gray roads. Flat tarmac, and flat, browned and burned grass. She saw a skew-eyed blonde girl with a roguish flash in her eyes writhe on the dance floor. She relived her first visit to the Green Rose, where she had met Kees and Renni. The seasoned woman realized startled that her life passed in review.

There… figures dressed in camouflage clothing slipped forward towards the place where the birds flying in the dark were hiding.

– They're coming, Judith related calmly. – They move in a random pattern, but there's little doubt they know where we are. A small group is leading on. They've been here for a while, studied the terrain, so to speak.

– For honor and medals, Elan spat.

Silence lingered in the very air… again, inside and outside the block. The chameleons out there hardly moved. No sound reached the ears of those inside. The window was slightly ajar. No falling needles were heard. Everybody cocked their guns. The spell was broken.

– They're about to use cannons, Kees exclaimed. – The shitheads.

They saw it, saw the barrels, saw the deadly batteries being deployed in the mist.

– I can't see any more emptyheads following those advancing, Kim said. – Backup may hide in the bushes, though.

– Good, Silverhair said, sounding pleased, her teeth gritted.

Gio smashed the windows. She fired her rifle, and killed the three who had made the most progress deploying the cannons.

Bullets rushed back and forth, like a horizontal waterfall. The screams of horror began. People woke up abruptly from their sleep, and were filled with lead and leaked blood when exposing themselves in the windows.

Somebody tried to escape at the front of the building. They were hit by the crossfire almost instantly. Some used their heads, and jumped from the balconies at the back. Nobody fired at them.

The Nightravens had pretty good protection behind the thick concrete wall, and held their position without much trouble… for a short while. They had to expose themselves to take proper aim. The *cannons*… if they were fired only once… Once would be enough.

– They haven't very much in terms of numbers yet, Gio commented breathless. – And we're just about holding our own. This isn't urban guerilla. We have no advantages here.

– Time to split then, Silverhair nodded, – while we're ahead.

They should have fled earlier, before the risk level had increased, but it was so hard to make all the right decisions all the time, make them in a fraction of a second.

Like the monster Hydra they charged, the army of decay. Perhaps there were ways to halt their march, but not one the five had in their possession at the time.

Kim fired and took cover. Elan took her place and fired his load. He hesitated a bit too long. He was hit by so many bullets that the blood jumped from all over his body. Kim saw him dissolve before her eyes. She didn't scream. Not aloud.

– All four simultaneously now, Silverhair shouted. She pulled Kim up with her. – FIRE!

They sent off their rockets. The same instant they turned and rushed towards the balcony. There was a low, undetermined sound. Kim heard, perhaps because she had her head half turned. She glimpsed the explosions out there. Huge holes appeared in the ground, huge craters in the decay's dying soil. She spotted the rocket with the horizontal fire farthest away. Saw it infinitely clear. She threw herself at Silverhair, hit her body, pushed her sideways into the hallway, before

(everything turned white and red)

The explosion made the entire giant building shake. The hulk shook on its stumbling foundations.

Judith crawled through the wreckage, towards Kim, shaking her head in an attempt to clear it. At the edge of her vision she saw the remains of Kees and Gio. It hurt to get close to her. Hurt so much. Kim was torn apart several places. It was miracle she was still alive.

Two pair of eyes filled with blood met. Judith couldn't fathom how she was still able to see.

– You know what you have to do, now. Kim coughed the words instead of speaking them. Judith knew what she had to do now, knew it too well. – You… must… escape.

Judith nodded, unable to speak. She attempted to remove blood from the face she knew so well.

– Do it. Kim gasped. – You have my consent.

– That solves one problem. Judith made her voice hard, closing off the pain. – But the decision is mine, and mine alone.

– *Show* them it is war. Show them they're fighting a WAR…

Those were her final words. Judith's eyes turned to the bloody hands. They held a hand grenade, and they pulled out the pin, and then hid the dangerous little thing. Silverhair rose and left the steaming body. Kimberly Russel was dead. Through sun and rain, during their endless days and nights she had helped her to hold out.

– I used to l-live here.

She heard a voice filled with hatred. She turned and stared into the hungry gap of a barrel.

– Perhaps I deserve it, Silverhair said. – We should have known how bloodthirsty they were, after being humiliated to the degree they were. But decide quickly. They will soon be over us.

He lowered the gun. She jumped light footed over the balcony fence and landed on the lane. He followed her, trailed her into the black and gray smoke hiding them, the panicked sea of animal-like creatures on the run obscuring their flight. The Sun shone in their faces. The sharp light made her eyes flow… but she didn't cry. She didn't know how to cry.

The first soldiers advanced slowly into the ruins of the block, advanced cautiously from cover to cover. It burned inside and they smelled burned flesh. It seemed safe, and more joined the first.

– There are remains everywhere. The lieutenant spoke in the radio. – It seems like everyone is here… sort of… here is Russel.

He kicked the body. Something rolled from its belly.

– A hand grenade… FUCK!

Silverhair and her companion didn't see the explosion, but they heard the crack, sensed the subtle tremor in the ground. She recognized the sound. The wind seemed cool after the hot flames. Judith felt it in every part of her face. If she was lucky they would believe she was among the dead. It would be very hard to disprove. And they wanted to believe she was no longer a threat to them.

She kept placing one foot in front of the other, kept making the effort. They were only two of many running head and toe from the battle. She didn't have the energy to look for enemies, but it wasn't such a big thing.

If there were agents of law and order in this assembly, they had more than enough trouble avoiding being stamped on. Thoughts came slowly. She was far outside the city now. It wouldn't take much to simply slip away, even if they kept searching for her, searching for a dead woman. She could rest. Perhaps she should have. But it wasn't in the cards. She had so much to do, so little time to do it.

The big rain would come. It had come, unstoppable. That was clear to her now. And it would flood everything in existence. Whether or not the rain was fire or water mattered little. It would probably be both, something including everybody, something nobody could escape, the true rain, drowning everything in its relentless waves. So the world, so mankind could rise again.

And grow freely, without any kind of management.

Silverhair was tired now. She felt the exhaustion in every bone in her body. *Close to ten years.* All that time she had carried on with this madness, had suffered and lived through fire, water, air and soil. Time to finish it… and she was the right one to do it. She had always been. She realized that with painful clarity. Her luck was about to run out, leak from her like heat from a dead body. One could only keep going for so long, until it grew increasingly difficult to avoid bullets. If she should do what was necessary she would have to do it soon.

Judith Breen vanished into the ever-increasing gray fog. Where she was headed now, she had always been, she realized, and that was merely one more bittersweet realization of many overwhelming her. The tired figure straightened. Her entire life had led her here, to this place between Time and Space. She was thirty-six

and her time had come.

Part three:
DREAMS IN STONE CITY

«You can blow out a candle
but you can't blow out a fire
once the flame begin to catch
the wind will blow it high»

Biko - Peter Gabriel

CHAPTER TWENTY

Judy Brevik rose early on constitution day. No one got out of bed before she did, except the servants - of course.

– Good morning, Mrs. Brevik. A nervous girl tripped by her when she walked down the marble stairs.

– Good morning, Tove, a distracted and distant Mrs. of the house replied.

The major domo greeted her with the same exquisite politeness. She replied to him preoccupied, automatically, in the same way, a bit colder.

– Does Madame desire an early breakfast? It will be ready in a few minutes. If Madame will wait in the living room…

– That won't be necessary, Thomas. Just make sure my car is ready, please.

– Right away, Madame. He bowed, hesitating a bit. – Tove didn't arrive in time to assist you in the bathroom today. Does Madame wish me to take disciplinary action? Such mindless laziness is unforgivable, of course…

– There's no need for that, she assured him. – It was I who woke up early, not she who was late.

Judy took a quick look in the mirror by the entrance. A satisfied smile touched her lips. She was dressed in a smart tight green dress. In an undefined way it fit her short hair. It had become a bit tight. Her lips curled, dissatisfied. She had grown… bigger lately. Time to get herself an entire new wardrobe. Most of what she wore these days was months' old, anyway.

The car waited for her outside. The boy who had taken the car out of the garage held open the door for her. She entered the driver's seat and started the engine. The car, a Lamborghini Mark IV raged across the extensive estate. The gate outside was opened at the last second. She left the private road on whining tires.

She drove the motorway to central Oslo with one hand on the wheel. The city rose around her. Buildings and concrete surrounded her. Silence still dominated in the streets. The children's parade had yet to start, start marching. The march and oath in the puppet king's honor was still in its tentative stages. She drove the car to the Brevik family's private garage close to the broad Karl Johan's Street. Just a selected few of the city's inhabitants had permission to use it.

Before leaving the car she drank the last drop of the bottle she had brought. It had been full just after she got out of bed. That would have to do for now. If she needed more she could just return to the car for more.

Judy Brevik stumbled through the morning streets. People and human beings passed by her in an endless stream. She feared she would be recognized. Experience made it easy to discover looks of envy and admiration. On the adjacent corner a brown-skinned man was grabbed and stopped by the police, was *asked* to show his papers. Racial profiling was used here, as it was all places, in yet another country of sharp and tall barbwire. What he eventually had wasn't sufficient. They dragged him inside the rolling cage and left with him. She turned away from it all.

The procession marched to the huge marble castle. The man on the balcony, a man that would have been dead many years ago without artificial ways of prolonging his life waved his raised hand a short distance back and forth, back and forth. He looked more dead than alive to anybody with a minimum of awareness and cognitive abilities intact. Machines kept him alive.

Judy blinked. For some reason it was as if her eyes were pulled towards three people, a woman and two men, standing a bit down the street from her. They simulated the king's waving in an obviously ironic and disrespectful way. But there was more. She recognized the signs in them. Eyes for a moment reclaiming their former astute look noticed the bags they carried. Throat tightened.

The three found, with a kind of eager calm their stuff, flags, one small and one big, something that had to be a law book, an electronic bullhorn and a can of gasoline. They splashed the flags and the law book, until everything was soaking wet. Then they immediately started speaking through the bullhorn. Judy didn't hear the words. Her eyes locked on to the flames rising from all the red. Slowly, very slowly people around them realized what was happening.

– Einstein was quite right when he stated that nationalism is a childhood disease, humanity's measles. On the other hand… In natural tribal societies the tribal identity has a function, since it is natural to protect the people closest to oneself. But on a national level we get such absurd and horrible expressions like «everything for norway», «deutchland uber alles», «my country right or wrong» and more…

– LET'S BURY THIS TRADITION ONCE AND FOR ALL

A guy dressed in red, white and blue kicked the smaller flag once and for all, his face distorted in anger. It didn't matter much, really, since the flag evidently was made of non-flammable material. Even when bathing in gasoline it didn't burn. The other, however, was another matter. When it was put close to the law book it caught fire instantly. Red, white and blue burned. People screamed. A pack of police officers charged the gathering.

The mood turned hysterical in moments. People ran to them and gesticulated wildly. The patrolmen started running.

The seven in the pack, quickly increasing to eleven started «handling» the three, who were told they were «participating in an illegal protest». A police patrol van appeared from nowhere. People formed a circle around the spectacle. Most with angry eyes, but some were also curious. The «protesters», after a brief argument followed the officers reluctantly to the patrol car. Everything seemed fairly relaxed, but the excessive honor escort looked anything but benign.

– There's supposed to be freedom of speech in this country, one of the three cried. – Have we truly done anything wrong? We're doing a peaceful, non-violent protest and are kept from expressing ourselves, also by representatives of official authorities.

– Are you now choosing to continue the illegal protest? A patrolman with a moustache said, clearly doing his best to look intimidating.

– What's your name and badge number? The woman asked cheerfully. – We've given you ours. Your own rules say you're supposed to give us yours.

– Nilsen, the dog patrol, that's all you need to know.

– There isn't a right to protest in this country, but a ban, the tallest of the three sniffed. – You may apply to the police for permission, to be «kindly» granted an exception from it.

– We're against anything smacking of police, of course, the other guy added.

– You stole our bullhorn, the woman complained.

– Evidence, Nilsen stated arrogantly.

– You're obviously getting away with anything. You've stolen…

– File charges, a stone-faced officer said in sadistic joy.

– That *is* a good one…

The tallest praised the officer for his sense of humor. Laughter. The patrolmen stared fuming at the crowd.

Judy stared big-eyed at what happened. She moved with the crowd, following the heretics to the patrol van and its cage. In a place inside her something screamed in wonder, admiration and despair. The three were so brave, so fearless… like she had been once.

She pulled back, away from there, while fighting an ever-increasing amount of panic. Judy hurried off, filled with a growing sense of despair, a deep, dark cloud expanding and filling her to the brim. Afterwards she never recalled how she had managed to get from the place of the spectacle, the scene of the crime and back to the quiet garage. Beyond the quiet twilight the silence screamed at her, making her whimper in growing terror. She threw herself into the car, onto one of the seats, wasn't certain of which and tore open the glove compartment door. She pulled on the screw in one of the bottles, in vain, of course. She was forced to unscrew it and it happened so slowly. She gulped huge sips to drown the sound of the whispering walls.

After that she recalled even less. Only that she drifted through the streets, glimpsing countless variations of a pale face in the store windows. Everything had turned silent, but the silent visions wouldn't let go. She froze badly. She ended up around a bonfire somewhere, with a gathering of leather clad youths. Most had the strangest hairdos and colors. Everybody sang from the heart, to the chords of a single guitar. Tears flowed unrestrained down her cheeks. It didn't help, no matter how much she attempted to dry her skin and sore eyes. There were always more tears. Fog spread. *Spread.* Whatever she did or didn't do. She fell, she knew she did, fell hard. Everything turned into one single burst of pain. *She knocked her head on the concrete and lay still.*

++++++++++++++++++++++++

Karine couldn't see the flowers and couldn't smell them. She had long since convinced herself that they crawled all over the neighbor cell. The nostrils were slowly being filled by snot. Again. They would wait until the last second, before giving her the spray, and then, after a while, the torture would begin anew. They had been eager, very eager to entertain her since her arrival here. She fought against despair and depression with every bit of resistance she had, but wasn't sure how much longer she could hold out. They were diabolical and diabolically sophisticated in their art. If they found one weakness in you, they exploited it for everything it was worth. They widened a crack to a ravine. And as long as she was imprisoned here, in this place, at their mercy, they had her exactly where they wanted her. If they had waited just a bit too long, just once, postponed the rescue operation a few more seconds her suffering would be done. No more suffering. Thus she thought. They had done this to her. How could they stand their own cruelty? She didn't get it. Only knew she would never let herself be put in a situation like this, *again*. They would never again gain any sort of power over her.

She stared blindly up into Judy Brevik's inexpressive face. Judy looked at her, and the irritation in the green eyes increased by the second.

– Hurry up with that damn spray, she roared at the guards quietly as a whisper.

He hurried to her with it. She pushed it into Karine's nostrils and the foggy eyes cleared. Karine kept coughing for minutes.

– From now on you will give her plenty in advance, to use as she sees fit, Silverhair announced coldly. – I intend to visit often and if I hear about more pranks from you naughty boys and girls… On the other hand I can be very generous…

– Everything will be done to your satisfaction, Mrs. Brevik, one nodded vigorously, a whipped, servile dog, a public servant eager to perform.

– Good. You will now leave us alone and enable us to speak uninterrupted.

She discharged them brusquely, by a wave of her hand.

– And remove those fucking flowers.

It turned quiet.

– Silverhair, Karine greeted her in acknowledgement. And then in a slightly different tone: – To what do I owe the pleasure?

– You are incarcerated, temporarily or not, for having protested illegally, and for a few other, unsubstantiated charges.

– I hope they will charge me with agitation and subversive activities, Karine grinned. – Only Einar Gerhardsen, one of our former prime ministers has been charged with that in our proud country. It will be quite an honor. Not to be compared with Gerhardsen, but the rarity of it all.

– You could have sought permission… The sarcasm was quite visible in Silverhair's eyes.

– We would never have been granted it, the prisoner snorted. – As you know there's a ban on protests in this country, in all countries. The police may grant an exception. It doesn't hold water. And we don't acknowledge the power law and order gives them, anyway.

– And there's a lot to be said about choosing constitution day as the day of protest…

– We knew we entered the lion's den, Karine said, without sounding too down. – Somebody must do it. Somebody must try.

Karine's penetrating eyes turned indistinct in Judith's vision.

… into the lion's den… at the center of the gray fog. One could be devoured in there.

– I can get you out of here, Judy said.

– You know where a few bodies are buried, right? Karine asked, a bit sarcastic.

– More than a few, Silverhair replied self-consciously. – You want out, right?

And now it was the green eyes that were intense. Karine shivered for a moment under that penetrating stare. It contained so much.

– Of course, this isn't exactly a prospective location, is it?

++

Dances, dances with wolves, two-legged wolves.

The room whirled round and round. The huge, main hall turned indistinct to Judy for a moment. She danced with the Mayor. The entire party was held in his honor. The Brevik Estate was excellently suited to the purpose. Today's little soirée didn't have the dimensions of that on his seventieth birthday, but it didn't really differ that much. Judy flowed between all the party clothes whirling on the floor. Sometimes she imagined these people were their clothes, and nothing besides. She had to strain hard to look beyond the luxury and façade to the person behind it. They all looked the same to her. This was no party, but a henhouse where all the hacking beaks hid behind masks.

Judy smiled automatically when the smiling man thanked her for the dance. Then Olav was there and pulled her away, and led them in another dance. They eventually got the floor to themselves, the two of them, entirely to themselves. She swallowed hard. He was so handsome in the dark clothes. They dominated the floor together, and they displayed raw power and elegance. There was no limit to what they could do or how far they could go together.

– The new dress looks nice on you, he said, giving her his praise.

– It does, doesn't it? She confirmed his words. – But you must have appraised me while I was asleep or something. I must say, my lord, that it seems a bit strange. You were never any good at it.

People applauded them in the humming silence after the dance. He bowed and she curtseyed, both with total control over themselves and their surroundings.

They circulated among the guests, the perfect hosts.

– Excellent party, a huge red-faced man remarked.

– Thank you. Judy smiled sweetly.

– Quite an ugly matter… the commotion outside the American embassy last week, Olav commented dryly, more than a bit patronizing. – Excellently handled, though.

– Thank you, the man resembling a pig frowned, clearly not quite convinced whether or not he had been praised.

Judy looked at Olav, but didn't add anything to his comment.

Some time later she sat with a few other wives and twittering hens, and was bored, bored beyond belief. She sat there with a strong impression that the hens didn't really hear a word she said. Not so strange that, perhaps. She didn't get much of what they said either.

– You're bored. Olav stood in front of her and reached out a hand. She accepted it.

– True words spoken. Do you have an anti-drug, my love?

She let herself be pulled into his arms, into her husband's arms. She was his woman.

Concrete and its associates plastic, glass and metal surrounded them on all sides, tangible and frightening beyond words.

She was trapped here. But what if she fled? What else was there?

He drew her attention to a man speaking in a circle of listeners. By their behavior and expression when they looked at him one could be tempted to believe gold flowed from his mouth.

– Dr. Kaspersen. She closed her mouth for a moment. – And admirers.

– Don't you want to take him down a peg or two? Olav teased her. – And it will give you something to do.

Take him down? She wanted that with a craving hurting her.

– Just don't cross the line, he admonished her.

Her response was a dignified glance, as if he should have known better.

On her way she heard the Smiling Mayor reply to a question from two wives conversing with him.

– Rumors and rumors only, he denied. – In such a large building as City Hall there will always be rumors. They have no foundation in the real world.

Not in the reality he wants to uphold.

And I, what reality do I want?

– Most and foremost the young need a firm touch. Dr. Kaspersen spoke as a person who had put all doubt behind him a long time ago. – Take these squatters, for instance… If they had been given regular beatings throughout their childhood they would most certainly have stayed at home and listened attentively to their parents instead of giving adults lip and roaming the streets.

– And they have certainly no valid reasons for their concerns and subsequent rebellion? Judy stated sarcastically.

– Certainly not, Mrs. Brevik, he snorted. – Nobody with their sanity intact would rebel against society's overwhelming majority. That's logical, isn't it.

– What about everyone who has enjoyed… the advantage of your methods, and still turned out… wrong?

She had already trouble containing her temper.

– Dear Judy, may I call you Judy? That's obvious. There are malcontents in all societies. It's just a matter of exposing and treating them. They must be held on a tight leash from the very first misdemeanor. Their misguided ways must never be allowed to grow. The lazy, the drug-addicts and other criminals should be sent to working camps, doing hard labor, until they're able to function in the society harboring them.

– Perhaps I would have been more impressed by your theories, Dr. Kaspersen - if they had been new - but the fact is that they aren't even very original.

– Oh?

– They have had a number of names during recorded history. The most recent is re-education camps. Have a nice evening.

The hens behaved even more reserved in her company after that. One of them showed a surprising level of reasoning by starting something that could have been the start of a discussion.

– I don't *understand* how you can criticize the good doctor. His conclusions are basically based on studies of the Japanese society, where respect for leaders is very common, and Japan is one of the world's most ordered societies.

– And one with the world's highest suicide rate, Silverhair snarled.

And that was that.

Judy didn't feel too bad, then. She reflected on the nights out she had enjoyed with Karine Lie, how she had managed to enjoy herself without drinking. Hearing Karine talk was like hearing herself in an echo originating long ago.

She grabbed another glass from a tray and despised herself.

She had to stop. She had to. Because she destroyed herself, and everything around her, everything not already destroyed.

– May I?

Someone grabbed her arm and led her back out on the dance floor. It was Peder. Peder Brevik, her dear father in law.

Her self-contempt truly hit bottom when she found herself smiling to him, to anyone she might take advantage of. A smile could be such a good thing. Here it was fake - like everything else.

He was an impressive figure, by any criteria. Or perhaps fearsome was a better word. Authority burned in his eyes. It made her fearful and hateful. Both emotions scared her.

– You've made excellent progress lately. He praised her. – You've finally begun to see what your position in society means, the infinite possibilities inherent in it and in your own strength. I've witnessed for years how you've squandered your potential. No one is happier than I, when it now seems to be a thing of the past. I had my doubts whether or not you were the right one for Olav, but that doubt is increasingly dissolving. You put that idiot Kaspersen in his place in an excellent way. Excellent!

She curtseyed proudly, couldn't help herself.

– Why do you put up with him? She asked curiously.

– Quite simply because he's a useful idiot, and can be even more so in the future.

– The «nobility» in Germany thought that of Hitler, too, she commented sarcastically.

– You have truly a poisonous tongue, sweetie. He nodded thoughtful. – An… uncanny ability to expose the essence in something… or someone. What you must learn, the final part of your education - my gift to you - is to go for the jugular, and not hesitate, when you with great skill have uncovered it.

– What make you so sure about what I want? She asked it sourly, subdued. – Perhaps I have entirely different plans?

– Everybody goes through a period of rebellion in their youth. Peder Bergli smiled his slight smile. – It may go on for a shorter or longer period of time, but it's just a passing curiosity or fancy. The question isn't *if* one surrenders, but when. And the price one has to pay.

– As with everything else it is a matter of price. In my experience, dear Judy, it's the strongest radicals, like you that often become the strongest turncoat. You and Olav have seen both sides of the fence, something that is an unconditional advantage. You're both rare and highly valued assets.

His words seemed so sensible. She listened to them, to him. Fragments of recent thoughts and memory resurfaced.

– There *is* practically permanent martial law in this country, right, especially in the cities? Those making that seemingly absurd claim are absolutely correct, aren't they? The police can, at any time choose what is illegal, whatever it is, backed by the law? And people allow themselves to be fooled, be easily fooled.

Bitterness overwhelmed her, and she pulled close to him.

– Bright girl, he nodded, acknowledging her intellect. – As I've implied, you and Olav will go far together, in spite of the minor… friction. We both know that the boy has his… eccentricities, but we also know that so have you. You're made for each other.

She let herself be caught in the hypnotic stare, like never before, in the haze of everything he promised her, wealth, position and power without limit. Any alternative sounded so silly spoken out loud that it stuck in her throat. Lights danced in the haze drifting above the concrete reality submerging them, lights putting themselves out and on, time and time again, constantly brightening and darkening, fading to pale embers in the gray landscape. He showed such confidence, also when he confronted her.

He thinks he can become a father figure to me. How stupid does he think I am?

She had rolled her hands into fists. He didn't notice.

– I mean… I would rather not keep picking dresses for you in the future, even wider than now.

– You picked the dress? She subconsciously raised her voice, inevitably. – The shoes, too, then, I gather?

– I had the overall supervision, he said, his typical aloof self. – As you know we have underlings taking care of such things.

He frowned lightly. Something jarred when she spoke, something in her voice when she had mentioned the shoes.

She rubbed the space between her eyebrows with a finger. This was simply too much. For a brief moment she saw herself and the surroundings clearly. Action followed thought magnificently fast. She kicked off her shoes in two swift moves.

– What are you…

He stopped, startled. She pulled in the straps making the dress stay in place. With a final pull they loosened and the dress fell off her. She was totally nude beneath. The cloth remained by her feet. She stepped out of it filled with contempt and walked to the door. The photographers present awakened, and charged her. The bravest first in line, but shortly it blinked in dozens of flashes. She gave them the finger, them, the guests, everybody.

She closed the door behind her, slammed one of many doors with a loud crack. She was seething in rage and emotions. What most of all stunned her was the fact that she hadn't felt any sort of embarrassment, she, who had always been shy.

Exhaling, she allowed herself the pleasure of a moment's respite. The empty bedroom seemed like a major anticlimax. She sat down in the armchair, rocking it back and forth, while memories kept assaulting her. It was on the same spot, the spot by the bed where the two had put it, laughing strong and hard, sharing the moment like two young lovers. She had sat there in the morning the first night they had lived and slept here and looked fondly at Olav, until he woke up, and then they had done far more than look at each other. Every morning, the entire year they had seen fit to indulge themselves in such acts, so sweet-filled, so longing, so desperate. They had tied themselves voluntarily to each other, with a thousand non-existing threads.

The party's hum no longer resounded in her ears. She had reached that point. Her hearing was sharp, and she heard nothing. Why, then, did it keep humming in her head?

His steps.

She knew she would recognize them everywhere. The sound gave her no comfort, as they once would have done. Loneliness could be okay occasionally, when one sought it, but not being lonely. And she had never felt more alone.

Her husband entered the room, and closed the door behind him. He looked so calm, so controlled.

– May I ask what that little performance was good for, and why the hell you did it?

– There was a time when you wouldn't have needed to ask that question. You would have known why the very second it happened and even joined in.

She searched his eyes for that awareness, imploring him, but if there was anything there, it flickered briefly and died, like her hope.

– Then there is this small matter of the clothes you gave me…

– Vanity, I knew it, he snorted in contempt. The face was without a shadow of a smile and a shadow of a shadow. – You were always naïve.

– More importantly are the realities behind it, the reasons for it. She couldn't keep the catching from her voice. It rose hard and pronounced. – He's forming us, forming me… You're forming me. I've HAD IT!

She rose and stood straight, proud and defiant before him.

He slapped her. Not hard, but it burned her cheek. She returned the strike, exposing her fangs. He was hit hard on the nose. Blood flowed, and he backed two steps.

– Damn bitch, making fools of us in front of all those important people. You'll pay for that. And for this…

He dried his muzzle.

– And for every other reason I can name.

She managed to avoid his attack, while he avoided hers with ridiculous ease. He hit her with a blow to the head. Dizziness almost overwhelmed her. She kicked out in pure instinct and he flew through the air, hitting the wall. He closed in on her once more, more cautious now, but like an unstoppable machine. Anything other then she felt like. She felt slow and weak. Moves that once had been fast as lightning were now visible, very visible and predictable.

In one single drive he hit her many times and paralyzed her. He could easily have finished it then, but delayed it, spiced it. She hated him. Threw herself at him with a snarl, hit him repeatedly. Her elbow closed an eye, before he snarling threw her off. They circled each other, now, while baring teeth. This performance wouldn't have led to scorn among the exalted guests. The rage revealed by the female and male would have frozen them to stone. They couldn't deal with what was pure, uncontrollable savagery.

His foot hit her in the soft belly, the way too soft belly. *Thousand devils!* She struck out with a fist at his head. He caught it easily, with such contemptuous ease. A knee followed his foot into her potbelly. The short, unequal engagement was done. He kept going a bit longer, before throwing her on the bed. She fought to get up and attack again. He pacified her with simple, but brutal kicks. Kicked out of her the small bursts of air she had left. She gasped and gasped helplessly. She crouched on the bed, paralyzed and weak, so damn vulnerable.

He started beating her up, holding her hair, while *punishing* her in a thousand big and small ways. It went on and on, without passion, without the slightest revelation of emotion. He was careful not to injure her, and didn't leave many marks. He frowned. The hair had become a bit too easy to hold onto. It had grown too long. She screamed and moaned, begged him to stop, cursed him. Nothing helped. Only when she finally started begging him to stop, and stopped fighting back, in any way he let go of the hair, and rose. He pulled out his belt. She understood. Huge, swollen eyes turned wet and round.

– You're my wife, my woman, and I'm going to make sure you start behaving that way from now on. We're superior to other people, and we're going to use that, benefit from it, in all possible ways. From this moment on, you will support me in everything. You will no longer show doubt. There will no longer be any doubt in you. One day, soon, you will thank me.

The first strike hit the unprotected skin. She cried short and sharp, and tears flowed from wide-open eyes, eyes staring uncomprehending at the world. She made small, pathetic attempts at escaping the burning pain. He followed her with it, and she didn't even get out of bed before he had whipped her into immobility. She shook every time the leather hit the skin, that's all. He turned her around, placed her in the position he wanted her to be, until he had covered all sides of the sore body.

Silence.

She waited passive, beaten. He had to be done by now? She begged silently that it was over and done with, knew in the silence it would never be.

– *Look at me!*

By his command her head turned. He removed his clothes. *No!* He pulled down his pants so she could see his large limb. It wasn't stiff, hadn't risen. She had almost… preferred if it was. He had a self-control that frightened her, made her feel even more fearful. Then it grew, his manhood, before her eyes, to its full size. *No!* She moaned, in despair, in pain, unable to stop herself. She decided just to lay still, submissive, and allow him to do anything he wished with her. He could take her body. She sniffed in despair. But he would never come close to the soul.

He put hands on the breasts - and squeezed. She howled, cried her pain with a voice already sore and weak. He started touching the sensitive skin, diabolically patient. He held her in his grip, proving his power over her, proving it further when she sensed the first indications of heat and softness in her body. She whined and complained in her bottomless despair and shame. He kissed her. Tight lips opened to his will. Unable to resist him she cried out her suffering with a long wail making him laugh in cruel triumph. He rubbed her at the back of the thighs, over the round ass. She attempted to pull her thighs together. He split them with a simple move, a few touches of fingers. More wasn't needed. Heat spread from her groin and to the body. The longing gasps and moans turned more intense, and the resistance faded quickly.

– No, she protested weakly.

– Don't even think about going there, ice-princess. I know you, you know, know about the volcano inside you and that you can't resist me, that you never will.

He pushed a hand in her cleft. From one moment to the next the glow turned to *heat*. He let her go. She fell down on the bed, while the body turned rigid against the hand touching her, touching her innermost being. She writhed beneath him in an effort to come closer to him. Tears flowed, but the inviting smile broke through the weeping. She was his.

She attempted to beg. The thick lips moved, but there was nothing but tiny, unintelligible sounds.

– What if I don't like icicles? He removed his hand.

She writhed wildly and reached out with her hands. He slapped both her cheeks, and the arms fell back. She begged him with her eyes, with every piece of her body.

– You are tamed, now, he declared. – From now on everything will go easier.

She wanted to say something, anything, but couldn't even make the effort.

– YES! He spat in triumph. – You *agree!*

He crawled on top of her, took her as his. She clung to the large, hard man in blind, helpless hunger. He knew how the world worked and would protect her, teach her everything she would need to learn in a hard and ruthless existence. The breasts and the hard nipples pushed at the broad chest. He pushed and pulled, moved back and forth, held her on the tight leash, constantly embracing her in his iron grip, and she howled in happiness. He played her with total control and she came when he did, erupted in a mindless rapture.

A while passed, feeling virtually instantaneous for the female. He placed himself on his knees and turned her over on her belly. He pulled up her ass and fucked her again. Her face was pulled and pushed back and forth on the bed. This time he pumped into her, and pulled out before her hot water flowed. Disappointment rattled her, but when he slapped her ass, and bid her to look at him, the lazy, content bitchy look was in place. He had to be pleased with her. He had to. She pulled close to him and offered herself.

– You've become a fat slut, he said displeased. Her smile faltered. He pushed her away. Tears erupted once again. – If I had allowed it to continue you would have turned unappetizing fairly soon. Be pleased that I certainly won't. We'll get you back into shape. The only one pumping you up from now on will be me. From this moment on you won't eat a single birth control pill. Do you *understand?*

– Yes, Olav, she replied cowed.

– I've *mastered* you, he said imperiously. – You'll obey me in all things. From now on you'll do what I command, when I command.

– Yes, Olav, she repeated, lowering her eyes in submission.

– Go to the floor and entertain your Master.

She danced, attempting to lose herself in the dance, but it was no use. He was always there.

– My honored father has repeatedly told me about the usefulness of training and a firm hand, he drawled. – He was right, as usual. Know that the punishment you have received so far is just peanuts compared to what will happen if you keep failing to please me. It's bad enough that police officers find you pissed drunk among the homeless, but such things can be covered up. While that today, on the other hand…

The smile froze on her face. She desperately wanted to please him. How could she allow this, the horrible things he was doing to her? If she had heard about it, been told about it, that another person had submitted to such callous treatment it would have struck her as completely ridiculous, and she would have dismissed it as unlikely and exaggerated. But this had happened and was happening. She was like blown away by a great and powerful storm. The paralyzing fear descended on her like a blanket, and kept her from acting, from opposing him. He was that strong, that terrible. And she? She compared herself with a brittle little doll he could do with as he wished. He had conquered her so easily, so thoroughly. Olav had been… bad for a long time, but not this beyond sinister and *mighty* creature. He had become all-powerful.

– Kneel, he bade her harshly, fully aware of what she was thinking, what was grinding through her feeble mind.

She gasped in fearful paralysis, and obeyed instantly. He smiled in triumph.

– There are two kinds of people in this world, he said. – I realized this some time ago. You're either master or slave. If you aren't one, you're the other. You, pathetic creature are a slave from now on, and until I tell you differently. You should use the coming weeks and months well, take my lessons to heart, unless you wish to be a slave until you die.

He signed for her to come to him, and she did. She crawled to the bedside. He grabbed the silver hair and pulled her head to his groin. She started petting him, showing him what a quick learner she was. It didn't take long before he had once more grown to his full strength.

– You're good at this, he praised her. – Such a cute pet.

He turned her, and with a few touches he had once more primed the female's body and mind. She longed desperately for him, and shivered all over her body when he pushed her forward, down on all fours. He grabbed the silver hair again, pushing his shaft teasingly between the wet thighs, before pushing forward.

– You have… sworn to… honor and obey me all your days, he breathed, – and… you shall.

He stopped a bit, but gave her no pause. Head was pulled back, the body held close to his. Her all-powerful Master touched her in insensitive and shameful ways, as he kept whispering forceful words into her ear, possessing her in beyond brutal and harsh ways.

– You look ravaging, my little pet, and ravage you is precisely what I intend to do with you.

Room faded. It didn't exist to her. She herself didn't exist. Only he and what he did to her mattered. He totally defined her reality. Every touch, every painful caress was a light in the endless dark. She sobbed, moaned and cheered every time he moved.

Aside from that she

(certainly)

didn't exist.

Smell… was gone.

Taste, too.

Sight, lights, too blinked and faded. Sounds faded. The sensations on her skin, the only thing that *was,* grew somewhere inside her to something resembling a million volcanoes and EXPLODED.

And everything was gone. Nothing was, nothing before, nothing after.

Eyes slid open when the Sun warmed her face… the morning after. She crouched on the carpet, the spot where he had left her, discarded her like rotten fruit. The large window between the windows showed her full figure.

Shame burned in her. She wanted to moan, but couldn't even make a single sound.

She had a vague recollection (true or false) of her serving him breakfast in bed, docile, obedient and eager to please him, terrified that he would wish to… correct her again. Crushed like she was, into tiny pieces she didn't know if there was any more resistance left in her to crush. There had to be… or were these thoughts merely the final ripples before the surface in the small pond would calm completely, the final hurdle before she became his creature, fully and irrevocably?

The mirror image scorned her. She was fat. Perhaps not compared to most people (she hoped), but clearly compared to what she had been. The belly could easily be bitten. He had done so easily (scorning her). Every second she stared at her (fat) body nausea rose another level in her throat. Her limbs were decisively rounder and softer, the muscles softer. She had weakened herself. *Stupid cow!* She had allowed herself to ripen to a fruit easily plucked and peeled.

Her entire body started shaking. She sniffed and crawled to the bar (her own private bar), where the bottles and decanters waited. Shivering hands filled to the brim the first and best glass from the first and best container she could find. She swallowed three major gulps. The strong liquor made her cough hard. It burned inside her like the ashes it had always been.

Later she rested in bed. She remained there, with a newly opened bottle in her hand. The fog descended on her, and she welcomed it. She was alone in the room, but she sensed him everywhere. Time extended, thick and dogged like porridge, like quicksand. She sobbed, and the tears started flowing once again. It pleased her when the room faded around the bed. She took another gulp from the bottle, bathing herself in the now so familiar bottomless despair and self contempt. Could this be the only thing she was good for; sobbing and drinking? The hand holding the bottle shook hard, a shaking spreading throughout the body. Nausea hit her somewhere. She crouched and threw up on the bed and on herself, spoiling herself even more. Dry, her throat felt like desert sand. Thirst grabbed her violently. She didn't really know what she did, but she reached the shower and drank greedily of the water there. So greedy the human being was. She soaped herself in with two pieces of soap, scrubbing her skin hard and frantic. Afterwards she had to lean against the wall, breathless. She stumbled back into the bedroom, and fell down by the bed. Completely beside herself, she struck her fist at the floor, without truly being conscious of her actions. Carpet turned wet beneath her. Fuck, she cried all the time. It had to end. Had to. Had to. *Had to!*

Judy Brevik had given him such cute, tiny smiles, smiled invitingly to him, *crawled for him,* because she desperately desired the reward he was more than willing to give. She wanted attention, proof of her existence, and he obliged her, granted the wish of a whore, the codependent slave with fake smiles. Claw-like fingers dug into the carpet. He fucked you over, you stupid doll, doll, doll… with his sweet words and promises. She looked into the mirror and felt contempt for what she saw. She had discovered something shocking about herself. It was clear to her, now, that she had, at least in part, taken him for the money, the money his father owned. Now, she didn't feel anything for him anymore.

Judy Brevik climbed on her two feet again. She pulled on another of the tight dresses her father in law had procured for her, drying her face thoroughly, painted her face and fixed her hair. Judy wanted to give her husband everything, everything he asked for, and one day she would push her favors deep down his throat.

There was a draft. The door was open. Judy turned and saw her daughter stand there. Lene was eight, tall, skinny and robust, everything at once. Judy curled her lips in resentment, wondering how long the rascal had stood there.

– Did he hit you? The girl whined.

– Children shouldn't interfere in adults' business, Judy replied icily. – Go to your room this instant, young lady and remain there for the rest of the day. If I see you elsewhere, I'll beat you senseless.

Lene shrank visibly. Tears jumped from her eyes. Crushed and uncomprehending she turned and ran off.

Judy turned once more to the mirror, her mind working in a cold and calculating manner. His forming… it struck both ways. She started forming, too, feeling the sweet itch of power.

She kept to her room. It was large and served her well. The servants came and removed the vomit-stinking sheets and clothes. This was no unusual task for them, and didn't take long. Soon new, fresh sheets covered the bed. And then they left her alone. She walked restlessly back and forth while waiting for her husband to return. He should have been here by now. She imagined how she received him, the independent, but supporting wife, how she, the spider tied him to her with a thousand strands of her web, just like he wanted to do with her. She would make herself even more indispensable to him. He would never choose a cheap tramp sometime in the future. Together they would be unstoppable.

Impatiently she pushed the remote control, turning on the TV. There was nothing on it, except the public radio broadcasting. The news, followed by Here and Now (behind the news). She switched to Text-TV, but left the sound on. She didn't really listen. It just paid off to be *informed,* that's all.

Nothing was happening, just the usual shit. The world never changed.

And if it did, it was for the worse.

She found one of the big, heavy decanters and a glass. There was noise somewhere. She was about to fill it up when something, something irritating at the back of her head stopped her. There had been some more unrest in town. Streets were blocked. The access to the motorway from the central parts of the city had been restricted. The smaller access roads had quickly been filled up with cars.

Mrs. Brevik, Lady of the manor, filled the glass, in a distant manner. They had a debate in the studio. She suspected that it was about… that the subject was the «riots». The «expert panel» would have to have been gathered in record time. Or it had been ready even before the riots began, as a backup, so to speak, ready and able the day it was needed. It was a fairly established bunch of people, that's for sure, yet another handpicked panel.

The host asked his question with just the right touch of eagerness and concern in his voice.

– Dr. Kaspersen, what is wrong with youths today?

– The youths are given what is basically a free rein. She heard the nasal voice, listened to it, realized it spoke with the mind of everybody wanting safety before freedom, no matter the cost, and who were destined to get none of it. – We must start early, already at home, in the kindergarten, at school. Teach them our safe, healthy values, about our democratic system, so no one develops their undoubtedly… skewed view on it later on. We must knock it into their heads if needed. And believe me, it is necessary. Corporal punishment should be reintroduced in school. Law and Order must be strengthened dramatically, to not leave any doubt about our resolve to stand against chaos and anarchy…

She switched off the sound, but left the thing on. There wasn't sufficient strength left in her hand to turn it off completely. She looked at the glass. Her hand had tilted it so much that the content flowed out of it. She let it flow and stared amazed at the tiny, ongoing waterfall.

– «We'll get you back in shape», she said aloud.

The abrupt laughter sounded horrible in her ears.

He had said that, assured, comforted and calmed her, knowing it would be too late, too late for her by then.

Swollen eyes looked quietly, timidly at the decanter. She could do like many cowed people, drink herself to oblivion, or let herself be guided or pushed there in other ways. The difference didn't matter.

Or she could fight with every fiber of her being.

She threw the decanter through the screen. Fire rose there and in her eyes.

I must get away from here, now, this instant.

She repeated the words, chanting them, like she would a spell.

Now, with the decision made, everything happened with a strange ease.

She removed her dress, and found one of her old shirts, with straps. Then she picked a pair of black jeans. The clothes didn't fit, but they would. She had to make it on her own, in all ways, from now on.

The wet hand caught her attention. She licked the liquor off the skin. It felt so good. She had a long way too go.

She sat down on the bed and called a cab. The softness she felt once more threatened to cast a counter-spell on her. She pulled her way up by the hair. In the closet she found the black jacket and the black, flat-brimmed hat. She entered the bathroom. There she cut and shaved off every piece of her hair. The silver threads fell into the toilet. She flushed everything down.

The mirror showed her twin, the woman only a flash or a heartbeat away. Who could say who was real and who was the reflection?

The leather jacket fit her well, over the shoulders and elsewhere. The hat did, too. It was like she had always worn these clothes. The dress was only a bad memory.

She packed a few clothes and belongings in a sports bag. When she zipped it, it was only about half full. She considered writing a note to Olav, but quickly rejected the notion. The message he would receive would be clear enough. She looked at herself in the mirror a final time. There was something explosive in her eyes. She smiled pleased.

I'm still me, she thought, both ashamed and hopeful.

Before leaving she visited her daughter's room. Lene crouched on the bed when seeing her, afraid of being punished for some imagined slight. *I'm her mother*. The girl was slightly comforted by the warm smile, but remained skeptical.

– You've seen and heard? The adult woman asked rhetorically.

The child hesitated, before nodding resolutely. They shared a kind of understanding. Not much, but to Judith it was enough.

– I'll be back for you, she said quietly. – It might take a long time, *but I will be back.*

She touched the child, and bestowed a brief kiss on her forehead. Then she left.

Judith Breen walked through the house, out of the door. Nobody seemed to notice her, really. They were probably just relieved that the Lady didn't notice them. She breathed deeply while walking the long way to the gate, through the gate and out on the public road, the quiet street. The taxi appeared after she had been walking twenty steps or so on the sidewalk. She opened the door, very determined, and sat down. Judith Breen didn't look back, striving to focus her attention forward, unable to stop herself from feeling the sensation of the wicked eyes in her back. She felt both fear and expectation when looking at the dark clouds in the horizon, beyond the smog and concrete, the vast gray desert everywhere and nowhere.

She had always known the Storm waited out there. She should have known a long time ago how determined it waited for her. Nobody paying attention could avoid hearing the heartbeats of the gods.

TEN YEARS LATER - OSLO

CHAPTER TWENTY-ONE

She had left the city ten years earlier. Little or nothing had changed, and only for the worse.

Silverhair turned off from the eastern motorway. The big Mercedes cruised lazily the last stretch towards central Oslo. There was nothing else to do, really, but cruise. Traffic was slow, painstakingly slow, in spite of it being in the middle of the night. The endless line of cars drove into the smog, a seemingly impenetrable soup, thick like porridge, pushing from all sides. Even the high-efficiency air-circulatory system designed to keep the stinking air out of the car failed. Silverhair couldn't stop coughing.

The concealed control post revealed itself behind a towering building. Only a few cars were allowed to pass without being checked first. Not many guards were visible for the drivers, but Silverhair knew that many soldiers in hiding awaited the signal of attack. She pushed a button automatically opening the window on the driver's side, and scowled at the heavily armed people out there.

– Do I need to show my ID *again?* She snorted and handed it to the soldier. – I've lost count of how many times I've done so since leaving Germany this morning.

– I'm afraid absolutely all of it is quite necessary, the guard replied politely. – Important things are happening in town these days, and we can't take any chances.

– I realize that, the Lady said exasperated. – With all these weirdoes running around one can never be cautious enough, I suppose. I don't know… I guess it is all the new EU-regulations that are making me nuts.

She couldn't resist. They represented no serious threat, but did piss her off.

Classy bitch, the guard thought.

She reminded him of someone. Probably he had seen her at the front cover of some magazine or something. He let her pass.

She drove further into the dreary, ever more depressing landscape. Dante's seven versions of hell, they were all present here. Having seen this from a distance all the lights had seemingly reached up like flames into the sky and nourished it. Here, the illusion being revealed for what it was, it was clear that the Gray Fog devoured everything, everything alive.

Humans stumbled through this landscape, pale, broken figures, into the twilight.

After patient reconnaissance she found a temporarily abandoned construction site. Tomorrow it would crawl with eager ants here. This was one of many projects began because of an abundance of available private funding. Norway Incorporated was styling these days, and had room for yet another huge shopping mall, what the former leader of the Oslo Governing Council, Thatzner, had once called «contemporary buildings and locations». The stock market was on its way up, and everything was right with the world.

Smugness was everywhere these days, and those opposing the hegemony were effectively ignored or marginalized. Very few even considered that the current course of action was wrong.

Or at least that was how it had been, years ago. The brief, triumphant smile played on her lips and the hands tightened into fists.

Nobody intruded upon her. She dressed in a wide coat. Thin and light, but solid. The only thing she brought from the car was the big backpack, the type used by travelers. She had made holes, both in the coat and the pack. In swift, certain moves she started pulling wires through the holes. At the end of the wires there were sensitive electrodes. She attached them to her body, to her naked skin, with clips. It didn't hurt really, not that much. Before leaving the place she sat down to pee. Warm air caressed the naked butt, and there wasn't any discernible difference between exposed and covered skin. Perhaps her mind was elsewhere.

(Mommy, I gotta pee)

She smiled. She recalled the walk she had had with Lene through this area, while it was still lively here.

– *Be patient, honey. We're close to a public toilet. It won't be much longer now.*

– *Mommy, I gotta pee.*

Mommy had sighed. A momentary hesitation and she had pulled down her daughter's pants, and placed the tiny ass on a waste bin. There hadn't been many people around, and strangely enough, no one had made a fuss about it. Mother and daughter had smiled to each other, as if they shared a big secret.

The young and innocent face faded, changing into an older, one on the edge of maturity.

++++++++++++

A room, a totally average room in a private school in Switzerland faded into her memory. Lene stood on the balcony and looked outside. Judith thought she looked painfully close through the binoculars.

Lene held on to a newspaper, *The European,* with hands still shaking and curling. She returned to the room, sat down in a chair and started reading everything word by word. She had read it many times already, two articles, two different editions published a week apart. The headline on the first was almost like war-types:

GOTHENBURG DESTROYED

And with smaller types:

THE NIGHTRAVENS' LAST BATTLE

The paper had detailed descriptions and pictures from the central parts of the city, where about one third of the buildings had become ruins. And the various battles, the uneven struggle were thoroughly described. How twenty people had fought an entire army, what impressions it had made. The soldiers falling in droves, while the Nightravens died one by one, fighting to their final breath.

And they had printed a surprisingly accurate account of the final battle. Nobody had managed to cover up the fact that the authority's forces had blown up an entire block of flats full of obvious non-combatants. The names of the five nightravens who had been killed there were also printed. Lene crushed the paper in her hands and threw it away.

The other newspaper, yesterday's edition, had a smaller headline. The article was about the relatively new Sonnezee nuclear plant outside Munich, at the center of Europe. It had blown itself up, entirely on its own. It burned and boiled there, and radioactive material flooded the area in an even flow. Munich was evacuated, but people already dropped dead like flies.

Lene philosophized over the cause of the… accident. It could be that the entrepreneur had «saved» money on construction materials, or straight out a mistake in the scientific foundations for the construction. Both were clearly true. But the main reason was technology in itself, the technological society. Accidents happened in complicated, modern societies. And they grew potentially bigger and worse for each passing year. Lene doubted that the truth, traditionally speaking, would ever see the light of day. It would come as a splintering darkness, all encompassing, merciless, impossible to ignore.

She dropped the second newspaper, too and left the room, a room she had never looked at as hers, anyway. She walked down the stairs to the exit, and into the day, the sunlight. One could see the Geneva Lake from here. Thought reached out, at the close and familiar, and the magical and mysterious. The water was still fairly clean. She had been swimming in it and surfing on it. It was truly something magical by surfing out there, under the mighty mountains. Lene had felt as one with herself and the surroundings, something she rarely did otherwise.

– Hi, Silverhair, a boy called to her. – I heard your bitch of a mother got it where it hurts.

She ignored him, ignored them all. Sighed. This could be such a peaceful spot. Not much was happening, but she saw it as an okay place to wait.

The narrow alley of trees led her to her little observation post. Benches had been placed in a half moon circle. Sand hummed under her feet. She wasn't the only one there, but she was alone. It felt like her place. She went here when she needed it, needed clarity. Lately she had come here often.

It had given her ever less peace.

She turned abruptly, and headed back. She didn't get far before the boy who thought he had scorned her, and five other boys and girls cornered her. Most were known to her. They were all irritating nuisances. They honored her by acknowledging her presence. It was just right for her to return the favor.

– We've had enough of your high and mighty attitude, one of the girls snarled.

And they dared say that do her.

They harassed her at any opportunity, and then, when she avoided them, they had the audacity to claim she was arrogant.

– We'll teach you a lesson, another grinned in expectation.

Silverhair attacked them. The young face didn't change expression. No emotions reached the surface. She felled two with the first kick, whirled around, and sent an elbow deep into a belly. Only one was skilled enough to avoid her first, wild attack. He hit her with a paralyzing strike at the shoulder muscle. She ignored it. Her kick paralyzed his thigh, and he lost his footing. She hit him with an extra fist in the head as he dropped to the ground.

She towered above them, pacified them with a few brutal, rough kicks. They looked scared at the fury, a face without expression, an expression containing so much.

– Listen carefully, she commanded with the chill in her voice. – I have a message for you, and I want you to listen. Never come near me or speak to me again.

– Hey, we didn't mean anything. One of the boys shook, his forehead wet, sickly shining in sweat.

She knelt by him.

– *You don't LISTEN*, she said kindly, holding a hand under his jaw, patting his hair. – *NEVER speak to me again.*

He and his compatriots shrank like a mouse before a cat. They hardly even dared nod in their desperation, in their sickening fear. The black eyes were like wells one might drown in, and never ever be found.

Lene walked away, light on her feet, the event already behind her.

She instantly noticed the man and the woman by the gate, the shadows mostly hidden by bushes. The rays of the Sun didn't reach them. They stood in twilight. She looked around to be certain nobody saw her. Then she sneaked outside the gate, outside the school's premises.

– Who are you? She frowned, clearly apprehensive.

– We participated joyfully when you crawled from your mother's belly, the man said. – We knew you before you knew yourself.

Hope confirmed coursed through her, sudden and glorious.

– Nelson? Tanya? They nodded. – Mummy showed me pictures of you all.

– Pictures taken so long ago, Tanya said softly. – We've all changed since then. Come with us, young Silverhair.

– Olav and Peder will look for me.

– The Journey is only a short one this time. And you don't need to worry about either Olav or Peder for much longer.

– I'm not, she said, sniffing in frustration. – But they don't stop worrying about me.

She joined them. A brief hesitation, and it was done.

They walked a short stretch, just down the slope from the school, and a little bit up again, and she was there… face to face with herself. An older Self, worn, and with black hair. Aside from that there were more similarities than differences.

– I knew you would come, you *promised.*

The embrace was brief and desperate.

– You've seen and heard? The teenager nodded eagerly. – Good, we don't have much time.

The words cut deep into the girl, and made her cold. She looked in pain at the woman who was her mother. But in the eyes, the black eyes, Judith read understanding.

– We will part soon, Judith said, – and never meet again. Soon you will be Silverhair, and you must be ready.

The girl's lips shivered. She shook her head back and forth several times, before she stopped.

– I will be. She swallowed hard.

Judith noted with satisfaction that the girl cast prolonged looks at the oblong linen package by the wall. Many had already lost their curiosity when they reached Lene's age. School and society did it to them, removed all wonder and supplanted it with cold cynicism and fear of «failure».

She studied and assessed her daughter, and was pleased with what she saw. It was amazing how much she resembled her father, how much she resembled them both, and yet didn't. She was a union of both parents and had many of their traits, but she was none of them. She would follow her own path.

– Warriors will gather around you, as they did me. Judith wanted to put a hand on her shoulder, but didn't. – Within us all is the key to victory. We couldn't find it, but you must. Don't use my method. Don't use any method but your own. There are those you can seek guidance from. They've all found their own way of fighting, but they're all doing it.

– How was it with you? Lene wondered. – How is it? Do you regret anything?

Judith realized that this was something the child wanted, needed to hear. Something Judith couldn't avoid replying to.

– It's both horrible and wonderful out there in the whirlwind, she replied with a remote look in the green eyes. – There's no way out. When you've taken that one, final step into the Storm, you can never leave it. But that's okay. It's out there you feel you're truly alive, that you're *human.* And you don't want to leave the path of the Green Rose, not deep inside, where it counts. The Green Rose is the entire scale of existence, everything that is. Roses and thorns, blood and clot, it is life and death. Not limited to the present's dual, limited view on existence. You can't pick and choose from it, without… loosing something. It's where you wander, dream and live. I've done and experienced things I've wanted to go back in time and change… But regrets… *Never!*

– You're so calm, Lene wondered. – So… relaxed.

I know I'm just me, Judith said. I know I can't expect aid from heavenly forces. There are none, no external powers, no almighty being. As soon as you realize this, you'll find your own peace, your own center. The answer, if it there is one, is found in ourselves. Remember that.

– I will, the younger Silverhair said eagerly. – I will!

– That's a good girl. Judith smiled to her, then, allowed herself that luxury. – It's time for me to go, but I have something for you first.

Lene accepted the oblong package. It was heavy, and she unwrapped it on the ground. Heart hammered in her chest. She couldn't help it. She pulled away the last few pieces of cloth in one move, and she saw what had been hidden. It made her gasp in wonder. The sword hilt glimmered in the Sun, but when she pulled the blade out the smooth, bright surface blinded her. The entire sword was brushed and oiled, and she could see her reflection in the blade.

– It has drawn blood from us all, daughter. We will be with you and yours, through wandering and dreams, until the end of time.

She said no more, just turned and left.

– Wait, what will you do? Lene cried after her.

– Something no one can ignore, Judith Breen said preoccupied, keeping her back to them as she kept walking. – Not even when it has all become history… A fire in nature clears the way for new growth, new life. That's the way it is. That's the way it must be. Fire is nature's way of cleansing itself. After it has burned itself out, everything sprouts anew.

They saw her just a few more meters. She vanished around a corner, and they saw her no more. They weren't sure they would have seen her even if they had run to the corner and looked beyond it. It almost felt like they had spoken to a spirit - or a ghost.

– Why does she leave us? Lene wondered in pain. – How can we make it without her?

– That we must, child, Tanya replied sadly. – We must all continue the life we're so badly suited to live.

– You have an interesting time ahead of you, Silverhair, Nelson said cheerfully, infectious. – We will be proud to be counted as your teachers.

– I will be proud to have you. Silverhair smiled and smiled brightly.

Nelson had studied Lene Brevik for a while, now, with both worry and excitement, but now, when he saw her sit on her heels, saw her eyes linger on the sword, he sensed the familiar calm descend on him. He didn't believe in fate, other than chains of coincidences, but now he felt it turn, the wheel of fortune. Life went on. That was both a cruel and wonderful truth.

Lene of the Green Rose grabbed the hilt with both hands and drew the sword. She strived a bit, inexperienced as she was… but lifted it high above her head. Nelson and Tanya felt how she there and then grew tall and proud. There was no melancholy, only a calm certainty of what was coming.

Lene Silverhair was eighteen, and her time had come.

++

Judith changed her mind a bit. She removed the coat and wore the black leatherjacket instead. When she left the «construction» site at dawn, she was dressed exactly as she had been ten years ago. Only the rucksack was new. She liked the black jacket. Hair reached far down on her back. She hadn't cut it much, since that day ten years ago.

Oslo Central Station remained true to its purpose, a cold, hostile and strictly efficient place. Silverhair looked through the huge windows at the sunrise outside. It had colors like rust and blood. Too much rust, too little blood. People filled the place, workers and clerks rushing off to work, people on vacation, also rushing somewhere. Just a very few showed anything even resembling calm and harmony.

She had a bit of trouble locating the toilets. Perhaps that was to her advantage, since others would have the same problem. They were empty right now, and served as a peaceful spot compared to the maelstrom outside. She washed the black color off her hair, without being interrupted. It was an easy and effortless process. She had always used color easy to wash off. Beneath, the Silverhair was exactly as she remembered it. She frowned, attempting to recall the last time it hadn't been dyed. It was like reaching far back, into the mists of time and existence. The familiar stranger shrugged in the mirror. She had forgotten so much that wasn't necessarily needed for the preservation of life, for survival.

I'm still young.

The equipment, its last bits and pieces, was easily assembled. She had assembled it with great skill. Gio, Karel, Willy and Sivert would have had reason to be proud or her.

She opened and closed her eyes, closed them hard… to open them slowly. She put the hat back on her head, and shook the long, fluffy hair.

Judith had been tired for so very long, but now it was as if she was filled with and glowed with (new) life.

The woman walking past the Narvesen kiosk displayed roguish eyes below the brim. She laughed at the world, and it felt good. Her eyes burned in defiance and rebellion and would keep doing so, to the end. The fire burned inside her and would keep doing so, until beyond the end of time.

She looked very young and stood out from everybody in the crowd, projecting something no one present possessed.

There were people around her, though, of both sexes that had colored their hair silver. People had started doing that in higher numbers recently, and that fact… pleased her. She couldn't say it didn't.

The newspapers' main stories, both domestic and international were about the major, crucial economic and political conference held in town. Everybody was here. Leonard Kaspersen, the leaders of the G7 group, the top brass of the ESF, prominent politicians from all over the world, Freuer - the head of the new, powerful European central bank, executives from far and close, handpicked scientists, who had in common that they received money and compensation to deny the facts about the environmental and sociological breakdown.

As if it was fated. Silverhair smiled cheerfully, ironically. Virtually every truly powerful clan on modern Earth had come here with a heavy representation to assure themselves and faithful slaves that there was nothing to fear. And to put a stop to anything that might threaten them. Extensive legislation would be prepared and passed during the coming week… «to better handle terrorism and the social disorder among misfits and unwilling workers». In corridors and dark hallways one whispered loud about extended use of general surveillance, video cameras on street level, computer registration and major increase in «pretrial confinement». The police cooperation within the Schengen Group was hailed as an example for everybody to follow. All polls showed that the general population would support any decision made by the delegates.

She felt the electronic eyes on her and the self-congratulating minds behind them, which eyes were certainly not much more human than their artificial helpers. Those people were hardly more than humanoids, people that had thrown their humanity away long ago.

They think they have all the bases covered. They don't know or realize, or won't realize…

… how far the rebellion had come, how far they had pushed it. They thought they were infallible in their management of the one-track-minded puppet theater.

And they believed they were invulnerable…

In spite of Gothenburg, in spite of the local feuds turning global.

Silverhair studied the civilian dressed guards. She almost laughed out aloud. The publication of her name in the news, on the list of fallen, was evidently not a trick. They had to be convinced she was dead. The old expression «out of sight, out of mind» was evidently still valid. The only way to be removed from clandestine archives was to die. She kept her body and mind on full alert, ready to act on a moment's warning, but nothing happened.

One second she was once more tempted. She could still take the train away from here, and disappear for good. It would work, too - now. But she had had that argument with herself long ago.

Two young women, two travelers stopped a few steps away from her. One had long, light and blond hair, and the other dark and short, with a cap on her head. The dark sat on a trolley, and the blonde pulled it. They had traveled far, and were clearly tired, though happy.

– Hey, you, do you have the right time? The blonde asked her.

Judith told them, with a happy grin, what the time was. She impulsively sought their company. She had a bit of time to kill, anyway.

– We thought we should see the world a few months… or years, the blonde said. – What about you? No offense, but you look like you've been around a few years.

– Yes, I have, Judith replied.

– It isn't anything in your face, the dark said quickly. – But something imperceptible… and the sense of having seen you… Will you be moving on today?

Moving on, Judith thought.

– Probably, but not yet… I've just arrived.

– There is something fam… Both pair of eyes opened wide.

– *Your train will leave soon?*

– Yes, jeez, in five minutes, the two choired.

– Good, Silverhair nodded. – Be on it.

She sent them a quick smile, before turning and leaving them.

– Do you know WHAT? One of them whispered aloud to the other. – We've just had a beyond interesting conversation with a ghost.

Silverhair's smile widened.

She sat down by the window, with a view to the hall, in the café on the upper floor. From there she could see the two, but they couldn't see her. Their departure had been delayed. She looked at her watch. She wasn't in a hurry.

A man approached her, openly, cautiously, as if he would make sure he wouldn't cause any… drastic reaction.

Light and shadow seemed to flicker around him, occasionally fading a bit, and then flare again, stronger than before. Judith recognized him, recognized Roland Vallens. He was in disguise, but the way he walked gave him away to her. When he started talking the remaining doubt dissolved. But it had, in truth done that the moment she spotted him.

– Don't fear for my health, he said with a crooked smile and a quick finger to his lips. – I'm on my way out of town.

– That's a relief, she admitted, after a brief hesitation. Or I would have needed to waste time in order to make you leave.

– I thought about taking the first train to Gothenburg, he said relaxed, leaning back in his chair. – The railroad is still working there. Aside from that I've heard that not much is working there these days.

He grinned the devil-may-care and sensual smile the entire world knew so well. No disguise could hide that. He seemed just as boyish as ever. Well, he wasn't more than twenty-seven. But he had started early, very early. Rumors claimed he had started small as early as at the age of ten, in Belgium and the Netherlands.

He leaned forward across the table, and grabbed her hands, totally unexpected, and held them tight. He had never acted «intimately» in her company before.

– If you don't want me to stay. I'm willing to do that.

What was it with him that made her feel this way, made her feel… feel that she *knew* him?

– I can't ask you to do that. She shook her head. – That would be unfair. You may claim I need moral support and such, and it would be true, but not that much. It would have been… wasteful. It's fantastic that you even risk coming here… How did you know I would by the way?

She fired it at him, to unbalance him. As expected, it didn't work. So many rumors circulated about him and so much would remain unsaid between them. He joked about it, like she had done. Just a tiny flare… of something lit his eyes.

– Call it an excellent educated guess, he said carefully. – I put myself in your position. It wasn't hard… for me.

It was in the eyes. What she saw there, she had seen before.

Dance the dance of Life, inside the circle of fire hot.

Confused imagery and impressions flowed through her mind. His eyes behind the eyes, they didn't just look alike, but exactly the same. She saw before her Anya each time they held an initiation. Saw the Ankh. Small threads of conversations she had had with Roland earlier, small hints, when he had slipped up. Perhaps neither slips ups nor hints, only thin strands, but long and endurable. They reached far and wide.

She knew. Knew with unwavering certainty where she had seen and met him before, from where she remembered him. Why she knew him the first time they met. He had looked completely different, then, but it was him. She had to pull herself together to sit still. It was something she had always known this, within, beyond the illusion, beyond the wretched and unnatural Gray Fog. Then as now, the *feeling* was the same.

– Have you seen the latest photographs of Earth from NASA? She asked.

– Yes, he replied quietly. – The fog is even thicker. The pollution is clearly visible.

– The revelation doesn't really help much, she said enraged. – Most people are so scared of being condemned by the majority, by their peers, both physically and mentally that they don't dare lift a finger to do anything worthwhile.

– Most people attempt to remove from themselves what they, what society see as unsavory aspects, what makes them unique, he stressed. – Even in death. But you're like me. You carry with you everything, without the artificial line between good and evil. We know well that nothing is truly right or wrong, true or false, in the Universe. Everything is merely a matter of perspective.

So much remained unsaid between them. Even though they seemingly spoke about different things… they really didn't, and it felt wonderful.

– I know about that, she nodded. – I was about to tell my daughter that she shouldn't care about what others might think of her and say about her, but she knew that already.

They enjoyed each other's company. That didn't feel weird. They had so much to talk about, to share.

– I find ever more similarities between the present and the Roman Empire, and its end, she said thoughtfully. – No outer enemies, but everything is just falling apart, a progressive inner rot, unable to carry anything. Except the way it looks the collapse then will look like a firecracker compared to the thunder that's coming.

They walked with each other for a while. They passed an assembly of white booths. She felt the heat of the many-colored lights in the face.

– Kurt and Susan escaped, he said.

– I know that. I haven't lived totally isolated lately.

– Janni, too, he told her. – And Jan.

– That I didn't know, she admitted. – It pleases me. Nothing is changed, but it pleases me.

A nod, a sore look she didn't see.

He walked into the ticket office and bought a one-way ticket. Finally, at this late hour he bought one. She felt a flare of anger, soon to fade into sadness. They parted shortly after that. He headed for the trains, she for the decaying heart of the Stone City, right at its jugular.

– Dreams belong to the night, he said, as solemn as one who didn't really take himself that seriously could be. – The moon burns and shines on us.

– Until dreams grow in daylight, she said lightly, in the same tone, – until the true dawn.

She followed him with sore eyes while he approached the two girls, the two young wanderers. It almost irritated her how easily he struck up a conversation with them. He turned and waved. She waved back.

They embraced once again, as they had done when standing close together. Distance meant little, time even less. It felt so good to live.

She chased after them, laughing softly. She easily caught up with them. It was something she had forgotten, something she couldn't resist doing. She kissed him on the cheek, and then she handed him her hat. And it was then the two young wanderers heard her say somber and in jest:

– *This is yours.*

++++++++++++

The forests and the fields were unchanged. The old cabin was no longer well held.

She walked determined on the now almost invisible trail. Almost twenty years had passed in silence and thunder since she had last walked here. The cabin's outer walls had large holes and had partly collapsed. Inside most of the furniture and stuff was gone. She shone a flashlight down the stairs to what had been the wine cellar. There were no doors anymore. The staircase was amazingly enough still standing and fairly well preserved. All the wine was gone, all the tasty wine. A few drops decorated the walls. The stench was quite tangible in her perception. The bolted door no one had managed to open or break appeared to her. There was hardly a mark on it. There, in the dark, beyond the destroyed wine cellar rested the secret, the weapon Jonas Bergli hadn't had the strength - or weakness - to use himself. He had left it to her, in her capable hands. She stopped before the door. It looked solid and the lock complicated, a long walk, with many twists and turns. Nobody had been able to get inside. But she would. To her there was no challenge… She had been shown how.

++

The small, cozy tavern was open twenty-four hours a day. Most of its clientele illustrated that in an excellent manner, as well, as they looked like they had indeed spent days and days there. Judith Breen - Silverhair - sipped the strong liquor. And waited… There was nothing. No unpleasantness, no craving for more. The smile spread on her lips, to her entire face, and to the eyes. She emptied the glass, rose, and left the place in a relaxed, steady walk. She noticed nothing of the poisonous liquid she had ingested. It had been her first drink in ten years - and the last. The alcohol quite simply dissolved inside her. There was no aftertaste, no smell. Nothing! Well, what was there to expect - from an active volcano?

She circled in on Stortinget, the national assembly, parliament slowly, but surely. This, of all places was where today's meeting of the economical/political conference was held. All the representatives, all the honored guests were present. How fitting, how very fitting that was. She moved as far away as to the SAS Scandinavian Hotel, before circling back.

He stood between the stone lions. The wind rocked and tore him. He spotted the long hair, shining in the Sun, flickering in the wind, saw her approach from the Castle Park, and followed her walk on Karl Johan's Street. She had almost reached the barriers. He started running.

She saw the antennas. She saw the snipers. Uniforms filled her vision no matter where she turned her head and directed her eyes. She walked casually, but had a goal. In a display window all the TV's showed footage from the Spanish/French border. Desperate people from the dry as a desert

Spain charged France's borders. Soldiers opened fire, cut them down. Finally it seemed to dawn on the starving people that they were shot at. Those who were able turned and ran the even tougher path back. Many remained on the ground dead or dying.

Judith Silverhair Breen stopped five meters before the line of security forces. She held her hands out from her body and smiled to them. They returned the smile. Her smile hardened.

– I carry a bomb, she enlightened them, – one with a Dead Man's switch. I'm sure you've heard the expression. If you come close to me it blows. If you shoot me or harm me in any way it's triggered. If you move significantly without my explicit permission, I will detonate it.

They froze in their tracks. Perhaps it was the quiet, impassionate speech that convinced them. And they recognized her. She saw it in their eyes.

She saw a bunch of VIP's arrive, saw them freeze in fear and indecision.

– Do as she says. The voice cut in after the soldiers had relented.

The man, Olav Brevik looked cheerfully at his wife.

– You're looking good… for a corpse.

– I don't need to quote Mark Twain, do I? She said joyfully.

– What do you want us to do for you, Princess? He asked ironically. – Tell us, and we will humbly obey your command.

– Not much, just let me in there. She nodded at the yellow building ahead. – I don't demand much, in my opinion.

– Why not? He grinned without warmth. – It might be fun.

– Sir, one of the guards protested nervously. – We can't… We need orders.

He finished lamely.

– So you aren't exactly the top dog here, huh? She grinned. He scowled. She turned to the guards again. – By all means, call your masters. Make it clear to them that this device is more than capable of disintegrating both the building over there, and all buildings in the immediate area… from *here*. And if you attempt to fuck with me my eyes and ears will tell me, and I will detonate the bomb.

– You're bluffing, Olav hissed.

– Try me, she hissed back. Once in the past his expression would certainly have scared her, but not anymore. – You're a *fool!* Do you truly believe that I, after what I've experienced, what I've done, fear death? That's the biggest flaw in you manipulators; you have no idea what desperation is.

The sergeant spoke in the phone. Judith waited, while her fate was decided. There was buzzing everywhere, while the situation was assessed and a decision was made. He nodded. The soldiers started moving aside.

The Red Sea divided in front of Silverhair, as it allegedly had done for Moses. The guards virtually formed an honor guard for Judith and Olav while the two of them walked the final stretch to what these days was the center of the Universe. The eyes of the world looked this way. For once Norway was what Norwegians faithfully believed it was; the navel of the world.

They stepped into the lion's den. Judith felt it. Something closed in on them, cutting off what she saw as important in life. The cold darkness surrounded her. Why her and not him? Was it because he held it back by allying himself with it?

– Never so bad that it isn't good for something. He brightened visibly. – Certain parties may take advantage of your presence here.

– You guys can just keep cutting each other's throats, she said indifferently, and to him irritatingly. – I don't care.

The dizziness almost overwhelmed her. She looked relaxed and almost felt that way, too, but she had moved on adrenaline since the start of her walk down Karl Johan. Skin tickled everywhere, a tickle growing more dangerous by the second. She meditated, repeated her secret sound, until she had reached a kind of stability in her glowing inside cauldron.

– After you, Princess, Olav said ironically, keeping his distance.

It won't last much longer, now, one way or the other.

She had known that for a long time, but the stubbornness kept hope burning.

The buzz grew louder, angry, frightened, the entire spectrum. The sea of eternity flooded Silverhair's vision. Green fire rose from the deep of her eyes. All chairs in the main hall, with only a few exceptions were taken. She knew who they were. The gathering was a Who's Who of the most prominent power hungry people in the world, a gallery of insanity. But best of all; even those who didn't usually stick their head out, pulling the strings behind the strings were present. What was happening here today was evidently too important to leave to underlings.

She had been headed towards the Citadel of Power for so long, and now she was finally here.

– Get her out of here, a woman howled hysterically. – She's a disgrace.

Judith knew of her. She had been a feminist. She was, depending on viewpoint.

Silverhair stopped behind the pulpit. She ordered three phones connected to separate lines put before her. Cameras whizzed, but she had to be certain it reached people.

The phones rang. She picked them up, pushed them at her ear briefly, got the necessary confirmation and hung up.

– *Can we trace them?* A hysterical chief of security asked.
– *Not a chance.*
– Dishonored gathering, she said scornfully.
– I just want to talk, to speak uninterrupted to you all. She looked at the camera where the red lamp was glowing. – I have come here to give a message, and that will be done.
The room, the hall did its best to act imposing and impressive. It didn't work. She felt like a giant.
– Some people claim it is sufficient to clean up a little, she began. The Fury stared at them and stared at them through the television screen, in Oslo, Norway, Europe, the world. Lene sat with Nelson and Tanya in a nondescript apartment. She was freezing. Anya sat on a naked hill, in unmovable meditation. Kurt sat with Sue and many others, in a dark room, where no one raised their voice. They all looked at something very far away and very close, in their hearts. They listened, both paralyzed and energized. – They betray, cheat and dominate. They keep denying the truth we all know. The pollution is only one of countless symptoms of a society sick and rotten to the core. We humans no longer live close to nature, but in poisonous and hostile surroundings, poisonous and hostile, not only to the body, but to the mind and soul as well. Society doesn't do anything to change it. Neither do the humans surrendering, submitting to it. They haven't even started peeling the apple, not a single bit, and far less reached the core. Everything mustn't merely be changed, but transformed. Or rather go, disappear. It isn't possible to build on a rotten foundation. This is something we all know, not just the architects. You can make the house stand a bit longer, perhaps, but when it goes, it goes that much faster, falling apart almost by itself. It's exposed like the house of cards it *is*.
Roland sat in the train compartment with the two girls. They looked at all of it on his watch-TV. He stared into the eyes. He so wanted to look into her eyes.
– We're nomads, seekers, wanderers in nature's twilight. To live in tune with nature is our only possible option if we want to stay human. It is, quite simply, our natural state. Nothing is static and there is *true* growth. Everything else is an illusion, a nightmare we can awake from at any time. We're all almighty beings playing out our drama of rot and decay. There are those who, at any cost desire to decide the rules of the game. Many «innocents» have been sacrificed already, but that's just peanuts compared to all the people who will croak, the millions, the *billions,* if we don't leave the insanity behind and return to sanity. There's only so much one person can do, even though we should always keep in mind that «a person can change the world with a bullet in the right place».

(Here she smiled her huge and broad smile).

– Fight for an end to the oppression, the injustice, the horror present everywhere, wherever you turn, if you just dare to look. Stop turning away. Too many do. They're just as guilty, just as much an integral part of the power structure as those sitting at the top of the Pyramid. Find your own value. Attack the power mad and their sheep, in all ways possible. Do it your way. No contribution is in vain, no matter how insignificant it seems at the time. But do keep in mind that words and thoughts about freedom become meaningless, if they aren't transformed into *action*. Don't learn to forget. Learn to remember. Throw away your existence in chains. It has no true value, and you know that, within, where it counts. All acts of conformity, however minor, are damnable. All acts of rebellion, however futile, are glorious. Remember… a prime mini$ter, queen, king, pre$ident, executive, $ergeant… huge buildings like this one are also merely dust in eternity, in the eternity of the Universe. Look through the lies, through the Lie of the shitty society, this inch deep «culture» they kill and destroy to keep going. It is *their* society, a lie, a world that must be torn apart brick by brick, wall by wall. You may tear down many bricks, many walls simultaneously, if you desire, the more the merrier.

– What is she *saying?* One whispered to another, understanding shit.

Olav couldn't put his finger at anything either, but he, too felt a sting of worry, of expectation. It was completely… wrong that Silverhair was here at all… But there was more…

– You're no god, he spat enraged at her. – When… if it goes bang, you'll die, just like the rest of us.

– Are you absolutely certain? She replied in her devil-may-care way.

She heard them, now, the Heartbeats of the Gods. She wasn't afraid anymore.

All this and what followed, was broadcasted on the world's networks this fateful day. Even a lot of what happened in the wings was.

– You listening out there may not know more about the Green Rose and the Nightravens than what you've «learned» through official channels. Or perhaps you've seen through public deceit and fraud, or you've heard something a lot closer to the truth, from friends, various associates or unofficial sources. I don't quite know what to tell you about us, there's so much I can say, that can be said. What I will state categorically is that this society, this world is a pyramid with the few at the top and the many at the bottom. We've been hounded and hunted… killed, both physically and mentally our entire life. They pushed us and pushed us, and kept pushing us, and finally they pushed us too far. We decided to strike back. It has been rough. Life is hard. But there have been good times, too. Those who live their lives at risk, live a richer life. We're true siblings. Not because we have the same parents, but by an inner unity transcending blood. The more the establishment hounded us, the more it strengthened us and they pushed us ever further, and we are so grateful. This is the end of the game, end of playing games. Too much is at stake. All oppression, all absence of life will cease. I won't set any time limit, though. I leave that in other capable hands…

The skewed smile was there all the time, side by side with the integral joy her presence revealed.

– A cornered animal gets desperate, turns savage. That's the message I'll send to those in charge. Give up the power voluntarily or be destroyed.

Fog floated into the room and created an unreal mood cutting and tearing in its reality. Blood boiled in the searing heat. Judith completed her task.

– … *I'm alive*, contrary to you cowardly assholes, long dead watching this, you dead people, even if you happen to walk and breathe. Well, perhaps there is hope for some of you, all you zombies, if you start using your ears to listen, your eyes to see. Blind faith in leaders will get you killed. Faith in leaders at all will get you killed. How long will you let yourself be fooled? Are you human beings or are you sheep? Tear down the pyramids and you will see. Build on yourself. It is correct that it is better to light a candle than to curse the darkness, but way too often this is used as a pretext, an excuse to not do anything. They don't want you to think for yourself, don't want you to realize that the best proof of independent thought is that you think *differently*. Many groups claiming to offer alternatives aren't more alternative than Rupert Murdoch. Like the majority of people calling themselves Green, and the many obscure remaining socialist clubs, tea drinkers with nothing more on their plate. They act as alibis to those in charge, like a kind of buffer between them and those fighting them, and don't do anything but pacifying true resistance. These charlatans are just as unwilling to give up their «safe» existence as you other cowards. Well, from now on you can forget safety. The time has come to choose sides. And as Freire said: « To wash one's hands of the conflict between the powerful and the powerless is not to be neutral, but to side with the powerful».

– We should light a candle *and* curse the darkness.

Half of the twenty cameras the producer had at his disposal were fixed at Silverhair, but the remaining ten spread his attention around. Five worked as surveillance cameras outside. He was sweating hard and let the image of Olav Brevik be broadcast. Brevik spoke with Erland Jostedt, quite… excitedly. Damn. It was impossible to catch what they were saying.

– She must die, Olav hissed. – Now! Shoot her to pieces.

– My dear Olav, you've always let yourself be governed by your emotions, Jostedt said calmly. – The last thing we need on our hands, right now, is a martyr. You don't seem to realize how Silverhair's reputation has grown to… mythical proportions after her «death» in Gothenburg. She's supposed to have been seen at a dozen places *simultaneously* around Europe. And after this disaster it won't be any better. She fucked us. We have to realize this, and cut our losses. By keeping our cool, we can yet triumph. We show our generosity. We let her walk out of here. She's dead. It's merely a matter of time, even if she, by a miracle, should get away this time. She's through, and she knows it. We can fix her death exactly as we desire, a method benefiting us, not her and her «cause».

Icy eyes stared Olav down. He hesitated briefly, before nodding in confirmation. Jostedt smiled and patted his back.

– I'm pleased this is reaching you, my boy. The alternative would have proven unpleasant to us both.

Olav remained, seemingly relaxed, but with his eyes fixed on Judith. She was so beautiful up there, so powerful. He wondered if the reason they had accomplished so much was that they were alone, with no ties, no obligations. Or would even more of their potential have been actualized if they had been together? He listened to what she was saying (what *was* she saying?), while he also listened with half of the other ear to what Jostedt and a subordinate talked about.

– We've succeeded in evacuating those in the restaurant. They should be far enough off by now, if she should… do the worst.

Olav stood there, unmoving. Suddenly the final piece fell in place. Suddenly he had it all figured out. Olav started laughing. He had to crouch and clutch his belly. He laughed that hard.

– I'm leaving you now. Judith stepped down from the dais.

She walked down the carpet-covered steps. The people in the hall stared at her as if she was a leper. To them she was. Except she was far more dangerous than any leper.

Olav grabbed a machinegun from a guard and charged her. He fired while running. Judith was hit many times, and fell on her back on the stairs, leaking everywhere. She lay on the rucksack and bled to death.

The powerful, all of them simultaneously was either frozen or ran in wild panic towards the exits. The cameras kept humming. No one operated them anymore. The producer attempted to look away from the screen. He couldn't.

Olav threw himself down by Judith's side. Both pair of eyes turned misty.

– It pleases me you're the same old Olav, she gasped, as she breathed for the last time. A single tear ran down her cheek

In a completely uncontrolled savagery he started tearing and pulling in the wires attached to her body, grabbing the entire her. Later all who had watched this in millions of homes could never agree if he tried to embrace her or tear her apart.

The screen turned black.

Color and lights, lights in spots and all colors. *Fog*. A mist in the surroundings and the soul, in all nuances of gray. The surroundings turned indistinct in the fog.

Smoke, lights in the air. It's easy to lose oneself in the fog and its flashes. You can look at the patterns forever. You may learn much, but you may also disappear in the infinite and eternal. Lights blink, and from the ashes smoke is rising anew. Lights blink anew. No beginning, no end. One beginning in a number of beginnings.

All the small lights turned into one.

The distorted mushroom cloud rose from the Stone City and reduced it to glass. The fire devoured everything and everyone, and spread like rings in the water to the entire world.

Amos Keppler
March 1st 1989 - August 15th 1991
237th Night 12046
In the first year in the time of Witchnight

July 27th 1995 - August 21st 1997
243rd day 12052
In the second year in the time of the Crimson Tide

Norwegian printed version ready 2002-03-17
86th Night 12057
In the second year in the time of the Twilight Storm

English translation completed 2003-12-30
9th Night 12059
In the fourth year in the time of the Twilight Storm

English printed version completed 2011-05-30
135. Night 12066
In the eleventh year in the time of the Twilight Storm

Author's word:

During 1987 I started musing over a story I initially called, with heavy emphasis on irony The Great European Novel. It was only a working title, of course. I never intended to actually call it that, even though I played with the idea. It would have been even more beautiful irony and even sarcasm (and it was).

I was writing on another novel at the time, of course, and knew I wouldn't start on The Great European Novel for at least a year, so I had quite a lot of time when it came to developing this one.

In those nights I didn't write on a thousand projects simultaneously.

There were just a few phrases and disconnected ideas. Sometimes I get almost the entire story in a flash. This wasn't one of those times.

I got the pieces one by one, really. It felt amazing as it happened and even more so in hindsight. I knew, as the months and years passed by that I wanted to do something More with this one, raising the stakes and do an EE, an Encompassing Everything story.

In September 1988 I moved to London, and stayed there for five years. Ironically (again) it was on one of my trips back to Norway a few months later a friend of mine asked me to join him on a trip to Copenhagen. He was chasing a girl, and the girl wanted to go with him, but she wanted to have her girlfriend with her, so he wanted to have me as a balance, I guess. I was amused, but intrigued, and we Went.

It soon came apparent to me that his efforts were quite hopeless, even though the reality of the matter didn't seem to get through to him. You see, the two girls were lesbians and clearly intimate, and just weren't interested in becoming romantically involved with a male at all.

To make a longer history shorter we ended up at a gay bar called Pan in the Copenhagen entertainment district. While he attempted all night to get in the pants of the girl, I sat there and studied my surroundings. It was my first time in a gay bar and it was quite a revelation. Everything looked very similar to an «ordinary» bar, except that the couples dancing together and having intimate conversation at the tables were of the same sex. Everything felt casual, so perfectly natural. The place had a great mood and was a fantastic setting in many ways, very inspiring. It did feel slightly awkward when males checked me out, but I just smiled and shook my head. It just was no big deal. Any preconception or bias I might have had about homosexuality faded away that night, and with less prejudice my mind opened further to new possibilities.

The book would have been a lot different if not for that brief trip to Copenhagen. It's hard for me, in hindsight to even measure how different. I realized that I had never touched the subject of homosexuality before and that I wanted to. Homosexuality isn't really a main subject in the story, though. Some of the characters just happen to be homosexuals and bisexuals, no big deal, really, except for those haters who want to make it one.

But with that visit to Pan and the two days and nights in the city came something more, the scenery and setting I had consciously and subconsciously been searching for. Copenhagen had been one of «my» cities for a few years, since I had first visited it as an adult in 1985, and I knew its streets and back alleys well. There was the entertainment district, there were its wide avenues… and there was Liberty City.

BANG, the stage was set.

I joined the Green Party in April 1989, first the Norwegian branch and then, later the British. Both were nascent organizations, given birth and momentum by the relative parliamentary success of the German sister party. I began writing Dreams Belong to the Night on March 1. Right from the start I wanted to make the book a kind of documentation of the process.

You see, I was already well aware of the pitfalls of a political party when I joined, against my better judgment, but hope against hope, and yearning for Change in a totally oppressive and destructive society made me join anyway. During the next thirty months I had the pleasure of having illustrated the truth of Ibsen's word on the matter almost constantly:

«A party is like a meat grinder. It grinds all the brains into one stew».

At first it was quite fun, or the fun lessened the aggravation. A lot of different people joined, everything from anarchists to true greens, like me, from people being in favor of legalizing all drugs to syndicalists. It was in many ways amazing, really, those first few months. As I shared my time between London and Bergen things proceeded in an amazingly similar manner.

In the novel I wrote about how it should have been, while struggling to deal with the very disappointing reality. To make the story shorter again: The good people, as they deserve to be called either quit in frustration or were driven out. It happened quickly, during just six months or so. I held out the longest, in thirty ever longer months. It was an ordeal, at least the Norwegian chapter. Things were slightly more open and tolerant in London, of course.

But my main lesson during my time as a politician was a confirmation of what I already knew: that the parliamentary system is an integrated part of the tyranny and can never be reformed, only destroyed. Democracy is the slickest tyranny in history, because it gives people the illusion of participation, on them being the part of the decision-making. If I hadn't spent months away from the circus I would surely have turned insane.

I started doing my street theater thing with a bunch of like-minded people, in and around London, and in Europe, and I wrote Dreams on the derelict old typewriter I dragged with me everywhere. The script was in stark danger many times, in many a squatted house, but survived.

My time with the Greens ended pretty much in September 1991. The novel, my Great European Novel and party diary was complete in August... When I returned to Europe and London in late September I felt totally wasted, used up, drained of energy. I felt like I was awakening from a nightmare, as I slowly realized that I had truly lived one. The members of the Norwegian Green Party were more like tea drinkers, doing their «rebellion» when they didn't have anything important to do, and they grew angry when anyone reminded them of that fact. They didn't want to change the world, but were perfectly happy with things like they were. They were small people, thinking small. Their British counterparts less so, but I pretty much drifted away from them, too, upon my return to the City of Cities, seeing the same horrible lack of desire for Change there. They were more red than green, stuck in a past that was never much to write home about. My life as a «politician» was over, and I rejoiced.

All this, a thorough documentation of «failure» is in the novel, albeit mostly in the first hundred pages or so (or perhaps in the hundred, mostly untold pages before the Copenhagen part of the story begins), before taking off in a completely different direction. The book is from the start a rejection of established truths, a story about true fighting spirit in a global society almost devoid of it, about seeing through illusions in a world filled with them, about leaving those illusions in shambles, as the shambles they are, leaving them broken, without possibility of repair. It's a guide for advanced rebels, for those who have rejected the deception and illusions of modern life and are ready to take the next step.

Judith Breen, the main protagonist in the book is part myself, part Ulrike Meinhof and part anyone who has ever stood up and fought with razor-sharp claws and fangs against oppression, and totally rejected the «values» and validity of the established society.

Put a bit simplistic Dreams is about politics, about radical politics and rebellion, while ShadowWalk, written practically simultaneously is about religion (and its vast antithesis rebellion and truly free and independent thinking), and the yet to be completed Phoenix Green Earth, the last book in the Janus Clan series… is about both.

I saw Dreams pretty much as my masterpiece, because it is a self-contained piece «with everything in it», just like I intended. It took years before I believed I could ever write anything that great again. It was the first time I felt that I was competing with myself, a strange notion many artists experience eventually.

I saw flashes of young boys and girls being initiated into the mysteries and joy of rebellion. I watched them clean their guns, saw them take their first nascent steps in a Norwegian forest and also in the streets and rebellious venues of Copenhagen, and I saw them as vastly different from a bunch of tea drinkers with delusions of grandeur, as people liberating themselves from all confines, confronting head on the vast corrupt forces ruling this world.

This is a story for rebels, warriors in all forms. The proud leaders of our society and Joe Public and others «enjoying» average books will in all likelihood puke if they read it. It's a kind of alternative history of the late Eighties and the Nineties, a parallel reality where scores of aware and passionate and truly rebellious activists and Human Beings run around destabilizing and creating havoc in the ever more modern day oppressive society. It's what should have been real, should be real.

One more thing to note about SW and Dreams is the high number of females and/or people with a darker hue of skin. I got sick and tired of the one female, one Asian/African-American/European quota in films/novels and decided to go completely overboard in order to distance myself from it.

It felt perfectly natural.

And yeah, the following is one reason why I feel grateful for the censorship of the established publishers. If my first three novels, the first three books in the Janus Clan series hadn't been rejected, I would probably never have written Dreams Belong to the Night, and not taken yet another step forward as an author and Human Being…

That was me being ironic and even sarcastic.

With the rejection of the first three I saw no reason to start on the fourth, though, not then, or for a long time. So I started writing one book, self contained stories, and that brought me eventually to the circumstances described in this article.

The reason I grew, also in this matter was because of my inborn stubbornness, not because I was encouraged to do so, in any way, except in the backward way it happened.

This is basically a translated, corrected and revised edition of the Norwegian edition, published in 2002. It's a strange thing to work on a novel I was very pleased with when I published it and see the need for improvements, now. During those nine years I've clearly grown further as an author and the demands I place on myself have grown subsequently. It is the same story, but those having read the original will notice the changes, and might also find them interesting.

So, after an evolution spanning twenty years, this is the ultimate and final version of the book.

The exterior and interior of the Gothenburg shopping mall Nordstan, with surroundings is described exactly like it was, June 6, 1997. I was there, that very day, making extensive notes.

Except for this and other markers of time, names and events linking the main parts of the story to the late Eighties and the Nineties, it's really a timeless tale.

Experience the defeat of civilization, of tyranny, of anti-life in:

Thunder Road - Book One: Ice and Fire

Damon Terrill is the Storm Child. He is born into the life hostile civilization's last years, as humanity starts on its return to nature, return to Life.

It started with the need for Freedom, the passion of life, and went from there, in new and unforeseen directions, in one, final attempt to get it right.

– It's the human being's path through life, Anya told them. – What challenges, destroys and strengthens it.

Burning Ice, Biting Flame… that's how life began, and that's how it will renew itself.

The Thunder Road is making a turn. It always is. No matter where humans are going. And now the blade is laid bare, ready to be tempered once more. Humanity's idiocy, their hubris has finally and fully been visited upon them. The End Time, the final hour, Ragnarok is here. The sea is rising. Winds are increasing in strength and numbers. A thoroughly rotten society is collapsing under its own weight.

Humans are natural nomads. Now they become nomads anew, pulled together in small tribes once more, pulled into a fellowship of fate in a final, desperate attempt to survive, to live the life humans are born to live. Finally! Damon, Anya, Andrè, Myriam and many others have started on their way Home.

Preliminary publication date June 21, 2015

Other novels and books by Amos Keppler from Midnight Fire Media:

Shadow Walk

The world is changing. They know this, in their core of cores, where everything moves and shifts. Night and fire have followed them all the days of their lives.

What they carry inside has always scared them, always intrigued them...

They have always felt different, apart from the crowd. And here, now, they get the confirmation they have always wanted, always yearned for, that they are truly different, a breed apart. The metamorphosis begins. Their minds, their bodies are changing in shocking and unpredictable ways, as what's on the inside is brought to the outside. And as they themselves are changing they are also changing the world.

Danger awaits them, Life awaits them, in the small, backward New England town. Magick and Mystery may be found beneath unturned stones.

People, young and old, are descending on the small, insignificant town of Northfield, New England.

Boys and girls, students at the school of Life, Seekers, yearning for what's different, what's hidden.

They're seeking within and without, high and low.

And here, in this dusty, remote place they're finding it, turning the stone, finding the strength within themselves to be themselves, to break out of confines, to the world beyond. And in time, after the initial, tentative steps, pushing down paths new and undreamed of.

And the present day order sees them for what they are... Agents of Change, a threat to any establishment, any imposed reality. The heatwave, the worst in living memory, is nothing compared to the boiling within the human heart. The Indian Summer heralds the twilight of mankind.

To be published October 31, 2011

The Defenseless

The two rivers meet and join in the city of Denver, becoming one...

The two dark brothers, growing up with their sister Linda in a mundane, average suburb, a place well entrenched in the modern United States and the world, have since their moment of birth, been at odds with the world... and with each other.

Mike and Ted Cousin are not who they are. There is a mystery here, one of birth and upbringing, one of fate. Violence and death, blood and fire follow them all the days of their lives. The fire is resting somewhere inside... waiting for the Spark.

Their parents know something, but are not telling. The policeman Mark Stewart and their aunt Trudy do, too. Everybody knows something, pieces of the whole, but nobody knows the whole truth, nobody telling it.

The ancient power is returning to the world, a world suffering massively from physical and spiritual poison, on the brink of collapse and a collective tailspin suicide run without peer in human history. Magick is returning from its long exile. Thus begins the story of the wild beasts rising from its ashes.

The Spark is struck, horrible and terrifying.

First book of ten in **the Janus Clan** series: Ten stories of the wild man in the modern world, forty years of wandering before the Phoenix is rising from its ashes.

ISBN 978-82-91693-08-8

Your Own Fate

In boca al loco - in the mouth of the wolf.
Italian salutation

From The Book of Fate:
In the Book of Fate there is everything. Every incident, all times, everything that has been, that is, that will ever be, everything that might be, everything that could have been.
But who is writing it? Who is penning it? Who is turning page by page, too many to be counted, blowing in the wind? Does it perhaps write itself, with a pen moving across the yellow sheets? Or is it a hand moving the pen, one unseen, one stretching back into the past, back to the time before everything was created, creating itself from nothing?

Timothy Joyce is an enigma, a man without a past, appearing from nowhere, to go on a rampage in an astonished world.

Jeremy Zahn is hunting Timothy Joyce. It seems like he has always been hunting him, from old London, from the island of angels, where it is said they met for the first time, to the city of angels, California, the new world.
Here, on this shaky ground, following confrontations spanning the world, its time and space the two will fight for the last time.
And the world is watching, its people shivering in their frozen hearts.

ISBN 978-82-91693-05-7

Night on Earth

This is said to be the age of enlightenment and reason...
A culmination of thousands of years' development and illumination.
The hunters are dying off, they say. Their day is done, in favor of the new, enlightened time of neon lights, technology and civilization.
But a hunter is stalking the streets of London. A creature without form, eyes and skin. In a city on the brink of chaos, of social and economic collapse, it's stalking cops, killing them in ever more horrible ways. Sheila Watts is a hunter. She's a cop.
Sheila is lost, losing herself further by the second. She's losing herself, finding herself, as she's closing in on the creature of the night, as it is closing in on her.
Sheila Watts can taste the sweet blood in her mouth...

ISBN 978-82-91693-07-1

Complete Poems 1989 - 2003

Venture into existence with Amos Keppler, into the rainbow, of red and green, shadow and pitch black. Experience Life through ShadowWalker's many senses.
That's all, folks.

Contains eight collections of poems, all 291 so far.

The Green Rose 1989 - 1993
Cry of the Jester 1993
Poems of the Hot Wind 1994 to 1996
Travels And Revels, Life and Magick, Tales from Hell and Beyond - Aleister Crowley 1995 - 1996
The Infinity Cycle 1995 - 1998
Chronicles of Our Dreams 1998 - 2001
Diary of a Traveling Man 2002
TheBeautifulExcitingWorldinPieces January to August 2003

Also included are author's remarks and background material.

ISBN 978-82-91693-06-4

Alarums of reality

The end is the beginning. The beginning is the end…

The once so great Caine Manor has become a ruin, one only fit for carrion birds and revenants. No one but daring children and crazed souls dare breach its confines.

The proud and shiny Caine Manor is an outstanding example of renovated architecture at the heart of the city.

Looking at the building, the house, resembling a castle, hidden in a strange, illuminated mist, squinting your eyes, it's often hard to tell what's illusion and what's real. Reality shifts and burns around the Caine Manor, either ruin or proud house, reaching out with strands of night and fire to the surrounding areas and to existence at large. It is the center, or at least one center, in an ever-shifting world.

Is Chloe Webster dead or alive? Is Marion Dexter? Is Marlon Caine? Or David Fallon Somby? Are they perhaps both? Or neither? What is the world? Is it a brick, a hard, impenetrable wall or closer to something akin to mist and shadow? Existence might make sense, to us, to them, but only in glimpses, only in passing, beyond a corner somewhere ahead. They may wonder. They may die clueless. Because they don't know, don't know why terror strikes them and makes their heart beat like a sledgehammer in their chest.

From a place unbound by time and space alarums of reality are reaching out to touch and ultimately engulf them all.

To be published February 29, 2012

www.ingramcontent.com/pod-product-compliance
Lightning Source LLC
Chambersburg PA
CBHW060605310726
48982CB00008B/1238/J

* 9 7 8 8 2 9 1 6 9 3 1 1 8 *